ON EDGE

BOOK #1
ROLLING ASYLUM MC

ASHLYNN PEARCE

Cover artist: Bella Media Management

Editor: Alicia Dean

Formatting: Unalive Promotions

2nd Edition

ISBN: 979-8-9909198-0-8 Paperback

979-8-9909198-1-5 Hardback

"There is nothing to writing. All you do is sit down at a typewriter and bleed."

ERNEST HEMINGWAY

To Chris ~ thank you for all your support. I Love you!
To Linda ~ what would I do without you cheering me on? LY!
To everyone who reads my books ~ you don't know what it means to be able to write my stories & share them with you. It's a personal experience for me.
Thank you!

AUTHOR NOTE

My characters deal with PTSD, C-PTSD, SA, PA, MA, & CA.

It's the story of my heart. It will pull at your heartstrings. This is a re-write of my first book, Rough Edges, that was published in 2010. It's a very expanded version & some things are different, but it's still the same Jake & Becca. I hope you enjoy!

ON EDGE PLAYLIST

This Time It's Different ~ Evans Blue
Down in a Hole ~ Alice in Chains
Burn MF ~ Five Finger Death Punch
Wreck Me ~ Jamie O'Neal
Dot Your Eyes ~ 5FDP
Need You Now ~ Lady A
Burning Bright ~ Shinedown
Broken ~ Seether
No End in Sight ~ Katrina Elam
Take it to the Edge ~ GodSmack
How Can I refuse ~ Heart
Smoke a Little Smoke ~ Eric Church
Falls on Me ~ Fuel
Inside ~ Soil
Doing Time ~ Avenged Sevenfold
My Own Hell ~ 5FDP
Pain ~ Three Days Grace
Crashed ~ Daughtry

ON EDGE

What if you lived, moment by moment, numb to everything and everyone?
How far would you take it just to feel?
I'm an adrenaline junkie searching those highs like a drug addict.
Being on edge kept me from jumping off the ledge of sanity.
Then she crashed into my world & flipped the script.
She makes me feel.
Real. Defenseless.
Alive. Exposed.
Animalistic. Possessive.
Can I really love her with my cold callous heart?
Can she be the anchor in my chaotic storm?

PROLOGUE

JAKE JAGGER KORTE

Who knew what would happen if they saw me?

I crouched behind the couch, and the smell of dingy fabric closed in on me. I covered my ears and squinted my eyes shut. But I heard it all. The screaming and crashing down the hall towards my parents' bedroom. My stomach cramped...I was hungry, but I remained frozen in my hiding spot. Eventually, the yelling got closer, and I tried to make myself smaller. I tucked into the far corner between the wall and the couch. Hoping it would be over soon, I rocked back and forth a tiny bit, trying to ease my nerves.

"You fucking bitch. I should get me a real woman and toss you and that brat out," Dad snarled.

"Oh, yeah? I should get me a real man. Not a drunk bastard," Mom screeched.

"You're going to pay for that," Dad said in a deadly calm voice I knew too well.

I heard slapping, followed by my mom's screams. My eyes popped wide open when she made a gurgling sound and the furniture slammed against the wall. It bounced off my body, but I was small

1

enough it wouldn't squish me. I bit my lip and breathed noisily through my nose, so I covered my mouth and nose with one hand. A few tears tracked down my face, and I hastily wiped them away, berating myself for being a baby. I heard Father's grunts and Mom sobbing as the couch banged into the wall.

Over and over and over.

And over and over, I flinched.

Then silence, followed by a loud slap and a scream from Mom.

"That will teach you, bitch."

Heavy footsteps and then a loud bang as the front door slammed. Hard enough that it shook the whole house. I was glad he was gone. When he was gone, I only had to deal with Mom. I wiped my nose, crept on the floor to the edge of the couch and peeked out. Mom was sniffling on the sofa, so I didn't dare leave my hiding place. I scooted back a little bit, lay on the dirty floor and waited. When mom got a beating, I knew I'd be next. So, I knew if I made my presence known now, she would take out all her anger on me. I didn't have to wait long until she was gone, too. Wary of any sound that warned me they were back, I crawled out from my hiding spot and stood up.

I hurried to the kitchen as painful cramps hurt my stomach and opened the fridge to find nothing except moldy butter. Scraping off the mold, I wiped it on my pants and ate the rest with my fingers. I opened the lower cabinets and scared away the cockroaches. Nothing. Scooting a chair near the cabinets, I climbed up. I found a handful of stale chips and ate them. On the floor once again, I wiped my eyes. But I didn't cry. Fending for myself was better than them being home.

It was almost dark when I left through the back door. I dug through the neighbor's trash and found a chicken bone with a little bit of meat on it. I sucked on it until it was clean. Accidentally, I dumped the trash over and an old black woman came out of the trailer.

"Get, you pesky cats," she hollered. I hid in the shadows, but she saw me. "Hey, what are you doing going through my trash?"

I wasn't quick enough to escape her grasp. I flayed my arms and kicked, but I made no sound. Beatings were worse if I cried.

"Boy, I ain't gonna hurt ya." She got down on my level, and I wiped the grime on my face. I was alert to any sudden moves, but all she did was look at me. "I'm Cellie. What's your name, boy?"

I hesitated. She had her hair in a tight bun and was wearing a pink fuzzy robe. She wasn't yelling at me like my parents did. I cleared my throat. "Jake."

"Don't you live at the end of the trailer park?"

I nodded, my stomach cramped again, and made a growl.

She peered at me for a few minutes. "I'll make you a deal. If you take a bath, I'll fix you some supper."

I wrinkled my nose. I hated baths but loved supper. Hesitantly, I nodded, and she smiled. She had a nice smile and pointed to her house. When I walked through the door, I stopped. Wide-eyed, I looked around her place. The floor was clean. There were colorful curtains hanging from her windows, and it smelled nice. There weren't holes in the walls or bugs crawling around. It was warm and soft. Not like my house at all. She led me to the bathroom.

"Do you need help with your bath?"

I huffed and crossed my arms over my chest. "I'm not a baby."

She smiled kindly and chuckled. "Okay. But wash everywhere, even behind your ears and in-between your toes. And I'll wash your clothes. You can put on an old tee of mine in the meantime. Deal?" She turned the water on in the bathtub.

I was barefoot and took off my pants and shirt and stepped into the tub.

"Do you not have any underwear, Jake?" She furrowed her brows as she looked at me. Water filled her eyes. She looked like she was about to cry, but I didn't know why.

I shook my head. She wiped away one tear and reached to pat my head. I immediately ducked and scrambled to the other side of the tub.

She pulled her hand back to cover her mouth. "You're safe here, Jake. I won't hurt you."

I blinked, then frowned. She nodded and left me alone. The water was warm and felt nice. My house only had cold water. I poured the soap into my hands and slapped it on my head. The soap smelled like flowers, so I hope she kept her promise. Cause I smelled like a girl. I froze when she came back in, but she only placed a shirt and towel in the bathroom, then left. She didn't try to touch me.

A little while later, I walked out of the bathroom with the shirt sticking to me and stopped at the table. It smelled so good. There were biscuits, gravy, eggs, and bacon. I sat at the table and shoved a whole biscuit in my mouth.

"There's no rush. Take your time so you won't get sick."

I spit half of the biscuit out in my hand, chewed the remaining half and swallowed and repeated the process with the other half. I scooped the gravy with my hand and put it in my mouth. It was so good and creamy. I closed my eyes briefly and looked at Cellie. Tears were rolling down her cheeks.

"I think this will help." She handed me a spoon.

I grabbed the spoon with a gravy-covered left hand and scooped up the eggs. I'd never tasted food so yummy. I gave her a small smile while I picked up some bacon and stuffed it all in my mouth.

She chuckled. "Do you like it?"

I nodded my head vigorously. "So good," I said with a mouthful.

11 YEARS LATER...

I sat on the threadbare sofa, smoking a joint. That, combined with the half-empty bottle of Jack, helped numb the pain. Not from my black eye, or even the bruised ribs, making me wince with every breath. More for the gash across my damned soul from the man who left the marks...my old man. The Prick.

But the fucker was out. Even though Mom was as bruised and beaten as I was, she still railed at me for making Dad leave. Made no damn sense. I was sixteen. I shouldn't have been the one to fight for her. I shouldn't be the one to tell Mom to shut the fuck up. Finally, I shoved her into the bedroom and locked her in, while she threw things at the door, screaming at me.

Yeah, that sick fucker had put sliding locks on the *outside* of every door in the run-down trailer. At the moment, it helped keep Mom from inflicting more damage to my body. But her words echoed crystal clear from her room down the hall.

"I should have aborted you when I had the chance," she yelled as another something crashed against the door.

I should've left. It would have been a hell of a lot easier. Why I even gave a shit about my mother was beyond me. Some tiny part I couldn't exorcise from my head wanted to protect her. Wanted what every child wants...at least one parent to love.

I inhaled another drag and followed it with another long drink. Yeah, I should've left her to rot. I eyed my swelling left wrist. That was going to be a problem. It was broken, or at the very least, cracked. I stubbed out the joint with a shaking right hand and stood.

Damn, that hurt too.

"Let me out, you lil bastard," she screamed again, and the door-frame rattled at her attempt to open it.

"You should thank me. He won't be beating on you anymore," I replied and leaned against the flimsy wood paneling lining the hallway.

"How are we going to pay the bills? We can't survive without him." She shook the doorknob again. "You've ruined everything!"

That was a lie. Prick didn't pay for shit. He drank the bill money, and Mom sold her body to feed her drug habit. I scrubbed a hand over my shaggy hair and dropped my head. Pain radiated through my body. I would have to work more to pay for the roof over our head. Mom was as worthless as Dad.

But first, I needed to get my wrist looked at. For that, I had to leave and if I left her locked in the room, she would bust out the window. Unlocking and opening it would never occur to her. I sighed, trudged down the hall, braced myself and slid the lock open.

The door flew open, and she slapped me so hard my ears rang. I turned on my heel and headed toward the door. Blows rained down on my back, but I barely felt her small fists hitting me. Her words, on the other hand, left marks no amount of time could undo.

I ducked out the door, hopped in my old truck, and took off. I hoped I stayed conscious long enough to reach my best friend's house. Tony didn't live far, but it might as well have been on the other side of the world.

5

It could have been hours, or moments, but somehow, I made it and climbed the steps to Tony's home. His parents, Maria and Carl, were more like my family every day.

I swayed on my feet and my bruised knuckles knocked on the pristine white wood. My vision swam. Not much longer. Soon oblivion would swallow me up. The door opened and Maria gasped.

"Carl! Come quick." She tried to catch me when I fell, but the most she could do was keep my head from bouncing off the floor. "Oh, my poor boy. What have they done to you this time?"

Her soft, caring words washed over me, and I could breathe. Darkness swamped me, carrying me into oblivion.

Later, I sat in the ER as the doctor scowled. "You say you were jumped, and your parents are out of town?"

"Yes, sir." Didn't take a genius to figure out the doc thought I was lying. I was. But no way in hell would I tell him the truth. My knee bounced, and I looked down at my casted wrist.

Of course…it was broken.

"This seems to happen quite often," the doc said as he looked through my chart. "Maybe you need to run with a different crowd or…"

I wasn't following that trail off. I was a lot of things, stupid wasn't one of them. They would put me in the system. They would take me away from the only family I knew…the Paganos. Tony's family. All I had to do was get through high school. I was locked into Automotive Service Tech for my last two years of high school. Fully paid. No way would I jeopardize my ticket to a secure future.

Maria and Carl stepped into the room. They wouldn't tell the doc the truth either. They wouldn't do that to me.

"He is free to go."

I slid off the table and tugged my dirty shirt over my bruised body. I wouldn't look at Maria. She'd seen me beaten before, but this time it was worse, and I couldn't face the tears I knew would be in her eyes.

The car ride back to their house remained silent except for a sniffle from Maria every now and then. Tony whipped open the front door when we rolled onto the gravel drive.

Tony crossed his arms over his chest. "They really did it this time."

I would have shrugged, but it hurt to breathe. As everyone walked in the house, the door snapped shut hard behind me, and I turned.

"That's it. You're moving in here." Maria's voice shook with anger. "I'll not tolerate this anymore. They've hurt you for the last time."

I lifted my gaze to Maria's, then Carl's. "I can't. I ran Tomas off. Jenny will need me." Which was true. Mom couldn't function without my old man around. She couldn't function with me around either...but that was an entirely different problem.

Maria's lips parted. "You kicked your dad out?"

"Yeah. I think he would've killed her this time. If I leave now, she will end up on the streets."

"You are a kid. She is the parent—"

"I know. It's fu—messed up." I cussed like a sailor most of the time, but I tried to rein it in around the Paganos. They deserved respect. The only people I had any respect for.

Carl put his hand on Maria's shoulder to silence her and said, "You're welcome here anytime, and if you need anything, let us know."

It was the same line of words he always said when I showed up busted and bleeding.

Defeat marred Maria's face. She walked toward me, and I stiffened. She wanted to hug me. Her arms reached up and then fell. I didn't hug. Didn't know how to accept them. Four years I'd been welcomed into their fold like family, and I still didn't know how to not flinch when she tried to touch me. She settled on patting my arm.

"Always. Anytime. Okay, baby."

I nodded, and my heart thumped like a drum. In my mind, Maria was my mom, even though I still didn't say much to her.

She'd been there through my nightmares.

Tended my wounds. Fed me. Made sure I had clean clothes. She even made a Christmas stocking with my name on it for the mantel. It matched Tony's and his sister, Andrea's. Pictures of me hung on their walls...I was in their family photo album. Like I was their son.

The only thing I had at home were holes in the wall where my old man missed my head, a sink full of dirty dishes, and an empty fridge. Unless you counted booze and drugs as food.

ONE
JAKE

14 YEARS LATER...

My pulse pumped through my body as I thrust into her.

Sensation.

Feeling.

I almost felt human. Alive.

Adrenaline and sweat drenched my body as I let go for only a moment. A brief glimpse of peace as I came.

A short-lived peace.

I opened my eyes to reality. Some no-name chick kneeled over the couch, her ass perched in the air, my dick buried in her. I pulled out and walked toward the bathroom. "Time for you to go."

"Oh, baby. Surely you don't mean that?" Her pouty voice did nothing but grate along my ragged nerves.

"Yeah. I do. Get the fuck out."

I shut the door, locked it, and dropped the condom in the trash before I stepped into the shower. I turned it on and let the cold drown me. If only it could. Finally, the water warmed, but I didn't care.

The emptiness was back.

It was always the same, but I couldn't stop the pattern. Not that I'd

11

know what to do if I did stop. It was amazing the lengths I went through to feel. Whether flying high in the sky on my dirt bike, doing 100 mph on my Harley, skydiving or fucking the never-ending line of nameless bitches who offered themselves up like prizes.

All of it gave me the same rush.

But it never lasted. Just a few moments of being alive before the numbness settled in around me like a black cloak. I looked at my watch...

11:17 p.m.

I braced my elbows on the shower wall, dropped my head and let the water wash over me. If only it could wash away the shit that clung to me and spiral down the drain as easily as the water.

Several minutes later, I stepped out of the bathroom and did a quick search through my house to make sure she was gone. Most didn't stick around. But every now and then, one would try to over-stay their welcome. Did that make me a heartless bastard? Probably. But I made no promises and rarely ever knew their name. Certainly, never remembered them. Just a long string of one-night stands.

They were using me just as much as I was using them.

I went to my fridge and snagged a beer. I had to work tomorrow, but as always, I wasn't tired. You'd think a good fucking would put me out...but it never did. I checked my watch.

11:28 p.m.

Tony gave me shit about wearing a watch. He said everyone had a phone, but you could lose it. I wanted...no, needed something attached to my body. You might say, I was obsessed with time. For good reason. I never knew when it would disappear.

I opened up my laptop and signed into a forum. Oddly enough, they were a good time suck. I very rarely engaged, just watched all the morons try to pick up chicks, talk shit and lie out their fucking asses. I sipped my beer and relaxed on the couch.

It was supposed to be a bike forum and now and then I would get some good info about bikes, but mostly it was just shit. All I knew, it was something that kept me from thinking too much. Kept my brain out of the shit I couldn't forget but tried my best to ignore.

I scanned through the conversation when I stopped on a name I'd seen for the last few weeks. A chick, or at least she claimed to be, named Bec2U. For some reason, I'd been keeping track of this one. Not talking to her, just watching her. She knew absolutely zero about motorcycles because she never even tried to pretend she was into bikes. My best guess...she was looking for a guy who rode a bike. Chicks really got into the whole bad-ass bike scene.

I wouldn't lie. It got me laid, but I didn't ride because of it. I rode because there was nothing like the wind in my face and the road flying under me. The faster, the better. Being on edge kept me from jumping off the ledge of sanity.

When my inbox beeped, I looked at the message...from Bec2U.

TWO
REBECCA ANN SAYLOR

I sat at my computer, stared at the crude messages I kept getting and deleted each one. This whole project was turning into a disaster. If I got one more dick pic, I was going to scream. I was here to do research for my novel, not collect raunchy pictures.

I blew at the bangs that hung in my face. So far, I haven't gotten any helpful information. When I'd ask a legitimate question, I got ignored. There were all different motorcycle forums, but I finally settled on a Harley one. Pretty much the same people came into the rooms at about the same time, but I still faced a constant stream of very explicit pictures I did not want to see.

Disgusted, I angrily shot a message to one offender.

BEC2U:

I do not want to see pics of your junk! Just stop already!!

MBFBJAKE13:

I didn't send you anything.

BEC2U:

Yes, you did. I have...omg. I'm so sorry. Wrong person.

MBFBJAKE13:

Getting lots of interesting pictures?

BEC2U:

Yeah...you might say that. Sorry.

WELL, WASN'T THAT JUST HUMILIATING? I'D MESSAGED THE WRONG GUY. Just my luck. He looked like he was thirteen years old. Perfect.

BEC2U:

Aren't you a little young to be in here?

MBFBJAKE13:

Young?

BEC2U:

13?

MBFBJAKE13:

Nope. I'm 30. That's my old # when I used to race dirt bikes.

BEC2U:

Wow, I just keep getting better. Sorry.

MAYBE THIS WASN'T MY BEST IDEA TO WRITE SOMETHING I KNEW absolutely nothing about. I didn't even know anyone who rode a motorcycle. I laid my forehead on the table and groaned. I'd had been at this for two weeks and had just a handful of facts about the biker life. If I didn't make some serious headway soon, I was going to trash the whole idea. But motorcycles had fascinated me since I was little. It was the story of my heart.

. . .

MBFBJAKE13:

Easy assumption to make.

BEC2U:

You know what they say about assumptions. It makes an ass out of me. Haha.

AS SOON AS I HIT SEND, I REALIZED IT WAS THE WRONG THING TO SAY. *Bluzty me.* It just invited him to make crude comments. I covered my hands over my face and peeked through my fingers, waiting for it.

MBFBJAKE13:

Hey you said it, not me.

I WAITED. AND WAITED. WHEN HE DIDN'T RESPOND LIKE I THOUGHT HE would, I dropped my hands.

BEC2U:

I was expecting a rude comment.

MBFBJAKE13:

Nah. I'm sure you get bombed with enough.

BEC2U:

Huh. Yeah, I do. I'm sure you'll laugh at me, but I know nothing about bikes or the biker lifestyle.

MBFBJAKE13:

I noticed.

BEC2U:

You noticed me? I haven't seen your name around.

MBFBJAKE13:

Nah. I just float, rarely respond.

BEC2U:

I'm here to gather information about a book I'm writing.

MBFBJAKE13:

What kind of book?

BEC2U:

A biker romance novel.

MBFBJAKE13:

Haha, good luck with that.

BEC2U:

I'm serious. But anytime I mention my purpose for being in here, I get flooded with inspiration pics.

MBFBJAKE13:

You're writing about sex with bikers. What did you think would happen?

BEC2U:

It's a love story. It's not just sex.

MBFBJAKE13:

I haven't read any romance lately, but are you telling me there's no sex in your book?

BEC2U:

U read romance? Omg. And yes, there's sex in my book.

MBFBJAKE13:

...............um no. Sarcasm. I see why you're getting dick pics. Are you blonde, too?

I STARED AT MY SCREEN AND HEAT HIT MY FACE. THE ONE GUY WHO WOULD talk to me thinks I'm a ditzy blonde...and my hair was blonde.

BEC2U:

Right. So, are you willing to answer my Q about biker life?

MBFBJAKE13:

I'm not patched in. Not in a club.

BEC2U:

You don't have to be.

MBFBJake13: What the hell. Shoot.

BEC2U:

I'm curious, what does your name mean, the MBFB?

MBFBJAKE13:

I ride a matte black fat boy Harley.

BEC2U:

Nice. FYI, I don't know anyone who rides motorcycles. All the info I know is from TV shows. So, please be patient with me. How long have you been riding? And how does it make you feel?

I WAS FINALLY GETTING SOMEWHERE. IF HE ANSWERED SOME OF MY questions, it would be more than I'd gotten from anyone else.

JAKE

I raised an eyebrow at the screen, a beer halfway to my lips. How does it make me feel? I downed the rest of it, got up, and threw it in the trash, and sat back down with a fresh one. It shouldn't be a prying question but for me? It was.

> **BEC2U:**
> Are you still there?

> **MBFBJAKE13:**
> 15 years. From dirt bikes, street bikes to Harleys.

> **BEC2U:**
> Wow. That's a long time. So why do you like it? How does it make you feel?

I'd HOPED SHE WOULD LET THAT LAST QUESTION GO. I STARED AT HER NAME on the screen and thought of answering truthfully. I didn't go for all that mushy-feely stuff. Honestly, I didn't engage with people at all. But hell, she didn't know me, and I didn't know her. It's not like we were going to meet.

> **BEC2U:**
> Jake?

HER SAYING MY NAME MADE MY BROWS FURROW. IT MADE ME UNEASY, BUT I didn't know why. So, I let it roll off and answered truthfully.

> **MBFBJAKE13:**
> It makes me feel free. Alive.

> **BEC2U:**
> What do you mean alive? I've never been on a motorcycle. I think it would be scary.

MBFBJAKE13:

You need to find someone to give you a ride. Nothing like it. You can see the sky overhead, the road whizzing beneath your feet. The faster the better. I can't explain it. You just have to experience it.

BEC2U:

I'll think about it.

SHE DIDN'T KNOW IT, BUT I NEVER OPENED UP LIKE THAT. IF ANYBODY asked me a question remotely personal, I stared at them. Was none of their fucking business. And I had the don't-fuck-with-me-look perfected.

BEC2U:

Do you wear a helmet?

MBFBJAKE13:

Nope. Don't want to live through a crash.

BEC2U:

What? That's awful!

MBFBJAKE13:

Saw a buddy crash hard. Wasn't his fault. The one time he wore a helmet, and he was in ICU for months. He lived, but his brain got scrambled and he needs 24/7 care. Not going out like that.

BEC2U:

I'm so sorry about your friend. Do most bikers wear helmets?

MBFBJAKE13:

Some states require it, some don't. Mine doesn't. I'd say 75% don't wear them here.

BEC2U:

It's getting late, and I have to go to work in the morning. Thanks for answering my questions. Are you available to answer more Q sometime?

MBFBJAKE13:

Yeah. You can DM me here.

BEC2U:

Great! I'll talk to you soon. Night!

MBFBJAKE13:

Night.

DURING THE FOLLOWING WEEK, I TALKED TO BEC EVERY FEW DAYS. Answering random questions about bikes. I didn't really know why I talked to her. Time suck, maybe? Who the fuck knew?

A week later, on Friday night, I pulled into Snookers and parked my bike near Tony's. I swung a leg over and put on my grip-lock and checked my watch.

10:15 p.m.

I heard a couple of female voices saying, "Hi, Jake."

"Hey," I replied without looking at them. I really didn't care who they were. I stepped inside and walked to the bar. Several female voices offered the same greeting, and I had the same reply. The place was packed. They had live music, a dance floor that I never used, and pool tables I did use. After I got a couple of beers, I made my way to the far corner pool table where Tony and my friends were.

Tony was loud and outgoing, and that's why we got into a fight after school eighteen years ago. Because of his loudmouth. He was one year older than me and he had won, but barely. Tony dragged us both home to get fixed up by Maria. I'd been a part of their family ever since.

I fist-bumped Tony and handed him a beer.

"Thanks, man," Tony grinned and bumped my elbow. "Did you scope out the new girls? They were by the front door."

"No. You're in charge of that. I just want to chill and drink."

Mack joined us, smiled and rubbed his hands together. "Did you see the new chicks?" I met Mack when we were going to automotive tech. "They're smoking."

I blew a breath out. "Like I trust your judgment, GMC freak."

Krista leaned against Tony. "Are you talking about the new girls?"

All three of us answered at the same time…two yeses and one no.

She rolled her eyes. "I knew what your answer would be, Jake."

I shrugged, sat on a barstool and drank my beer. Honestly, I didn't give two flying shits about the new girls. Krista belonged to Aaron, one of Tony's friends. She was cool, and unlike most girls, not annoying. Most of the female population was irritating as fuck.

Krista patted Mack's and Tony's shoulders. "Seems like you're too late." And moved to sit on a barstool beside me.

"What? Ah, hell no," Tony said. He was taller than most anyone, so he spotted them easily. "It's those weasel dicks. We can take them easy. You in, Jake?"

"Nah. You go ahead, man. I'll sit this one out."

He grinned and shook his head. "Your loss." And he and Mack made a beeline for the new girls.

I pulled out my phone when it vibrated. It was a DM from Bec.

BEC2U:

Are you available for chat?

I ASSUMED SHE'D BE BUSY ON A FRIDAY NIGHT. FAMILY OR SOMETHING. BUT she hadn't told me her age or any information, not that it mattered. I thought about blowing her off, but what-the-hell.

MBFBJAKE13:

Sure.

BEC2U:

If you're busy, it's fine.

MBFBJAKE13:

If I was, then I'd tell you.

WHY DID PEOPLE HAVE TO MAKE IT SO COMPLICATED? SAY WHAT YOU meant and mean what you say. Simple. Although everyone told me I had social issues. The girls mostly. I looked up in time to see Tony and Mack escorting the three new girls to our table.

"Hi, I'm Krista and this is Jake and we're not a couple." She smiled sweetly at me as though she did me a favor.

I looked each girl up and down, not even trying to hide I was checking them out. And each one of them blushed.

Tony draped his arm over the tallest one. "She's Megan, and Emma and Bella."

They all said hi, and I gave them a chin lift. "Hey."

Then my phone vibrated, and I turned my attention to it.

BEC2U:

Ok. I heard the term, cager. Does that mean all cars and trucks?

MBFBJAKE13:

Yeah. Means 4 wheels or more.

BEC2U:

Are bikers dangerous?

MACK TURNED HIS BACK TO THE GIRLS AND NUDGED ME.

"Which one do you want?"

I glanced over at them. "Pass."

"Seriously? They're hot." Mack raised his eyebrows.

The girls were young. I bet they were barely over twenty-one. "Nah," I said and looked at my phone.

MBFBJAKE13:

Most aren't. But as with all people, some are.

BEC2U:

Are you?

I smirked at the question. I wasn't known for causing fights, but I never backed down from one. Ever. The last one I lost was to Tony... when I was twelve. I didn't count Prick.

11:12 p.m.

MBFBJAKE13:

To some.

BEC2U:

Lol. What does that mean?

MBFBJAKE13:

Just what I said. And I don't ever say things I don't mean.

BEC2U:

Right. Everyone says stuff they don't mean.

MBFBJAKE13:

I'm brutally honest. With the emphasis on brutal.

"Hey," Tony said, and I looked up. "Who are you talking to?"

"A girl."

"Hello? There's a hot girl here who needs attention."

I looked toward the girl watching me with a hopeful expression on her face. Was she Emma or Bella? Didn't matter because I wasn't touching that. I glanced at Tony and then back to her. "Pass."

By her crestfallen face, she had heard me. Good. She appeared

25

innocent, and I didn't play with those types of girls. They expected things I couldn't give them. Like a heart. Even I had some morals.

Tony shook his head. "Damn. Even for you, that was cold."

I sighed and studied her peeling the label off her beer bottle. "Hey," I snagged her attention. Her instant smile made me regret it. "No offense, I'm an asshole." I downed my beer, tossed it in the trash can and walked to the restroom. She was getting ready to argue with me. I could see it on her face.

When I stepped out of the john, three weasel dicks met me and attempted to block me in. But I shoved through them. A hand clamped down on my shoulder, I grabbed it, twisted it around and pinned it behind weasel's back. Then I grabbed him by the back of his neck and smashed his face into the wall and sighed.

"Listen here, weasel. I'm gonna walk away, and you better let me."

"You're outnumbered," came the muffled voice.

I looked around, not seeing anyone but not that it would've mattered. I was trained by the best. My old man. "Your buds scattered." I released him, backed up a few steps, turned around and strode to my friends' table. One girl was hanging on Tony. Bella? Fuck if I knew.

"Heads up. Weasels tried to start some shit. I'm gonna get out of here."

"Those fuckin' weasels. Did they scare you off?" Tony tried to suppress a laugh.

I gave him a bored look. "Right. See ya'll." When I was unlocking my bike, heels clicked right up to me and stopped. I put the lock in my hard bags, rested a hand on my handlebars and faced her. Not surprised to see the girl I dissed inside the bar.

I arched a brow when she moved her lips to lick them and fidgeted.

"Go back inside." I swung a leg over my bike.

"Can I have a ride?" she asked timidly.

"Do you see a back seat? No." She gaped at my response. I leaned an arm on the gas tank. "I told you I was an asshole. Unless you want to follow me home to fuck me, I'm not interested."

Her eyes got as big as saucers.

I chuckled. "That's what I thought." I started my Harley and took the long way home.

11:47 p.m.

The loud rumble of the bike soothed my senses. It blocked everything I didn't want to think about. I stopped at a gas station\liquor store. My phone vibrated.

BEC2U:

Brutal, huh?

BEC2U:

Do you have a different mindset when you're on your bike vs in your car?

BEC2U:

Hello?

BEC2U:

Sighs, I hope I didn't run you off.

MBFBJAKE13:

Nah. I was at a pool hall and didn't want to stay, so I took a ride. I'll be home in 15, and I'll answer your Q.

BEC2U:

Oh, you're back! I thought I'd lost you

I SMIRKED AT THE SMILEY FACE. IT WOULD BE SOMETHING MARIA OR Andrea would do. I didn't give out my phone number to girls. Never got personal enough to keep in touch. Hell, I only had a handful of numbers in my phone total. I didn't have accounts on social media, either. Only a couple of accounts on bike forums.

THREE
BECCA

I smiled. He hadn't ghosted me after all. It was almost one in the morning, but he said he'd be home soon to answer my questions. My best friend, Summer, had invited me for drinks at a club, but I'd messaged Jake before answering her. When he said he'd be around, I begged off. I loved Summer, but the club scene was not my thing. It was always the same routine.

We would get into the club quickly, thanks to Summer's looks. We'd get swarmed by guys, also thanks to Summer's looks, and immediately she'd hit the dance floor and come to the table for air or a drink. I would be left to guard our drinks and type notes in my phone for an article I was working on or, lately, for my first novel. I wasn't jealous, but we were two totally different people.

We had become fast friends in high school. Summer was Latina, a model, tall, dark skin and stunning. Whereas I was short and blonde. We couldn't be more opposite, but our bond was airtight.

I fixed a fresh cup of coffee, settled on the couch with my laptop and waited for Jake to come home.

MBFBJAKE13:

I'm here.

BEC2U:

Welcome back. I appreciate you taking the time to answer my Qs.

MBFBJAKE13:

Np.

BEC2U:

Do you take on a different persona when you are on your bike vs in your car?

MBFBJAKE13:

I'm not sure what you're asking. Do I become a different person?

BEC2U:

Sorta.

MBFBJAKE13:

Never thought about it. Me, I don't change. I'm an asshole everywhere.

BEC2U:

Lol. I'm sure you're not an asshole everywhere.

MBFBJAKE13:

Yeah. I am.

BEC2U:

You're not to me.

MBFBJAKE13:

You don't really know me.

BEC2U:

Hmm, true. Do you think most bikers do that? Take on a different persona.

MBFBJAKE13:

I'm not sure what the percentage would be, but I know a lot of weasel dicks.

BEC2U:

Lol, what?

I LAUGHED OUT LOUD AT THE 'WEASEL' PHRASE. WHERE ON EARTH DID HE come up with that?

MBFBJAKE13:

It's a term we've come up with. It describes sport bike riders who are young punk ass bitches who are full of themselves.

BEC2U:

When you say we, who are you talking about?

MBFBJAKE13:

Me and our friends. Idk if it's a universal term, but it's accurate. I had to teach a couple of them a lesson tonight.

BEC2U:

You got in a fight?

MBFBJAKE13:

Nah. They thought they wanted to fight, but I convinced them otherwise.

I SIPPED MY COFFEE AND TRIED TO DETERMINE IF HE WAS BEING TRUTHFUL. Or if he was exaggerating. I couldn't decide, and I realized that he could tell me anything. Anything at all.

BEC2U:

Can you tell me where you're from? Doesn't have to be specific but a general area. I just thought some areas would have different lingo.

MBFBJAKE13:

I have nothing to hide. Tulsa, OK.

BEC2U:

Wow. Ok. I'm on the east coast. Divorced, by the way.

MBFBJAKE13:

Single.

WHY DID I TELL HIM I WAS DIVORCED? STUPID. I PRESSED A HAND TO MY forehead. He didn't need to know that. I was getting off track. I had this annoying habit of not saying anything or saying everything.

BEC2U:

Back to my original question, would you say most are different people on bikes vs cagers?

MBFBJAKE13:

I know a lot of bikers patched and not, and I'd say no, except weasels. Most bikers are who they say they are. But I've been drinking.

BEC2U:

Hehe. I'm drinking coffee to keep me awake.

MBFBJAKE13:

I rarely sleep.

BEC2U:

That's not good for you.

MBFBJAKE13:

Most things aren't good for you.

BEC2U:

True. Well, I can't think of any more questions tonight.

MBFBJAKE13:

I have a Q.

. . .

AND HERE'S WHERE IT GOES SOUTH. A TIPSY BIKER AND AN ADMITTED asshole, although he didn't seem an asshole so far. I waited for the dreaded dick pic or some sexting.

MBFBJAKE13:

Why did you get divorced?

OUT OF ALL THE THINGS I THOUGHT HE'D ASK, THAT WAS NOT ON MY LIST. I chewed my lip and debated how to answer. Whether to give a simple line like I gave most people or, to be brutally honest, to use a page out of his book. I thought he'd been honest, though I didn't have proof of that. It was just instinct.

BEC2U:

He was extremely controlling, and he hit me.

MBFBJAKE13:

That motherfucker.

A FEW TEARS SEEPED FROM MY EYES, AND I HUGGED MYSELF. I DIDN'T TELL most people that. I didn't want to see the pity in their eyes or hear them question why I had put up with it for so long. So, I avoided it all together. It wasn't worth it. I didn't know why I told Jake the truth. Maybe it was because I really didn't know him. A safe place. From Jake's response, he seemed mad about it. I didn't know what I expected, but it wasn't anger.

MBFBJAKE13:

My dad beat my mom and me.

I GASPED AND COVERED MY MOUTH AND STARED AT HIS TYPED WORDS. HE understood. He actually understood what I went through. Wait a minute…

BEC2U:

When you were a child?

MBFBJAKE13:

Yep. Mom, too.

BEC2U: Y

ou mean your mom beat you too?

MBFBJAKE13:

Yep.

No. I DIDN'T REMOTELY UNDERSTAND HOW YOUR PARENTS COULD BEAT their own child. I knew fear. I had learned to anticipate my ex's moods. Well, at least, I tried to. How could a child learn to live like that? And from *both* parents.

BEC2U:

…I'm speechless.

MBFBJAKE13:

Yep.

BEC2U:

I'm so sorry.

MBFBJAKE13:

I don't need or want your pity. Just facts.

BEC2U:

I don't pity you. I admire you.

~

JAKE

I PACED BEHIND THE COUCH. I SHOULD HAVE NEVER ASKED HER WHY SHE got divorced, but I was curious and was tipsy enough. I had asked... like a dumbass. And why go into my past? An image flashed in my mind, unwanted and unbidden, of my old man beating a faceless girl.

Bec.

Then me.

The image in my mind was so bright, I flinched. My vision went in and out, and I gripped the back of the couch to get some kind of grounding.

"YOU WORTHLESS, PUNY ASS WIMP," DAD SPIT AT ME. I COVERED MY HEAD as blows rained down on my small body. I tried to wad up to become smaller, but it was no use.

MY VISION CLEARED A BIT, AND I TRIED TO ORIENT MYSELF. I RETURNED TO the couch and fisted my trembling hands. I checked my watch.

12:38 a.m.

MBFBJAKE13:

I have to go.

BEC2U:

Wait, are you ok?

35

MBFBJAKE13:

Night.

I SHUT MY LAPTOP AND GRIPPED MY HAIR. THIS WAS GONNA BE A LONG night. I abruptly shot off the couch, went to the bedroom, stripped and changed into loose shorts. Grabbing my phone and earbuds, walked down the hall to my garage and flipped on the light. Stuck my earbuds in and selected a playlist on my phone. Time to let off some steam.

I swung at the punching bag that hung in the garage, but I didn't bother to put my gloves on. I wanted to feel the pain. Needed it. I alternated between punches and kicks as sweat glistened on my skin and poured in my face. As the lyrics blared and my blood pumped to the erratic beat of the music, I faded away.

I was on autopilot. Not really there...

Numb...

Nothing...

I found myself sitting on one of two barstools in my garage. I looked down at the sting of my hands. My knuckles were raw, and blood dripped off them to the floor. I blinked. My music had stopped. I didn't know for how long. I blinked again. My two motorcycles were sitting in the garage. I vaguely recalled talking to Bec.

Fuck.

It had been a long time since I had a blackout. I raked a hand through my hair and checked my watch.

3:32 a.m.

I lost a little over two hours and scraped a hand through my short beard. I stumbled into the house and stepped into the shower, adjusted the temp till was ice cold and ducked under the spray. Leaning on my elbows on the shower wall, I shivered. Trying to be present.

Then I remembered. Her ex had beaten her.

I shivered more, and not from the freezing water.

That was what triggered me. More like a bomb had been dropped.

I stood in the shower for a few more minutes, got out, toweled off, hung it on a hook and walked naked through the house. Downing a bottle of Gatorade, I leaned against the counter and inhaled a few deep breaths.

Fuck.

I was used to the numbness, that wasn't the problem. It had been a few years since I had a blackout. But the way I was feeling lately, I was surprised it wasn't sooner. I rubbed the back of my neck. She had no clue of my background, at least she didn't until I ran my fucking mouth. I grabbed some shorts, phone, and sat down on the couch again and opened my laptop.

3:57 a.m.

There were exactly five messages from Bec.

> BEC2U:
>
> Jake?
>
> BEC2U:
>
> Are you ok?
>
> BEC2U:
>
> Message me as soon as you can, so I know you're all right.
>
> BEC2U:
>
> I know about triggers. I get them too.
>
> BEC2U:
>
> Please be all right.

STARING AT THE SCREEN, I SAT BACK. I DIDN'T KNOW WHETHER TO BE thankful she understood or mad as hell she understood. I ran a hand over my face. It was after five in the morning where she was, but I answered anyway. I was sure she'd get it in the morning, but I wasn't going to sleep anytime soon.

MBFBJAKE13:

I'm fine.

BEC2U:

Thank goodness.

MY BROWS FURROWED. SHE ANSWERED IMMEDIATELY. LIKE SHE WAS waiting up for me.

MBFBJAKE13:

Why are you still up? I thought you'd be asleep.

BEC2U:

I was worried about you.

MBFBJAKE13:

But you don't know me.

BEC2U:

I know what it feels like to suffer from trauma and to feel like you're alone.

I FROWNED AT THE SCREEN. FOR ALL SHE KNEW, I COULD BE FEEDING HER bullshit. My jaw clenched and my fist tightened. I tried to figure out what to say, but I didn't really talk to real people, much less cyber people.

MBFBJAKE13:

Ok.

BEC2U:

You don't have to talk about it if you don't want to, but the door is open if you do.

MBFBJAKE13:

Ok.

WAS SHE FOR REAL? OR WAS SHE A SHRINK? I FROWNED HARDER AT THE screen. Maria tried several times to get me to see a therapist. She had even offered to pay for it when I was a teen. Fuck that shit. I didn't need some psych doc poking around in my head. They'd probably lock me up and throw away the key.

BEC2U:

Ok. I work at a paper, and, as you know, an aspiring author.

I FROWNED HARDER. WHAT THE FUCK? IT WAS FINE WHEN SHE WAS ASKING questions about bikes, but she was fishing for information about me. But it was my fault for prying into her life and opening my mouth to parts about me. Dumbass.

MBFBJAKE13:

What are you doing?

BEC2U:

I assume you can't sleep, and you want a distraction from yourself. At least, that's what I want when I've been triggered.

SHE WAS RIGHT, AND I DID NEED A DISTRACTION FROM MYSELF.

MBFBJAKE13:

I'm a mechanic.

BEC2U:

Bike mechanic?

MBFBJAKE13:

No. Ford. But I could be. I've worked on construction sites, too.

BEC2U:

Cool. You work with your hands. I've always admired people who can build and fix things.

I LOOKED DOWN AT MY HANDS. THE SESSION WITH THE PUNCHING BAG rubbed my knuckles raw and red. They hurt, but I really didn't feel it unless I focused on them.

MBFBJAKE13:

It's no big deal.

BEC2U:

I'm sure to you it's no big deal, but something simple can turn into a big headache for me. Like putting together a desk. I had to eventually hire somebody.

MBFBJAKE13:

So, you tried to put it together?

BEC2U:

Yeah. It didn't work out...if you're laughing. Stop.

MBFBJAKE13:

Not laughing. But it's funny.

BEC2U:

Haha, not.

MBFBJAKE13:

Haha, I better let you go get some sleep. It's 6 a.m. where you are.

BEC2U:

You sure you're okay?

MBFBJAKE13:

I'm good. Night.

BEC2U:

Goodnight, Jake.

I STARED AT THOSE LAST WORDS. FOR SOME REASON, IT DID SOMETHING TO my gut. I didn't have a clue what it was. I couldn't even explain it. Hoping to crash for a few hours, I headed to the bedroom and rubbed my chest absently.

"YOU FUCKIN' FAGGOT!" DAD FLUNG ME AGAINST THE WALL, AND I crumpled to the floor. I bit my lip to hold back the scream. The taste of blood filled my mouth as I held my arm at an awkward angle. I stayed right there, on the floor where I fell. I squeezed my eyes shut, but I could hear everything.

"This is the way to treat a woman," Dad grated out with a chuckle. "Take it, bitch." A slap against skin. And another. I flinched with every slap, even though I wasn't the one being hit—yet.

I JERKED AWAKE, SWINGING, AS MY FIST SLAMMED INTO THE MATTRESS. MY eyes popped open. Sweat poured off of me. I clenched my hand in my wet hair and gasped for air. Blood filled my mouth where I bit my lip.

Fuck.

The covers and pillows were on the floor, and I glanced at my watch.

7:28 a.m.

I only got two hours of sleep. I scrubbed a hand over my face and beard. After taking another cold shower, I loaded up my dirt bike and went to Maria and Carl's. They owned forty acres and me and Tony built a dirt track out there. Complete with jumps, whoops and sharp turns.

I wanted to fly.

Not think. Just feel.

Feel free.

Soon, I was at the track. I turned the corner, revved the throttle and flew high in the air on a jump. The higher I went, the better I felt. Adrenaline pumped through my veins, and I concentrated on the ride. Nothing else. Just the dirt in front of me. Lap after lap. I didn't know how long I'd been riding. It didn't matter. I spotted Maria standing beside the track. I slowed down and stopped right in front of her, turned the bike off. Removed my goggles and helmet and hung them on the handlebars.

She smiled at me and handed me a glass of iced tea. "Good morning."

I took the hem of my t-shirt and mopped the sweat on my face. "Morning. Thanks." I downed it. She made the best sweet tea on the planet.

"You're up early for a Saturday." She peered into my face.

I looked away towards the track. "Good riding weather." It was mid-March, and the weather was perfect.

She sighed. "Yes. It's going to be a lovely day. Do you need to talk about anything? Has your mom been bothering you?"

"Nope." I looked down and hoped the conversation didn't go any further. She meant well, but she was the only person who could read me like a book. At least, when I was younger. She was witness to my nightmares and bruises. And I didn't want to talk about any of it. I was thirty for fucks sake. I should be over it.

She pursed her lips. "Andrea is supposed to be here any time to do wedding stuff. I don't know what I'm gonna do when she moves to Virginia."

"She's really going through with it?" I didn't know why anyone got married anymore, and I handed her back the glass. Hell, I'd only had a couple of girlfriends.

She chuckled. "Yes."

Andrea pulled up and parked, spotted us and headed in our direction. She was only ten when Tony dragged me reluctantly home to Maria to be fixed up, and she had the same black hair and blue eyes as Tony did.

"Hi, Mom." Andrea pulled her in for a hug. "Hi, Jake. You want to do wedding stuff with us?" she asked with a smile.

"Nope. I don't know why you're doing wedding stuff."

She rolled her eyes and huffed. "Because I'm getting married, that's why."

I got off my bike and started pushing it towards my truck. "Why get married at all? Waste of money."

Maria put her hands on her hips like Andrea was doing. "Don't you be filling my girl with that nonsense. And just you wait. A girl is gonna come along and change your views."

Andrea laughed. "I don't know, Mom. Jake doesn't even date."

"One day. Mark my words," Maria declared.

I shook my head. Right. When hell froze over.

FOUR
BECCA

I rushed out the door, late for my lunch date with Summer. I had stayed up way later than normal. Like, *all night*. I couldn't ever remember staying up all night. And for a virtual stranger.

It was Summer's turn to choose the place, so, of course, she chose Cooper's because they had a fantastic wine list. I rushed to the table and about ran over a waitress carrying a huge tray of food. "So sorry," I told the waitress. I plopped down at Summer's table and blew the bangs hanging in my face.

"Sorry I'm late."

She smiled. "Don't worry. See, I have a glass of wine for you. And it's excellent." She pursed her lips and kissed her fingers exaggeratedly.

I laughed. "Did you have fun last night?"

"Mmm girl, did I ever." She crossed her long legs. "But by the end of the night, he was too handsy. I snuck out the back."

I shook my head as she sipped her wine. "You know you'll have to take a chance eventually, right?"

She looked down and fidgeted with her napkin. "I'm not ready yet."

"I know." I grasped her hand and gave her a reassuring squeeze.

With my crazy wife beater ex and Summer's fiancé, who had been dead for years, we were quite a pair.

The waitress came and took our order.

"So how did motorcycle research go?" Summer asked, abruptly changing the subject.

I tucked some hair behind my ear. "It went good." I sipped the wine.

"Why are you hiding behind your wine glass?" She arched a perfectly groomed brow. "What's his name?"

"Jake."

"And?"

"And what?"

Just then, our food was delivered.

She tapped her red nails and studied me. "I know you too well. Spill it."

"He's a mechanic in Oklahoma. And I kind of let it slip I was divorced."

"So? A lot of people are divorced."

"He asked why."

She nodded. "And you told him the real reason."

"Yeah." I debated telling her his reaction, and the why of it. But it wasn't my story to tell. I'd only known him a couple of weeks, and I already felt some loyalty to him. I worried about him. Stayed up all night because of him. It made little sense.

"And?"

"He seemed mad about it."

"Good. That's the right reaction."

The rest of lunch sped by, and Summer had a model booking to go to. I stopped by the bookstore to check out some motorcycle magazines. But the information was mostly technical and went right over my head. I yawned. I hoped Jake got some rest. Right after I split with Nick, I was constantly triggered. I spent a lot of sleepless nights hanging on the edge. I couldn't imagine living like that your whole life. He hadn't told me much, but he didn't have to. My gut instinct told me it was bad.

After getting home to my apartment, I changed into loose cotton pants and a t-shirt. I sat on the couch sipping on some wine and opened my laptop. I went over all the notes for my story, but what I really wanted to do was check on Jake. See how he was.

BEC2U:

Hi, Jake. Hope you're doing well.

MBFBJAKE13:

Good. U?

I SMILED WHEN HE ANSWERED PROMPTLY.

BEC2U:

I had a lunch date with my best friend. I hope you got some rest.

MBFBJAKE13:

No.

I FROWNED AT HIS CURT RESPONSE AND HIS ANSWER.

BEC2U:

I'm sorry. Is this a bad time?

MBFBJAKE13:

No.

I ARCHED A BROW AT THE SCREEN. HE SAID IF HE WAS BUSY, HE'D TELL ME.

BEC2U:

Do you have time for more Qs?

MBFBJAKE13:

Yup.

BEC2U:

I stopped by the bookstore to look at biker magazines, but all of them were so technical. Nothing I've found in books or the net give me the info I was looking for. What do bikers do?

MBFBJAKE13:

Do? What do u mean?

BEC2U:

Like what kind of activities do you do?

MBFBJAKE13:

You mean like pokers runs?

BEC2U:

Exactly. Lol. What are they?

THIS WAS THE KIND OF INFORMATION I WAS LOOKING FOR. I'D SEEN several posts in different places about poker runs, but I didn't have a clue what they were. I had asked, but it seemed if you didn't have a bike or rode on the back of one, you were shut out.

MBFBJAKE13:

A poker run consists of 3 to 5 stops and you buy a 'hand', a piece of paper. At each stop, you draw a chip with a # on it and they write down the #. At the last stop, we turn in our papers. The highest & lowest hands win a prize. Most of the time, it's money.

BEC2U:

Where are the stops at?

MBFBJAKE13:

Usually, bars.

BEC2U:

So, it's a party drink fest and some money.

MBFBJAKE13:

No. It's usually to raise money to help
someone or charities for kids. Or, if a biker is
hurt, the money goes to help. Most of the time
there's a silent auction and 50/50 tickets too.
All the extra money goes to the cause.

MY JAW DROPPED. BIKERS DID CHARITY WORK? THIS OPENED MY UP MIND
to the whole biker community. It made me think there was a good
heart under all those tattoos and leather.

BEC2U:

I had no idea. I'm shocked.

MBFBJAKE13:

Most bikers are very generous of their time and
money. If you are on their good side, they'll
give the shirts off their backs. If you get on
their bad side, they'll burn it with you in it.
Except weasel dicks. No one likes a WD.

BEC2U:

Lol. That term cracks me up. I would love to go
on a run sometime. That's sounds amazing.
And I'll remember to stay on their good side.

MBFBJAKE13:

It's great. Especially the longer runs.

BEC2U:

What do you mean longer?

MBFBJAKE13:

Miles between stops.

BEC2U:

Gotcha. Do you go to many?

MBFBJAKE13:

A few. A lot of bikers are vets or in the service.

BEC2U:

That's interesting. Why do you think that is?

MBFBJAKE13:

Something to do with brotherhood. IDK. I'm drinking FYI.

BEC2U:

Buts it's only 4 p.m.

MBFBJAKE13:

3 here and it's been a shit 24 hours.

I FROWNED. THAT'S WHY HE WAS OFFERING INFORMATION WITHOUT ME asking. I was sure it had something to do with his trigger. At least he was home drinking. He was safe.

MBFBJAKE13:

I did a few laps on my dirt bike at 8 this morn.

BEC2U:

This morning? You didn't get ANY sleep then.

MBFBJAKE13:

2 hours of nightmares.

I COVERED MY MOUTH. MY HEART BROKE FOR HIM. YES, HE COULD BE feeding me all lies, but I didn't think so. He felt too real to be fake, although that didn't make much sense either.

BEC2U:

I'm sorry I triggered you. I didn't mean to do that.

MBFBJAKE13:

Hell, you couldn't have known.

BEC2U:

What are you drinking? If you don't mind me asking.

MBFBJAKE13:

Oilfire with a splash of coke.

BEC2U:

What's Oilfire? I'm drinking wine and had some at lunch.

MBFBJAKE13:

Whiskey. With your gf?

BEC2U:

Yeah, Summer. Are you planning on going out tonight?

I HOPED NOT. HE WAS DRINKING THE HEAVY STUFF, BUT HE WAS A bachelor, so who knew?

MBFBJAKE13:

No. you?

BEC2U:

No.

AND THEN SILENCE. I BIT MY LIP AND LOOKED DOWN. I HAD ONLY GONE ON a handful of dates since I got divorced three years ago. And every one of them were disasters. A guy that I worked with was interested in me, but I felt nothing for him. He was smart, successful, good looking and we could talk for hours. We had kissed on our second date, but it felt like I was kissing my brother. Yuck.

BEC2U:

Do you have any siblings?

MBFBJAKE13:

No. do U?

BEC2U:

No.

MBFBJAKE13:

Tony is like a bro to me, and his sister, Andrea, is like my sis.

BEC2U:

How long have you known him?

MBFBJAKE13:

Since I was 12, and we got in a fight. He's 1 year older than me and Andrea is 2 younger. I don't tell anyone this shit. Maybe cause I'm drunk.

BEC2U:

Lol, but you really haven't told me much.

MBFBJAKE13:

More than I've told people who have known me for years.

THAT STOPPED ME. WAS HE SERIOUS? THIS WAS BASIC INFORMATION, BUT I decided to not press it.

BEC2U:

I've known Summer since I was 13. And only guys could become best friends after a fight.

MBFBJAKE13:

I almost won. Afterward, he dragged my ass to his mom to get fixed up.

BEC2U:

Why did you get into it, anyway?

MBFBJAKE13:

Cause he's a loudmouth. Still is.

BEC2U:

LOL That's the funniest thing.

MBFBJAKE13:

Haha.

BEC2U:

I went to a private school and Summer was the new girl. She's Latina, had broken English and was picked on for that. I helped her learn the language. We've been friends ever since.

MBFBJAKE13:

Are you from money?

BEC2U:

No. Should I be?

MBFBJAKE13:

You went to a private school.

BEC2U:

The public schools are crap here.

MBFBJAKE13:

So? Around here, only the kids that have money go to private schools.

BEC2U:

My mom died from cancer when I was 5. Her life insurance paid for my school.

. . .

I HAD TOLD NO ONE THAT, EXCEPT FOR SUMMER. I DIDN'T KNOW WHY I told Jake. Mom's greatest wish for me was to get a good education. I only had vague memories of her now.

MBFBJAKE13:

Ah shit. Sorry, I didn't know. I told you I was an asshole.

BEC2U:

You couldn't have known. Everyone has demons they are haunted by.

MBFBJAKE13:

You're probably right.

BEC2U:

Truth, I've only told Summer about how my schooling was paid.

MBFBJAKE13:

Truth, I NEVER talk this much to anyone. Not even Tony.

MY EYES WIDENED. SURELY, HE WAS EXAGGERATING.

BEC2U:

Haha. Right.

MBFBJAKE13:

I'm deadly serious. You can ask Tony. I seldom talk.

BEC2U:

Only when you're drunk, right?

MBFBJAKE13:

I only drink heavily when I'm at home alone. I wouldn't know.

BEC2U:

Then why are you talking to me?

MBFBJAKE13:

Fuck if I know.

BEC2U:

Lol. You're funny.

MBFBJAKE13:

Not in person.

BEC2U:

You're an asshole, right?

MBFBJAKE13:

Yup.

BEC2U:

I don't think you're an asshole, and you say you've talked to me more than anyone.

MBFBJAKE13:

Huh.

BEC2U:

Yeah, huh.

I SMILED. HE WASN'T AN ASSHOLE. FAR FROM IT. HE WAS JUST misunderstood, and people saw only what he allowed them to see. It was a defense mechanism. I would tell him that, but it would probably make him mad. But I was curious about one thing—what he looked like. He didn't have a picture on his profile, and I was itching to put a face with the name. But to be fair, I didn't have a picture on my profile either. I finished the glass of wine and refilled it. I friended Jake, turned the profile to private, and uploaded a picture of myself. And waited.

MBFBJAKE13:

Nice pic. I knew you were blonde.

BEC2U:

Lol. Shut up!

MBFBJAKE13:

Okay.

MBFBJAKE13:

I sent you one. I promise it's not a dick pic.

I WAS ALMOST SCARED TO LOOK, BUT THE CURIOSITY WAS KILLING ME. I opened it. My lips parted as I stared. It was a head shot, and he had an angular face with a squared jaw. His black hair was hanging partially in his face, and he had a short beard. His skin was darker, maybe a dark tan, and his brows were low over his eyes. I couldn't tell his eye color. He wasn't the All-American-Boy material, but the bad-boy... correction, man. You could never ever mistake him for a boy. He was rugged. I swallowed. I couldn't look away for a few moments. He was the exact opposite of every guy I had dated. I remembered all he had told me...this image seemed to fit. My heart did this weird flip, and I jerked my gaze away.

Becca, calm down. He's cyber...not real. But he felt real to me.

JAKE

I was sitting on the couch, my laptop was on the coffee table, and I was nursing a bottle of Oilfire whiskey. I had a can of Coke for a chaser, but it had been a while since I'd touched it. I was more than tipsy...I was plastered. And it took more than most to get this way. Thanks to Prick's bloodline. I was talking to Bec. Still. It was the longest conversation I'd ever had. The fuck if I knew why.

I saw the friend request from Bec and accepted it. There was a photo of her that had not been there previously. I clicked on it to make it bigger. She was sitting on the floor, her leg drawn up, and she was smiling. Blonde hair and big brown eyes. I didn't judge anyone by their looks. Looks could be deceiving. If that was really her.

I smirked and took another swig and set it down on the coffee table and thought about uploading one. That had to be why she loaded one. What the hell. I scrolled through my phone. Did I even have a picture of myself? I clicked on one and sent it directly to her.

BEC2U:

Um, what's the color of your eyes? It's hard to tell.

MBFBJAKE13:

Blue-green, but Andrea says hazel. She took the pic. Who the fuck knows why she sent it to me?

BEC2U:

Tony's sister?

MBFBJAKE13:

Yeah. Do you think I take selfies? Lol. Nope.

BEC2U:

You'd be amazed at how many guys take selfies.

MBFBJAKE13:

I bet they're weasel dicks, though.

BEC2U:

Lol. I laugh out loud every time you say that.

I GRINNED AT THAT. NOW I HAD AN IMAGE TO GO WITH THE LAUGH. I looked down at my phone when it vibrated.

6:56 p.m.

. . .

TONY:

Are you coming or what?

JAKE:

Where?

TONY:

Snookers. I texted you.

JAKE:

Must have missed it. No.

TONY:

Why the fuck not? Emma's asking for you.

JAKE:

Who?

TONY:

The girl you dissed last night.

JAKE:

Not interested. And I'm shitfaced.

TONY:

I could come get you.

JAKE:

No.

TONY:

Or we could come to you?

JAKE:

No. Don't you fucking dare. I'll lock you out. I don't want to see anybody. Not in the mood.

TONY COULD BE A PERSISTENT ASSHOLE SOMETIMES. I WANTED TO BE LEFT alone. Except, I was talking to Bec. But she wasn't an asshole.

BEC2U:

Jake? Have you passed out?

MBFBJAKE13:

No. Tony's blowing up my phone.

BEC2U:

Do you need me to let you go?

MBFBJAKE13:

No. He wants me to go to Snookers. And I don't want to.

BEC2U:

What's that? I don't think you should drive.

MBFBJAKE13:

It's a pool hall and bar. I told him that. He offered to come get me. I told him to fuck off.

BEC2U:

Lol.

MBFBJAKE13:

Apparently this girl is asking for me. Like I fucking care. BRB.

THIS TEXT FROM TONY RILED ME. I WENT TO THE GARAGE AND FLIPPED ON the light and called Tony.

The background noise of Snookers was loud when Tony answered.

"Hey, Jake. It's Jake everybody."

I could hear everybody say hi. Tony was lit. "Don't come to my house, asshole. I'm dealing with some shit." I didn't have to tell him what that shit was. Tony knew. "Are you sober enough to understand?"

"Ah, man. Hell. Sorry. Do you need anything?"

"No. I need to be alone. I'm not safe to be around anyone." I hated to admit it, but I didn't need people to be invading my space right now. Anything could set me off. I had to get my head twisted on right to let people in my personal space, and that didn't happen often.

"Got it. Message heard."

"Thanks." I hung up and, with a shaking hand, put my phone in my pocket.

I directed my attention to the punching bag and hit it numerous times. My phone chimed.

"Fuck."

I pulled it from my pocket to fling it but stopped once I saw it wasn't Tony.

7:42 p.m.

BEC2U:

Hey, you seem to be busy, so I'll let you go.

MBFBJAKE13:

I'm not busy, just had to make a phone call to make sure the asshole didn't show up at my house with that girl I couldn't remember.

WHY DIDN'T I LET HER THINK I WAS BUSY? IT WOULD HAVE BEEN THE EASY way out. I walked to the kitchen sink, turned on the faucet and stuck my head under the ice-cold water and let it drown me for a few minutes. I turned the faucet off, grabbed a hand towel and dried my hair off. When I sat back on the couch, my hair still dripped, but I didn't care.

BEC2U:

Did you meet her last night?

MBFBJAKE13:

Yeah.

BEC2U:

Why couldn't you remember her?

MBFBJAKE13:

Are you sure you want me to answer this Q?

BEC2U:

Try me.

MBFBJAKE13:

I don't remember girl's names, usually. They're just to fuck. That's it. And this one had the deer-in-headlights-look when she looked at me. I don't go for those types of girls. Even I have morals. Somewhat. Just remember, you asked.

BEC2U:

Wow. Umm, I don't know what to say. That's pretty harsh.

MBFBJAKE13:

I told you I was an asshole. Told her that, too. No one listens. And then when I prove it, everybody is shocked.

BEC2U:

Do you treat all girls that way?

MBFBJAKE13:

Mostly. Exceptions being Maria, Andrea and a couple of friends' girls.

BEC2U:

You don't treat me that way.

MBFBJAKE13:

You don't know me in person.

BEC2U:

But you don't know me in person, either.

MBFBJAKE13:

Good point.

. . .

I EYED THE BOTTLE OF OILFIRE AND DEBATED WHETHER OR NOT TO FINISH IT off. A typical hangover had you worshiping a toilet bowl and hiding in your bed the next day. Not me. I would drink till I passed out and, in a few hours, wake sober as shit. Tony was jealous of it, but I knew it was nothing to be jealous of. I was the son of an alcoholic...a sadistic son-of-a-bitch who got off on other people's pain. The pain of animals, too. Prick liked to torture pets, so I gave them away.

Hate was too simple.

I loathed him with an all-consuming passion and thought several times about killing him. That fucking prick was a waste of breath. As I stared at the bottle, my breathing echoed in the living room and a roar pounded in my ears.

BEC2U:

I don't think you'd treat me that way.

BEC2U:

Are you there?

BEC2U:

Jake?

I GRABBED THE BOTTLE AND THREW IT AGAINST THE WALL. THE GLASS shattered and amber liquid ran down to the floor. I scrubbed my face and beard. My vision, blurry and unfocused, and I tried unsuccessfully to get control of my thoughts and emotions.

8:23 p.m.

BEC2U:

Jake, are you ok?

． ． ．

I FOCUSED ON MY LAPTOP, AND BEC'S WORDS.

MBFBJAKE13:

No.

SHE DIDN'T KNOW IT, BUT THAT WAS THE FIRST TIME I'D EVER ADMITTED IT. I was not okay. Never had been okay. My leg bounced, and I put my head in my hands as waves of emotions and memories crashed into me.

BEC2U:

Listen to me, take really deep belly breaths. I know it sounds stupid, but it really helps. Okay?

MBFBJAKE13:

I should be over all this shit. Fucking stupid.

BEC2U:

You're not stupid.

MBFBJAKE13:

I don't want to talk about this anymore. It serves no purpose. Just a vicious circle.

BEC2U:

You're right. So, how tall are you?

MBFBJAKE13:

6'1".

BEC2U:

What's your favorite color?

MBFBJAKE13:

Black. Are you just gonna ask me question after question?

BEC2U:

Yes. Lol

MBFBJAKE13:

Yours?

BEC2U:

Pink. What kind of cage do you drive?

MBFBJAKE13:

Black Ford truck. You?

BEC2U:

A bright yellow Jeep I love. Nick made me buy a boring gray Buick, but as soon as the divorce went through, I traded it in.

MBFBJAKE13:

Nick was an asshole.

BEC2U:

Yup. You're not. He wanted me to quit my job because it didn't 'fit' with what he thought his wife should do. Tried everything he could to control my every thought and action.

MBFBJAKE13:

How long were you married?

BEC2U:

4 years. Too damn long. It was gradual. He appeared caring at first, but it was all an act.

I REALIZED, AS SHE TALKED, I CALMED DOWN. NO LONGER FOCUSING ON my shit. No longer breathing hard. No longer grinding my teeth. And that...amazed me. She knew I'd been through some shit, but she demanded nothing from me. Like information. If she had, I wouldn't be talking to her right now.

. . .

MBFBJAKE13:

I'm a different kind of asshole. Good on you to get out.

BEC2U:

I'm proud of myself. So many girls stay stuck. And I'm gonna let the asshole comment slide for now. What are your hobbies?

MBFBJAKE13:

Still with 20 Qs? Anything to get my blood pumping.

FIVE
BECCA

I bit my bottom lip and shook my head. Why did I immediately think dirty thoughts? Maybe because if the picture he sent was really him, he was dead sexy, in an unconventional way. But he could have snagged that image anywhere.

BEC2U:

Like?

MBFBJAKE13:

Riding my bikes, bungee jumping, skydiving and parachuting, ziplines, water skiing and fucking.

HEAT HIT MY FACE. I DIDN'T THINK HE WOULD SAY IT, BUT I WAS THINKING about it. I refused to comment on it, though.

BEC2U:

Sounds like you are an adrenaline junkie.

MBFBJAKE13:

I suppose so. What's yours?

BEC2U:

Boring stuff. Haha.

MBFBJAKE13:

Try me.

BEC2U:

Okay, just remember you asked. Antique stores, old bookstores, Starbucks and riding in my Jeep with the top down to let the wind mess up my hair.

MBFBJAKE13:

You would definitely love motorcycle rides then, and it seems all you white girls love Starbucks.

BEC2U:

Lol. Just remember, you asked. I would love to go on a motorcycle ride sometime.

I DIDN'T SAY, *WITH YOU*. THAT WOULD BE TOTALLY STUPID. NOT TO mention, he was in Oklahoma, and I was in Virginia. He couldn't possibly give me a ride, and if what he said was true, he probably wouldn't offer, anyway. He said girls were just to fuck, and that's it. Seemed hard to believe.

MBFBJAKE13:

What's your favorite food?

BEC2U:

Now you're asking me Qs? Hehe. Peel and eat shrimp, crab, and pasta. You?

MBFBJAKE13:

BBQ and pizza. Turnabout is fair play.

BEC2U:

Favorite music?

MBFBJAKE13:

5 Finger Death Punch, Slipknot and Alice in Chains.

BEC2U:

Wow. I wouldn't have guessed that being in Oklahoma.

MBFBJAKE13:

Not everybody here likes country. You?

BEC2U:

Brantley Gilbert, Lady A and Eric Church.

MBFBJAKE13:

No offense, but your music sucks. Gags.

BEC2U:

Lol. Stop it. I think the same thing about yours.

MBFBJAKE13:

But mine is actually good.

BEC2U:

We're going to have to agree to disagree on that one.

MBFBJAKE13:

Nope. Yours sux.

BEC2U:

Lol. I can't believe you're still awake.

MBFBJAKE13:

Barely. I don't sleep much.

BEC2U:

I'll let you go so you can sleep. Night, Jake.

MBFBJAKE13:

Night.

AFTER I SHUT MY LAPTOP, I CURLED UP IN BED. JAKE WAS STILL AT THE forefront of my mind. It went from me asking question about bikes to becoming very personal, very fast. He understood my pain and triggers. But his pain went even deeper. I snuggled in to my soft body pillow, and my arms wrapped around it. I drifted off to sleep with his image in my head.

MY ALARM STARTLED ME AWAKE. I SHUT IT OFF AND PUT MY HAND AGAINST my head. I was dreaming. Of Jake. I squeezed my thighs together. It had been three years since I had been with a man. Not that I didn't like sex but getting myself off seemed safer than actually being with a man. I had wet dreams before, but not with a specific man or image. Jake's face was there. His calloused hands skimming over my flesh. Well, I imagined his hands were rough, because he was a mechanic. I flopped on my back and blew my long bangs out of my face. I glanced at the time: eight-thirty. It wouldn't be right if I got off on him. Would it? We would never meet, I reasoned. I could blush all I wanted behind a screen, and he would never know it.

I bent my legs, pressed my heels into the mattress, moved a hand under my panties and slid a finger in. Still wet from the dream, I moved my fingers so they grazed my clit. In and out. I panted and arched my hips in time. I cupped my breast and tweaked a nipple. Before long, it was a frantic pace. I saw his face in my mind, and I rolled my fingers around my clit. I groaned, convulsed and squeezed my legs together tightly. My breath rushed past my lips. I blinked and sighed.

Suddenly, tears seeped into my pillow. I had been with only two men. The first one when I had been fifteen and only twice. The second was Nick, whom I had been with since I was seventeen. Belatedly, I realized, Nick saw me as only a vassal to satisfy him. To obey his every command. My wants, needs, likes, and dislikes were irrelevant. I wiped at my eyes and got dressed for my run.

Keeping trim was another thing he insisted on. I quickly recognized it was a way to escape his orders. I would put my earbuds in, and he would leave me in peace while I pounded on the treadmill. To stay trim for him. He never caught on I did it to avoid his demands on me.

A short time later, I was at my desk with a cup of coffee, trying to work out a plot for my biker novel. I tapped my pen absently.

BEC2U:

Are you around for more Qs?

MBFBJAKE13:

Yeah.

I DIDN'T EXPECT A REPLY SO QUICKLY.

BEC2U:

Did you get any rest?

MBFBJAKE13:

I thought you were gonna ask bike Qs?

I PULLED MY HEAD BACK. IT WAS A STARK DIFFERENCE BETWEEN THE JAKE last night, and the Jake today.

BEC2U:

Is this a bad time?

MBFBJAKE13:

If it was, I would've said.

71

BEC2U:

Okay...not all bikers are patched, obviously. What's the difference in the mentality between bikers who are not patched and those who are?

MBFBJAKE13:

IDFK. They want to be accepted in some way. Maybe.

BEC2U:

But you and Tony don't?

MBFBJAKE13:

No. IDFK.

THE CHANGE WAS SO STARK. MAYBE HE WAS AN ASSHOLE, LIKE HE SAID.

BEC2U:

Do you need to get something off your chest?

MBFBJAKE13:

Are you a fucking shrink? Because, trust me, no one wants to be in my head. Including me.

BEC2U:

No, I'm not a shrink. I would be a crappy one if I was, and let Nick reduce me to nothing.

MBFBJAKE13:

You're not nothing.

BEC2U:

He made me feel that way. My dad died when I was 17, and it was unexpected. I was in a fog when I met Nick. I thought he was my hero because he took care of everything, then I came out of the fog too late to see who he really was.

. . .

Why did I tell him that? I seemed to word 'vomit stuff' I held in my heart. But he wasn't real. He was just a name on a screen. *Oh, that's why you got off on him?* Right.

MBFBJAKE13:

It wasn't too late. You're free.

BEC2U:

Hmm...I am, aren't I? Thanks for pointing that out.

MBFBJAKE13:

That girl showed up at my house last night. Tony, the fucker, gave her my address as a 'present'. I told him I was not in the right frame of mind. Fucker wouldn't listen.

The thought of someone else with him left a sour taste in my mouth. And that was just ridiculous. Earth to Becca? He's an online guy. He's not really real. Even though I didn't want to know what happened, I assumed he was going to tell me.

BEC2U:

Did something bad happen?

MBFBJAKE13:

Yeah. I fucked her, and she got all pissy, because I said a name that wasn't hers.

BEC2U:

Wow.

MBFBJAKE13:

After you and I talked, I smoked a blunt to get some sleep. I was fucking high as a kite and plastered when she showed up, then I called her Bec.

MY EYES WIDENED AS I STARED AT THE SCREEN. HE SMOKED WEED. AND fucked a girl, and he called her Bec. The blood drained from my face and then filled it. Then…I recalled this morning.

Oh, boy.

BEC2U:

I don't know what to say.

MBFBJAKE13:

I was high and drunk. I saw your name on the screen and didn't know what her name. Easy mistake.

BEC2U:

That was not an easy mistake. That's horrible, and I bet she was offended.

MBFBJAKE13:

The last time I saw her, I said, 'If you're not going to follow me home to fuck me, I'm not interested'. She made her choice last night.

BEC2U:

You weren't lying about your treatment of girls.

MBFBJAKE13:

Nope.

BEC2U:

At least you know her name now.

MBFBJAKE13:

Nope.

BEC2U:

You're lying.

MBFBJAKE13:

Lol. Nope.

BEC2U:

Jake! That's awful.

MBFBJAKE13:

Maybe I'll use your name in place of name-less bitches every time.

THE THOUGHT OF HIM USING MY NAME EVERY TIME HE WAS HAVING SEX with other girls both disgusted me and perversely aroused me. But I would not admit to him or, for that matter, myself. And I would not address the nameless-bitch description either.

BEC2U:

Um. I'd prefer you not.

MBFBJAKE13:

Okay.

BEC2U:

Okay.

MBFBJAKE13:

Lol.

BEC2U:

You are, aren't you?

MBFBJAKE13:

You'll never know. Haha.

Damn. I realized I'd never know the truth of the matter. And I would not admit to myself or him that my panties were wet just thinking about.

BEC2U:

You don't play fair. Back to my bike Q. Why are you not patched?

MBFBJAKE13:

I don't want to be.

BEC2U:

Okay. But why have you decided not to be?

MBFBJAKE13:

I don't want to be responsible for anyone, and I'm really shitty at taking orders.

BEC2U:

Not surprising you wouldn't take orders well, but why would you be responsible for anyone?

MBFBJAKE13:

The club is a brotherhood. They have each other's back. I don't rely on anyone, and I don't want people relying on me.

BEC2U:

The clubs seem to be tightknit groups.

MBFBJAKE13:

There are several clubs that tried to talk me into it. A few of my friends. Just not interested in that lifestyle. One club offered to cut my time as a prospect in half.

BEC2U:

Why do they want you?

MBFBJAKE13:

Cause I know how to fight.

THAT SURPRISED ME. ALTHOUGH, I SHOULDN'T BE. HE WAS A BIKER WHO was an admitted asshole, smoked weed, drank excessively, and had sex with nameless random women. It fit the profile. On the surface, he was an asshole, but I sensed something deeper. Something he wanted to keep hidden.

BEC2U:

Have you been trained?

MBFBJAKE13:

Yeah. By my old man. The hard way.

I FROZE. I DIDN'T WANT TO TRIGGER HIM AGAIN, BUT I HAD SO MANY questions. He was the most complex person I had ever met. There were so many edges to him. I wondered if I would, eventually, cut myself on one of his edges.

BEC2U:

I'm sorry.

MBFBJAKE13:

I don't want or need your pity.

BEC2U:

I don't pity you. You're a survivor.

MBFNJAKE13:

No biggie.

BEC2U:

You're wrong, but I'll let it slide. Why would they want you because you know how to fight?

MBFBJAKE13:

To make me an enforcer.

BEC2U:

To carry out orders by any means necessary.

MBFBJAKE13:

You've done your research.

BEC2U:

Lol. Yes, I have. But what I've read about Club Enforcers is, to be a good one, you have to be cold. Indifferent. And have questionable morals.

MBFBJAKE13:

Yup.

BEC2U:

You don't seem to be cold. I would say you run hot.

MBFBJAKE13:

Are you saying I'm hot?

BEC2U:

Uhm...I'm gonna plead the fifth.

HEAT HIT MY FACE, AND I SHOOK MY HEAD. YEAH, HE WAS HOT. BUT HE seemed to not care either way. No matter what angle I took, it always turned back around to personal questions about him.

MBFBJAKE13:

An enforcer needs to be cold to a point, then when action begins, he needs to 'run hot'. I've been called the coldest bastard around.

BEC2U:

I get that about the enforcer, but I don't think you're cold at all. Harsh. Maybe brutal. But not cold.

MBFBJAKE13:

That's because you think I'm hot. Lol.

BEC2U:

Jake, stop it! Lol.

MBFBJAKE13:

I've fought in some underground fights and some bikers saw me. Rumors spread pretty fast.

BEC2U:

What do you mean, underground?

MBFBJAKE13:

Illegal.

BEC2U:

Right.

MBFBJAKE13:

I gotta go. Bye.

BEC2U:

Bye, Jake.

JAKE

12:46 P.M.

I stared at the screen, and my brows furrowed. The last thing she said was 'Bye, Jake'. I couldn't identify what or why there was a tingling at the back of my neck when she said my name. *Every time* she said my name. Being hyperaware saved my ass countless times, but it was just a named typed on a screen. I couldn't, obviously, hear her voice to read any inflections that would change with her moods. I'd became an expert at that, thanks to my parents. Words on a screen shouldn't affect me at all. I closed my laptop, changed clothes and hopped on my Harley.

It was pristine weather for a ride, and I would've taken the long way, but Bec had pulled me into another conversation. She knew more about me than *anyone* in just a few days. Why I let her in, I didn't fucking know. Maybe because she wasn't real in my mind. But last night, 'Bec' was way too real when I fucked that nameless bitch.

She, whatever her name was, had a nice ass. I pulled her hair, and she gushed all over me. She looked innocent, but she liked it rough. I made her come twice more before I nutted. Even when I said Bec's name, she was pissed and cussed me out, but she didn't stop. Only moaned louder. And when we were done, she straightened her clothes, slipped her number to me and left. She never gave her name or fixed the screw-up, which told me she didn't care what I called her. Maybe I'd call her for round two if she acted like that every time.

I whipped my bike into the parking lot of Psycho Tattoos. I shoved my kickstand down, put on my grip-lock and walked in. Psycho was putting plastic wrap on the roll around-table.

"What up, brother," he said.

No matter how many times I told him I wasn't getting patched into his club, he still called me brother.

"Not much." I took off my leather jacket and t-shirt and laid it over a chair.

"Ooowee," Hails said, as she came from the back. "Mmm. I don't know how you do it, but the older you get, the sexier you get."

As she went in for a hug, I stiffened up. I had to learn to accept hugs over the years, but I never received them easily. She patted my chest a little longer than necessary.

"How are you doing, Hails?"

"Can't complain."

"Quit feeling up my client," Psycho said and muttered under his breath about crazy bitches.

"I heard that. And I would do more than feel him up if he'd let me." She gave me a wink.

She would. And the whole Rolling Asylum MC would be after my ass if I so much as sniffed her direction. "I don't need to be castrated, Hails."

"Smart man," Psycho said. "I've worked up a couple of different drawings for you to look at."

I leaned down and grinned. "They're both badass. But the kid's face sold me on this one. On my back, left side."

"You got it. Let me do the stencil, and we'll get to work."

I moved to stand at the window and watched the traffic roll by. A couple of girls came in, but I didn't spare them a second glance. Hails was a sister to Psycho, and she was a tattoo artist, too. She was good, but not Psycho good. He worked in layers. Like a painter. It was not long until I was sitting backwards in the chair, getting poked over and over again with needles. Ink therapy. Nothing like it.

"You thought about our offer?" Psycho asked.

"No."

"I'm telling you, joining the club would be dope. You go to our events anyway."

"If you weren't a sic tat artist, I'd find somebody else. No. You won't talk me into it." I shook my head.

"If you let anyone else mark up your skin, I'll burn it off of you."

I blew out a breath. "You could try."

"Hey, it might take half the MC to take you down, but it'd be worth it." We shared a laugh. "It would be easier if you had a girl. Hold her for ransom, or some shit."

"When hell freezes over," I muttered.

"I'm up for the job," Hails said loudly, and the girls giggled.

"Not a chance, Hails," I replied.

A few hours later, he was done with the first of many sessions to follow. I backed in front of a mirror and held a handheld mirror over my back to view Psycho's handiwork.

"I outlined the face and did all the contrast red first," Psycho said.

It was a skull with a slack jaw and a child's creepy face inside. It said Hell at the top and had one ram's horn coming out of the skull.

"That's sic. Thanks, man."

"I'll see you in about a month, but I'll probably see you on the bikes sooner."

I shrugged on my shirt and jacket, waved, and then headed out. It was dusk, and I let the rumble from my bike and the sting from my fresh art soothe me. I didn't know why the pain from tattoos calmed my soul, but it did. Maybe it had something to do with being an adrenaline junkie, like Bec said.

I pulled into Snookers, parked right beside Tony's bike, and went to our normal table. It was the same girl from two nights ago hanging beside Tony. If she was going to be a regular thing, I might have to remember her name. I bumped fists with Tony.

"How did Psycho's go?" Tony said and sipped his beer.

I shook my head. "That fucker fixed me up. As always."

"Let's see it."

I slid my jacket off, pulled my left arm through my shirt and turned my back towards them.

"No way," Tony exclaimed in the loudest voice possible. "Dude, that's cool as shit, but Mom won't like it."

"No. Mom won't like it at all." I slid my arm back through my shirt and caught the expression on the girl's face who was hanging off Tony. Seems I didn't have to remember her name after all, because she was eyeing me up and down and licking her lips.

I clapped Tony's shoulder and said in a low voice next to his head, "She's 'fishing'."

"You serious?"

"Sorry, man."

"Fuck. I thought she was different," Tony said. He dropped his head and put his hands on his hips.

'Fishing' is a term me and Tony came up with for women who appeared to be disloyal. I had a total of two girlfriends, and that was enough for me. I never tried again for a steady girl, but Tony did from time to time. I glanced at Tony, and he turned just in time to catch her eye-fucking me. She played it off well, focused on Tony quick. Not quick enough, though.

I wondered why girls were so wishy-washy. I hadn't met one loyal one. Except, Maria. Even Andrea wasn't loyal. She changed men like she changed socks. Maybe me and Tony caused some of that, but most of the men she seemed to get with were douche-canoes. Kevin seemed the only one who stuck around, despite me and Tony trying to scare him off.

I shrugged on my jacket, got a beer from the bar and noticed a pair of eyes staring at me. It was the same girl who I had bent over my couch early this morning. What the fuck? She had that deer-in-head-lights look again and looked hella nervous. It was such a one-eighty—it gave me whiplash. She timidly walked up to me, and I was so confused, I let her.

"I need to talk to you," she said. "Privately."

"Okay." I furrowed my brow and let her drag me off to a quieter section of the bar.

Her face was flushed pink, like she was embarrassed, and it was freaking me the fuck out, because this was not an act. I knew when somebody was fake.

"Did we do anything last night?"

I rubbed the back of my neck. "You don't remember?"

Her eyes filled with tears, and she shook her head.

Fuck. "Did you do drugs last night?"

She shook her head again, wiped a lone tear and looked down. "I have a personality disorder," she said, just barely over a whisper.

SIX
JAKE

How come I always attract the crazy bitches? "Yeah. You came to my house, and we fucked."

Her hand covered her mouth, and her eyes widened. "Did you use protection?"

I stared hard at her. "Yeah. I always do. Do I look stupid?"

"No." She swallowed. "Did I at least enjoy it?"

Was she for real? I didn't bother to answer and started to walk off, but she grabbed my arm and stopped me.

"Please? Tell me."

This was the most fucked up conversation I'd had in my life. And I'd had some doozies. "Yes. You gushed all over me three times before I nutted. Straightened your clothes, gave me your number and walked out."

She took a step back with wide eyes and then blinked.

I thought of the conversation with Bec this morning about names and groaned. I put my hand on my hip...fuckin' Bec. "Tell me your name." I lifted my eyes to look at her.

"You don't even know my name?" she asked with irritation.

"If I did, I wouldn't be asking it." And that's why they called me antisocial. I raised an eyebrow and waited.

She straightened her spine and looked me in the eye. "Emma."

I downed my beer, tossed it in the trash and made my way back to our table. When I did, I noticed Emma was my tag-along, and I shook my head. If she had designs on me, she was in for a rude awakening. We reached the table in the back in time to hear the no-name-girl yelling at Tony. I was too sober for this shit.

7:52 p.m.

"That's Meagan," Emma said from right next to me. "I assumed you didn't know her name, either."

"No, I didn't." I didn't add. I really didn't fucking care either.

Tony laughed and said to Meagan. "It's cool. All the girls want Jake at least once."

And Aaron, Krista and Mack laughed. I glanced lamely at each of them. "Right."

Tony clapped me on the back and looked at the girl beside me. "Hey, Emma. If you want a go at it, Jake," Tony pointed to Meagan. "You're welcome to her. She has a nice ass."

Emma gaped. "Do you guys pass around girls like they're nothing?"

I looked at Meagan. "If the shoe fits."

Everyone laughed loudly at Meagan's outraged face, and both she and Emma left.

"That's why you're called a cold bastard," Krista said as she shook her head and smiled.

I shrugged. "Call it like I see it. Oh, if you guys were thinking of fucking Emma." I looked at Tony and Mack. "Heads up, she's got a personality disorder. She didn't remember last night."

"No way," Mack said. "Did you fuck her?"

"Yeah, and won't be making that mistake again," I answered, as I walked over to Tony, who was laughing his ass off. I punched him in the gut, and he was still laughing despite being hit. "When I tell you I'm going through shit, leave me the fuck alone, and that means alone, from everyone. You got me?"

He looked up and stopped laughing. "Did you tell me that?"

"Yeah, I did." I leveled a look at him.

"Sorry, man. I was piss-ass drunk." Tony crossed his arms over his chest. "It's been a while, hasn't it?"

"Yup." I didn't tell Tony I'd blacked out. He'd been witness to a couple of them. Each time, I would 'waken' to me tied to a chair and to a post in the barn. Carl and Tony were beaten and bloody messes from my fists. Friday night, I had to assume I'd just beaten up the punching bag. Judging by the bloodstain on it, and my torn-up knuckles, which were still sore.

"I'm headed out." I fist-bumped him.

Tony grabbed my hand, looked at it and then looked at me. "Something you want to tell me?"

"I forgot to put on my gloves."

I waved bye to our friends and headed out to my bike. This weekend was a shit storm from hell. I was glad it was finally over. I took the long way home and ignored the vibration in my pocket. It was Bec. I knew because I hadn't turned off notifications for the forum. Everyone else was turned off.

I pulled into my garage and made a quick change of clothes into loose shorts, got a beer and slapped together a sandwich. I settled on my couch and opened up my laptop.

BEC2U:

Are you around?

I ATE SLOWLY AND WONDERED ABOUT RESPONDING. DECISION MADE, I closed my laptop, finished my sandwich, got up and went to the garage. Music blasted in my ears, and I focused on the blood coursing through my body. With every rep. With every punch. I felt more alive. Numbness slowly dissipated.

Until she crept in.

Bec's image.

I hung onto the bag and stared at the floor as sweat dripped off me. She was there in my mind, like I'd actually seen her. I didn't know what it meant, and that bugged the shit out of me. For someone I had never met in real life, she sure occupied a lot of space in my brain. Hell, that might be a fake pic for all I knew. At least, that's what I told myself.

8:46 p.m.

"Fuck," I muttered, then hit the bag one last time. I pulled off my gloves, took a cold shower and settled back on the couch.

> MBFBJAKE13:
> I'm here.

BEC2U:
Hi, Jake.

EVERY TIME SHE SAID MY NAME. *EVERY FUCKING TIME*, IT HIT ME STRONGER. It was so frustrating. I wanted to throw my laptop—I wanted to know why.

> MBFBJAKE13:
> Have more Qs?

BEC2U: Y
es. Who gives orders? The president of the MC?

> MBFBJAKE13:
> He can, but the board votes on it. It has to have the approval of the board.

BEC2U:
Members of the board, would be positions?

> MBFBJAKE13:
> Yep. Her name was Emma.

BEC2U:
Who are we talking about...Ooh. Nameless girl. Right.

MBFBJAKE13:

I saw her tonight at Snookers. Turns out, she didn't remember last night.

BEC2U:

What do you mean? She didn't remember.

MBFBJAKE13:

She has a personality disorder.

BEC2U:

What??

MBFBJAKE13:

That's what I said. Fact. I felt bad not knowing her name, thanks to you, and I told her to tell me.

BEC2U:

Wait...you told her, to tell you, her name?

MBFBJAKE13:

I already said that. Point is, you and I are the only ones that know I called her Bec.

BEC2U:

Right. And that's supposed to make me feel relief? That she doesn't remember.

MBFBJAKE13:

That she doesn't remember me calling her Bec.

BEC2U:

Wow. Lol. I don't know what to say. I got nothing.

MBFBJAKE13:

Thanks? Maybe.

BEC2U:

That's not the word I'd use. But it's something.

MBFBJAKE13:

It's late. Night.

BEC2U:

Lol Goodnight, Jake.

~

FOR THE NEXT FEW DAYS, I TALKED TO HER EVERY NIGHT, AND SOMETIME, during the day. I was trying to figure her out. And we were talking about random stuff. Not just about bikes. I told her about 'fishing', and she told me about a guy she worked for who she dated a couple of times. She told me more about Nick, and I told her about my parents. It would start off as questions about bikes but went way off course. Quick.

IT WAS THURSDAY AND BIKE NIGHT AT SNOOKERS. I GREETED PEOPLE WITH the usual hey and chin lift. I was only here for the cheap beer, nothing more, nothing less.

"About time you got here." Tony fist bumped me.

The usual crowd was here. Aaron, Krista, Travis, Sami and Mack with a no-name girl. Bec tried to get me remember names more, but it didn't seem important. Tony racked balls on the pool table.

"Are you still talking to that chick?" Tony asked me.

"Yep." I pulled a stick out of the rack and eyed it. Not the straightest, but not bad.

"What chick?" Sami asked.

I put chalk on the cue and didn't bother to answer.

"Tony, what chick?" Sami repeated.

Tony grinned, and I gave him a death glare. He knew better than to tell people my personal shit.

"Just a chick," I said.

"I wanna see your new tat, Jake," Mack said.

I took off my leather jacket, hung it on a barstool and pulled my left arm out my tee and turned my back to them.

"That's awesome, dude. It's gonna be wicked when it's done. Psycho does such good work."

"I don't know why anyone would tattoo 'hell' on their skin," the girl with Mack said.

Everyone, including Mack, stepped back.

I looked over my shoulder at her. "It's not your skin, and I don't remember asking you."

She huffed. "What does your mom think about it?"

My friends all looked anywhere but at us, as I slipped my arm back through my tee.

"I don't remember asking her either." I leaned down, aimed and broke the play.

Mack tried unsuccessfully to distract her. "So, what you're saying, you don't care what your mom thinks?"

"That's exactly what I'm saying. I don't give a fuck what you or anybody think." I gritted my teeth. "And if you don't mind, I would like to enjoy my beer in peace."

"Get her out of here, Mack," Tony told him, all trace of humor gone.

"Got it." Mack said. "Come on, let's get some air." He told the girl and proceeded to drag the protesting woman out the door.

Tony walked toward me. "It's cool, man."

I looked down at the pool stick in my hands. I let it go, just moments before snapping it. "Fuck," I muttered and let Tony grab the stick out of my hands.

I raked a hand through my hair and grabbed the jacket off of the barstool. "I gotta go."

Tony put a hand on my shoulder and looked me in the eye. "You good?"

"Yeah. Yeah, I gotta split." I walked out and was unlocking my bike when my phone vibrated. I pulled it out.

BEC2U:

Um, do you have time to talk?

THE HAIRS ON MY NECK STOOD ON END.

Fuck.

. . .

MBFBJAKE13:
I'll be home in 15.

I MADE IT IN TEN. I RUSHED IN AND CHANGED MY CLOTHES INTO LOOSE shorts.

MBFBJAKE13:
I'm here.

Bec2U: Okay.

SILENCE. I COCKED MY HEAD. THE TINGLES WERE BACK, AND MY KNEE bounced with nervous energy.

10:16 p.m.

MBFBJAKE13:
You seem quiet. Are you okay?

NOTHING. ALARM BELLS WERE SETTING MY BRAIN ON FIRE.

MBFBJAKE13:
What's wrong? Talk to me.

BEC2U:
I saw Nick tonight.

> **MBFBJAKE13:**
>
> What did he do?

NOTHING. THE SILENCE WAS DRIVING ME MAD. I DIDN'T ANALYZE HOW SHE was just a name on a screen. Or that she could be pulling my chain. I trusted my gut. It had never been wrong.

> **MBFBJAKE13:**
>
> Tell me what he did. Tell me something.

BEC2U:

He showed up at my door, even though there is a restraining order. He wanted to talk about something.

> **MBFBJAKE13:**
>
> And?

I KNEW IT WASN'T TO TALK. NO. I PACED BETWEEN THE COUCH AND THE coffee table. Chills ran up and down my spine. No. Nick didn't want to just talk.

> **MBFBJAKE13:**
>
> He hit you, didn't he?

BEC2U:

Yes.

> **MBFBJAKE13:**
>
> That motherfucker.
>
> **MBFBJAKE13:**
>
> Call me. 918-365-1845

BEC2U:

What? I don't think that's a good idea.

MBFBJAKE13:

IDC. He hit you. Call me.

BECCA

NICK NOT ONLY HIT ME...*HE TRIED TO RAPE ME.*

I stared at the computer screen as tears streaked down my face. I sucked in my bottom lip, that was partially swollen. Should I? There were so many reasons it was a bad idea.

When the cops finally left, all I wanted was Jake. I didn't want my family or Summer. I just wanted him. If he was real and telling the truth, he'd been through it. Not exactly the same, but close. He knew the type of fear I'd experienced. I picked up my phone with shaking hands and downed the whiskey I was sipping on. Knowing my number was blocked, I felt safe in calling him. I dialed his number before I backed out, and he answered it on half a ring.

"Hello, Bec?"

"Hi, Jake," I said in a cracked voice.

"Are you okay? What did he do?"

His voice matched the pic he sent. Low and rough. "Um,"

I got up from my desk, strode into the living room and stopped. I choked. Sitting on the couch wasn't happening. It was where the scene played out. I hurried to the bedroom, shut and locked the door.

"He's gone, right?" Jake asked.

"Cops took him away."

"Good. You're safe."

I took a deep breath and let his voice wrap around me like a cloak. I settled on the bed, pulled the covers up to my shoulders, and rested against a cocoon of pillows.

"You're safe, Bec. Better?"

I blinked away tears. "A little."

"How bad are you hurt?"

"Um, just a couple of bruises." I said it lightly, but in reality, it was more. The only thing that saved me from being raped was the gawd-awful heavy lamp Nick bought when we were together. I'd whacked it against his head.

"I know he did more than a couple of bruises. I've been there. Tell me the truth."

Fresh tears swam in my eyes and my vision became blurry. "He tried…" The words stuck in my throat.

"That motherfucker," he grated out, and I heard a loud thump.

"Jake? What are you doing?"

"Where are you at? He won't touch you again."

Steel laced his words, and I realized he was deadly serious. "The cops have him."

"But he'll get out. They always do. I'll take care of it if you want me to. Just say the word."

The protection I felt with just his words floored me. As much as I wanted to make Nick go away, I couldn't ask that of him. "No. Thanks, though."

"I'm serious. You don't even have to see me. I'll make that mother-fucker pay."

At a loss for words, I didn't know what to say. No one had offered me physical protection before, other than Summer's father. Never thought I'd need it until a few years ago. I had only known Jake about a month, but it felt like longer. Even so, I couldn't ask him to do that. He would get in trouble.

"I appreciate it, but no," I said in hushed tones and buried my head deeper into the pillows.

The silence dragged. "Jake?"

"I'm here," he said in a ragged voice.

"Are you ok?"

"I'm fine. It's you I'm worried about."

I couldn't help the small smile. He was worried about me, and yet, he claimed he was cold-hearted. I was right about my earlier observa-tion…he was only misunderstood. "I'm okay. Just mostly scared."

"I get that."

"It helps to talk to someone who really gets it." I absently picked at my covers. "I'm sorry if it triggers you."

"Darlin', don't worry about me. I've dealt with them for years."

I gasped when he said 'darlin'. Maybe it was the accent, but it did all sorts of gushy things to my insides.

"You, okay?" he asked.

I licked my lips. "Yes." My voice squeaked higher than normal, and I covered my face, even though I knew he couldn't see me.

"Are you crying?"

"No."

"Something sounds off."

"No, I'm not crying. It's your accent." My cheeks heated, and if Summer saw me, she would die laughing.

"My accent? I don't have an accent."

"Just certain words."

"Like what?"

"Darlin'."

"Darlin'?"

I gasped again, covered my mouth, so he didn't hear it.

"That's what that sound was. I thought you were crying. Glad you're not."

"I was. Earlier."

"He doesn't deserve your tears, darlin'."

"You're doing it on purpose now."

His slight chuckle edged up my spine. "Yup."

"Your voice matches your picture."

"Yours does too. You sound light and airy."

I smiled. "I can't see you saying that."

"Well, you do. I call it like it is."

"Well. Your voice sounds low and rough."

"Huh. Probably because I don't use my voice often. Darlin'."

"Ugh. Stop that." No doubt about it, his accent was cranking my libido into overdrive. Despite getting slapped around, he could make me smile...make me want him. And that was crazy thinking. I put the phone on speakerphone and laid it on the bedside table.

"Anything to distract you."

I smiled and cuddled with my pillow. "You're doing that, all right."

"What am I doing?"

His voice dropped an octave lower, and I swallowed. "I'm not really sure," I breathed.

"You're not?" After a long pause, he said, "Darlin'."

I expected him to say that, but it still affected me. I squeezed my legs together. "Is this your plan? Talk to a girl online and get an excuse for them to call you—"

"No. If you think I'm faking this shit, I'll hang up right now. I've never met someone online, much less talked to them on the phone. You could be filling me full of shit, too."

"You're right. I don't think you're faking anything, and I'm not either. I just..." Tears tracked down my face and soaked into my pillow. *I don't know why I wanted you.*

"Don't cry."

My eyes widened. "How did you know I'm crying?"

"I hear tears in your voice."

"I'm not making a sound. Do you have a sixth-spidey sense I should know about? Cause I didn't even sniffle."

"No. I'm hyper-aware of everything. Product of my environment. Another reason why clubs want me." I heard a loud bang. "And I don't tell this shit to anyone. Ever."

"Why do you tell me?" By the sounds in the background, he wasn't happy about it.

"Fuck if I know. You know more than...anyone."

"That's a little hard to believe." I heard another big crash. "What are you doing?"

"Threw a beer in the trash. And yeah, you are. Darlin'."

"I told you to stop that." I buried my head in the pillow.

"By the breathy way you respond, I'm guessing it's needy."

I lifted my head up and blew at my long bangs. "Needy?"

"Do you need something?"

My jaw dropped. How did he know? It's like he knew I fantasized about him. I groaned and let my head fall.

"I could make you groan in a different kind of way."

My head popped up. "A groan is a groan. They don't have different groans."

"I beg to differ. The groan you made was a frustrated groan."

"You *are* really hyper-aware." I stared at my phone, like I was staring at Jake.

"Yup."

He was unreal. If he was here, I would tackle him right now. And I'd never felt the need to do that to anyone. "It can't be good living every moment of your life like that."

"It's the only way I know."

"I was expecting darlin' after that."

"If I do it every time, it will lose its effect."

"You want to keep me guessing, huh?" I smiled into the pillow, even though it hurt to smile with my busted lip.

"Yes, ma'am."

"Your accent is showing there. It pops up at random times."

"Are you complaining?"

"No. Just making an observation."

"Darlin'."

"Dammit, Jake."

His response was a deep chuckle over the phone. It was almost as much of a turn on as his, darlin'. But I hadn't been with a man in so long, I'd almost forgotten what it was like. Nick was never concerned about my pleasure.

"You sound needy again," he said in a low, guttural voice.

I paused before answering. "I just want to forget Nick and erase his touch." I'd never admitted that to anyone, but it was freeing to be able to voice it.

"If I was there, you wouldn't have any problem forgetting him."

"Cocky much?"

"No. Just facts."

"I believe you," I whispered. And I did. I didn't know why, but I had this gut feeling everything he said was the truth. I licked my lips and, braver than I had ever been in my life, I said with tears streaking down my face, "Make me forget. Please."

SEVEN
JAKE

I stilled on the phone. She was crying again and sounded lost. I wanted so badly to make that fucker pay, but I couldn't. I didn't even know where she was on the east coast. She could be anywhere from Maine to Florida. If she wanted me to know, she would say. I hid my rage from her because I couldn't help her if I let it control me. She was hurting, and I wanted to ease her pain. I completely ignored how out of character it was for me.

"Are you asking what I think you're asking?" I didn't want to misunderstand and piss her off. I went back into the house from the garage, turned on some music and sat on the couch.

"Yes," she said in a small voice.

I paused and reflected on all she'd told me. She proved she was a girl by calling me, and there was no way she could fake the tears I'd heard. My instincts were never wrong. She was in pain...physical and mental.

I propped a foot on the coffee table. "What are you wearing, darlin'?" Her gasp on the phone every time I said that had my blood heading south.

"A pink tank top and pj pants."

"What are you wearing under them?" I'd never had phone sex

before. Didn't talk to anybody long enough for that. But I was willing to do what she asked because...she needed it. I didn't question why I wanted to give her what she needed. Maybe it was the pain in her voice. I recognized her pain. And proceeded to tell her what I'd do if I was there.

"Some boy shorts." She paused and then said, "no bra."

"Close your eyes. I would cup the back of your neck and barely bite it, and I'd soothe it with my tongue. All the way down. Are you with me?"

"Yes," she said, just above a whisper.

"I would cup one breast through your shirt and my lips would travel over your shoulder."

"Oh, yes," she muttered.

"Is your hand cupping your tit?"

"Mmm."

"My hand is under your shirt, and I tug your nipple. My mouth sucks the other one through your tee."

"Oh gawd. I was dreaming," she panted.

"Of me? I shove up your shirt and tweak a nipple with my teeth."

"Yes."

Her yes was drawn out like a hiss, and it had my dick tenting in my shorts. "My hand skims down your stomach and traces the hem of your panties."

"Yes. With your rough hands."

I smirked. She *was* dreaming of me. *Damn.* "Tell me what I do next."

"You strip me."

There was a rustle of covers on the other end, and I pulled my dick out. I fisted it at the base of my cock and held it there. "Are you naked, Bec?"

"Yes. But you call me Becca in my dream."

I could only guess, but the image in my head of her naked was fine as fuck. "Do I taste you, Becca, darlin'?"

"Oh, yes."

"Do I tongue it?"

"Yes," she panted. "Please tell me I'm not alone in this. I can't believe I'm asking this, but are you hard?"

"Damn right I am." I stroked down my length, turned on by her little pants and moans. "Are you with me?"

"Yes, Jake," she hissed.

My name off her lips was like a sucker punch to the gut and an instant turn on. I turned the speakerphone on and dropped it on the couch. "Are your fingers wet?"

"Yes." She panted faster, and I stroked faster.

"Ride that clit, darlin'."

"Oh, gawd." Her high pitch moan had me wound up. "I'm coming," she said.

"Fuck." Blood rushed in my ears as I came and caught it with my shorts. Gripping my cock through the fabric, it throbbed and sweat beaded on my skin. I never thought phone sex would be such a turn on. I leaned my head back and tried to calm my jacked-up pulse.

"You better, Becca?" With her voice alone, she disoriented me. I had trouble identifying what about her was so different.

"Yes. Are you?"

"Did you really dream about me?"

"Mmm. And I," she paused. "Got off on your image."

I raised a brow and sat forward. "You had a wet dream about me, then masturbated to my pic?"

"Oh, gawd. When you say it like that, I sound awful."

"What? No. That's hot as fuck." *Damn.*

"I didn't mean to tell you." She blew out a breath. "I'm so embarrassed."

"Did you think it would bother me? Hell, no. Did you wake up with wet panties?"

Silence hung on the phone for a beat. "Yes, I did," she squeaked.

"Then my job here is done." I smirked.

"You don't need to get any cockier."

"Facts are facts, baby doll."

She hissed in a breath loud enough I heard it. "Why does everything you say turn me on?"

"I don't know." I got up, grabbed a towel from the kitchen and snagged a beer on the way to the couch. Why was she able to get my pulse up without having even met her?

"Do you live alone?" I asked.

"Yeah. Summer and my aunt and uncle offered to let me stay at their place for a time, but I wanted to do something on my own. To prove to myself I could. Nick made me feel so helpless."

Her voice got small as she talked. I knew how abuse could make one feel useless. I got called every vile name in the book...every day. It just turned me cold. I didn't want that for Becca. It was a shit way to live.

12:05 a.m.

"I understand more than you can imagine, but it's not about proving anything, baby. It's about staying safe."

"I plan on getting a security system on Saturday."

I breathed. "Good."

"Do you live alone?" she asked.

"Yup. I can't tolerate people in my space. The only person I would let move in is Tony. But I can't stand the fucker most of the time. So, it wouldn't be for long."

"But isn't Tony your best friend?"

"Yeah."

"That's an awful way to talk about your best friend."

"Nah. He'd say the same thing about me."

She laughed and had a pleasant one. Most girls irritated the piss out of me, and I couldn't be around them long. Even Andrea. Come to think of it, when I added up all the time we had talked, this was the longest conversation I'd had with a girl or guy...ever.

"Guys are weird." She uttered a small little laugh.

I shook my head and smirked. "We say the same thing about women." I glanced at the time. "Do you have to work tomorrow? Or are you going to take off because of asshole?"

She sighed. "I would normally, but I don't want to hide anymore. I didn't cause this, and I refuse to let his actions dictate my life."

"You got balls." Unlike my mother, who cowed down and accepted it. She let my asshole of a father do whatever the fuck he wanted and never fought back. I fought him for her, but I got hit because of it. By Dad and Mom, if you could even call them that.

"Rest assured, I don't, but unlike you, I need sleep to function."

"Call whenever you want. If I can't talk, I'll message you."

"Good night, Jake, and...thanks."

"Anytime, night darlin'." I smirked, knowing what it did to her.

She groaned. "You don't play fair."

When she clicked off, the smirk on my face dissipated and the black cloak settled around me again. Heavy. Numb. How quickly it overtook me. I felt alive when I was on the phone with her. Just talking to her did the trick. I orgasmed quicker, and I felt *more* with her, somehow. It made no sense whatsoever. I leaned back and stared at the ceiling. The impact of her saying my name on the phone was multiplied by a hundred versus chat. There was something about her I couldn't pin it down, and that bothered me.

The tingling that had me on edge when we chatted...I knew before I knew.

I stripped and took a cold shower, and I didn't bother with the hot water. It was the *shock* I needed to wake up my system. But it didn't work. *Becca did.* Fuck, if I knew why. I had to work tomorrow, but I'd be lucky if I went two hours of sleep without nightmares. Becca's life brought up chunks of my life, but that was nothing new.

Triggers were just a part of my life. The smell of certain alcohol, a time of day, a date, a song, a familiar street or section of town—and for the most part, I acted like I wasn't affected at all. The bitch at the pool hall tonight triggered me, but it was a rare occurrence that I lost control in public. Slipping into madness seemed to be the direction I was headed. I built walls around me for a damn good reason. The outside world only saw what I wanted them to see. A cold son-of-a-bitch just like the water pouring over me.

≈

BECCA

The blaring of my alarm on the phone woke me, and when I went to grab it off the bedside table, it tumbled to the floor. As I stretched to get it, I fell to the floor, knocking off the bottle of lotion and nail polish that was on the bedside table. I blew at the hair in my face and finally clicked off the alarm. If this was a prediction of my day, I would be better off not getting out of bed at all. I stood up, put the lotion and nail polish back on the table and glanced at my phone.

Jake.

I couldn't believe we'd talked and had phone sex. Gawd, just thinking about it was embarrassing. I was *never* like that. Never that forward. Never that bold. I was shy. Timid. Reserved. That's how Summer would describe me. Where was Rebecca Saylor last night? Obviously, not there. I had been replaced by a sex kitten. I groaned and rolled my eyes. Jake would call that a frustrated groan. Yes, I definitely felt frustrated.

I went into the bathroom and stared in the mirror. Half of my lip and left eye swelled up, and I couldn't cover it all with make-up. I sighed, got ready for work and tried not to think about Jake, which made me think of him more. Did he get some rest? I hoped so. As I walked toward my bright yellow Jeep, it never failed to bring a smile to my face. Tripping on the parking curb and stumbling into my car, setting off the car alarm, I searched through my purse to find my keys, while the alarmed honked loudly. Finally finding it, I pressed the button to silence it. I could hear Nick's condescending voice...

You're such a klutz. Good thing I married you because no one would want a Bluzty.

I wiped at tears and winced when I touched my bruised face. That was Nick's nickname for me because I was naturally clumsy. Dad told me that was an endearing trait mom had. But Nick made me feel self-conscious about it and, in turn, it got worse.

Finally, I reached my office building, and I looked up at the large letters that hung on the façade of Richmond Dispatch.

"Morning, Becca," several people said as I walked towards my cubicle. I greeted everyone but didn't take off my sunglasses.

"So, how is Becca this fine morning?" Pat, Patty as he was known to most, asked.

I took off my glasses and was mentally preparing myself for the twenty questions. It automatically reminded me of Jake. He had made a significant impact on my life in an extremely short amount of time. I looked up into Patty's face.

He squealed, disappeared and reappeared in my cubicle. "What happened? Who did this?" he asked as he lifted my chin so he could inspect my face. "Oh, dear! Did you put ice on it? I bet it was that awful man, Nick. Did you call the police?" Patty rattled in his high-pitched voice until half the Dispatch was crowded around us.

A hundred different questions hit me all at once.

"I'm okay," I tried to explain. It made me re-think my decision to come in.

"Oh, my goodness, that is going to swell something awful!" Patty tsked. "You should be at home putting some ice on it. John, go get this poor thing a bag of ice." He gave John a shove to get him moving.

"I didn't want to stay home," I said.

"Of course you didn't! Why would you want to do that? You need your people around you." Patty nodded. "Mn-hmm. You gots to be more careful, doll. Why did you even go around him?" Then John handed him a bag of ice. "Oh, thank you. Here you go, honey." He placed it in my hand.

"What the hell is going on here? Why aren't you people working?"

Everyone jumped when they heard our boss's booming voice and employees scattered.

"Patty, you better get back to work," I said.

He pursed his lips. "I want you to know, I'm not afraid of the big, bad boss." He returned to his cubicle as I heard Robert's heavy footsteps.

I hesitantly looked up.

His beady blue eyes stared at me, and he crossed his arms over his chest. "In my office," he ordered and walked away without another word.

I sighed and followed him. Once in his office, I closed the door and looked at my uncle. He stood there, his bald pate shiny under the fluorescent lights, his lips set in a firm thin line. Robert was a tough man and most said a hard-ass boss, but he was always fair.

"Nick?" he asked.

I nodded. Robert never minced words and was always direct and to the point.

"Do you want to tell me the details, or do I have to call the station to figure it out?"

"He came to my apartment and wanted to talk about something. I tried to refuse him, but he shoved his way inside." I wasn't going to tell him anything else. The bruises said it all.

"I see." He paced behind his desk before stopping to look at me. "Are you okay?"

I shrugged and willed myself not to cry. I was strong, capable, and I didn't need to be coddled. At least, I kept telling myself that. I recalled something that Jake told me last night...I had balls. I wiped my face and smiled.

"You can come live with us, you know. You don't have to live alone," he said.

"No. I want...need to do this on my own." For once, I wanted to stand on my own two feet.

He nodded. "I get it. But think about your safety."

"I will. Thanks," I replied.

"Do you have your column done?"

Relieved there were no more questions about Nick, I let out a long breath. I could always count on Robert to get back to business. "Yes, I do. I'll send it straightaway."

"Good."

But before I could leave, he came around his desk, embraced me in a big hug and then turned around and shuffled some papers on his desk. "I want that column pronto," he said in a gruff voice.

I somehow managed not to cry. "Yes, sir," I said and left his office. I made my way to my desk and emailed it to him.

Getting through the day at work was better than sitting at home thinking about everything. I was munching a cracker at lunchtime when my cell rang. I smiled when I saw it was Summer.

"Hey."

"Hey, girlfriend. I thought I could come crash at your place this evening with some wine and Chinese takeout. What do you say?"

"I'd really like that." I paused and knew I had better say something about the purple mark on my face *before* Summer saw me. "Nick showed up last night."

"Oh, please tell me you shut the door in his face. Or better yet, did you go after him with a filet knife? That would make my day."

"Yeah. That's a nice thought, but no." It still took everything I had to admit to his abuse, even though I knew it wasn't my fault. I took a deep breath and said, "He shoved his way inside—"

"What?"

"Yeah. He—"

"Hit you. Didn't he? That bastard. Are you okay? And why the hell didn't you call me?"

"Yeah, he did. But it's okay. He's with the police now. I didn't want to stay at home, and I didn't want to bother you." That was a lame answer, but how was I supposed to explain that I only wanted Jake instead of my best friend? I dropped my head in my hand.

"You didn't want to bother me? Are you serious? Girl, you know better. I'll take care of you tonight."

"That would be great. I'll be home about six."

"It's a date," Summer replied and hung up.

The rest of the day flew by, but I was glad when work was over. Patty was driving me nuts and several other coworkers whispered until I walked up. I was putting my laptop into its bright pink bag when I felt eyes on me. I turned to see Clay leaning casually against the cubicle wall.

"You want to get some coffee?" he asked.

He was a good-looking guy, brown hair, blue eyes that usually twinkled with mischief. But his expression was solemn, and he had been avoiding me all day. "I have a date," I said. "With Summer."

His tense expression eased a bit, and he nodded. "Is there anything I can do?"

He had been pursuing me off and on since my divorce. But I didn't want to get involved with someone else and especially not someone at work. Even though girls seemed to like Clay and he was a decent guy.

We'd gone out twice, but there was no chemistry. At least, not on my part.

"No, thanks. I'll manage."

"If you need anything...all you have to do is ask."

It was a shame I didn't feel more for him. "I know."

He looked almost defeated before he nodded and walked off. Frowning, I gathered my purse and laptop bag and headed out the door.

"It's me!" Summer yelled from the other side of the door and knocked.

I opened it and smiled. "About time. I was beginning to think you stood me up."

"You wouldn't believe the people at the liquor store," Summer said as she breezed past me in heels and a short skirt. "Then some guy was talking to me, and he was so funny," she said, a smile curving her lips.

"Did he ask you out?" That was a redundant question because men always asked Summer out. The girl was a knockout with her long legs and full lips. Guys, literally, drooled on themselves when she walked by.

"Yeah, but you know, I wasn't interested."

I shook my head as she grabbed two plates and two wineglasses from the cabinets. "Eventually, you will have to go out with one of them. You know this, right?"

"Yeah, whateve'," Summer replied and poured two glasses of wine.

It broke my heart that Summer wouldn't even take a chance. I knew it was more than a dead fiancé. He hid his scheming ways from Summer...he was just after her dad's money to pay for his drugs. I wrapped her in a hug. We've leaned on each other through so much.

Summer released me first. "Let's take a look at this." She eyed my cheek and lip. "Someone needs to serve his ass on a platter for what he's done to you.

"I think Jake wanted to do something like that," I replied and realized my mistake when Summer narrowed her eyes.

"Jake? Who's Jake?"

"Oh, um." I tucked my head to my chest.

Summer smacked the table with her hand. "Oh, it's that motorcycle guy, isn't it? Did you talk to him again?"

I filled my plate with sweet-n-sour chicken and wondered how I was going to explain. I knew better than to lie because Summer knew me too well. "Er, yeah. He's the motorcycle guy. I called him."

Summer's dark brown eyes went round, and she almost choked on her chow mien. "You what? Girl, what were you thinking? He could be some lunatic, for all you know."

"Hey, give me some credit. I didn't give him my number and my number is blocked, remember? If I don't want to call him again, I won't." I shrugged and took a bite of sweet-n-sour chicken.

"But why did you call him? I thought he was just a research assignment for your book?"

I squirmed and sighed. "I shouldn't tell you this because it's not my story to tell. His mom and dad beat him."

When Summer remained silent and stared at me, I got nervous. The girl had that knack for seeing right through me.

"I'm sorry that happened to him, but I think something else is going on," Summer said as she leaned back in her chair and crossed her legs. When her foot started tapping air, I knew I was in trouble. "You like him."

I tried to brush it off and nodded. "He seems like a good guy."

But Summer pointed her fork at me and shook her head. "Uh-huh. But you really like him. I can see it in your face. What have you been keeping from me? I think there's more going on than just a little research."

Heat filled my face, and I looked down. There was no way I was telling Summer what happened last night. I couldn't believe it myself.

"Rebecca Saylor, I want deets, and I want them now. Just how involved are you with this Jake character?"

"Just talking. That's it."

"Uh-huh. That would explain why your face is my absolute favorite nail color—red-hot. You might as well give it up. You'll tell me eventually."

"Really. We just talk."

"About what?"

"Motorcycles."

"Sex?"

I jerked my head up and stared at my smiling friend.

"That's what I thought." Summer laughed. "What? You think you're the only girl to have cyber-sex? That's nothing new, honey. But you took it a step further, didn't you? Is phone sex better? I haven't tried that yet."

"We didn't have cyber-sex. That would be stupid." I was never one to talk about things like this. Not with Summer or anyone else for that matter. But Summer never had trouble talking about anything, and she loved details. So, I tried to change the subject. "He was worried about mean and knew Nick had hurt me. We've suffered abuse." But that's all I was willing to say about that.

"Wow. After the cops took A-hole away, you talked to him about it instead of me? And even though he might understand you, it doesn't trump your best friend of forever. Sounds to me like this is a relationship, not just *talking*."

"No, we're not in a relationship. I know. It's nuts." I took a long drink of wine. "I hadn't talked to him on the phone until last night. Before that, it was just chat. I don't know. I guess I wasn't thinking straight with everything that happened."

Summer tapped her red nail on the table. "Do you have a picture of him? I want to see."

I might as well as tell her everything. "You're not mad at me, are you?"

"Sister, we've been through too much for me to be mad at you over this. Did you have phone sex?" Summer grinned.

I sheepishly looked down.

"The first time you talked to him, and you had phone sex?" She leaned her head back and laughed. "This is more than talking, girlfriend. I wanna see him."

Hiding behind my wineglass, I wasn't adding more details about it, although Summer would probably try. I picked up my phone and scrolled through my photos and clicked on his picture. "Here he is, if the pic's real."

Summer's eyes widened. "Damn, girl. How tall is he?"

"Six-one." I went to the bathroom and inspected the bruises in the mirror. They were angry red and swollen, and I needed to put some more ice on it. When Nick lived here, I had a freezer full of ice packs, but when I threw him out, I'd trashed all of them. I vowed I wouldn't need them anymore. How easily he forced his way inside caused me to panic.

Breathe. Breathe.

First thing tomorrow, I was going to the hardware store and checking into a security system and have it installed ASAP. Jake could do it. His name popped into my mind more and more. So easily and so swiftly. I realized he hadn't left my mind since we'd met. I put a hand on my forehead and stared into the mirror. Getting tangled up over a guy just screamed stupidity.

What are you doing?

Blowing out a breath, I walked back into the living room and stopped. Summer was on the phone. My phone.

"Hi. Are you Jake? Good, this is Summer."

My mouth gaped. "What are you doing?"

"Could you hold on a minute?" Summer said into the phone, covered the mouthpiece and looked at me. "I'm talking to Jake. Don't interrupt." Removing her hand, she continued. "Sorry. Becca's not thrilled with me right now."

I stomped my foot and glared. How could she do this? I mouthed at her—just you wait.

Summer smiled. "Oh, you've heard about me. All good, I hope? But the reason for my call is I want to know something about you. Seems my friend has been keeping you under wraps."

I couldn't hear Jake's replies, but Summer kept smiling as she started writing stuff down. I was going to kill her when she got off the phone.

"Hm. You do realize if you hurt her, I'll hunt you down?"

"Summer!" I really couldn't believe this. But Summer ignored me and laughed into the phone.

"Nice talking to you, too. Bye, Jake."

"What do you think you're doing? How could you call him like that?" I all but yelled, appalled at what Summer had done.

"Oh, calm down. I wanted to find out a few things about your Jake."

"What does it matter? It's not like he knows where to find me."

"Now we can double check his info."

"Are you serious?" I asked, stunned.

"Deadly. Because I care about you, girlfriend. So, hush and deal."

I fumed as I watched Summer do a reverse image search. Honestly, I hadn't even thought of that. We both were surprised it didn't come up with anything.

"Hmm…that seems to be the real him," Summer said, and she typed Jake Korte into the computer.

"I feel like I'm creeping on him. This feels so wrong." I sighed and downed my wine.

Summer smiled at me. "He was very forthcoming with information. He said he didn't care what you knew."

"He said the same thing to me." I groaned. "That means everything he's told me was the truth." I got the wine bottle and didn't bother with the glass, just drank straight from the bottle.

Summer laughed and swiveled to face me. "Isn't that good? That he's honest."

"Brutally honest. His words." I leaned my head on the back of the couch, so I was looking at the ceiling. "And I had phone sex with him."

Summer burst out laughing. "Was it at least good?"

I peeked at Summer. "Well, I mean, I don't have any experience with whether it was good or bad. I have nothing to compare it to."

"Did you orgasm?"

I covered my face with my hand. "Oh gawd, did I."

We both burst into a fit of giggles. It had to be the wine that was getting to me, but I needed this. Just to unapologetically be myself. I was repressed under Nick's thumb when we were married…it was crushing my spirit. He was eroding who I was without me realizing it. Even though it had been three years since the divorce, I sometimes fell in line with what Nick wanted without recognizing it. I could drink more than I needed to sometimes. Could get loose and crazy some-times. I was an adult. And I *wasn't* under Nick's ridiculous rules anymore. And if Jake wanted to have phone sex with me, and me with him, I could. I wasn't hurting myself or anybody else.

I was free, as Jake reminded me.

EIGHT
JAKE

I hung up the phone and shook my head.

"Who was that?" Tony asked and took a drink of his beer.

"Summer, Becca's friend. She wanted information about me."

Tony laughed. "That's a good ploy. Get the friend to get info."

"Naw. I heard Becca in the background. She wasn't happy. At least someone is looking out for her. And hell, I don't care what she knows." I frowned and clenched my hand. "Her ex-husband beat her. That's why she divorced his ass. He shoved his way into her place last night and hit her." I downed my beer. Just thinking about his hands on her got my blood boiling.

"Fuck, you're kidding me? Did you tell her we could make her problem go away?"

"Yeah, I did. But I don't think she took me seriously."

Tony crushed his beer can with his hands. I knew he had an intense hate for people who preyed on another's weaknesses. He had his own demons. Like Bec said, everyone was fighting their own battles.

"I could take your ole man out too, and they'd never find the body." he leveled a look at me as cold as I felt most of the time. When he was honorably discharged with an injury he acquired in Iraq with his SEAL team, he didn't come home the same man. His time over there gave him a lethal edge. He didn't mention his time as a SEAL often, but I knew that look. As easy going as Tony was most of the time, you'd never guess what lurked below the surface.

Tony was deadly. I knew that look because it stared back at me every day.

"I know."

"Has she sent you a picture of her yet?" Just like a flipped switch, Tony grinned and returned to his easy-going nature.

"Yup." I flipped open my laptop, brought up her picture and turned it to him.

"Not bad. Have you done a reverse image search of her?"

"What's that?"

"Here I'll show you." He typed on my laptop. "You need to get with the times, man. You upload the pic, and it looks for that pic on the web."

"And why do that?" People said I'm behind with the times because I don't have the social media bullshit. But I'm a wiz at tracking wiring problems in cars. To me, that's useful.

He laughed. "To see if she swiped the pic off the web. And it looks like she hasn't."

He was surprised, but I wasn't.

"Did she tell you where she was at?"

"Nope. And I'm not going to ask. If she feels safer that way…" I let my words trail off, shrugged and stared at the big screen that took up most of the living room.

"Maybe you should worry about flesh and blood girls instead of this one."

"And maybe you should mind your own damn business."

"I would. But you get that lost look on your face sometimes and it's scaring me. It's like you've fallen for some cyber chick," he said, grinning like an idiot.

I snorted. "You know damn well I'm not capable of that."

"Yeah, but someone has to give you shit about it." He glanced at his phone. "Speaking of shit, I have to get out of here." He headed out the door. "Later."

"Later, man."

I gathered up the empty beer cans, took them to the kitchen, and dropped them in the trash. Leaning against the counter, I stared outside at the steady rain. It was unusually hot for mid-April. But the rain hadn't cooled anything off, just made it sticky and hard to breathe. I checked my watch.

9:02 p.m.

When I heard someone banging on my door, I walked to it and pulled it open. Frowning, I stared at the woman on my doorstep. Her over-bleached blonde hair with dark roots hung in wet, scraggly strands around her life-worn face.

"Are you just going to stand there and let your mother get soaked or are you going to let me in?"

I hesitated and thought about it. If I left her there, would she go away? No, she would stand out there and raise hell until I let her in, or someone called the cops. Been there, done that. So, I stepped aside without a word.

"Well, hello to you too, son," she said, as she walked in and sat on the black leather couch.

I crossed my arms over my chest and waited.

"I thought you might want to hear this in person. Your daddy's out."

"Why do I care?" I figured it was about time my old man was released from prison.

"You should. He's your daddy." Her bright red lips pursed in a thin line. "You should show a little respect for your elders."

Her tone grated on my stretched nerves. "I do. To those who deserve it." Evidently, she had been working. She was wearing a skirt that almost let her secret out. And just the thought of being born of that made me want to puke. "If that's all you had to say, then get out."

"I need some money."

"Whore for it." I was tired of giving her money for her booze and drugs and whatever else she did with it.

The sneer on her face said it all. "Oh, yeah. You are such a great son, the way you take care of your mother. If it wasn't for you, I wouldn't have to whore for it!" She stood and pointed her finger at me. "It's all your fault he left. Ungrateful bastard. I should have—"

"Aborted me? I get it. So, get the hell out of my house," I said with surprising calm. But my fingernails cut into my palms to keep from lashing out at her. I wouldn't let her get to me. At least, I tried not to. Wouldn't let her see the pain she caused with each word.

"Are you really not going to give me any money? My rent is due."

I ground my teeth, walked to a side table, grabbed my wallet and pulled out a couple of hundreds. Gripping her arm, I wadded the cash into her hand and immediately released her. "Now leave."

She nodded and stared at the money greedily. "I'll leave. But I know your daddy will want to see you soon." She glanced back up at me.

"Tell him I said fuck off."

"That's no way to talk to your flesh and blood!"

"Get. Out." I shook with anger, and it was all I could do not to bodily throw her out.

"I wouldn't want to stay here, anyway." She banged out the door into the rain.

Rage boiled inside, and my head pounded with the race of my heart. I paced the length of my living room, trying to slow my breathing, but memories flooded me. They always did after an encounter with her.

DAD'S FACE CONTORTED WITH FURY, AND I COVERED MY HEAD AS FISTS *pummeled me. Hitting my arms, face, legs. Nothing was left unmarred. All because the old man was drunk and mad. Later, Mom yelled at me, telling me it was my fault Dad was so angry all the time, while blood dripped from my split lip.*

I SAT ON THE COUCH AND PUT MY HEAD IN MY HANDS. I WAS THIRTY. NONE of this shit should bother me anymore. I was an adult.

Responsible. Had a job. Paid my bills.

It didn't matter what my parents thought. I had done something with my life.

You'll always be a fucking loser.

How many times had they told me that? I got up, grabbed a beer out of the fridge and walked to the garage. It was time to let off some steam.

10:14 p.m.

It wasn't long before I was dripping with sweat. I opened the overhead garage door to let air in, but it was so muggy it didn't do any good. Hands on my hips and breathing hard, I stared out into the rain that fell in straight sheets. The sky was a dull gray with a few angry black clouds. Matched my mood perfectly.

When my cell rang and vibrated on my workbench, I walked over and grabbed it. I didn't want to talk to anyone right now, but the screen said, 'blocked number'.

Becca's number was blocked.

"Hello," I said, hoping it was her.

"Hi. I'm so sorry Summer called you. I had no idea. I hope you're not mad."

I relaxed at the sound of her voice. "Hey, don't worry about. She's obviously worried about you."

"Yes, but she's extremely nosy."

"Most friends are." I sat on a barstool and glanced at my motorcycles. "You doing all right?"

"Yeah. I'm okay. You sure you're fine with Summer calling you? I couldn't believe it. I was so pissed at her."

"Seriously, Becca. It's cool." I wondered why I had to reassure her so much. Probably had everything to do with her asshat ex. "So did she google me?"

"Of course. That girl, I swear. She wanted to make sure you were being honest."

"And?"

"Well, you know what we found. Jake Korte lives in Bixby, Oklahoma, thirty years old."

"Anything else?"

"Just a couple arrests, but it didn't say what for. But you've mentioned them, so I wasn't surprised. Although, I thought you lived in Tulsa."

"Yup. Tulsa blends in with Bixby. So close you can't tell them apart.

I told you I was arrested. I'm not trying to hide anything. Everybody does stupid shit when they're young and dumb."

Her light laughter lifted my mood a little.

"Summer also did a reverse image search. And you know what we found. Nothing. Seems you are who you say you are."

"Tony was here when Summer called and he did a reverse image search on you, too. I didn't know there was such a thing."

"And?"

"You're real," I replied and smirked. "But I wasn't surprised."

"You weren't?"

"Nope. I knew you weren't lying."

"So, what are you doing?"

"Beating the piss out of my punching bag. I had an unwanted and unexpected visitor."

"Is this a bad time?" Her voice was hesitant.

"No, I'm glad you called." And I was. She was exactly what I needed. It was no different when we chatted online. She could calm me down and no one had been able to do that. The fuck if I knew why.

"Good," she said, and I heard the smile that I couldn't see.

"Did you find out any other details about me?"

"No. Was I supposed to?"

"I have no clue what you would find. I've never had the need to search myself."

She laughed loudly, and it was nice to hear. "I could search you," she said in a breathy voice.

"And I'd let ya." I twirled a screwdriver absently in my hand and smirked. Oh, yeah. I would let her search me. All over.

"Mmm. That's a pleasant thought. How would you like me to search you?"

I got up, hit the garage door button, walked into my house and sat on the couch. "Any way you want." I grabbed the remote and pushed play, so Slipknot played low in the background, but I didn't bother turning on the lights.

"Just to warn you, I may have had too much wine tonight."

I smirked. "Are you saying you're sloshed?"

She laughed, then hiccupped. "Yeah."

"Ya think?"

"Could we go back to the searching you subject?"

"By all means."

"I could start with your chest. I assume you don't have a shirt on, do you?"

"No. Too hot."

"Are you?" Becca's voice was low and sexy, which forced me to adjust my too tight shorts.

"Nighty-four degrees with a hundred percent humidity, and I've been working out. So, yeah, I'm hot. Darlin.'"

I heard a gasp. "I like a man who's a bit steamy."

I raised a brow. "Are you trying to seduce me?"

"Hmmm. Is it working?"

"Maybe." I smirked. Oh, it was working all right.

"I would run my hands over your shoulders, chest and across your stomach. Maybe tug at your shorts."

My abs tightened, and I grabbed my cock through my shorts. "Are your nipples hard?"

"They weren't until you asked." Her words were just above a whisper.

"Tug on your nipples, darlin'."

"Mmm," she groaned.

"That was a needy groan. Are you needy?" I clicked on speaker-phone and dropped my cell on the couch.

"Yes," she breathed.

"What do you need?" I stroked my dick slowly.

"You."

I looked down at the phone. "Do have your fingers in your pussy?"

"Oh, gawd yes."

"You're fuckin' sexy, you know that darlin'?" I stroked faster. Just the image of her fingers buried in her wet slit made my blood simmer. "Is your tit heavy and full? My teeth would graze back and forth."

"Oh, gawd." She was panting hard. "Please."

Tension coiled and my balls tightened. "Do you feel the walls around your fingers quiver? Press your thumb on your clit."

"Oh, fuck."

"Do you feel it?"

"Ah. Gawd, yes. I want you," her breath heaved in my ear.

"Come, baby."

"Yes," she hissed and groaned.

Her 'yes' had me coming in my shorts…again. *Fuck.*

"Mmm," she whispered. "You are hot."

"At your service." I forced my words to be even. Once again, I had to fight for control of my body. My pulse. My breathing.

"You service so well." Her words were purely feminine, and my protective urges sprung to life. She wasn't the only one who was satisfied.

"Did I distract you enough?" I heard the smile in her voice.

"Mission accomplished."

She laughed, a deep throaty sound, and my dick twitched.

"I wanted to repay the favor."

"You did that. But I thought you were drunk and horny, so I was doing you a favor."

"I wasn't horny," she huffed.

"Yeah, right."

"Well, maybe I was a little bit. Are you complaining?"

"Hell, no. Matter of fact, call me every time you're horny."

She giggled. "Every time?"

"Are you saying you're horny all the time?"

"Just when I'm talking to you…I should've not said that. Nope. Pretend you didn't hear that."

I smirked. "Oh, I heard it. And I'll remember it. Unlike you, I'm not drunk this time."

"Even if I say please?"

"Maybe." I paused and added, "Darlin'."

"Dammit, Jake. Ugh," she sighed. "You don't play fair."

I chuckled until she said, Jake. And it felt like a hammer punch against my chest. What the fuck was that? And why? Plenty of girls knew my name, and I barely blinked. I rubbed my chest. There was no way in hell I was telling Bec what it did to me.

"Are you staying home tonight?" I asked as I got cleaned up and grabbed another pair of shorts. I made a pit stop by the kitchen to grab a beer and plopped on the couch.

"It's midnight here. I'm not going anywhere this late. And besides, I had a date with Summer tonight. She was upset I didn't call her last night."

"Don't do that." Her voice got small when she talked about anything having to do with that asshole.

"What?"

"You shouldn't feel ashamed about what he did to you. You didn't cause any of it." I sipped my beer. "You barely whisper when you talk about him and the abuse."

"Oh. I didn't realize I was. Are you going out?"

"Naw." I almost said I preferred talking to her than going out. My hide was a tough outer shell, nearly impenetrable, but somehow this woman, whom I've never met, was breaking through.

"Won't the nameless babes miss you?"

I grunted. "No. They'll find some other nameless cock to ride."

"You sure don't mince words."

"What do you mean?"

"You say things bluntly."

"People say too damn many words." I downed my beer. Like I was doing? I didn't recognize myself when I talked to her. It was making me antsy. My knee started bouncing. Nope. Not getting sleep tonight. "I gotta go. Bye."

I barely heard her say bye and clicked off. I needed a long night ride. The wind on my face and the rumble of my Harley. I took a quick cold shower, got dressed, and as I straddled my bike, my phone vibrated. It could only be Bec. I started my bike and pulled out my phone.

12:29 a.m.

BEC2U:

Did I do something wrong?

I SIGHED. SHE DID NOTHING WRONG, BUT I WAS ALL WRONG.

MBFBJAKE13:

No. It's me. I'm headed out on my bike for a long ride. I'll be MIA for the next several hours.

BEC2U:

Are you sure you should? It's very late.

MBFBJAKE13:

No worries, darlin'. I do this all the time.

BEC2U:

Okay. You be careful.

MBFBJAKE13:

Did you gasp?

BEC2U:

Ugh...yes.

MBFBJAKE13:

Lol. My job here is done. Talk to you later, babe.

BEC2U:

Bye, Jake.

DAMN. IT HIT ME AGAIN. I RUBBED MY CHEST AND POCKETED MY PHONE. I took off and took the long way to Fort Gibson Lake and stopped at the Git Lost Bar. I hadn't been here in a while since the floods tried to wipe it from the map, but I went on the poker run to help raise money to rebuild it.

They'd done it up nice. It was better than the original. I didn't recognize anyone, and that suited me just fine. I sat at a back table along the wall, and just chilled. I didn't want to think about anything, but Bec dominated my thoughts. It might have been a good thing if she turned out to be fake. Then I'd have an excuse to wash my hands of her. As it was, she was slowly getting under my leather skin. No. I needed to put a stop to it. Just ghost her. I downed my one beer, straddled my bike and left.

I backtracked a little way and did a U-turn on 80. The winding road followed the edges of the lake. I took my time, because it wasn't well lit, and animals were known for being on this stretch of road. I was daring but not stupid. It was colder here because of the lake, and I welcomed the chill on my face. It made me feel alive. Bec made me feel more alive.

1:47 a.m.

Suddenly, flashes and memories spun in my head.

"THIS BITCH WILL CURE YOU, YOU FUCKING FAGGOT." PRICK SHOVED ME *into my bedroom as he slid the lock on the outside of my door. There lay a naked teenage girl who was high on something. Her eyes were unfocused, and she was limp. "I won't let you out until you fuck her," Prick screamed.*

I BLINKED AND TRIED TO ORIENT MYSELF. I STILL SAT ON MY HARLEY, IT was running and parked at a gas station. Trying to cling to the present, I tried to focus on the rumble and breathed in the rain.

When did it start raining?

When did I pull over?

Fuck.

I looked at my watch.

4:13 a.m.

Double fuck.

I lost two and a half hours. After turning off my bike, I realized I was soaked to the skin. Even my socks were soppy. Stepping inside the gas station to get a coffee, I pulled out my phone and clicked on the GPS.

Springdale, Arkansas.

I'd never blacked out on the bike. Ever. I could only assume I drove straight here. Hopefully. I gathered some snacks, paid for them, and then crashed at the nearest hotel.

I woke to the sound of my phone vibrating, then glanced at my watch.

9:32 a.m.

"Hello?" I rubbed my eyes.

"Hi. I hope I didn't wake you up, but I was worried about you. The last message you sent was alarming."

I sat up and leaned against the headboard. "What do you mean?"

"You said, 'I won't hurt you. Don't worry. I'll let you go'."

Wide awake now, I put her on speakerphone and looked at my last messages.

> MBFBJAKE13:
> I won't hurt you.

> BEC2U:
> I know you won't hurt me.

> MBFBJAKE13:
> Don't worry, I'll let you go.

> BEC2U:
> What?

> MBFBJAKE13:
> You're safe.

> BEC2U:
> Wait? What are you talking about?

"Gawd dammit," I yelled and punched the bed. I got out of it and paced frantically.

"Jake, what were you talking about? Are you okay?" she asked in a panicked voice.

I raked both hands over my face and beard. I was far from okay. I checked if my clothes were dry...nope. "Fuck." I yanked the damp jeans on anyway.

"Jake. Talk to me."

"I don't know what to fucking say. Ignore those messages." I pulled on a shirt. At least it was dry.

"No."

I stopped and stared at the phone. "Did you say no?"

"Yes, I did. Tell me what's going on."

My socks were still soaked, and I threw them in the trash. I pulled on my boots and laced them.

"I'm waiting."

"Well, you'll be waiting forever. Cause I'm not talking about it." I went to the bathroom and didn't shut the door.

"Wait, are you peeing?"

"Nope. Pissing. Girl's pee." I flushed the toilet.

"Seriously?" she huffed. "Jake, please. Talk to me."

It was like a physical blow when she said my name. Impulsively, I picked up a lamp and threw it at a picture on the wall. They both crashed to the floor. I sighed and looked up at the ceiling with hands on my hips. "I'm gonna have to pay for that."

"What did you do?"

"I'm in Springdale, Arkansas at a hotel, and I'm gonna have to pay for that lamp and picture I just broke." Fucking hell.

NINE
BECCA

"What? Why are you there?" He said last night he wasn't going anywhere, and he ended up in a whole other state.

"I have no idea. Fuck." He sighed heavily.

"Well, since you went there...you had to have some reason." I was getting more perplexed by the minute.

"I don't know. You really don't want me to answer that question. You really don't."

"Please. Talk to me." I was scared for him, and I really believed he didn't know why he ended up there.

He blew out a ragged breath. "I get blackouts. From flashbacks. I've never had one on my bike, though."

I covered my mouth. I'd read about them, but I'd never experienced one. Flashbacks, of course, but never blackouts. "Tell me about them."

"Why? Are you really a shrink?"

I heard a frantic tapping and swallowed. "Breathe. Just breathe."

"You are, aren't you?"

"No. And if you thought that, you would hang up."

"Damn right," he snorted.

"Tell me. Please." He didn't know it but pushing through the pain was the only way he was ever going to be able to put it behind him. I'd read a ton of self-help books on PTSD and Complex-PTSD.

"Prick was convinced I was gay because of what I didn't do at ten years old. I gotta be out of my mind for telling you this. I've never told anyone."

Silent tears tracked down my cheeks, and I hoped he couldn't sense it. I didn't comment, just waited for him to continue. He sounded like he was pacing. He would get louder, then softer.

"Prick put sliding locks outside every door. I was fourteen. I came home from school, he shoved me in the bedroom and locked me in. Fuck, Bec. I can't..."

My eyes widened as I stared at my phone. He was about to tell me something horrific. I didn't want to hear it, but he needed me. He needed to let it go. I swallowed. "You can."

He released a heavy breath. "He had put a girl in my room. She was naked and high on something. She was like a rag doll. He said he wouldn't let me out until I fucked her."

I wasn't prepared for that. My vision went blurry from the horror, and I hugged a pillow tight against my chest.

"I couldn't. So, I waited until she was somewhat lucid, gave her a shirt and let her go out through the window."

"You're a good man, Jake." I wiped away tears. "What happened to you, since you let her go?"

I heard another crash.

"Fuck. Two lamps and a picture. I should be over this shit. You can probably guess."

"I don't want to guess...I want to know."

"Is that why you're crying? Cause you want to know?"

"I thought I was hiding it well." I buried my face in the pillow and dried my tears on it.

"You don't wanna hear my nightmare life. I don't know why I told you as much as I did. No one knows that."

I leaned my head on the pillow. "I'm glad you trusted me enough to tell me. But your story is not done."

"My story will never be done. One day in my life would give you nightmares for life. I'm fucked in the head."

"Tell me. Please."

"Shit. You're persistent, I'll give you that." He sighed, and he stopped pacing, as far as I could tell. "I ended up in the ER. Some broke bones. Maria and Carl took me."

I licked my dry lips. "I assume Carl is Tony's dad."

"Yeah. My parents didn't give two shits worth about me. They would have let them heal disfigured."

"What did you do before you met Tony?" I couldn't even fathom that. It was so far from reality...it sounded like fiction.

"Stayed hidden. Mostly. A neighbor in my trailer park helped me." He sighed audibly again. "My checkout time is at 11 a.m., so I need to get out of here and pay for damages."

"You sure it's safe?"

"Safe as I'll ever be."

"My number is 804-251-6478. We can text, if you want to, instead of going through the forum." I felt safe with him. Trusted him. A biker. A crude biker who had morals...somewhat.

"804? I recognize that area code...Oh, Andrea is getting married to a douche from there. Fuckin' married. That's some stupid shit right there."

"Plenty of people get married and are happy. Yes, it's Virginia. Let me know when you get home safe."

"Yeah, right." He grunted. "Are you my mother and a shrink?"

"No. I don't think they would do what we did the last two nights." I smiled and bit my lip.

"No, they wouldn't, darlin'."

"Ugh, you're not fair." I planted my face in the pillow.

"On that note, I gotta go. Two hours more or less to get home. Later."

"Bye, Jake."

I couldn't hold back a smile, but it slowly turned into worry. How could I help him? I knew I couldn't heal him. That was his responsibility, but I could help. I wouldn't even ask him to seek therapy because I knew what his answer would be. A cuss word of his choice and no.

Jake was blunt. Like my uncle, Robert. I was pretty sure if the work-place was laxer, he would cuss. He had to get creative. He once called a co-worker, twiddlebaned, under his breath, of course. But I heard it and had a hard time not laughing. It wasn't much different from 'Weasel Dicks' and 'Fishing' Jake and his friends used.

THE PHONE VIBRATING BY MY HEAD STARTLED ME. I WIPED THE SLEEP FROM my eyes and looked at my phone.

JAKE:

I'm home.

BECCA:

Thank you for letting me know.

JAKE:

Yup.

AT LEAST HE WAS HOME SAFE. I'D FALLEN ASLEEP DOING RESEARCH FOR blackouts. All I'd found was what I already knew. Jake needed to process through the memory. But, by the sound of it, his whole life was a big scary flashback. I would help all I could, but ultimately it was up to him to kill his demons.

Sighing, I got dressed to run some errands. As I pulled up at a stop-light, two motorcycles were alongside of me. I rolled the window down to listen to the rumble of their engines. How would it feel to be on a bike? To see sky overhead and the road beneath your feet. It looked highly dangerous to ride a flammable gas tank over an engine. I realized I was staring only when they stared back. I flushed, and the two male riders grinned at me and revved the bikes. When the light turned green, they peeled out and one did a small wheelie. My mouth dropped, and I shook my head and went to do my boring errands.

Seemed especially tame compared to what they went off to do…whatever that was.

The first place I stopped was to get an alarmed installed. No way I was letting a repeat of Thursday night happen. When the guy said it would be two weeks, I pointed at my face, and he said he'd do it Tuesday. That was better, but still wasn't soon enough for me, but I made the appointment, anyway.

I went to the grocery store and felt eyes on me. When I scanned the crowd, I paled at the familiar face. I swallowed bile and wiped my sweaty palm on my jeans. Nick smiled at me over the crowd.

He was out…so soon?

Didn't they know he was dangerous?

How could my bruises mean so little?

I wanted to run and hide. I could still feel his fist and the hand that grabbed me by the throat. I took a deep breath…he was in the wrong. I straightened my spine, looked him dead in the eyes. He wouldn't terrorize me anymore. Although, I wanted to bolt the second I spotted him. I finished my shopping, and he followed me. With shaking hands, I checked out and requested a manager. Nick stayed a fair distance away, but I knew if I left the store, he'd follow. I explained the situation to the manager and indicated my face and pointed to Nick. The manager and another bulky employee followed me to my car, loaded the groceries, and I thanked them. But as soon as I drove out of the parking lot, I lost it.

Tears streamed down my face, making a mess out of my mascara. I didn't know if he followed, but he knew I was headed home and he knew where I lived, obviously. I pressed the button to lock the doors every five seconds. Every minute I scanned the streets, looking for his car. Pulling into a busy gas station, I wondered what to do. Summer was on a shoot again, and I could call Robert, but he would tell me to come to their house. Maybe Summer's dad, Alan.

Alan was very protective of Summer. Once my dad died, Alan appointed himself my guardian. Not legally, of course, but Robert and Alan stepped in to fill my dad's shoes. Alan didn't like Nick at all, and he tried to warn me. He never said I-told-you-so, but I felt like an idiot for not heeding his warning. He tried to warn Summer too about her fiancé, and it turned into a fiasco. Alan was a brilliant man who owned a vast company, so I called him. He picked up on a couple of rings.

"Hi, sweetheart. How are you doing?"

I smiled, despite the tears. "Hi. Are you busy?"

His voice became immediately stern. "What's wrong?"

He had the same spidey-sense Jake did. I dreaded to tell him this, but I didn't know where else to turn. "I have a slight problem."

"Why are you crying?"

I exhaled loudly. "Thursday night Nick pushed his way into my apartment. He—"

"He hit you, didn't he? Why are you just now telling me this?"

"Yes." I leaned back on the headrest. "I've already arranged for a security system to be installed on Tuesday, but I spotted Nick in the grocery store, and he was following me. I'm scared to go home." I hated to admit it, and I couldn't stop the tears from clogging my throat and staining my cheeks.

"Where are you? I'll send security to follow you home and *my* guys will have a system installed today."

I shared my location with him through the phone. "But I've already—"

"No. It will be installed today. Becca, you should have called me after you called the cops. I'd have made sure he didn't walk out with only a slap on his wrists."

"I really thought he would stay in jail longer," I sniffed.

"Sadly, that's not the case. It never is."

"But he tried…" I still couldn't say it.

"Rape you? Did you tell the cops?" Alan sounded furious.

"Mhmm." I was beyond words right now and terrified.

"A black car pulled in behind you and he'll follow you home. He will stay with you until your alarm is installed. Are you able to drive?"

I nodded, wiped the tears and blew out a breath. I looked in the rear-view mirror and sure enough, a black car was behind me. "Yes." I heard Jake's voice in my head…*You're safe. You're safe, Bec.*

When I clicked off the phone, I drove home but couldn't stop trembling. When we parked, the man emerged from the car, and Chad Bennett introduced himself in a military manner and helped carry my groceries. Chad, and the security team that followed us, Mark and Keith, all wore black and had some serious muscle. As they installed the alarm, I put away the groceries, then curled up in an overstuffed chair and wrapped a blanket around me. It wasn't cold, but I couldn't stop shivering. I just wanted to talk to Jake.

How did he deal with the fear as a child? How did his own father and mother treat him like that? Sounded like they never took him to the doctor. I couldn't imagine the physical and emotional wounds he suffered. He was lucky to be alive. I sat cross-legged with my head against the cushion and watched the three guys sightlessly.

"Miss Saylor, we're finished."

I blinked and cleared my throat. "How much do I owe you?"

Chad shook his head. "Nothing. We're employed by Larkin. And we'd do it for free to stop those bruises."

"Um, thank you." I ducked my head, ashamed, although I shouldn't be.

"We need you to understand how the system works."

After the run through, they handed me their cards and said if I had questions at all, call them. As I read all three business cards, The Bennett Brothers, was embossed in silver font on top, and then realized they were brothers. But they looked nothing alike. They made sure I understood if I feared for my safety, at any time, to text or call one of them.

"Arm the door when we leave and keep it armed when you're home, not just when you're away," Chad said.

"I'll do that. Thank you."

"No problem. Stay safe."

They filed out the door and I armed it. And breathed. No one would come in unless I wanted them to. They had installed a video camera, so I'd know who they were, and it was connected to my phone. I blew out a breath. Even though I felt safer, I was still chilled to the bone. I called to report it, and let the police know I was terrified. But they acted bored as they took the information down. How could they act like this was normal? Just an everyday occurrence. I also cancelled the appointment I made earlier with the alarm company.

I pulled out a journal where I kept all the abuse I had experienced at the hands of Nick. Getting it out was the only way to cleanse my soul. I wrote in graphic detail everything he did, how I felt.... sobbing while doing it. After my tears were spent, I fixed a bath, dropped a bath bomb and sank down while it fizzled my fears away. At least, it tried too.

Jake.

He never left my thoughts. An idea popped in my head. What if he wrote all his demons on paper? Would it have the same effect on him as it had on me? I smiled. He'd probably shred and burn it afterwards.

I had the strong urge to send him a picture. Not a sexy one, but he'd know I was in the bath. I bit my lip and grabbed my phone, smiled for the pic and looked at it...and stopped. It would have been a good one if there wasn't a large bruise on the left side of my face. It reminded me of Nick at the store following me. Reminded me of the fear. I couldn't send it. In fact, I deleted it and put my phone down. I wiped away a tear and let the water drain. It was getting chilly anyway.

It was early, but I snuggled down in my bed with my laptop and a glass of wine. I knew where to start the story...beginning with those two bikers I saw. Armed with the information Jake gave me, and my imagination, I took off to an impressive start. Time flew by. When my phone rang, it startled me, and I knocked over my wineglass. Thankfully, it was empty. I blew out a breath and tried to calm my racing heart. When I saw it was Jake, I smiled.

"Hi you."

"What did you do to my friend?"

I was taken aback by the unfamiliar voice. "Who are you?"

"I'm Tony. What did you do to Jake?"

"I don't know what you mean." I didn't have a clue what he was talking about. "I didn't do anything to him."

He barked out a laugh. "No. You did something to him. He's shit-faced and talking about you."

The noise was loud on the phone indicating a bar or something. Maybe Snookers. "He got himself drunk. I didn't do that."

"He always gets drunk at home. Alone. Not out and certainly not talking about a chick," Tony said over the commotion going on there.

"Like I said, I didn't cause anything."

"Why the fuck are you on my phone?" Jake said in the background.

"Because I wanna know what she did to you," Tony said.

I heard some scuffling in the background, a few curses were thrown about, and I raised my eyebrows and was laughing softly into the phone.

"You think this is funny, darlin'?" Jake said into the phone.

When he said that, my insides turned to mush. I gasped and sucked in my bottom lip.

"Just the response I was looking for."

"Tony said you were drunk."

"Yup."

"He asked me what I did to you."

"Fucking asshole." He snorted. "I don't usually get drunk in public places cause I have exceptionally low tolerance for bullshit and assholes."

"You're talking very well for someone who is drunk." He was. Not a slur one.

"I can thank dear ole Prick for that one."

I nodded. "Your father. And I'm guessing your low tolerance would mean you can get in fights easy." The background noise disappeared.

"Yup. Tony lined up a friend to take me home in a cage, and he's following on my bike. Nobody but me rides my bike. I don't like that shit one bit."

"Are you in a cage now?"

"Yup. Don't like this shit either. Krista is taking me home, so I don't beat somebody's ass."

I was immediately jealous, and that was crazy. "Would you beat someone?"

"Eventually. Say hi, Krista."

A female voice said, "Hi, Bec." And she laughed in the background. Evidently, he had turned the speakerphone on.

I saw red and closed my eyes to suppress it. "Hi, Krista."

"Don't worry," Krista said. "We're not together. I have a boyfriend."

"Why do you always tell people that?" Jake asked Krista.

"I don't want to give people the wrong impression," Krista said.

"Whatever the fuck that means. Krista doesn't dig. I can tolerate her."

"Tolerate?" Krista snickered. "I take that as a compliment coming from you."

I was beginning to wonder why I was even on the phone with him to begin with. I didn't think 'tolerate' was a compliment. "She's taking you home. Be nice," I chided.

The silence on the other end had me wondering if he had hung up. I was about to say something when Jake spoke up.

"Fine. Thank you for taking me home."

Silence.

"You must be completely trashed to say that," Krista said, and burst out laughing like it was the funniest thing in the world.

"What? I can be nice," Jake said. "I just choose not to be most of the time."

Krista continued to laugh, and I didn't know what to say.

"Thank fuck I'm home," Jake said. "Later."

"Bye, Bec," Krista said.

"Um, bye, Krista," I replied and heard a car door shut.

"You asshole. You better not have scratched it," Jake said sternly.

Tony huffed. "If I did, it would be your fault, fucktard."

My mouth dropped. They were supposed to be best friends, but they sounded like enemies.

"Bye, Bec," Tony said, and another car door shut.

I heard the garage door shut and then, silence. He said nothing to me, but some music came on and turned low. I didn't recognize the music, but that wasn't surprising.

"What did you turn on?"

"Music," he replied.

I rolled my eyes. "What band?"

"Oh, Stone Sour."

"I haven't heard of them."

He snorted. "The mellow version of Slipknot."

"Gotcha." I heard a clank and asked, "What was that sound?"

"My wallet. I'm changing clothes."

I bit my lip. "Um, does your wallet have a chain?"

"Yup."

I imagined him. What would he look like? He'd only sent me a headshot, but I was curious about the rest of him. He hadn't given clues to his physical appearance, but he worked out a lot. "Do you have any tattoos?"

"Have we moved on from motorcycle research to personal shit?"

"I was curious. I'll let you go."

"Why?"

"Why what?"

"Why do you want to go?"

I paused. I couldn't get a read on him at all, and it was confusing. "I don't know, honestly. I can't judge your mood and can't tell if you want to talk to me. Tony called me. You didn't."

"Oh. I got a couple of tattoos."

I huffed. "Do you want to talk to me or not?"

"Yup. I would've told you if I didn't."

I put him on speakerphone and laughed. The way he was raised probably made him that way. He was probably doing the best he could with what social and emotional tools he owned. His world was just survival. No wonder he had social issues.

"Are you laughing at me, darlin'?"

"Ugh, you don't play fair."

"The world isn't fair."

"You're right." I paused, "Tony said you were talking about me. What did you say?"

TEN
JAKE

I settled on the couch with a Gatorade. As much as I drank tonight would have put a normal person in the hospital. Thanks to Prick, I would be sober in a few hours. I really didn't want to answer her question, but she was probably going to pester me until I told her.

11:18 p.m.

"I told Tony more about you and the fact that you were in Virginia. He urged me to set up a meet. Andrea is getting married on Virginia Beach."

"She is? And you're going to be there?"

"Yup. On orders from Maria. I tried to get out of it. She wasn't having it." My brows furrowed. Nobody but Maria had gotten me to do what I didn't want to. Until Bec. I rubbed the back of my neck because it was prickling again. "But I told him you wouldn't want to meet me, cause I'm an asshole."

"What if I told you...you're wrong."

"You don't have any business meeting me." I shook my head. Yeah, I wanted to meet her, but the sensible side of me knew it wouldn't be a good idea.

"Are you saying you don't want to?" she asked in a small voice.

Gawd dammit. I ran a hand through my hair and blew out a breath. I should've never told her. "No. That's not what I'm saying."

"I'm in Richmond, only about an hour and a half drive from there," she said and paused. "We could meet, only if you want to."

I stared at my phone. "Are you serious? After all I've told you about me? I'm a fucked-up mess." I was badly considering downing a bottle of Oilfire.

"Yes."

She sounded breathless and needy, and it had my blood rushing south. I got up immediately and went to the kitchen and grabbed a bottle of Oilfire and a can of Coke. Fuck the Gatorade. I fell back on the couch. I swallowed the liquor and chased it with a sip of Coke.

"If you don't want to. I'm not mad. I'll understand."

I swallowed another drink of whiskey. Alarm bells were firing off so loudly in my head I could hardly hear her. I couldn't decide if they were warning me to back off or to take a leap off the edge.

"Jake, are you there?"

Like always, my name on her lips sent my heart racing. The way she said it differed from anyone else. Decision made...the edge it is. "Yeah. I'll meet you. It's May first at ten A.M."

"Are you sure? You seem hesitant."

"Not anymore."

"Okay," she said, and I heard a smile in her voice. "Me and Summer usually go to the Rockfish Bar. It's right on the coast and easy to find."

"If you want, bring Summer. I'm sure Tony, the asshole, will tag along whether I want him to or not."

She laughed. "I can't get over the way you talk about Tony. And Summer will insist on coming, anyway. What time do you want to meet?"

"I'm not sure. I'll ask Mom when I can cut out of there. Hopefully, eleven."

"I'm sure it will be longer. I'm going to guess, one. At least."

"Fuck. Really?" I groaned. She giggled, and it wasn't annoying. Most girls' giggles were annoying as fuck.

"Have you ever been to a wedding?"

"No. As far as I'm concerned, they're a waste of time and money. And it's outdated anyway."

"Let's see, there's the wedding ceremony, then its pictures, cake, then a dance and a meal. I think that's it."

"You gotta be kidding me? I gotta sit through this shitdig for hours? They'll probably fight on the way to the airport for their honeymoon cruise." As I was saying this, she bubbled over with laughter. "It's not funny."

"You said shitdig. It's shindig." She burst out laughing.

I shook my head. "Same difference. If I have to be there, it's a shit-dig. Glad you find this so humorous."

"I do. We have a few weeks, so let me know when you know."

She became quiet suddenly, and it made my skin crawl. The silence stretched. She was still there because I heard her breathing. "Why are you crying?"

"Um, I saw Nick."

I jerked and bolted off the couch. "What did he do?"

"Nothing. I saw him in the store, and he was following me as I shopped. When I checked out, I asked to see a manager, and they walked me to my car."

"Smart girl. And?" There was always a...and. When dealing with the shit stains of human life, the story never really ends.

"He knew I was headed home because of the groceries." Her voice became small. "I called Alan, Summer's dad, to help. I was so scared."

I clenched my fists. If that mother fucker even touched a hair on her head, he was dead. "And?" I ground out.

"When my dad died, Alan stepped in, along with my uncle Robert. Alan is the head and owner of a huge company. He sent a car to follow me home and had an alarm system installed." She sniffed, and I sat back down. "I was so scared, Jake."

She was crying in earnest now. "Just breathe. You're safe now, Becca." I wanted so bad to be there... *What the fuck?*

It hit me. Hard. Stunned, I stared into the dark.

"I remember you saying that Thursday night. Your voice telling me I'm safe. It calmed me."

I was rendered mute. I was glad Alan helped her, and I felt thankful for his protection, but I couldn't stop the feeling that it was my job. It was so far off anything I'd ever felt before, it left me dumbstruck.

"Are you there?" Becca asked.

"Yeah. Glad Alan helped and got an alarm system for you." My voice sounded foreign. Hollow. Even to me. I scraped a hand over my beard, went to the kitchen, turned the faucet on cold and ducked my head under the spray. I waited till I shivered, turned the water off and checked my watch.

1:04 a.m.

I grabbed a kitchen towel and turned the faucet off. I ran the towel over my head and threw it on the counter.

"Jake? Are you okay? Is that running water?"

"It was the sink." My head was clearer, but the thought still remained…it was my job.

It least I hadn't blacked out. For the moment. I could almost tell when I was about to black out. I couldn't explain it. But I didn't have a warning last night on my bike. The wind in my face and the rumble of my bike always grounded me. I knew all about PTSD. I'd done research and knew how truly wacked I was.

"Jake?"

I rubbed my chest. "I'm here." I took a drink of Gatorade and let the bottle of Oilfire stare at me.

"I write down every abuse incident in a journal. In graphic detail. And I cry, scream and hit a pillow, sometimes imagining it's Nick's face. I have to get it out or it will destroy me. Maybe something like that will help you."

"Write in a journal like a girl? I don't want a book about my life lying around. Fuck that."

"I thought you may say something like that. How about you write it down and burn it," she said. "When you get a flashback or blackout, write it out. And burn it or shred it. You need to get it out."

I propped a foot on the coffee table. "I knew you were a fucking shrink."

She laughed. "And I knew you would say that. I went to see a therapist for a while. She gave me some tools to cope."

"I'll think about it." I ran a hand through my wet hair. The only way I dealt with it was beating the shit out of my bag or being an adrenalin junkie. But lately, it wasn't enough. Even before Bec, I felt like a ticking time bomb.

"Good. I wasn't sure how you would receive the advice."

"I've done research. I know I have PTSD and other issues. Nothing that I haven't figured out."

"Really?" She sounded surprised.

"Yup. Really."

1:54 a.m.

I was still good. Surprisingly.

"I've started writing my novel. I saw two bikers today, and they gave me inspiration. With the information you gave me, I'm putting all the pieces together." She yawned.

"Good. I better let you go. It's late where you are."

"Okay. Try to get some sleep."

"Sleeps overrated."

"Says you."

"Night, darlin'."

"Ugh," she groaned. "I wish I had a word that affected you. Night, Jake."

She clicked off, and she didn't know she already had a word...*my name.*

2:10 a.m.

Dad grabbed my wrists and dragged me down the hall. "I need to teach you something," he said.

I learned to stay silent, so the beatings were shorter. He got off on my cries. Pulling me into my parents' bedroom, there was a girl lying naked on the bed. My ears rang so loud, and my breath strangled my throat. I fought to get loose.

Dad hit me on the back of the head. "Calm down, you little shit. You're gonna like this." He grabbed me by the back of my neck, shoved me closer to the bed and the girl. "See? You can do anything you want to her. Go on, boy. Touch her tits."

. . .

I woke up when I punched through the headboard into the wall. Sweat covered my body, my throat parched and the ringing in my ears overwhelming. I blinked and looked at my watch.

5:13 a.m.

Motherfucker.

I flung myself out of the bed and took a cold shower...again. I was trembling but not from the frigid water. Could I not get a moment's peace? Anywhere? I leaned on my elbows. I couldn't erase that image out of my head. That girl couldn't have been over fifteen. Blonde. *Just like Becca.* My stomach churned, and I barely made it to the toilet, where I promptly threw up.

I sat on the floor and leaned against the tub. The shower was still on, and I was dripping wet. Staring at the ceiling, I knew that girl wasn't Becca. But I couldn't separate the girl who laid on the bed, from Bec. My eyes burned, and I swallowed hard. I got up, turned the shower off, and toweled off.

The mirror reflected a perfect image of Tomas. There could be no doubt I was my father's son. The only difference was my eye color. I barely contained my rage and didn't shatter the mirror like I wanted to. I put on some shorts and sat on the bed.

I was dead tired and raked a hand through my wet hair. I was used to little sleep, but I wasn't getting *any* lately. All the things that worked previously...weren't. As I reflected on Becca's advice, I thought it sounded counterproductive. I sure as fuck didn't want to relive that scene. I did everything to *avoid* those memories, but it wasn't working anymore. No matter how hard I tried, I couldn't escape my real life nightmares.

I blew out a heavy breath, laced my hands on top of my head and paced the bedroom. How did I do it and come out on the other side intact?

What if I went mad?

What if I immersed myself that way and had a blackout and hurt someone? That was the real fear. I couldn't do it yet. I looked at my watch.

6:33 a.m.

I shot a text to Tony asking him to come over as soon as he woke up. He was the only one I trusted to keep me, and anybody else, safe. I was pacing in the living room when there was a knock on the door.

8:14 a.m.

I opened the door and continued pacing. Tony walked in and shut the door behind him.

"You look like shit," Tony said.

"Well," I stopped. "I feel worse."

Tony narrowed his eyes. "What haven't you been telling me?"

I blew out a breath. "The blackouts are back."

"Geezus. I knew there was something going on with you. How long?"

"Two months or so. Friday night I went for a ride, 'woke up' in Springdale, Arkansas. Lost, at least, two hours." I hated talking about this shit.

His eyes widened. "No shit? And you were on your bike?"

I nodded. "I've never had a blackout on my bike. And the nightmares are back. It's bad." I looked down at the floor. Rage boiled just below the surface. At life. At my parents. "Becca said she has flashbacks—"

"You sure talk to her more than you ever do with us." Tony crossed his arms over his chest.

I began pacing again and ignored that comment. "She writes down all of her flashbacks and suggested I do the same and burn it."

Tony raised his brows. "Might be helpful."

"But she doesn't have blackouts." I leveled a look at him and struggled to continue.

He nodded. "You're afraid it might make you blackout and hurt someone."

This is what my life consisted of...avoiding and distracting myself from myself, essentially. "Fuck. The normal stuff I did to cope is not working anymore."

"The only safe place would be the barn, but you are bigger now. Me and Dad had trouble even when you were smaller."

I gripped the back of the couch. "Tie me before and leave one hand loose where I can write. That way, you have only one arm to control."

"Are you sure you want to do this?" Tony asked.

I looked at him. "Do you have any better ideas? You know what they'd do to me in a mental hospital? If it doesn't work, it doesn't work."

"But what if it does?" Tony said. "All right. Let's do this."

A COUPLE HOURS LATER, I WAS TIED TO A CHAIR AND BOTH ME AND THE chair were tied to a pole in the barn. All except my left arm. Carl and Tony stood back.

Tony grinned, clapped and rubbed his hands together. "All right, are you ready for the exorcism?"

"You're enjoying this, aren't you, fucker?" Tony tied me tight enough.

"Immensely." He laughed.

"Make sure Mom and Andrea don't see this. No one is to see this or hear about this." I glared at Tony.

"I'll make sure," Carl said.

I nodded and blew out a breath. I didn't like being restrained. It was almost enough to make me back out. Carl handed me a notepad and pen and sat in a foldout chair near the door. Tony sat in a similar chair closer to me but facing away.

I must be out of my mind to try something as drastic as this. I wiped at the sweat on my face and stared at the dirt floor. Carl and Tony were silent. It was just me and my chaotic thoughts.

I started to write...

TEN YEARS OLD. TOMAS DRAGGED ME TO MY PARENTS' BEDROOM. I WAS filled with dread, and I had no clue what awaited me inside. A naked girl on the bed. Blonde. Young. Drugged. Prick forced my hand on her tit. I fought. Kicked. Tried everything to get away. But I remained silent...

MY HEART RACED. MY MOUTH WENT DRY, AND I FOUGHT TO KEEP A HOLD of reality.

11:14 a.m.

. . .

"LICK IT," TOMAS SAID. "BITE IT. ALL WOMEN LIKE THIS."

I fought to get loose. I didn't want any part of this.

"What's wrong with you, boy? Are you one those filthy faggots?"

Tomas forced my hand between the girl's legs...

"JAKE KORTE! I'M SAFE. I'M NOT THAT GIRL. I NEVER WAS THAT GIRL," SHE stated firmly between sniffles.

"Becca?" I said in a hoarse voice that cracked. "You're safe?"

Disoriented and woozy, my vision went in and out of focus, and I found it hard to swallow. My clothes were soaked to the skin from sweat or water, I didn't know which. I remained in the chair, but either Carl or Tony had tied my left arm.

"Yes, I'm safe. I wasn't that girl," Becca sobbed.

I looked at Carl, who had a tormented expression and tears in his eyes. I stared at Tony, realizing he had called Becca.

"You mother fucker, I told you I didn't want anyone else to know about it," I yelled at Tony and pulled the restraints.

"Look at your watch, dickhead," Tony shouted.

I tilted my wrist up, and I closed my eyes momentarily. "Fuck," I said raggedly.

"Yup. Four fucking hours we been trying to wake you up. Becca could have done it in five minutes," Tony said. "I need a fucking drink." And he walked out of the barn.

Carl untied me. As the ropes came loose, I could see how hard I struggled to get free. Rope burns crisscrossed my chest, and my shirt was in shreds. And evidently, they had tried to wake me by dumping water on my head because my clothes were soaked.

"You good, son?" Carl asked me and gripped my shoulders.

No, I wasn't good, but I nodded anyway. "When you can, Maria will get you fixed up and you can rest." Carl handed me two bottles of water, clapped me on the shoulder and headed to the house.

I downed one water and ran a shaky hand through my hair. The only thing I could hear were the sounds of Becca crying. I tore off the rest of my shirt.

"I'm so sorry, Jake," Becca sniffled.

"Nah. Not your fault. Now we know." Physically and emotionally, I was done. Not to mention I could hardly talk. Maybe I could get some sleep. I picked up my phone and eyed the yellow pad. I thought about leaving it, but I grabbed that too and got in my truck. Every muscle in my body felt like it was pulled. It hurt to even breathe. "How much do you know?" I asked Becca as I pulled out of the drive.

"Not much," she answered. "Weren't you supposed to go in the house?"

"Don't want to."

"I'm not sure it's safe for you to be alone."

"I'm not, you're here," I croaked out. My throat felt like it was bleeding. It was so raw. "I want to know what he told you."

"Tony only said that you thought I was that girl in your flashback, because you were screaming my name."

"That's the second time I've used your name in place of a blonde." Tony's name flashed on my phone. "Fuck. I'll call you back."

"What?" I barked. Or I would've if I had my full voice.

"Where the fuck are you going, asshole?"

"Home." My body was barely functioning, but I needed to be home. I assumed Maria knew what was going on and didn't want to see the horror on her face. My whole life was a creepy freak fest.

"I'll be there." Tony hung up.

I wanted to argue, but I didn't have the energy. I called Becca back.

"Hello," she answered in a small voice.

"I don't know how long my voice is gonna hold out, so listen. You didn't cause this. Tomas did. You were only trying to help." I sighed. "Don't cry."

"I heard you screaming. You sounded like an animal being tortured," she sobbed.

I parked in my driveway and hung my head. I never liked drama, but it always found me. Tony pulled beside me and unlocked the door to my house like he owned it. I gave him a key for emergencies, but Tony barely glanced in my direction.

"I…" What could I really say? I needed to ghost her. She'd be better off. "I need to go. Bye, Bec."

I hung up without giving her a chance to say bye and thought about deleting her number. But I couldn't do it. I went into the house with Tony lounging on the loveseat with a beer. I flung the pad and my phone down on the coffee table without a word to Tony.

"Take a shower and come back in here. Mom bagged up some stuff for those rope burns."

"Does Mom know?" I asked wearily.

He nodded. "We tried Mom before Becca. She was our last resort before we got the hospital involved. We didn't know what to do."

I looked at the ceiling. "Yeah."

5:42 p.m.

Cold water rushed over me. I didn't shiver. Nothing. I felt nothing. I didn't even feel the rope burns. I went into the living room and let Tony put the salve on. Without words. The silence was welcoming. There was no buzzing in my ears. Or roaring in my head. Or racing thoughts. Just…nothing. When Tony finished, I took three headache pills and fell in bed.

Finally.

I woke to a darkened room and checked the time.

11:23 p.m.

Uninterrupted sleep did wonders, but I felt the sting from the rope burns and every muscle was sore. I stretched, sat up and rubbed the back of my neck. Hold up…did I hear a girl's laughter? Surely, Tony didn't have a girl over. I walked into the living room where Becca, on speakerphone, was cracking up at something Tony said.

"Well, look who returned from the dead," Tony said with a mouthful of popcorn.

"Hi, Jake," Becca said, hiccupped and giggled.

Tony laughed. "She's drunk."

"I'm not. Just tipsy. Are you feeling better, Jake?"

I stared at Tony and my phone. "Do you feel the need to use my phone whenever you want?"

Tony shrugged. "Bec was blowing up your phone because she was worried about you after you rudely hung up on her."

Becca hiccupped again. "It's the wine," she giggled. "Are you feeling better?"

I sighed. "Yeah, I am."

"On that note, I'm fairly certain you won't be skinny dippin' in your crazy anymore tonight. I'm outta here. Bye, Becca."

"Bye. Nice talking to you."

I rubbed my head as Tony left. "How long...never mind. I don't wanna know." I went in the kitchen to make a sandwich and sat on the couch.

"Were you going to ask how long me and Tony were talking? About an hour, or maybe two."

"It doesn't matter."

"Right. I know you said it wasn't my—"

"It wasn't you, Bec. You didn't cause it. And I don't want to talk right now." I knew I was being rude, but knew I wasn't good for her. I hurt her from a thousand miles away. My black soul stretched beyond that.

"Okay," she said, hesitantly. "I'll let you go. Bye, Jake."

"Bye."

We clicked off, and I leaned back. My name from her lips had me all twisted inside. I should cut me out of her life, it would be for the best. Finishing my sandwich, the yellow pad of paper screamed at me. I didn't know how far I'd gotten into that tale, but Tony and Carl had read it. I wanted to know what they knew. I picked it up.

I FRANTICALLY PULLED MY HAND BACK, BUT TOMAS MADE ME TOUCH IT.

"What kind of boy doesn't like pussy?" He snarled. He flung me away by my arm and I crashed into a wall and slid to the floor. My arm was broken, but I wouldn't dare make a sound or move. My eyes squeezed shut, and I tried to block out the sounds, but I heard everything. The slaps of Tomas' hand on the girl. The grunts from him.

"This is how you treat a woman, boy."

She was blonde...Bec...

. . .

AND THE STORY STOPPED THERE. MY HANDS SHOOK AS I FLUNG THE PAD onto the coffee table, and it skated to the floor. I raked both hands through my hair. And that was just one of many stories that was my life. I abruptly got up, picked up the pad, tore my words out and put it in the sink. And promptly set it on fire.

I took a long, deep breath. Seeing the flames turn into ash and eventually die out was oddly satisfying. Maybe it did work. If It did, I had the emotional and, now physical, scars to prove it.

I knew I would never be completely free. The scars were bone deep. I would have to be dead to be completely rid of them. And hell awaited me. I might give Satan a break from the hellish things he did. A vacation, so-to-speak. I shook my head and strode to the bedroom, hopefully to get more sleep.

ELEVEN
BECCA

Wiping my puffy eyes, I curled up in a ball and stared at my phone. The screams from Jake were etched in my mind and fresh tears fell. After Jake got home and hung up on me, I texted him. When he didn't answer, I panicked, until Tony called and reassured me Jake was okay. I asked Tony to read me what Jake wrote, and Tony tried to warn me, but I insisted. And when he finally read it word for word, I was shocked by the horror of it.

That's why his father locked him in a room with a drugged-up girl when he was fourteen. When he told me that story, I couldn't imagine a worse flashback. But no. It wasn't the worst. He was just a boy…ten years old. I couldn't begin to comprehend it. Jake's father was a psychopath, and his mother was just as bad. How many real-life nightmares would he have to endure to get some peace? Honestly, I was surprised he was still alive. It probably had to do with Tony and his family. They were probably the only thing that kept those demons from swallowing him up.

I glanced at the time and shook my head. Three a.m. and I had to get up for work in only a few hours. I clicked off my lamp and snuggled down in bed. Between the wine and mental exhaustion, I fell promptly asleep.

. . .

MONDAY WAS HARD. I KEPT ZONING IN AND OUT ALL DAY, WONDERING IF
Jake was okay. I texted him but hadn't got a reply. When I got home, I
ate dinner, poured a glass of wine, and called him.

It went straight to voicemail. I left a short message, but when an
hour dragged by, I messaged him on the forum. By nine that evening, I
was starting to panic. He never took this long to respond. I wanted to
know if he was all right. If he was breathing. He told me I wasn't the
cause of anything yesterday, but somehow it seemed like I was.

When my phone rang, it scared me so much I jumped and
screamed. My phone slipped between the couch cushions, and I frantically reached for it.

"Hello," I answered breathless.

"Hey," Jake answered.

I blew out a breath of relief and put my hand on my head. "Thank
goodness."

"Why do you say that?"

"You're okay. I just wanted to make sure you were okay." I wiped a
stray tear.

"Why are you crying?" Jake asked in a stern voice.

I rolled my eyes. "Nothing gets past you."

"I hurt you. And never meant to." He sighed. "I'm no good for
you."

My breath seized. Was this why he hadn't answered all day? Was
he wanting to end things? Whatever thing we were doing. "I needed to
make sure you were okay. That's all. I understand if you don't want to
talk or text or anything. I'm not here to make demands on you. I just
needed to know you were safe."

Silence. I waited, albeit impatiently, but I waited. And waited.

"Okay. That's fair."

I blinked. What did one say to that? What possible reply was I to
respond with? "Okay. I'll let you go. Just needed to know that."

"Okay. Bye."

"Bye, Jake."

I laid the phone down on the coffee table, put my elbows on my knees, threaded my hands in my hair and stared at the phone. Why did it feel like we broke up? Tears slipped down my face. Maybe he needed some breathing room. Maybe I did too.

I abruptly got up and ran a bath. Then turned on some music by Eric Church and sang along with lyrics, "Drink a little drink, smoke a little smoke, yeah." I couldn't sing a lick, and Nick said I sounded like a dying cat. To hell with him and men. And I sang louder just for spite.

A FEW DAYS LATER, I'D ONLY HEARD FROM JAKE SPORADICALLY. IT WAS A stark difference from a week ago when we texted each other throughout the day, every day. I didn't even know if he still wanted to meet after the wedding. It was Friday night when Jake popped up on the screen of my phone, making me instantly smile.

"Hey you."

"He did it again," Tony answered.

There was a lot of noise in the background, and I assumed it was Snookers. I sighed and wished Jake would have called instead of Tony. "I swear I didn't do anything this time. We've barely talked in the last few days."

Tony laughed loudly, and I could hear some scuffling.

"Give me my phone, you fucker," Jake muttered. "I'll call you back, Becca."

He hung up, and I blew the bangs out of my face. I shook my head. Those guys acted like toddlers most of the time. I'd gotten to know Tony somewhat when we talked when Jake was sleeping last Sunday. He said he used to be a SEAL, but now he was a pilot and a helicopter mechanic. I'd asked him some of the same biker questions I asked Jake. And he was shocked by the amount of information Jake gave me. Tony said he never talked about much of anything. That meant, I honestly knew more about him than anyone else. And that was sad. A virtual stranger knew more about him than his family and friends.

But I'd told Jake some stuff about Nick that no one knew. Not even Summer. I ran my hand over my phone absently and clicked on Jake's pic. I didn't know if he'd call me back or not, so I got ready for bed. I had just clicked off the light when my phone rang. Keeping the light off, I answered, "Hello."

～

JAKE

"Hey. Sorry about Tony calling you," I said. "He's a pain in my ass."

"That's okay."

It was great to hear her voice.

"Did you just get home?" Becca asked.

"Yeah. I should've stayed home. I don't know why I bother going out when everybody aggravates me." I clunked down my wallet, keys, and phone and changed into loose shorts. "Hell, I can drink beer at the house, and it would be cheaper. And less peoply."

"What do you mean, you don't like people? Shocker."

I smirked. She always made me feel better. So why was my dumbass trying to ghost her? "Are you being a smartass?"

"Maybe."

"What are you doing? Writing?"

"No, I just got in bed. I didn't know if you would call me back or not."

I frowned and plopped on the couch. "I said I would."

"Yeah, but we've not really talked in the last couple of days."

"But I said I would. I take my word seriously." I had explained that…I thought. "If I give my word, you can count on it, except in emergencies."

"Okay."

I blew out a breath. "Forget about Sunday."

"I can't do that."

I closed my eyes. "I'm sorry you had to hear that. I'm no—"

"Were you planning on ghosting me?" she asked in a small voice.

I dropped my head. That was the plan I started to put in motion. Until Tony called her. And I heard her voice… "I won't lie, I thought about it."

"Oh. Uhm—"

"But my reasons were valid. You cried because of me." I put the phone on speaker and my knee bounced.

"I hurt with you, not because of you. There's a difference."

I looked at the phone, like I was looking at her. She was right, there was a difference. Like I wanted to beat Nick to a bloody pulp because the pain she had suffered at his hands. Bec didn't cause Nick to beat her, any more than I caused my parents' abuse.

"You're right." I sat back with my hands laced behind my head and tried to see it through her eyes.

"I am?" she asked in an awed voice.

"Why do you sound surprised? I thought women just assumed they were right about everything."

"No. Uhm, Nick never thought I was right about anything," she whispered.

"Becca, I'm not Nick. I don't have a holier-than-thou mindset. I make a lot of mistakes, but I at least own up to them. Or I think I do."

"I know you're not Nick, but I fall back in those patterns, and I don't even realize I do it."

"I get that." It was hard not to flinch when you expected to get hit. Every time.

"If you want, we could stop talking. But I'm not okay with you ghosting me. That would be unfair to me."

I barely heard her...she was talking so softly. "Do you wanna stop?"

"No."

She was crying again, but she tried to conceal it. I clenched my fist. This time, I caused those tears. "I'm no good for you. You do realize that?"

"No. I don't. You push people away on purpose." She sniffled. "But I don't blame you. You have your reasons, and they're logical."

"Are you positive you're not a shrink?"

"You know the answer to that."

I sighed. "I don't want to stop talking to you. And I don't know why. But you'd be better off without all my chaos."

"I think I can handle your chaos."

"Oh, you do?" I smirked. She was like a drug I couldn't stop taking. "You really think you can handle me?"

"Yes. Do you think you can handle me?" she asked, and I heard the smile in her voice.

"I'm positive I can handle you, darlin'." I smirked when she gasped.

"You don't play fair." She groaned. "And don't say anything about my groan."

I laughed. "But it's needy."

She huffed. "I told you not to say anything."

"What do you need, darlin'?" I set my foot on the coffee table and imagined her hair in my hands. Pictured her big brown eyes widening.

"Nothing," she squeaked.

I laced my hands behind my head. "All right," I said and waited.

The silence stretched.

"Jake, you there?"

It hit me, almost like a physical blow. I rubbed my chest. "I'm here. Just waiting."

"Waiting for what?"

"You to tell me what you need." I knew what I needed...I needed to be with her. I raked a hand through my hair. *Gawd damn.* I breathed through my wayward thoughts.

"I want you here," she said.

"What would you want me to do if I were there, baby?" I couldn't steer away from her, no matter how hard I tried. Couldn't fight her pull.

"Gawd...everything." She panted.

"Is your neck sensitive? If I breathed along it, would you like that, darlin'?" I liked to watch a woman's neck, almost as much as their ass. If one paid attention, every thought started with the pulse in their necks.

"Yes," she hissed. "Everything about you turns me on."

"Turning you on gets my pulse jacked," I rumbled. And it did, by the tent in my shorts. "Are you wet?"

"Mmm."

"Check."

"Umm…"

"You were already there, weren't you?" I pulled out my dick and fisted it.

"Yes," she hissed.

She was panting in my ear so hot and heavy a little bit of precum leaked out of my cock. "Tell me what you feel."

"Slick. Hot. Are you?" she asked between pants.

"Fuck yeah. It's hard for you, darlin'."

"Oh, gawd," she moaned.

"Are your walls quivering? Are your fingers sliding over your clit?" I pictured her…head thrown back, fingers buried in her pussy. *Fucking hell.*

"Ahh, yes, I'm…"

"Fuck." I barely caught the cum with my shorts. I leaned my head back, and my dick pulsed in my hand through the flimsy fabric. This girl had me wound up tight, and I hadn't even touched her.

"Jake," she said on a sigh and my dick twitched so hard I had half a chub.

*What the fuck…*I heard of guys led around by their cocks, but this was taking it to the extreme. "Shit. Be right back." I shot off the couch and quickly changed my shorts and grabbed a bottle of Oilfire and a can of Coke. "I'm back."

She let out a contented sigh.

I couldn't help but grin. And I rarely smiled. "Better?"

"Mmm, yeah. You?"

"Oh yeah." I was going to ghost her, delete her number and disappear but instead had phone sex. That's how very little control I had when it came to her. What would it be like when I met her? Would she be the same in person?

"You were right," I said.

"Right about what?"

"Mom said one-ish when the shitdig would be over."

She laughed. "I thought as much. Do you still want to meet? I understand if you don't."

"Yeah, if you do. You've heard how whacked I am, and I wouldn't blame you if you backed out."

"Yes. I do," she said. "I'm looking forward to it,"

"You sure? If you changed your mind at the last minute, I'll understand." I didn't have any idea why she wanted to meet me.

"Jake, I will not back out. I will be there. I should be there by three." She yawned.

"Okay. I'm gonna let you go since you're sleepy."

She yawned again. "I haven't been sleeping well the past few days, and I think it caught up with me."

"All right, darlin'. Night."

"Ugh, it's like kryptonite when you say that. Good night, Jake."

When she clicked off, it was back. The thump in my chest and the big black cloak that I couldn't shed permanently. The numbness. The emptiness. I noticed it a lot more because talking to Bec I didn't feel like a walking dead person. I didn't know if that was a good thing or not.

That's when I realized I hadn't checked the time in hours.

11:17 p.m.

I got up, went to my garage to beat the hell out of my bag.

"Jake, would you like some potato salad?" Maria asked.

I glanced up at her and nodded. "Thanks." Scooping a heap onto my plate, I listened to Andrea talk.

"Mom, I'm so excited. But I will miss you all so much."

"I don't know why your fiancé can't move here. Why do you have to move to Virginia?" Tony asked. "I don't know why you have to give up everything."

Andrea's lips pursed familiarly. It meant she was getting ready to go on a rant, and it made me want to duck.

"You know why he can't move here, Tony. He has a job. A good one. You know, people move across the country all the time. I don't know why you have such a hang-up about it. It's not like you can't visit."

"Yeah. But how am I supposed to keep an eye on you all the way in Virginia? Trouble is your middle name, husband or not," Tony replied.

"You don't need to keep an eye on me. I'll have a husband. And you and Jake are the troublemakers. Not me. I swear, the last time I went to Snookers with you, there was a girl fight. Over you two. Can you believe it?" She looked at her mom. "Why in the world would anyone want to fight over those two?"

When Maria turned and looked at us, Tony said innocently, "What? I didn't tell them to fight. Did you, Jake?"

"Hey, don't get me in on this. I just want to enjoy the food." I took a bite out of my charcoaled cheeseburger so I wouldn't have to say anything else.

"One of these days, you two will get caught in your own game. A girl will come along and there you will be. None of your dashing charm to save you. Just mark my words, one day it will happen." Maria waggled a finger at us.

"It won't happen to me." Tony elbowed me. "But it might have already happened to my friend here."

I glared at a grinning Tony. "Yeah, right. When hell has frozen over."

"Is that why you're meeting Becca in Virginia?"

I wanted to pummel Tony. Why in the hell had he brought Becca up with our family around? "Whatever," I said, trying to ignore it.

Andrea placed both hands on the table and leaned forward, her pale blue eyes wide. "You're bringing a girl to my wedding? Oh, my Gawd. Hell did freeze."

"No. I'm not bringing a girl to your wedding." I frowned. "She's a girl I'm meeting in Virginia."

"She's not flying down with you?" Andrea asked, being her nosy self.

"No. She lives in Virginia."

"How did you meet a girl in Virginia? Did you go on a trip and not tell me?"

I fought the urge to roll my eyes and glanced at Maria for support. But she was sporting a smile that said she wanted to know as well. I looked at Carl and he just shrugged. No help there. Carl knew about Becca because he was there when I lost my shit.

"She's a girl he met online," Tony blurted out.

I choked on my burger and jabbed him hard in the side, which only made Tony laugh.

"You're online dating? Why in the world would you do that?" Andrea asked. "You have your pick of females...although I have no idea what they see in you. You never talk and—"

"That's enough, Andrea," Maria said. "Do we get to meet this girl, Jake?"

"I didn't go on a dating site, Andrea. No, you don't get to meet her." I had no intention of revealing any more information.

"They've been talking for about two months. We're meeting her at the beach." Tony offered.

"Two months?" Maria asked, and I didn't meet her gaze. "My, that's a long time for you. And Tony is going with you?"

Did Tony have a death wish? What the hell was the matter with him? I shook my head and glanced at Maria when I heard the hope in her voice. The woman had tried everything to get me to settle down with a girl. I knew she wanted me happy, but I had given up on that dream a long time ago.

"Don't even think it. I'll probably never see her again." Which was true. I had no idea what she would think of me, and I planned on it being a onetime thing. "I told her to bring a friend, so I invited idiot here. She seemed to feel safer that way."

Andrea burst out laughing. "She won't once she gets a look at you two. Did you tell her to bring her daddy? That's the only way she would be safe."

I wanted to thump her on the head. She was like a little sister to me and just as irritating. "Maybe I should've warned Kevin about you. Heaven help the poor man who has to put up with you 24/7."

"You exaggerate, Andrea. They are good boys."

Andrea choked on her drink and, strangely, so did Carl.

"Did you hear what he said about me?" Andrea dramatized. "You stick up for him, but not for me?" When she stuck her tongue out at me, I winked at her, and she smiled.

"Always a circus at this table," Carl muttered.

Maria patted his arm. "You like it that way, dear."

I listened to them rattle on, mostly Andrea, Tony and Maria. I contributed little, just added a word or two when necessary. Carl leaned back, drank his iced tea and watched us.

This was home, not my mom's drug infested trailer park.

TWELVE
BECCA

I had been trying to think of a way to tell Summer about me meeting Jake. But it was Wednesday now and in only three days I would see him. I swallowed the lump in my throat. Summer sat across from me at our favorite club, Sunsets. We met here frequently for a few drinks and to catch up. Music thumped in the background and although the place wasn't packed, there were a few bodies moving on the dance floor.

"Quit thinking about phone sex with Jake," Summer said, interrupting my thoughts.

"What? I was not!" I said, heat filling my face.

"Don't lie to me, chica. I know that faraway look."

I couldn't deny it. I talked to Jake often. And several times it led to some serious orgasms. I bit my lip, remembering his deep voice over the phone. What was I going to do when I finally met him in person? I looked at Summer, who was nodding her head to the music and sipping her margarita.

"I'm meeting him," I blurted out.

Summer froze and stared wide-eyed at me. "You're what?"

"He's going to be at Virginia Beach this Saturday."

"I knew it. I knew there was more going on. There is no way I can let you meet him by yourself, even if you are meeting him for some hot sex."

"It's not about sex, Summer," I said in shock. "He's going to be down here for a wedding, not to meet me for that."

"Mmhmm. So, you're telling me that if something pops up, you're not going to jump on it?" Her eyebrows wiggled at me, and I laughed.

"We're just going to talk."

"Sure, you are, babe. And does he know this?"

Blanching at the thought, I said, "Gawd, what am I doing? I should know better than this." Putting my head in my hands, I stared at the table. I didn't think he would expect it…would he?

Summer touched my shoulder, and I looked up into her smiling face. "No worries. I'll be there. Nothing will happen unless you want it to."

"He's bringing his friend, Tony, and I have talked to him a few times. Surely, Jake doesn't think I'll just fall into bed with him."

"Honey, that's what all guys think. Look at it this way, if you do end up in the sack with him, he has to go back to Oklahoma eventually." Tapping the table with a brightly polished nail, Summer smiled. "And, you know, a one-nighter might do you some good."

"I don't know. I've never done anything like this before. I have a feeling I'm in over my head." This was a bad idea. How many women got killed because they went to meet someone they met online? But he was Jake. And I felt like I really got him.

Summer leaned in close, her face suddenly serious. "All you've really known is Nick. You need to do this. You need to see what it's like with someone else. Someone who doesn't control every damn move you make."

Summer winked at me and turned toward a guy who had walked up to us. I barely noticed when they wandered off onto the dance floor.

I sighed. Summer was right. I had been with Nick since my senior year in high school and hadn't really dated much before that. My life had been a whirlwind since my dad had died when I was seventeen. Wrapped up in my grief when Nick stepped into my life, I followed his lead. He seemed to be what I needed at the time. Looking back, I realized he just filled an empty hole. Had I ever really loved the guy?

He didn't make you feel like Jake does.
I inhaled sharply at the thought.

LATER, WHEN I WAS HOME LYING IN BED, I STARED AT THE PHONE. SHOULD I call him? It had been a few days since we had actually talked, but we had texted most every day. I put a pillow over my head and tried to sleep. But I was too wired, and my thoughts kept straying back to Jake. Every time I moved, the soft sheets slid against my skin, and I groaned. I kicked off the covers and flopped over on to my back. Oh hell, who was I fooling? I wanted to hear his voice. I grabbed the phone and dialed.

"Hi," I said when he picked up.

"Hey, darlin'. How are you?" Jake answered.

"I'm good." Stretching out on my bed, I stared up into the dark and smiled, feeling instantly relaxed now that I could hear his voice. "How have you been?"

"Okay," he said flatly.

"That doesn't sound good. What happened?"

"Fight. That's all."

"A fight? Are you okay?" I asked and instantly sat up in bed.

"Oh, yeah. I'm cool. The other dude...not so much."

"What happened?"

"Tony and I were at Snookers and some guy started shoving around a girl. No one seemed to notice, so I told him to stop." He said it like he was reading facts from a book.

"You told him?"

"Maybe I did more than tell him. But he did stop."

I laughed. "I bet he did. That was a nice thing to do."

"Yeah. Whatever."

I could almost hear his shrug. "Not whatever. Most people don't like to get involved and wouldn't have done anything about it."

"Yeah?"

"Yeah. And don't use that tone with me. You are not like your dad, Jake." It made me mad he seemed intent on thinking that. "He would have been the guy pushing the girl around. Am I right?"

Silence hung on the phone before he finally answered. "Sure. But don't be putting me on some pedestal, Bec. I don't deserve it. I stopped some guy from hitting a girl...so what? It's one incident and I'm sure all my other fuck-ups make up for it."

Shoving my hair out of my face, I got up and paced my bedroom in anger. His parents were the fuck-ups. How could they treat their only child the way they had Jake? It boggled my mind. It made me want to pull him close and help heal those wounds. He was a good man. But he didn't believe it.

"You are not a bad guy like you seem to think."

"So, how was your day?"

Sighing at his change of subject and knowing it was his way of dealing, I said, "It was good. Summer and I went to Sunsets tonight."

"Your usual Wednesday nighter. Just good?"

How could I tell him I'd thought about him the whole time? That he stayed in my thoughts like an addiction? "It was fun." I laid back down on the bed.

"You're lying."

"Fine. But I didn't have a bad time."

"But no fun?"

"No. Not really. I had things on my mind." *Like you*...I didn't say.

"Thinking about the beach," Jake said, and it wasn't a question.

"Your spidey-sense is active today."

"It never shuts off, but you know that. Second guessing?"

"No." I wasn't sure about a lot of things, but I knew I'd meet him, regardless of how nervous I was. "Summer's coming with me."

"Good. Asshole is coming too. I couldn't talk him out of it," he grumbled.

I laughed. "Summer insisted on coming. It's good Tony's coming to distract her. She would ask you a million questions otherwise. Don't back out on me."

"I gave my word. I'll be there," he said in a low voice, a promise that almost sounded like a threat.

A shiver ran through me, and something hot settled between my legs. I closed my eyes and squeezed my thighs together. I didn't know what it was about him, but when his voice dropped like that, all I could think of was sex. He had said nothing even remotely sexy, but it didn't stop my body from reacting to it.

"Good." I licked my lips.

"I thought about you last night."

"I thought about you too," I said.

"What were you thinking?"

"I was dreaming, actually."

"Interesting. Were we together?"

"Yeah." Oh gawd, were we together. I didn't think I would have the courage to have sex with him on Saturday, but that didn't stop my mind from conjuring the scenario while I slept.

"I want to make it clear…I don't expect sex when we meet. That's not my goal."

"It's not mine either." I bit my lip. "Summer said you'd expect it."

"No, but I really figure you'll back out at the last minute. That would be the smart thing to do. And if you do, I won't be mad."

"Jake, I'll be there. No doubts."

He really didn't know how badly I wanted to meet him. I would have to be dead not to. I was dying to know him in person. Touch him. Not just a voice or chat. To see if we had the same chemistry in person as we had on the phone. I couldn't imagine it would be less. And if it was more, I'd have a hard time keeping my hands off him. And I never felt like that. I'd thought about video chatting but couldn't bring myself to ask. And he never brought it up.

THE NEXT FEW DAYS FLEW BY. WE TEXTED A LOT BUT NOT TALKED, THANKS to Summer. She had me busy…shopping, tanning, facials, waxing, hair, and nails. I didn't normally go all out, but Summer insisted it was necessary. It was turning a new chapter, she said. And after I thought about it, she might be right. Whatever happened Saturday, it was a fresh start to my life.

SATURDAY

I got out of my Jeep and stared at the beach. The dark blue ocean lapped against the sandy shores and the sun glared off the water. I always loved coming here. The air was crisp and tangy, and all the stress seemed to melt away, usually…except today.

Today, I was meeting Jake.

I blew out a nervous breath and looked at Summer. The girl could make anything look good. She wore an orange halter top and a flouncy skirt that stopped mid-thigh. It made her already long legs seem longer. Especially since she wore thick, heeled sandals with straps that wrapped about her ankles several times.

Smoothing down my pale pink sundress, I almost wished I had worn heels. I was too short without them, but my nerves were ragged, hence I was clumsier than my regular awkwardness. As it was, I'd already tripped countless times in my brown and pink flip-flops.

"We're so late." I glanced at my phone for the hundredth time. "Do you think he gave up on us?"

"Are you kidding?" Summer rolled her eyes. "Call him. Let him know we're here. I can't wait to meet, the stud."

"Would you stop calling him that!" Every time Summer called him that, I felt heat flood my face.

"Oh, you know I'm teasing you. So, call him already."

I bit my lip. We were late, by an hour and a half, because of a traffic jam that had me grinding my teeth. I had called earlier and let him know but had only gotten his voicemail. I prayed he was still around.

Scrolling through my contacts, I called him.

"Hey, Bec."

"Hi, Jake."

"Babe, just a sec," he said, sounding slightly out of breath. "Time out guys, phone. Okay, back. Sorry about that."

Loving how he always called me babe or baby, I smiled. "We're finally here."

"Cool. Don't worry about being late. We've been here for a bit. Got out of family duty early. We're a little way from the restaurant playing volleyball with some guys. You want to walk down here?"

"Sure. Family duty? You make it sound like you were in jail." I slid one sandaled foot back and forth in the sand.

"It was. The shit they made me wear...ugh. Was ugly. Real ugly."

I laughed at his exaggeration. "It couldn't have been that bad."

"You have no idea. Come on down here."

"Okay. We're on our way."

I clicked off and Summer had a funny grin on her face.

"What?"

"You should see your face when you talk to him."

"Oh, gawd. Don't embarrass me when I'm just getting ready to meet him. I'm nervous enough as it is."

"Nothing to be embarrassed about. But if you don't want to know..." Summer turned to walk away.

"Okay. Fine. What did I look like?" I was sure I would hate the answer.

Summer turned back around. "You go soft, and smile. I mean really smile. Your eyes light up and you have this look like all is right in the world. Something you never did with Nick."

"I knew I shouldn't have asked," I said, as more heat hit my face.

"I'm not saying he's your new boyfriend. I'm saying let yourself recognize what it's supposed to feel like with a guy. That's all. And hey, no worries. I'm right here. For as long as you want me to be." When Summer winked, I laughed. I didn't know what I would do without her. No matter what happened tonight, Summer was looking out for me.

"They're down the beach playing volleyball," I said.

We linked arms and headed off at a leisurely stroll down the boardwalk. I ignored the catcalls guys hollered at us. I had gotten used to it. When I was with Summer, guys always ogled us. Or more to the point, Summer. I was just the tag-along friend, no matter how much she argued about that.

It was warm, but not overly hot. A perfect day. Looking up at the blue sky streaked with an occasional cloud, I relaxed under the warmth of the sun. Until, I saw volleyball nets in the distance.

"Relax, Becca. He won't bite. Or he might, but I'm sure it wouldn't be too hard," she said, making me laugh.

"Okay. I can do this," I breathed. We unlinked arms as we got closer to the nets.

Jake and I had been talking for almost two months, shared secrets, been there for each other when we needed someone...and had phone sex. I knew him. It should be easy meeting for the first time.

Right?

My pounding pulse and sweaty hands proved otherwise.

There were several sets of nets set up and teams of two to four people. A lot of the guys were pretty big, with muscles and biceps flexing as they hit the ball. Some bigger than others, and some sporting hot tans—none had shirts, and all were sweaty.

I had no idea which one was Jake. He had only shared a couple of head shots. I only knew how tall he was, had a couple of tattoos and worked out a lot. Black hair and blue-green eyes. Glancing up and down the line of teams, I spotted one guy I would guess to be about his height and coloring.

When the team paused for a break, I raised my voice above the noise. "Are you Jake?" I asked a guy in swim trunks.

"No. Sorry," he said, glanced at me, then fixed his gaze on Summer. "But I can be whoever you want me to be, sweet thang."

A sudden movement caught my attention from the corner of my eye, and I turned to look at two guys. Both were looking in my direction. One was grinning at Summer, but the other was staring at me. At least, I thought he was. It was hard to tell with the dark glasses covering his eyes. Then he shoved up his glasses, and I inhaled.

Jake.

My breath lodged in my throat as I saw him walk with purposeful strides in my direction. His muscles moved easily with his frame, making my heart race. He was dark complected, his black shorts clinging low on his hips, emphasizing an honest to gawd vee. I swallowed. My gaze traveled up the length of him, over the muscled abs and broad chest. He told me he had a couple tattoos...he had two full sleeves up each arm, a large tribal medallion took up most of his chest and even his hands were tatted. He was so much bigger than I had imagined. He was supposedly the exact same height as my ex. *Not on this planet.*

He had a black beard clipped close and his brows were low over his eyes. He wore a hat backwards, and I could see a hint of his dark hair peeking underneath, barely brushing down his nape. His lips seemed to tempt me, even though he was still a few steps away. He wasn't handsome in the traditional sense. There was a ruggedness about him that was hard to explain. An intensity that a simple picture couldn't convey. As he came closer, all I could think about was all the moments we had together on chat, on the phone. I was sure my mouth was gaping a little. If I didn't know him, I would have never approached a man like him.

But I did know him.

And he knew me.

He was just so much *more* to take in. More than I ever anticipated.

His voice was seared into my mind. Telling me what to do, bringing me to orgasm each and every time with very little effort. My breasts tightened and became heavy and full, and I resisted the urge to clamp my legs together where I was hot and wanting already.

"Becca, look out," he said.

I caught sight of a ball flying in my direction, and when I moved to get out of the way, I tripped and collided with Jake, as he batted the ball away.

Gawd, he smelled good. Musk, sweat and all male. His arms steadied me, and I looked up. His light-colored eyes were stark against his dark skin. Dark full lashes fringed each one, giving them depth.

I licked my lips instead of his chest. "I'm sorry. I'm such a klutz." I put my hand on his abs and reluctantly backed up a couple of steps.

One side of his lip quirked up. "It's all good," he said in a low voice that had my libido flaring.

Did I measure up? I didn't think I would feel this way, but he was so imposing. No one would overlook him. He was just so striking. I could see him with someone like Summer...not plain Rebecca Saylor.

His gaze swept me, and I tried not to sway from the intensity of it. Good gawd, the man could make me come right now with only a look. Nervously, I tucked a strand of my hair behind my ear.

"Ooowee!" Summer exclaimed.

I jerked my head toward her. *Oh, don't do it*, Summer.

Summer circled the guys, eyed them up and down and smiled devilishly. "Are all men in Oklahoma built like you two? I'd say they are far from fugly, Bec."

I covered my face with one hand, one eye peeking through, mortified.

"No, sweetheart. We're the best Oklahoma has to offer." The other guy had a grin to match Summer's. "Hi. I'm Tony and you must be Summer. This moron is Jake," he said, nodding toward him.

"Hey," Jake said.

"You're right, cutie. I'm Summer and that's Becca," Summer said as she shook Tony's hand.

"It's nice to meet you in person, Bec." Tony shook my hand. "Sorry about all those times I called ya from Jake's phone."

"Nice to meet you too, Tony." I hesitantly smiled up at him. Tony was taller than Jake and just as big and fit. "Don't worry about it."

I looked back up at Jake, who wore a crooked grin that made my knees weak. Holy hell. That little grin made him look like he was up to something mischievous. Damn if my panties didn't get wetter.

"Hi," he said.

"Hi, Jake," I replied and grappled for something else to say. "If you want to finish your game, you can."

"Naw. It's cool. Would you like a bottle of water? We have a few in a cooler."

I nodded in mute agreement, unable to think coherently. He turned to walk away, and that's when I got a good look at his back. My mouth dropped. A tattoo covered most of the left side of his back. It was a skull and inside was a child's scary face. A ram's horn was coming out of the skull's head. The word 'hell' was written on top of the skull surrounded by red.

"Psycho did that." Tony pointed at it. "It's not done yet, though."

Summer laughed. "Psycho?"

"He's the best tat artist in Oklahoma. Maybe the tri-state area," Tony said.

Jake walked back to us and handed me a bottled water, then gave one to Tony and Summer.

"One or two sessions and it will be done," Jake said. "It's warm, and you looked flushed," he said and tilted the bottle back and downed half.

Looked flushed, hell I was more than flushed.

"Does that hurt?" I asked Jake.

"What? The tattoos?"

I nodded.

"Needles poked in your skin over and over for hours." He smirked. "Hurts like a bitch."

I tilted my head. "So why do it?"

"Adrenaline." His lips quirked up in a way that spoke volumes, and he winked.

I swallowed, twisted the cap off the water bottle and took a drink. The look he gave me made my mouth dry.

"So, the wedding was good?" I asked, not knowing what else to say, but needing to say something because his focused gaze on me was sending my pulse into overdrive.

"Yeah. I guess. Andrea seemed happy. As long as she stays that way, I'll be happy for her."

"You worried she might not?"

"If she isn't, he'll answer to us," Tony barked a short laugh. "And he doesn't want that, I can assure you."

Jake and Tony shared a chuckle.

I put one hand on my hip. "What did you guys do?" They both shrugged, and I looked in-between Jake and Tony a few times.

"I mean, we were only looking out for our baby sister," Tony said.

"Wait a minute," Summer interrupted. "You guys are brothers?"

Tony blew out a breath. "Basically."

"Not by blood," Jake said.

"What did you do?" I asked again.

"She's persistent, isn't she?" Tony said to Jake.

He shook his head. "You have no idea."

Summer leaned back her head and laughed aloud. "He's already got your number, Bec."

I crossed my arms and ignored Summer. "Out with it."

"We just gave him a little talk." Jake lowered his head and arched a brow.

Why did everything about him turn me on? I completely lost my train of thought and placed the cold bottle against my cheek.

"Would you mind if Tony and I went back to our hotel to get cleaned up? It's across from the restaurant," he asked. But his voice had dropped in that low octave I knew so well.

"No, that's fine. We have plenty of time. You want to meet us at the restaurant?" I fidgeted.

"That will work."

"We'll probably be sitting on the patio facing the water. That's where we always sit."

"Great. We'll see you in about twenty minutes, tops."

When I smiled at him, his crooked grin appeared. He winked at me, then punched Tony's arm.

"Hey, lover boy. Let's hit the hotel and get cleaned up. Last thing the girls want is to smell a couple sweaty guys."

"Ow… What the hell was that for?" Tony punched him back.

"It's to keep you from drooling on Summer."

"Oh, I don't mind." Summer smiled.

"See. She doesn't mind."

"Yeah, well. She doesn't know what kind of cooties you have either," Jake said.

I bit my lip as I watched him bend over to pick up the cooler, straighten and look directly at me.

"I'll be right back, babe." Then, with one last flash of his smirk, he turned and walked towards the hotel.

I watched him walk away and noticed his gait rolled with his shoulders and ass. And what a fine ass he had.

Summer draped an arm over my shoulder. "If all the men in Oklahoma look like that, we're in the wrong state."

I looked at her and then we both started laughing.

THIRTEEN
JAKE

I made myself walk away from Becca, and it had taken all my discipline to do so. She was so damn tempting standing there in her dress. I thought it was white, but on closer inspection; it was a pale pink. And she was so tiny. The woman couldn't have been much over five feet tall. Those big brown eyes looked up at me, and I heard the soft hunger in her voice. When she said my name, my heart stopped, then thundered in my chest. Just like the chat and the phone calls.

5:15 p.m.

"That Summer is damn fine. Why didn't you tell me she was such a hot piece?" Tony asked with a grin.

"I didn't know. I had no idea what she looked like." We stepped into the elevator, and I hit the twelfth-floor button. I didn't want to talk. I needed a cold shower. Now.

"Becca sure is a little thing."

"Yeah. I noticed."

When the elevator doors opened, I shot into the hallway and walked toward my room. Tony's was just a few doors down from mine and across the hall. "I'll meet you in the lobby in ten," I said.

"Got it," he replied.

Safely in my room, I tossed off my cap, glasses, stripped and stepped into an ice-cold shower. Tension coiled in my stomach. She had looked so fresh and sweet...innocent. Her damn toenails were even pink. Heaven knew I walked a fine line between hell and damnation. She even knew of my hellish ways. What was she doing meeting me? Raking a hand through my hair, I looked up at the ceiling, suddenly remembering the first night she had called me and the why of it—*her bastard of an ex had hit her and attempted to rape her.*

As little as she was, the man could have killed her with one good hit. She wasn't much bigger than a kid. I only got protective of Andrea and Maria.

This? It was so much more. I would kill that bastard if he ever laid a hand on her again. I wouldn't ask her permission next time. No doubt about it. They'd never find his body.

And she wanted me. She wanted to talk to *me*...not her friends or her family. Me.

Taking a deep breath, I closed my eyes. A part of me wanted to get on the first plane out of here, and another part of me itched to get back to her. Talk to her. Touch her. Listen to her voice. Watch her smile. My thoughts were so out of character, it dumbfounded me.

TWENTY MINUTES LATER, WE WALKED INTO THE ROCKFISH BAR AND GRILL and made our way to the back patio. I saw her before she saw me. Her lightly tanned legs were crossed, a flip-flop dangling from her foot. One hand was curled around a drink, and she was laughing at something Summer had said. Her shoulders were bare except for the tiny straps that held up her dress. When she glanced in my direction, her smile softened.

Something tightened in my chest, and I wondered if she knew the effect she had on me. Summer was looking at us now, and I would be the first to admit she was a knockout, but she wasn't Becca. There was something about the girl that had gotten to me from the moment I met her online. She was different, and I didn't have a clue why.

"Hi guys," Becca said as we reached their table.

"Maybe now we won't offend you with our stench," I said.

She laughed and sniffed at me. "You pass the test."

I smirked and slid into a chair next to her, while Tony sat next to Summer.

"A lovely sight to see. Two pretty girls waiting on us," Tony said with his trademark smile in place.

"Welcome back, boys," Summer said.

A waitress came up, took our drink orders and walked off.

"What are you drinking?" I asked Becca.

"Bahama Mama. They're great. You should try one," she said as she took a sip.

"Naw. Think I'll stick with beer."

The waitress brought the beers for us and then took our food order.

Becca pointed at my shirt. "Not surprising. You're wearing a Harley shirt."

"That's my entire wardrobe," I said.

She smiled. "I believe it."

My gaze lingered on the slope of her neck and shoulder. The thin gold necklace around her throat and the tiny earrings in the shape of a bird. Her rapid pulse beat at her neck as she caught me staring. But I didn't look away. Just focused on her face and the way she licked her lips in nervousness. The way she shoved her hair behind her ear and captured the straw between her lips. I noticed it all when it suited me. And it definitely suited me now.

When she got the deer-in-headlights look, it confirmed what I already knew. She was too good for me. But the bitch was...she already knew my demons, and I knew hers. And I didn't know why she got me to open up like that. I didn't understand it at all.

I didn't bother trying to keep up with the conversation—My priority was seated next to me.

And when she covertly tried to study me, I noticed. The way her gaze traveled down my arm and glanced away. She would study me hiding behind her drink. When she looked at her phone, typed in it, she would flush and glance at me. I'd bet money she was talking to Summer.

When our food was delivered, she stared at my plate and bit her lip.

"Do you want to trade?" I arched a brow.

She shook her head like she was embarrassed and looked down.

"She's clumsy," Summer piped up.

I narrowed my eyes at Summer. If somebody had said that other than her, I would deck them.

Her eyes widened. "Damn, that escalated quick. What I meant to say—"

"I'm clumsy," Becca said, and raised her gaze to mine. "I inherited it from my mom. I love snow crab, but it's so hard to get it out of the shell...see that table way over there?" She pointed to it.

My brow furrowed. "Yeah?"

"I might of, sorta, flung the crab fork in a man's drink."

Summer nodded. "I've seen it. First-hand."

My eyebrow arched high. "Seriously?"

She sighed and looked toward the sky, and I was looking at her neck. The need to press my lips to that track of delicate skin was almost irresistible. Fuck, it was hard to stay in my chair.

"And now you know. It's the worst trait." She peeked at me with flushed cheeks. "I really hate it. I'm surprised I haven't spilled my drink on me. Or yours."

"Don't jinx it." Summer waved her fork. "Don't worry though, she always brings an extra set of clothes. Always."

"Summer," she exclaimed and threw up her hands.

Tony laughed. "If that's your worst trait, darlin', compared to Jake, you're a saint."

When Tony said darlin', I watched her closely for some sort of reaction. But she didn't pause or gasp. I found that curious. As the conversation went around the three of them, I was cracking the crab legs open. I speared some meat and held the fork for her to take a bite, saying nothing.

When she noticed it, she stopped and stared. I focused on her lips. The way she licked them and sucked in her bottom lip slightly. She parted her lips and took the bite.

She rolled her eyes and fell back in the chair. "So good."

Summer and Tony burst out laughing at her exaggerated response.

"Shut up. Let me have my little moment of bliss."

I squashed the memories that floated to the surface and smirked at her reaction. "That good, huh?"

"You have no idea." She glanced sideways and gave me a little smile that lit up her eyes. "Thank you."

If she acted like this every time she ate crab, I'd feed it to her all night.

Summer checked her phone. "I'm stuffed. Tony, you want to walk down the boardwalk and listen to some music?"

"Sure. You guys coming?" Tony asked.

Becca glanced at me.

"Whatever you want to do," I told her.

"No. I'll think we'll stay here for a bit. Take care of my girl, Tony." Becca glanced at her phone.

"You got it, doll," Tony said.

And they left the restaurant.

I leaned sideways. "I like that."

"What?"

"Summer checking her phone, and you checking yours."

She blushed. "You caught that, did you?"

I nodded. "I don't mind." I speared the last chunk of crab and held it up to her. She hesitated, and I chuckled. "You know you want it, babe."

She quickly took it and closed her eyes. "Every bite is as good as the last."

"You want to order more?"

Her brown eyes popped open. "You would do that?"

"As long as you want." I sat back and rested my forearm on the table.

She stared down. "Nick would order crab and wouldn't share it. He called me Braceless, for graceless or Blutzy because I'm klutzy."

"Look up." I leaned toward her. "I would never do that, and I'd deck anyone who would."

She nodded. "I know. I saw how you looked at Summer when she said it."

"You ready to go?" The antsy feeling creeped in. It wasn't in my nature to sit still for very long, even for dinners. I would if she wanted more crab, but I had the feeling she didn't.

She nodded and gave me a barely there smile.

I snagged her hand, and she tripped when she got up. I steadied her and waited patiently for her to get her bearings and caught myself when my instinct was to kiss her forehead. I didn't do forehead kisses. Neither did I hold hands. I fucked. That's it.

So why did I do this with her?

BECCA

My nerves were shot, although I tried to hide it. He was openly staring at me throughout dinner. Summers's text said she was going to leave us alone to have hot monkey sex, and if I changed my mind, to call.

We left the restaurant about dusk and strolled down the boardwalk. I took a deep breath of the crisp salty air and could actually hear the ocean again. Its gentle lap—lap—lap against the shore.

He didn't ask me if I wanted to listen to music, and honestly, I didn't want to. I looked down at our entwined hands. His large, dark, tattooed hand engulfed mine, and it gave me tingles. When he stopped, I looked up. I liked he wasn't wearing a hat. His hair fell into his face like it needed to be trimmed. It tempted me to touch it.

"Your picture didn't do you justice," he said.

I huffed. "Like yours did?" I never expected him to be this intense.

He released my hand and grabbed the rail that lined the boardwalk and looked out to sea. He slowly turned his head towards me. "What were you thinking to meet me?"

"What do you mean?" I cocked my head and leaned back on the railing.

"You're sweet. Innocent." He rubbed the back of his neck. "Whole-some and so damn little. You know my life. It's the farthest away from sweet as you can get."

I huffed. "I'm far from innocent."

"You're too good to be with the likes of me." He gave me a hard stare.

I pursed my lips at him. "That's bullshit."

The muscle in his arm tightened as he gripped the railing. "Is it? If you knew what I wanted to do when I saw you, then you might realize the truth. Hell, if you knew what I wanted to do right now, you would take off at a dead run. And I wouldn't blame you."

I didn't know if he was trying to warn me away from him or daring me to stay. Either way, I wasn't leaving.

"Jake, it was probably the exact thing I wanted to do to you." My reward was his shocked expression.

"I highly doubt it," he muttered.

I ducked under his arms and faced him. His body heat came off him in waves. Tension was so thick between us—it was almost suffocating. I put my hands on his forearms and scanned his face. All I could smell was him, earthy male and dark musk.

A sound emitted from him that was animalistic, and he leaned back so we were at eye level. "What are you doing, Bec?"

"What I wanted to do when I saw you," I murmured.

I didn't know where I found the courage because I was never this forward. Maybe it was because I knew he wouldn't make a move, or maybe it was because I wasn't sure if I'd ever see him again. Or maybe it was because, gawd, I wanted to touch him. See if we had that same connection in real life.

My heart thudded in my chest as my fingertips followed his tattooed arms and brushed over his shoulders. I was amazed at the thickness and lines of muscle I could feel through his t-shirt. The air thickened. His stare never left my face, but he didn't stop me. Swallowing hard, I reached up with one hand and my thumb drifted across his jaw.

His arms locked, and I felt him shudder, but he still didn't move. I sucked my bottom lip and reached to touch his hair but stopped.

"Um, can I touch your hair?" I asked timidly.

He cocked his head. "What?"

"Nick—"

"Gawd dammit." He turned and walked away a few steps with hands on his hips.

I looked down and was on the brink of tears. "Jake—"

He swiveled and took two steps back to me. Crushing my hair in his hands, he molded himself to my slight frame, and he pierced me with a gaze so intense all the air left my lungs in a rush.

"You can touch me however and wherever you want, darlin'."

I gasped at the darlin', and his mouth was on mine, devouring me. I didn't have time to react, and the heat from his body seared into my skin. I couldn't breathe, think. All I understood was he was finally kissing me. His large hands tilted my head so he could taste deeper. His tongue swept across my lips, and I opened for him. I had to.

Gawd, I needed to be closer. Wrapping my arms around his neck, I leaned against him. His arm curled around my waist and his leg slid between my thighs. The movement pushed my dress up dangerously, but I didn't care. My vivid dreams of us together were a sad comparison to reality. Not just a typed message or just a voice. In the flesh. Touching me, making me feel.

When he finally broke the kiss and trailed his lips down the curve of my neck, I gasped for air...not that I could get any. I shoved my hands in his hair to bring him closer. His teeth left small little pinches, his tongue swirled over the bite, and he repeated it down my neck. His hands gripped my hips and rocked me on his thigh, creating a friction that had my head spinning. I was beyond wet, and beyond caring who saw.

"You did this when—" I panted.

He nodded and his beard scraped against my skin. "Do you like it?" His teeth sank into the skin between my shoulder and neck.

My yes was drawn out, and I arched my head back to give him better access. He was hard everywhere, and I clung to him like a lifeline. Nothing prepared me for Jake and the way he made me feel. From the very start, I had been helpless against him. I was completely lost now.

"I want you," I said on a moan.

He lifted his head. He still had a hold on my hips but held them still, and I desperately wanted to move. "I can feel how wet you are," he whispered. "Are you that close?"

"Yes," I whispered in return. I pulled his head down and meshed his lips to mine. He finally started moving my hips again, and I groaned into his mouth.

He broke the kiss and his mouth pressed to my ear. "You are so fucking sexy, Bec." He increased the pressure of his leg between my thighs.

I hung onto his hair and sucked my bottom lip in. The pleasure was excruciating. Sensation after sensation bombarded me. There wasn't any room for thinking, only feeling. I heard myself whimper and blood surged through my body.

"That's it, darlin'," he said, and crushed his lips to mine.

My body tensed for the biggest orgasm of my life, and he caught my cries of passion with his mouth. I had a death grip on his hair as I shuddered. Little aftershocks swept through me, and I opened my eyes and broke the kiss.

I stared into those hungry eyes. His big body tense while mine was boneless. His breath was harsh, and I realized where I was.

On a public beach. Out in the open.

I blushed and looked at him. All he did was arch a brow.

"Um…I don't know what to say. I've never acted like that." I put a hand on my face, feeling the heat there.

He chuckled, and I smacked him playfully and buried my head in his chest. "This is all your fault."

His arm came around me. "I tend to have that effect."

"Really?" My hands snuck under his shirt and my fingers traced around to his back. I felt muscles tense and flex under my fingertips.

His growl vibrated through him into me. "If you don't wanna be fucked here and now—"

"Take me to your room." I tilted my head up.

"Are you sure?" He crowded me back against the railing, his breath hot on my skin.

"Jake—"

He kissed me savagely. Brutally. I whimpered because the fire he doused came roaring back to life as though he didn't make me come a few moments ago. Then he captured my hand without a word and quickly led me to his hotel.

He stopped abruptly and turned to face me. "Do you need to call Summer?"

My face flushed, and I shook my head.

He quirked his lips. "Right."

I trailed along behind, but when I tripped for the third time today, he steadied me. "I'm sorry. I'm such a—"

"Don't say it," he interrupted. He flung me over his shoulder but clamped an arm over my dress, so I wasn't mooning everybody. I screamed and then laughed.

"Jake, I don't think this is necessary."

People were staring, and I was still perched on his shoulder when I said, "So sorry, guys. Honeymoon."

He paused, and his chest rumbled a short laugh, then resumed his fast pace. He only set me down when we reached the entrance, but then he snagged my hand and led me to an elevator. Once inside, he backed me in a corner and lifted me up till I had no choice but to lock my legs around his waist and loop my arms over his neck.

His lips met my skin just below my ear, and he pressed his arousal to my core. My hands tangled in his hair as all the air rushed out of me. I'd never been this overwhelmed in my life.

"I'm gonna fuck you, then eat you and then fuck you again. Not necessarily in that order."

"Oh," I squeaked. "Is that all?"

He half-chuckled, half-growled, and it sent shivers up and down my spine. When the doors opened, he set me down, and I tripped over the elevator threshold.

I held up my hands. "I'm good."

He smirked, led me down the corridor, then he opened the door and held it for me. I paused in the hallway and looked at Jake from inside the room. With his messy hair, black shorts, Harley shirt and his black and white sneakers, it was an understated style. His hand held the top of the door as he leaned on it and crossed his ankles. He didn't say a word. But the heat from his stare was blistering. I somehow knew this decision would change my life. But trying to play it safe got me Nick. And his abuse. I was done being timid and afraid.

It was time to take my life back.

I held my head high, walked inside, put my palm on his chest and backed him up. He arched a brow, let go of the door, and it swung shut. It was dark, but the bathroom light was on, and the curtains were wide open, so moonlight spilled in.

Braver than I'd ever been in my life, I kicked my sandals off, peeled my dress over my head and dropped it.

FOURTEEN
JAKE

Her actions surprised me, causing me to back up a step and be stopped by the bed.

She wore a pink lace strapless bra and matching panties. No doubt about it, she was small, but all woman and had curves to match. Raising her chin, she sucked in her lower lip and peeled the bra off over her head.

Shocked, I sat down on the bed. "Holy shit, woman. You can't be real."

"These? They're real," she said in a high-pitched voice.

I shook my head. "No. You…"

"I'm real. And yours, Jake," she said and tripped.

I caught her, grabbed her by her hips, and brought her the rest of the way in. "You're so gawddamn, perfect."

Her cheeks pinkened. "I didn't mean to trip—"

"Don't say it," I warned her.

Her skin felt silky smooth under my rough hands. I trailed a fingertip over her hip and up her back. She arched and shoved her hands through my hair.

"I need to touch you," she stated, hunger in her voice.

I picked her up to straddle my lap. "Then touch me."

She ground down on my dick, clawed my shirt off, and I groaned. It was a struggle to maintain control. I cupped her perfect breast, kissed her collarbone, and she trembled in my arms.

I paused…something was off.

The trembling didn't seem to be all pleasure. I could let it go, and my body was egging me on. But this was Bec. I closed my eyes briefly and tried to ignore those delicious tits in front of my face.

"Becca?" I looked her in the eyes.

Her eyes were half-hooded, but they immediately flew open. "Did I do something wrong? Did I come on too strong? I was trying to be confident. I always screw everything up," she said and covered her breasts with her arms and ducked low, like she was expecting to be hit.

I knew there was something.

"Hey, shh." I cupped her face. Tears pooled in her brown eyes. "You did nothing wrong." I hated like hell to ask, but I had to. "Was Nick your only?" I couldn't say lover, that mother fucker didn't deserve that title. I treated nameless bitches better than Nick did Bec.

She looked down and shook her head. "One other one, twice when I was fifteen. I did, didn't I? I screwed everything up—"

"No, darlin'. You didn't. That fucking asshole did." That fucker took something perfect and beautiful and treated her like trash. "Do you trust me?"

She met my eyes squarely. "Yes. I would be nuts to go to your hotel room if I didn't." She hung her head low and tightened her arms around herself. "I'm messed up, aren't I? And not only by the physical abuse."

"Hey," I gently pushed her hair back to peer in her face. "If you want to continue, you need to give yourself permission to feel good. Not think of anyone or anything else."

I had learned to focus on one thing. Just one. It helped me block out something horrendous and replace it with something good. For a few moments, at least. The adrenaline junkie that Bec said I was.

On the other hand, I ought to be out of my fucking mind. I had an almost naked and gorgeous woman in my arms, and I was giving her the option of walking away.

She peeked at me. "What about you?"

"What about me?"

"About your pleasure," she said in a small voice and looked down.

My lip quirked. "Darlin', don't worry about me. Giving you pleasure gets my world rocking."

She looked up and frowned, as though she were confused. "But…"

"Forget that asshole. Shitcan all his fuckin' rules. All his bullshit. And I mean it, touch wherever and however you want. There's just one rule with me…keep my dick and balls intact and we're golden."

She was thinking about it. I could see it in her face. I ran a hand through my hair, waiting for her to get up and leave. Without ever tasting those mouthwatering tits, which were *still* in my face.

She startled me by tackling me and pushing me flat on my back. She fused her lips to mine, and I immediately noticed a difference. No longer timid, she took the initiative. Her tongue tangled with mine, and her hands shoved in my hair. With my hands on her hips, I ground up into the vee of her legs.

Scraping her nails across my scalp, she moaned in my ear and pressed her breasts against my chest. I growled and flipped her so that she was on her back, me on top, and I captured a nipple in my mouth…finally.

"Oh, gawd," she moaned, tilted her head back and locked her legs around my waist. "Please."

I lifted my head to watch her face as I ground my dick against her pussy. "Please what?"

"Need," she said and nipped at my lip.

"Let's see if you're ready or not."

~

BECCA

He said to focus on pleasure, not anything else. Not to worry about his pleasure. That was so foreign to me it seemed unnatural. He lifted his body from mine and quickly flipped me over, so that I was lying on my stomach.

"Gawd damn."

I tensed, afraid I did something wrong. "What?"

"I don't know which is better. Your ass or your boobs."

I smiled, but it was short-lived because his hands were on me. His rough, calloused hands setting fire to every nerve cell in my being. He traced my spine and grabbed my ass. As he dragged me backwards, I tightened my hands in the sheets until my feet were on the floor.

"What are you—" I gasped as my boy shorts were stripped off, and his fingers traced the insides of my legs, making my insides quake.

He leaned down to my ear and said in that low voice that always got my libido going. "Let's see how ready you are, darlin'." His hand slid down my stomach and slowly inched his way down and stopped short just above my pubic bone.

My breath came out in small pants. "Oh, gawd. Please, Jake."

His finger slid in and up, and I gasped as he slowly fucked me with his finger. His other hand was around my neck. Not tight, but enough to keep me locked in place with my head arched. The pleasure was so intense I didn't have brain power left to worry about Nick's so-called rules.

His teeth grazed my shoulder. "Hmm. You're so wet."

I whimpered when he pushed two fingers in me and sped up. His arousal pressed against my ass in sync with the thrust of his fingers. My hips bucked to the tempo he set. Never had I experienced such agonizing pleasure. I was shaking with it and fisted the sheet in my hands.

"That's it," he said in my ear.

I moaned, and he growled. My body clenched, and I squeezed my legs together as I came. He immediately flipped me over, so that I was on my back. I couldn't even begin to catch my breath.

"I can't fucking wait to be inside you," he said. "And fucking you."

I blinked at the blunt words. He stripped off his shorts, rolled on a condom and slid me up in the bed.

"Please." I didn't recognize the wanton he turned me into. I kissed his neck and thrust my hips, seeking fulfillment. I had never been so hungry. He slid in and paused. I was so full…of him.

He was staring into my eyes when he moved his hips a tiny fraction. I saw stars and gripped his broad shoulders.

"You're tight, and I don't want to hurt you," he said, breath hot and heavy against my cheek.

I didn't answer him because I was beyond speech. He moved in small thrusts, and my breath left as he slowly increased the speed. I felt the muscles in his back bunch and flex with each drive. He was so gentle, the opposite of what I expected, as wave after wave of pleasure coursed through me.

"Are you okay?" he asked in a familiar, low voice that edged up my spine.

"Yes," I hissed and met his thrusts.

He rumbled, slid one hand to my hip, gripped my leg and hiked it up. He was deeper and made every nerve ending come alive.

"Oh, gawd," I moaned.

"Do you like that, darlin'?" He breathed along my neck.

"Uh-huh." Heat spread throughout my body. His voice needed to be on lockdown. It was like taking shots of whiskey in rapid succession.

"Now, I'm gonna fuck you," he growled.

Wait...*what*? I thought we already were...

His fingers dug into my hips as he moved quickly and relentlessly in and out, holding me still so all I could do was feel. Oh, lord, could I feel. Every stroke, every ridge. I gripped the pillow under my head tightly and didn't recognize the sounds coming out of me. All I could do was endure the thrill of a man who knew exactly what he was doing.

I bowed my head back and expelled a high-pitched note.

"That's it, darlin'."

I opened my eyes and saw that he was watching my every move. His nostrils were flaring with his breath. Every muscle was taut and the light from the window and bathroom ricocheted off the sheen of sweat, highlighting his impressive frame.

"Jake," I keened out and my body shook from the all-consuming peaks that kept getting higher and higher. I bowed tightly from my toes that curled, to my hips, and to the tips of my hair. "Oh, gawd," I pleaded, as he kept thrusting at a frantic pace. When I felt him get bigger inside me, I hit another peak. My eyes flew wide, and my mouth formed an O, but it was silent.

"Fuck," he ground out.

I felt him pulse inside me, and he moved in short, slow thrusts. I shuddered and couldn't move. He gradually lowered my hips to the bed, and he laid his head between my breasts as he slowly slipped out.

Stunned, I released the death grip I had on the pillow and ran my fingers through his incredibly thick hair. His breath tickled over my breast and beard scraped my over sensitized skin down along my stomach. He planted one kiss just above my pubic bone, leaned up on his knees, and slid the condom off, tied it and tossed it in the trash nearby.

He stayed on his knees, and his gaze deliberately traveled over my legs, to the junction of my thighs, lingered, and moved up my stomach. He focused on my breasts so long they tightly pebbled and he finally made it to my face. My flushed face. I swallowed and sucked in my bottom lip.

His hands rested on his thighs, and he cocked his head. "You keep looking at me that way, I'm gonna have to fuck you again or eat you."

I gasped and struggled to get words out. I moved to cover myself, becoming self-conscious.

"No." He placed his hands on either side of me and pinned me with his eyes. "You're stunning." His fingers slid gently through my hair, and he said softly, "angel."

Tears pricked my eyes, and I struggled to reject Nick's voice in my head. "I'm no angel," I whispered. I recalled all the names Nick called me in private.

Too stupid. Too short. Too emotional. Too loud. Too quiet. Too thin. Too fat. Too slobby. Too neat.

He cussed me on a daily basis. The list went on and on. In private, of course, he was the perfect gentleman when we were around others.

He stretched his body on mine and rolled me so that I was on top. He did it so quickly, I inhaled.

"Forget that weasel dick," he smirked, and I bubbled with suppressed laughter. He threaded his hand in my hair. "Don't tone down your laugh, your smile. Your fire. For anyone."

I blinked and stared. That was what I did. I toned down everything for Nick. And it took Jake saying it to really hit home. "I did, didn't I?"

One side of his lip quirked up. "You did, but not anymore."

I smiled, sat up on my knees to straddle him. Curious, I tentatively traced the large medallion on his chest. "You said a couple of tattoos."

He shrugged. "A couple dozen."

I rolled my eyes and pushed my hair out of my face. "If you'd have told me about them, I would've spotted you easily."

"Hmm. Didn't really think about that."

JAKE

I watched her face with rapt attention, as she lightly traced my tats. I could read her every thought. Most people were a closed book, but I had a knack for figuring them out, eventually. But Bec? She wore her heart on her sleeve. She was an angel. Sweet. Innocent. And I had no clue how she hung onto that because of that bastard. She was the epitome of girls I steered clear of. If I'd met her on the street, she would barely get a glance. Not because of her looks, but because she was a pure soul.

"You're deeply intimidating," she said, as she captured my left hand and studied it. "If I didn't know you as well as I do, I wouldn't have the courage to approach you."

There she sat, straddling my lap, naked and looking like she belonged on my lap, which gawd damn bewildered me. "You're perfect."

She rolled her eyes again. "I bet you say that to all the girls."

I couldn't hold back a half-chuckle. "No. Not by a long shot."

"What is this?" she asked, touching my left hand.

"A ball bearing." Her brows drew together. "Car part."

"Why are all your tattoos black and red?" she asked.

I thought about giving her a bullshit answer...but this was Bec. And she was different. I scrubbed my hand over my beard. "Black for my soul, red for all the blood I've shed."

She narrowed her eyes. "Jake, stop it. You do not have a black soul. Your parents do, but you don't."

Fuck. I should have given her the BS answer. I didn't want to talk about my shit life, especially not now when I had a hot babe in my lap.

I slid my hands up her thighs, over her hips, dipped to her waist and cupped her tits.

She hissed in a breath. "I know…what you're…trying to do." Her head fell back, and she leaned forward to increase the pressure of my hands.

I sat up and licked a nipple. "Is it working?"

"Yes," she whispered and grabbed fistfuls of my hair to keep me there.

"I think I've created a greedy monster," I mumbled and rolled her nipple with my teeth, while a hand slid over her ass to reach her pussy.

"Ooh," she moaned.

"Do you like that?" I asked and studied her face.

She tilted her head to mine and kissed me. I broke the kiss and nipped her ear.

"I wanna taste you," I growled.

I laid down and shoved her forward, so she straddled my face. Her eyes widened and her mouth gaped.

"Uhm," she started to say.

My tongue swiped her delicate flesh, tasting her. She was sweet. Tangy. Fucking delicious.

"Oh, gawd," she panted and placed her hands flat on the wall. "I've never, I mean…"

I stopped and looked at her face between her tits. "You've never had anyone eat your pussy?"

She licked her lips and shook her head.

"I'm the first?"

She nodded, and her body trembled.

"Just relax, darlin'. Just feel." I saw her eyes close, and she took a deep breath. "That's it. Do what comes natural. Let go of control."

Knowing I'd be the first to taste her gave me a sense of possession. I kept my eyes on her face as I resumed. I tasted her slowly. Deliberately.

To bring her nothing but pleasure. My tongue swept up, and my teeth grazed her clit.

"Oh, hell," she moaned.

My hand traced her ass, and I slid a finger back and forth in her slit and sucked her clit, all the while watching her face.

"Oh, gawd," she muttered.

Pretty soon she was riding my face. Watching her tits bounce, the rapture on her face was so fucking sexy. Those loud sounds she made. I was rock hard and couldn't wait to fuck her after she got hers. She gripped my hair and ground on my face as she gushed. She tasted sweet. Like candy. She shuddered one last time, and I pulled her down my body, so we were chest to chest.

"Jake, is it always like that?" She murmured against my lips, and her fingertips grazed my beard.

My chest thumped when she said my name like that. My hand laced through her blonde hair. I couldn't help but think that I stained her halo with my dark soul. "No. Not everybody knows what they're doing."

She slanted her eyes at me. "Is this male ego talking?"

"Naw." I brushed my beard along her cheeks. "It's fact, darlin'."

She gasped and meshed her lips to mine. I let her lead the way and matched her hunger. When she broke the kiss and shoved a tit in my face, I latched on to it with a chuckle. My hands raked down her body and followed the curve of her ass and squeezed.

"Becca," I growled. "Fuck me."

She stopped, looked at me with half-hooded eyes, and said, "Yes." She moved lower, and I grabbed a wrap off the side table and felt her hand on me. I froze. She sat on my thighs, the light from the bathroom and moonlight making her hair silver. She looked at me, bit her lower lip and with sure strokes, stroked down my length and ended with a twist.

Shocked, I laid back, and she did it again. "Fuck me," I grit out. She didn't grip my dick too tight or too loose. Over and over. Her hand worked me like a ten-dollar clock, till some precum leaked out of the tip and I was sweating. "Stop," I snapped.

She jumped and stared at me with big eyes.

"Fucking hell." I closed my eyes briefly and sat up. I wrapped an arm around her and gathered her close. "I'm sorry."

"Did I—"

"No. You did everything right." I burned with anger. That fucker taught her how to give pleasure but didn't give her an ounce of it.

"Are you sure?" She tucked her chin to her chest.

"Hey." I raised her chin back up and caressed her cheek. I knew well how a person was conditioned to jump at sudden noises. To cower when a voice was raised or shy away from touch. Those habits were hard to break even after the threat was gone. I kissed the corner of her lips. "You're safe, angel," I murmured.

Her lips parted, and her eyes widened. Tears pooled in her eyes, but they didn't fall.

"I want you," she panted against my lips. "Make me forget," she whispered.

She sounded just as lost as that first phone call.

"My pleasure." I tore the foil packet while she bit my neck. I growled, rolled down the wrap, picked her up and lowered her on my dick.

She gripped my arms. "Jake," she whimpered.

My name off her lips had my hips driving up. I lifted her hips, forced her down and drove up again. Her nails left marks, and I was mindless, until she put her hands on my chest and pushed me flat.

She sat up, looked at me through the fall of her blonde hair and hissed as she slowly slid down on me and back up. The slow pace was going to kill me, but I could endure it. I clenched my jaw. I never gave up control, but Bec more than deserved this. She looked so gawddamn perfect riding my dick. Like she belonged there.

It wasn't long, and she moved quicker. She mesmerized me. The little sounds she made. The expressions on her face as she abandoned control and gave into passion. I cupped a breast and her hand closed over mine to keep it there.

"Do you like me touching your tit?" I asked and rolled a nipple between my fingers.

"Yes," she hissed. "I like you touching me everywhere."

At that, I tensed and stilled before I flipped us over and drove in hard. She clawed at my back and arched her hips to my thrusts.

"More?"

"Gawd yes," she moaned.

I hooked one leg on my hip and drove in deeper. When I felt her walls tighten around me, and she made those high pitched mewls, I hooked both of her legs over my arms.

"Come on, Angel. Come for me," I demanded, as I watched her face contort with ecstasy.

"Oh, hell," she said, as she tipped her head back.

I groaned as I pulsed inside her and watched the tension release from her body. Through heavy-lidded eyes, she peered at me. I slipped out, took off the condom and tossed it in the trash. I laid flat on my back, an arm behind my head, put one foot on the mattress so my knee was bent and stared at her. She automatically snuggled into my side, and I unconsciously put an arm around her.

I was stunned by my own actions. I swallowed and stared at the ceiling. *What the fuck?*

She traced patterns on my chest. "Thank you," she murmured and lowered her lashes.

I pulled my head back and narrowed my eyes. "For what?" If she said for fucking her…

"For being patient." She looked back up. "You are very understanding."

I thought about replying, but to say what? *You're welcome…*didn't seem right. As I struggled for what to say, she leaned up on her elbow and studied me.

"You are captivating." She ran her hands over my abs and up my chest. My brows furrowed. A pretty package could hide shit, just like a paper bag.

"I almost believe that coming from an angel." I rubbed a few strands of her hair in my hand.

She shook her head. "I don't know why you call me that."

"Just facts." She looked down again and hid her face. I tipped her chin up to look at me and tightened my hand in her hair. "I don't lie, darlin'."

She gasped, sucked in her bottom lip, and I growled.

FIFTEEN
BECCA

H is chest rumbled beneath my chin, and I squeaked when I was pulled up level to his face. His hands tilted my head, so his breath and beard grazed my skin and left tingles in their wake.

"What did...I do..." I stumbled over the words because the world wasn't making much sense at the moment. The way he made me feel was astonishing. I never knew sex could be like this in real life.

"You."

That's all he said and left a fiery trail of kisses down my neck. I panted in-between words. "That's not an answer."

He stopped, abruptly got out of bed and grabbed my hand. He led me toward the bathroom, and I stopped. "The lights are on."

"So?"

I blinked and hesitated. "Um..."

He grabbed my hand again and led me in. I avoided looking in the mirror and, instead, stared at the tile floor. He turned me so I faced the mirror, and he leaned his hands on the sink on either side of me, effectively trapping me. I scrunched my eyes shut and clasped my hands in front of me.

"Open your eyes, darlin'."

His voice was level with my ear. I shook my head and crossed my arms over my chest. An unpleasant knot formed in my stomach.

"Do you trust me?"

There was no hesitation of trust. I knew he wouldn't hurt me, but I hadn't looked in the mirror naked for years. Thanks to Nick eroding my self-confidence about everything, including my body. "Yes," I answered.

"Open your eyes, Angel. And I'll show you what I see."

I opened my eyes, but I had my gaze trained on the floor. Heart beating out of my chest, I bit my lip and slowly lifted my head. I looked at Jake behind me in the mirror, and I was momentarily shocked at how he dwarfed me. The size difference was startling, and my pale skin looked bright against his dark one.

"Don't look at me, look at you."

My eyes darted around, not focused on anything. Then he brushed aside my hair, and I tracked his movement with our reflection. He kissed my shoulder, and I swayed back against him. He skated his hands over my shoulders and partially down my back. My hands gripped the countertop for balance. My heart was pounding out of my chest, and I licked my lips.

I heard a rumble behind me. "Do that again and watch yourself."

"What?" I locked my gaze to his.

"Just do it."

It was ridiculous. I wasn't sure what I would accomplish by doing what he asked. Hell, I didn't even know why I was standing here naked with him at all. But I watched myself lick my lips and immediately heard his reaction. And I did it again, unbidden. His hands circled my waist and slowly moved down along my stomach.

"What I see is the lines of your neck tempting me," he whispered in my ear. "And every time you lick your lips, I have the intense urge to fuck you senseless."

I gasped at his words and watched him cup my breasts. He didn't touch my nipples, but they hardened at the feel of his rough hands. I automatically leaned my hips back against him and his hard body. He growled in a sexy way that made my pulse jump.

I tilted my head back against his chest and looked up at him. My hand curled around his head. "You make me feel beautiful."

"Because you are."

I turned to face him and studied him. My gaze traveled from lean hips, his large arousal, that vee, to his abs, his muscular chest, and finally to his face.

"I'm lucky because I accidentally messaged the wrong guy, which turned out to be the best mistake ever."

He cocked his head and narrowed his eyes. "Don't pin a fairytale on me, Bec."

"I'm not." I glanced at the floor, then back to his face. "I don't know anyone who would be as patient and understanding as you have." I placed my hands on either side of his face, stood on my tiptoes, and lightly kissed him.

His jaw twitched when I leaned back. I would love to know what was going on in his mind. He didn't have an impassive look but didn't look happy either. But he was aroused. That was evident.

Then he smirked. "If you're trying to puzzle me out, you're wasting your time."

I pursed my lips. "How did you know?"

"You wear your thoughts on your face," he said in a low voice and reached up and traced my shoulder.

The delicate way his calloused fingers glided across my skin left goose-bumps. "When your voice drops like that, all I can think about is sex."

His eyes fixed on my neck, but swiftly shifted back to my face. "That's good, because right now, that's all I'm thinking about. Stay put." And he swiftly left the bathroom.

"What—"

He came back in with a chair and a condom. He set the chair against the counter, backwards, picked me up, set me in the chair so I was facing the mirror.

"What—" I repeated. Then he scraped his rugged hands along my back, making my pulse flutter.

"Get on your knees." His hot breath was against my ear. "So you can see how fucking perfect you are."

I felt overexposed like this, but I did as he asked. I wanted to cover myself, but his lips were on my skin, biting and teasing. And his hands created a storm of sensations. I didn't have time to think about anything.

"Just feel. And watch."

I caught his eyes in the mirror, and I whimpered when his fingers tugged my nipples. While his other hand dipped lower and his finger disappeared. In and out. His finger grazed my clit with every move.

I panted and gripped his hair. It was the most erotic sight. "Oh, gawd." I shook as my eyes clung to his. I felt like I was someone else. He played my body perfectly. He rubbed tight circles on my clit, then dipped into my body. Over and over, he repeated the pattern.

His hand moved from my breast to my neck, pinning me against his body. "That's it. Come for me, Angel."

My cry of passion echoed in the bathroom. I held nothing back. My hips bucked to the frantic pace of his finger. I quaked and trembled from the force of it. I wasn't in control. He was. "Jake," I screamed.

"Gawd damn, I need in you now," he rasped out.

He let me go, and my hands hit the counter for balance. I looked up in the mirror. His dark tattooed body was behind me, and I looked at myself. I got a glimpse of what Jake saw.

My flushed face. My body arched. Pale delicate skin. Blonde hair.

"You see now?" Jake said as he paused, breathing hard.

"Yes," I hissed and licked my lips. "Fuck me, Jake."

A growl was all I got, and he plunged in. He put his hands on my shoulders and slammed in and out. But our eyes met and clung in the reflection. I didn't do anything except feel. There wasn't room for anything more. Just me and Jake existed for this moment. Nothing and nobody else.

I felt alive. More alive than I'd ever felt in my life. It seemed life led me to this very moment in time. I felt like he was letting me out of the cage Nick locked me in. I was finally free.

I flung my head back and every muscle in my body clenched as the magnitude of my orgasm combined with the feeling of being free sent me soaring.

~

JAKE

I looked into the mirror at the most beautiful sight I had ever seen.

Becca.

Her head flung back, her mouth forming the perfect O, her face flushed, and her eyes narrowed to mere slits. Her body tensed and her walls squeezed me, so much I lost control and came right there on the spot. Geezus. I pulsed in her, and our gazes locked. That's when I noticed I trembled as much as she did. I blinked and tried to get myself contained. Composed. Repeating in my head, she was just a fuck. She wasn't, but I kept up the litany anyway. I slipped out, threw the condom in the trash, picked her up and placed her in bed, slid in, and rolled on my side. She cuddled up to me, chest to chest. My arm came around her and pulled her in tighter. Her little contented sigh was about my undoing. She didn't know it, but I never did this. Ever. It was so far from my norm—my mind scrambled for an answer. So, why did I? Cuddle and shit?

Her breath tickled my chest. "I didn't expect this."

"I didn't either." That was, off the charts, a flipping fact.

She looked at me with sleepy eyes, and I didn't stop her from dragging her fingernails in my beard. "I believe you, despite knowing your track record."

I arched a brow. "I didn't meet you for sex. But I wasn't gonna turn it down, either."

She giggled. "Now, that's a Jake answer."

I couldn't stop myself from brushing a few strands of her hair off her face. I didn't recognize that scent in her hair. My brow furrowed. Why did I even notice? She didn't know I never did that. Or the way I cupped the back of her neck so I could see her eyes and caress the skin of her cheek.

Nope.

Not me.

Not till *her.*

"What's that scent in your hair?" *What the fuck? Was I bi-fucking-polar?*

"Is it bad?"

"No."

She was still playing with my beard and a smile toyed with her lips. "My shampoo smells like mangos. Do you ask all the girls that question?"

I smirked. "Yeah, I do." *Fuck no, I didn't.*

Her eyes widened, and her mouth gaped. When I said nothing, she smacked my arm playfully.

"You had me going there for a second. You don't." When I didn't answer, she cocked her head. "You don't, do you?"

"No. Never." I trailed a finger over her arm. She was silky everywhere. I'd never noticed with other women, just her. She scared the holy fuck out of me. But I couldn't pry myself away. I was just digging myself a deeper hole.

She gasped. "I can't think when you're touching me."

"Good." I raised up on my elbow and continued the path over her waist and onto her hip. I glanced into her face and the way her pulse beat at her neck. Her small little pants got the job done, and I was fully erect. But she had to be sore. "Am I the only one since Nick?"

She bit her lip, nodded and lowered her lashes.

"But you've tried." It wasn't a question. Her eyes flew open, and she nodded. "And it didn't go well." Again, it wasn't a question. She'd had some shitty experiences with men.

"Why do you trust me? When you know my history. My life. How screwed in the head I am. How I treat women." She knew everything. She was even the voice that kept me out of the mental ward. I was certain that, once locked up, I'd never be free again.

She captured my hand and laced it with hers. "I know for a fact you would never hurt me. But I never dreamed you'd be this patient."

"I'm not usually."

She tilted her head. "Why are you with me?"

"I don't know." I stretched our laced hands above her head. "Maybe because you're an Angel." I breathed the words against her skin.

She shoved her loose hand in my hair and arched back to give me better access. "No. An angel would never crave a man like I crave you."

She had my heart hammering, and I groaned in frustration. "You have to be sore."

"My muscles are sore." She nodded. "But that's all."

I laid my head between her breasts. "I've been too rough."

"Jake—"

I tightened my hold on her hand and breathed through the power she had just uttering my name. That breathy voice. Needful. I stayed right where I was, head resting between her breasts. Her body needed a break.

When I tensed, she tensed.

"Did I do something wrong?" she asked.

I shook my head. "No." But I couldn't relax, and I breathed, trying to think straight. Trying not to take her. Hard. Fast.

She let go of my hand and laid her hands on either side of my face to make me look at her. Silence hung in the air. She leaned down to kiss my lips, but I pulled back.

"Bec, you need—"

She mashed her lips to mine, and her little tongue darted into my mouth. That's when I lost the will to fight it. Her tongue sparred with mine, and she broke the kiss and pressed her tits in my face. Her legs locked around my waist.

"I *know* I created a monster," I said before I rolled a nipple between my teeth.

"Yes," she cried.

I kissed over her stomach and spread her legs. I bit the inside of her thigh, not hard but hard enough to make her gasp.

"Please," she panted.

"What do you want?" My tongue swept her wet slit and stopped. "Do you want me to suck it or fuck it?"

"Yes," she groaned.

"That's a needy groan. Both?"

"Gawd, just do something, dammit."

I pressed her legs wide, did a couple sweeps with my tongue and just grazed her clit. Her hands gripped my hair and kept me between her thighs. I chuckled at her demands. She was so gawd damn beautiful everywhere. I slowly enjoyed tasting her as my tongue grazed her wet slit. I watched her face as I slid two fingers in…and out. A slow repetition while my tongue worked her clit. She was sopping wet already.

"Oh, my gawd," she exclaimed as her body bowed off the mattress.

My teeth nipped at her clit, then suckled it, and she came apart. I lapped it up, enjoying every second of her pleasure.

"Jake," she yelled and clawed my hair and brought my head up. "I need more."

She licked my neck when I reached over to grab another wrap. "Bec, you have to let me go, to put it on."

She groaned in frustration. "Ugh. Fine." She flung her hands over her head in a huff.

As I rolled it on, her hair looked like a halo around her head. My hands followed the curves up her body, laced with hers over our head and pinned them there. I slowly slid in and out.

"What are you doing to me?" she asked as she locked her legs around my waist.

"I don't want to hurt you." That might be true, but I didn't fuck slow. Ever. I memorized how her body fit with mine. The little sounds she made as I kissed her shoulder. I still had her hands restrained with mine above our heads. "Look at me, darlin'."

She gasped and her eyes flew open. "Jake," she moaned. "Please."

"Please what? What do you need?" I knew what I needed. To taste her. To not let an inch of skin go untouched. To make a permanent impression on her body she wouldn't be able to wash off.

To make her mine.

I shook with the intensity of my thoughts. A roaring erupted in my mind, and I slammed my lips against hers. She matched my ferocity—I released her hands so I could grab her ass. She immediately clawed my back, and her hips matched my thrusts. She leaned her head back to let loose a high pitch cry, and I felt the vibration through her.

I couldn't hold back, and she milked me dry. Geezus. This tiny thing somehow handled me in a way that no one else could. I couldn't control my breathing—my pulse was erratic. My mind was chaotic. I looked at her in amazement as her fingers traced my beard. I got rid of the wrap, laid back down and gathered her close. Her contented sigh was all I heard from her as she nuzzled into my chest.

My lips pressed to her forehead, and I threaded my hand in her hair. I looked sightlessly out the window. I ought to get up right now, block her number and disappear. I really should...but I didn't. I let her wrap an arm around my waist and get as close as she wanted. Which was skin to skin. When her breath slowed, I knew she was asleep.

That's when I realized I hadn't checked the time and looked at my watch.

3:12 a.m.

Bec was not what I had expected and so much more. She was pure. Even after her shit experiences with men. She had found a way under my tough hide, climbed all my walls, and became important to me in a quick amount of time. I didn't know what to do with that. I had let the Paganos in, but Becca? She trumped even them. I wasn't in the habit of lying to myself, but I wouldn't tell her. Or anyone else, for that matter.

Fuck no.

She deserved a whole hell of a lot more than I could give. So, I'd get a little slice of heaven here, fly home and cut her off. She could do better, and she deserved better. And she'd never know what she meant to me. I pulled back a fraction to see her face. I called it right. She was an Angel.

Her brows furrowed, and she mumbled my name in her sleep.

I tightened my arm around her, and her eyes fluttered open.

"Jake, you're here," she murmured and nestled down against my chest and fell back asleep.

I wouldn't be for long. Our flight was at eight a.m.

~ *BECCA*

"Becca. Darlin'." I heard a voice, then felt a hand slide through my hair. I blinked open my eyes and abruptly sat up. Jake sat on the edge of the bed, a hat on backward and fully dressed.

I clutched the sheet to my chest, although it made little sense after the way we spent the night. He knew every inch of me, and we had sex countless number of times.

"Babe, I gotta go. Our flight leaves out early."

I frowned. "You have to leave?" I glanced out the still open drapes where the sun hinted at rising over the water.

"Yeah." He pulled me closer, and his thumb grazed my lower lip.

I resisted the urge to ask him to stay longer. Like, forever. I swallowed hard at how ridiculous that was. But I was sure it was in my eyes because he gripped the back of my neck and pulled me in close for a deep kiss. He tasted of mint and his clean scent wrapped around me. Forgetting about the sheet, I clenched his shoulders, letting all the words I knew I wouldn't say come through in my kiss.

When his phone vibrated in his pocket, he pulled back. "Damn. I really have to go."

I nodded, not trusting my voice. As stupid as it was, I felt like I was splitting in two. Like a part of me was going to trot out the door with him. He kissed me again, and I tried not to cling. But gawd, it was hard.

He stared at me as he headed toward the door, stopped suddenly, then walked back to me. The intensity in his gaze as he looked down at me made my breath catch.

"Fuck it." He blew out a breath. "There's a poker run in two weeks. Do you wanna ride?"

"What?" I asked, my stomach doing a nervous flip-flop.

"I'm not gonna ask again." He pulled off his hat and raked a hand through his damp hair before shoving it back on.

He was serious. He wanted me to come to him, and I found myself nodding. "Yes." My heart was thundering. Be on the back of his bike? "Yes," I said in a stronger voice.

He leaned down to kiss me firmly once more. This time, he had that sexy half-smile on his face as he walked out the door.

I stared at the shut door, my hands fisting in the sheets. I must be out of my mind. Why had I agreed to fly to him?

Because I already miss him.

I swallowed hard. Oh, gawd, I did. Biting my lip, I stared at the mess of the room. Most of the blankets were on the floor and only one pillow was on the bed. Wrapping the sheet around me and tucking it under my arms, I got up and padded towards the sliding glass door. Every muscle in my body ached deliciously as I opened the door and stepped out onto the balcony. I curled up in a chair. The sun slowly rose, a bright orange ball reflecting off the deep blue of the ocean.

Muscles weren't the only thing that ached. Somewhere inside, I felt a loss. I wanted him with me to watch the sunrise. How could I feel like I was missing something important when we hadn't even shared one full day together?

I rested my chin on my knees. The light breeze tugged at my tangled hair...I knew exactly why. Because I knew him. Even before meeting him in person, I knew him. All that time we spent in chat, on the phone...he knew me better than anyone. Even better than Summer.

A tear slipped down my cheek. Missing him already, and he hadn't been gone an hour. Just two weeks until I saw him again. But that seemed like an eternity.

JAKE

I sat on the plane and watched the landscape get smaller and smaller. My fist clenched as we soared into the sky. Why had I invited her to Tulsa? I must be out of my damn mind. Just because I could see the hunger in her face when I told her I was leaving didn't mean I had to invite her out. The woman sat there, her hair in disarray, the sheet hiding nothing from view, her big brown eyes begging me to stay, even if she didn't voice the words, and I had cracked. I rubbed my eyes.

The plan was to ghost her—for her own good.

Not invite her out on a poker run. I didn't even have a back seat or footpegs for a passenger. But that was the smaller issue. It was totally out of character for me.

I rarely ever saw a woman more than once. It was always a onetime thing, no strings, no phone numbers, no other contact. Just a fuck and nothing more—I didn't want or need more.

Could I really delude myself and say Becca was just a fuck?

Tension coiled like a snake in the pit of my stomach, answering my question.

SIXTEEN
BECCA

I hummed as I walked through the cubicles at Richmond Dispatch. My coworkers were staring at me, but I didn't care. I felt happy, light, and it was all because of Jake, and I'd see him in two weeks.

"Mmm-hmm. If I didn't know better, I would think you got laid, sister." Patty said as he leaned over the flimsy wall.

I was terrible at hiding stuff and couldn't stop the blush before it hit my cheeks.

"O-M-G!" His dark eyes widened. "You did get laid." He disappeared, only to reappear and perch on my desk. "Okay. Give me the deets! Was it hot?"

"Patty! Shh. Not so loud," I said, trying to get him to be a little less flamboyant. Like that was possible. The man was wearing a bright pink kerchief around his neck. One didn't get any flashier than Patty.

"But, girl. I approve. You know I do. It's about time, is all I can say. So, who was it?"

I laughed as his eyebrows waggled comically. "His name is Jake."

"Oooo, sounds scrumptious. Did he have a nice, firm—"

"I have a delivery for Rebecca Saylor," a man called from the front of the office.

Patty pointed at me as I stood up. "Here she is, the lucky girl."

My mouth dropped at the size of the bouquet. At least two dozen pale pink roses filled a lavender vase that was tied with a lovely pink bow. The delivery guy brought them to me. The bouquet barely fit on my desk and the aroma filled the office. A couple of my coworkers let out a whistle.

The white card seemed to glare from in between the blooms.

"Go on. Read it," Patty said, his wide grin infectious.

I slid the card from its holder and took a deep breath. I couldn't believe Jake had sent—my breath stopped as I re-read the card and felt the blood drain from my face.

Surprise. Bet you thought they were from your new lover. Your husband, Nick.

HOW DID HE KNOW? HOW COULD HE KNOW? I DIDN'T EVEN NOTICE WHEN Patty plucked the card out of my hand and read it.

"That sorry son-of-a-bitch," he said. "And how could he even dare to say he's your husband? That man is a lunatic."

When my business phone rang, I answered in a daze.

"Hello, this is Rebecca with Richmond Dispatch."

"Hello, Rebecca." The familiar voice sent a chill down my spine.

"What do you want, Nick? You're not supposed to talk to me. Restraining order, remember?" Although that didn't stop him the last time, did it?

"I wanted to make sure you got my note."

My hands shook, and I gripped the phone tighter. "I don't want to talk to you."

I was about to hang up when he said, "Don't you want to know how I know about your little affair? You should be more discreet. A coworker of mine saw you at the Rockfish Bar. How could you?"

"Nick, get out of my life. I don't care what you think. We're divorced, remember?" Bile rose in my throat, and I wondered what I ever saw in the man.

"You are my wife," he yelled. "No flimsy piece of paper will change that!"

I slammed the phone down and looked at Patty, who had his arms crossed over his chest. His lips slashed in an angry line.

"He is vile," Patty said.

"Yeah." I couldn't agree more. Grabbing the vase of flowers, I stalked to the back room where there was a large wastebasket and dropped them in. The vase shattered, but what I wanted to do was run each rose through the shredder. Shaking, I walked back to my cubicle and slid into my chair. A steaming cup of coffee sat on my desk.

"Drink it. Then call the cops," Patty said from behind the wall.

"Thanks." The aroma tickled my nose and when I took a sip, it had a bitter bite. I stared at the PC screen, took a deep breath, and called the cops. I was to report any contact he made with me, and even if they wouldn't necessarily do anything about it, at least they would have a report of it.

Over the next few days, Nick left notes on my car, was following my every move, and I called the Bennett brothers. Then Nick would disappear. But when I didn't have the protection of the brothers, he would always show up. It had my nerves frayed to the breaking point. Alan made a call to the police department and demanded something be done about it. I even stayed with Summer a few nights to give my overwrought nerves some peace. Alan said he would take care of it and the police had issued a BOLO on Nick.

It made my decision more concrete to fly to Jake. I wanted more of how he made me feel. I felt free to be myself. He was tough, big, gentle, and patient. He was full of contradictions. And I couldn't wait to see him again.

~

JAKE

I inspected my bike. I replaced the solo seat with a two-seater, added a quick disconnect sissy bar and back foot pegs. It didn't look bad, but I was used to seeing it with only a solo seat. Leaning against my workbench and drinking a beer, I studied it. The garage door was up, so I heard the bikes before I saw Tony and Mack roll up and park in my driveway.

They dismounted, stopped and stared at my bike.

"What the fuck did you do to your bike?" Tony asked in obvious shock.

"Bec is going on the poker run Saturday." I downed my beer and tossed it in the trash.

Mack looked confused. "Who's Bec?"

"Since when?" Tony asked.

"Since May second." I crossed my arms and ankles.

"And you didn't think to mention it sooner?"

"Who's Bec?" Mack repeated.

I shrugged. I didn't want to tell anyone for this reason right here. I never talked about my personal shit with anybody but Becca. Why she was different, I had no clue. I didn't want to be grilled about it from Tony or anyone else. "Didn't think to mention it."

"She's a good girl, Jake." Tony stepped closer and locked his jaw.

My brows lowered over my eyes, and I cocked my head. "I know that."

"Don't play with her."

My hackles stood up. "I'm not."

We stared at each other. I wasn't sure what Tony was doing by giving me a death glare, but if we fought, I would win, but it would be bloody. And we both might end up in the hospital.

"Do her right."

I scowled. "What the fuck are you getting at?"

"You know what I mean. I like her, and she'd be good for you, but don't treat her like you treat most girls."

"She's not like most girls," I said under my breath.

Then, like a switch, Tony grinned and clapped me on the shoulder. "Good. When is she flying in?"

"About noon Friday." I checked my watch in frustration.

7:43 p.m.

"Hello? There's another person here. Who's Bec? Since when do you have a girl?" Mack asked.

I looked at Mack. "I don't. She's just a friend."

Tony leaned back and laughed. "Yeah, right. Bec is your girl, you just don't want to admit it."

"Someone tell me who Bec is?" Mack looked back and forth between us.

I sighed. "A girl I met on a bike forum." I didn't plan on saying anything else about it.

"She lives in Virginia, and when we went up there for Andrea's wedding, we met in person," Tony offered. "They've been talking for two months."

"Woah, you do have a girl." Mack laughed.

I glared at a grinning Tony. "You're still a fucking loudmouth, and I oughta deck you."

"But you won't," Tony said. "Let's roll."

I grumbled and took off the sissy bar, fired up my bike and all three of us roared down Memorial. It wasn't far to Snookers but traffic this time a day was brutal, and there was always road construction. We pulled in, parked and I put my grip-lock on.

The weather was pristine for the middle of May. The weather in Oklahoma was a bit on the humid side, which was expected for the middle of May, but it looked good for Saturday. I had conflicting feelings about her coming here. On the one hand, I wanted to see her, on the other, she would be around my friends and family. I'd never had a girl around them. And Tony was wrong. She was just a friend— *wasn't she?*

We filed into the pool hall, grabbed some beers, and headed to our usual table. Aaron, Krista, Travis, and Sami were all there.

"Hey, guys," Tony said as we walked up to our usual spot. "Jake is having Becca fly in for the poker run."

My beer stopped halfway to my lips, and I looked at the ceiling to give me patience. "What the hell is wrong with you?"

"Just trying to help you out." Tony grinned.

"By spreading my business?" He just looked amused.

"Is this the girl I talked to on the phone?" Krista asked.

"Yeah." I downed the beer like a shot and tossed it in the trash.

She laughed. "She made you be nice to me."

"Yeah," I grumbled.

Sami's eyes lit up. "I heard about her through Krista. So, you do have a girlfriend."

Travis leaned his arm across Sami's shoulders. "Jake, you might as well accept it. We all go down sometime."

"No, she's just a friend," I insisted, for it seemed like the millionth time.

Tony and Mack laughed.

"No, she's his girl," Tony said. "He just won't admit it."

"He even put a passenger seat, foot pegs and a sissy bar on his bike," Mack added.

The girl's eyes widened. "Shut up," Sami said. "No way."

I sat on a stool and looked at my so-called friends. The red headed Sami looked at me in awe and the brunette, Krista, had a wide smile, and Aaron and Travis were smirking. They were eating this shit up like candy. I was going to castrate Tony and Mack.

"She's doing research for a book she's writing. That's it." I yanked off my hat, ran my hand through my hair in agitation and slapped it back on backwards.

8:54 p.m.

Tony busted out laughing. "That's it?"

"What kind of book is she writing?" Sami asked.

"Biker romance, she said." I didn't know why I came here every week. "She knows nothing about bikes."

"And you know about romance?" Krista asked and shook her head.

I sighed. It was a bad idea inviting Becca here. "She asked me about bikes. Don't give her shit like you give me." I eyed each one of them.

"Oooh, she *is* your girl." Krista patted my arm. "Don't worry, we'll treat her right."

"Becca's a good girl. Too good for the likes of this asshole," Tony said as he racked some balls.

"That's something we can agree on," I replied.

"Can I see her picture?" Sami asked.

"Why do you want to see her picture?" I looked around the group and muttered out a curse. I scrolled on my phone and clicked on Bec's pic.

Sami took my phone, her eyebrows rose, and she blinked. "Is that really her?"

"Lemme see." Tony glanced at the picture. He grinned. "Yep."

I watched as they took turns passing my phone around, their expressions shocked.

"And she wanted to fly out here?" Krista asked in amazement.

My brows lowered, and I took my phone back. "Yeah." There was no need to ask why they were shocked. I knew.

Tony came closer to me and whispered, "That's why I told them to give them a heads up."

Tony might be right, because the way our friends were looking at me, like I was the devil himself, confirmed what I already knew. What the hell was an angel doing with the likes of me?

"She's beautiful and looks sweet," Sami said.

"She is," I replied.

"I'm sorry, but I can't believe she agreed to fly here after she met you in person." Sami added. "No offense, but you're kinda scary."

"None taken." I scared off the sweet girls just by being me, but she knew me before I met her in person. She should have got in her Jeep and hightailed it out of there. But instead, she went to my room and blew my damn mind.

"Where is she staying?" Krista asked.

I leveled a look at her. "With me."

Hers and Sami's eyes bugged out. "And she knows this?"

I sighed and clenched my jaw. "Are you girls done with the interrogation," I said, and it wasn't a question.

"Okay, okay," Krista said. "It caught us by surprise."

"If she's staying with you, then she's your girl," Mack said with a laugh. "I'm just saying." He held up his hands.

I glared at him. "I don't know why I hang out with you fuckers."

Aaron leaned over to take a shot and then stood up as it missed the pocket. "You might as well face it. She's your girl and fuck what other people think."

Aaron was ten years older than Krista and they took a lot of heat because of it. From their families mostly. Aaron met Krista when she was barely eighteen, so they went through a lot of bullshit to be together.

But I wasn't willing to saddle Becca like that. Bottom line, she deserved better. She was way out of my league, and I knew it.

FRIDAY 10:36 A.M.

I took Friday and Monday off work so I could spend it with Becca. Her flight was supposed to be in about noon. I looked around my house to make sure I didn't miss anything, but it was never messy. Growing up, I was never clean. Insects and rodents everywhere. Cellie was the one who taught me hygiene, not my worthless ass parents. They were too busy getting their latest fix. Booze, drugs and stealing shit so they could afford their habit.

Needless to say, I was a picky bitch about cleanliness.

I was just about to leave when there was a knock on my door. I looked out the window and my blood boiled. What perfect fucking timing. I called Tony.

"Hey man," Tony said. "Shouldn't you be picking up Bec?"

"My fucking parents showed up at my door. I don't know what they want yet, but it never ends well."

"Wait, you said parents. Tomas too?"

"Yup."

"Ah, fuck. Yea, I can go get Bec. No problem."

He knew why I called without me even asking. "I appreciate it, man."

I clicked off while the knocking got louder. I rolled my shoulders, whipped open the door, stepped outside and shut the door behind me. No way in hell was I letting that prick in my home.

"What the fuck do you want?" I asked with a scowl on my face.

I hadn't seen my old man in years, not since I was seventeen. Tomas had been in and out of jail and he landed in prison. Last time, I was smaller than him. Now, I could look him dead in the eye and I was just as big. There was no doubt I was Tomas's boy. We were built the same, dark complected, and same black hair.

"Oh-ho," Tomas backed up. "You're the big man on campus now."

I crossed my arms over my chest. "I don't know why you're here, and I don't care. Get off my property."

Tomas cackled. "Looks like you got too big for your britches." He stepped up to me. Eye to eye. "Do I need to teach you a lesson 'bout manners, boy?"

"Is that any way to treat your elders?" Jenny spat. "Just give us some money and we'll be on our way."

I never took my eyes off the asshole standing before me. "You could try, but you'll lose." I was seething inside, and it was all I could do to remain calm. I wanted to rip his throat out. Jenny continued to screech, but I ignored her. Flashes from my past tried to overtake me, but I was determined to keep it together. Bec was coming today. Just the thought of her seemed to smooth my frayed ends.

Tomas sneered at me. "Boy, you're too cocky for your own good. How about I knock you down a notch or two?"

"So far, you've only run your mouth." I watched as Prick's face twitched, his pulse pounded in his neck and his fists clenched. He wanted to hit me, but there was a hesitation. And that pause told me I had the upper hand. "I suggest you leave before Jenny's shrieks make the neighbors call the cops."

"You think you're so much better than us," Jenny screamed.

I didn't bother to answer. There was no point. I'd learned long ago not to reason with the old bat. Tomas sneered, and I ducked to miss his thrown fist. I landed a punch to the ole man's ribs. Jenny's small fists rained down on my back, but I ignored her.

"You're gonna pay for that," Tomas said and tried to hit me with an uppercut, but I dodged it and landed a blow to his face. Blood spurted from Tomas's lip.

Tomas growled and tried to tackle me around the waist, and I could have avoided it, but when I stepped back, I tripped over Jenny and we all three went down. I automatically rolled, and Tomas landed a punch to my back.

Right about then, I heard the sirens.

BECCA

When I stepped off the plane, I was a bundle of nerves. I was supposed to meet him at baggage claim. Seeing my bag coming up the conveyer belt, I reached over to grab it when someone picked it up. I looked up at the smiling face of Tony.

"So glad to see you, Becca." I returned his smile and searched behind him for Jake. "He's not here," Tony said. "And he wanted me to tell you he was sorry. Something came up and he couldn't make it here on time. So, I'm in charge of taking you to him."

Disappointment and doubt settled in my chest.

"Hey, it's cool." Tony's reassurance did nothing for me.

"It's fine," I replied, not meaning it.

"Come on. I'll tell you about it on the way to his place."

I followed him, and when we stepped outside, heat and humidity hit me in the face. The air was so thick and heavy it got stuck in my throat. I was happy to get in his bright blue four-door truck.

"Nice." I glanced at the gray interior.

"Thanks," he said as he put it in drive. "But I'm sure you don't want to talk about my truck. Jake," he spun the wheel to make a left turn and glanced at me, "was waylaid by his parents when he was getting ready to come get you."

I gasped. "Tomas is there?"

"Yeah," Tony replied, as his lips compressed in a thin line. "I don't know what the outcome is yet, but it never ends well."

"Jake told me he was released from prison recently." I sucked in my bottom lip. I never wanted to encounter Tomas. The things he did to Jake were horrifying. I shifted in the seat and held the seatbelt so it wouldn't strangle me, one of the many disadvantages of being so short.

Tony glanced at me. "I was shocked when Jake said you were flying in. He told me Wednesday."

"Really? He invited me out before he left. I assumed you knew." I chewed the inside of my lip. He talked openly with me, so it was surprising Tony didn't know. Although Jake said he didn't talk to people. Ever. Maybe there was some truth to that if he didn't even tell his best friend.

"I like ya, and he needs someone like you."

Heat invaded my face. "I don't—I mean, there is nothing going on. We're not a couple or anything," I said, trying to blow it off. I felt like a stuttering fool.

His blue eyes twinkled. "Right. Sure, you're not."

Tony turned the conversation to more mundane subjects, and I relaxed a bit. The last thing I wanted to do was voice how confused I felt when it came to Jake. My feelings were about as clear as mud.

As we exited the highway, I was amazed at how busy the intersections were. I had always thought Tulsa a small town, but I was wrong. Businesses lined the streets and cars darted in and out. When we passed a row of car dealerships of every make, Tony pointed out the Ford one. "Jake works there."

Soon, we made a left turn into a neighborhood with larger lots. The homes were older, some more run-down than others, but most were well kept, with clipped, bright green grass.

That's when we spotted cop cars with blue and red flashing lights.

"Fuck." Tony hit his steering wheel. "Why can't they just leave him alone."

I felt the blood drain from my face, and I covered my mouth. What did they do? I didn't spot an ambulance, but there was a fire truck.

Tony stopped his truck well down the street. "Listen," Tony leveled a look at me. "Stay in the truck till it's safe to get out."

I looked at the lights, then at Tony. "But there are cops there."

He shook his head. "Don't get out of the car until me or Jake come get you. And lock the doors when I get out."

"Surely it's safe because the authorities are here."

"If Jake thinks you're threatened in any way, he will lose his shit. Trust me on this. You remember the barn? It will go like that."

I couldn't forget the barn incident as long as I lived. I'd only listened to it. It had to be horrible thing to witness. Tony and his dad had seen it all. I nodded and pushed some of my hair behind my ear.

I gripped the seatbelt tighter as Tony drove and parked as close as he could.

"Lock the doors when I get out," Tony reminded me. He got out and jogged to Jake's yard.

I locked the doors and searched for a glimpse of Jake. My stomach was in knots at the thought of him harmed in some way. Physical or emotional. I wanted to rush to his side, hold his hand and be there for him. But Tony was right. I needed to be safe, so Jake was safe. My phone beeped, and I dug in my purse to retrieve it.

THIS IS TONY, YOU CAN COME OUT NOW.

I GRABBED MY PHONE AND SCRAMBLED OUT OF THE TRUCK AND RAN TO Jake's yard. I didn't pay any attention to the policemen getting in their cars and leaving. And I didn't bother to look if they had arrested his parents. Never would be too soon to see them. But I wanted to see Jake, and there he was. I inspected him for injuries and threw myself into his arms.

"I was so scared," I mumbled. There were no physical injuries I could see, but the emotional damage had to have hurt him. His arms came around me and the feel of him was incredible when he pulled me snugly against him.

"Bec," he whispered against my cheek, and his large frame shuddered.

When his lips brushed my neck in a purely devotional fashion, I melted into him, and his arms tightened. My heart skipped a beat as he clung to me. He might be bigger, and he might be holding me up, but he clung to me. The thought was devastating to my senses. I'd never felt so needed in my life.

I peered up at him and put my hand on his face. "Are you okay?"

He nodded. "I'm fine." He tucked some strands of my hair behind my ear. "Better now that you're here."

I smiled at him. His hands cupped my face, his thumbs tracing across my cheeks, making me forget to breathe. His head lowered as though giving me time to change my mind. But I was rooted to the ground as his lips touched mine—just a faint brush across.

Tony cleared his throat. "Friends? Righttt." He laughed and set my bags on the walkway and put my purse on top of them.

I blushed, but Jake was cupping the back of my neck, keeping me close.

"Thanks, man," Jake said in a rough voice.

"Everyone is going to be at Snookers tonight. If you want, come on out."

"Thanks, Tony," I said.

"Anytime, doll." He got in his truck and drove away.

"Come on." Jake grabbed my bags and went inside.

I noticed a black Ford truck sitting in the driveway while I followed him in. His place was cleaner than I had expected a bachelor's place to be. A black leather sofa and love seat took up most of the space. The huge TV wasn't a surprise. An XBOX remote was on a sturdy black coffee table. The man obviously liked black.

The windows had no curtains, just mini-blinds, and the walls were white with no decoration except for two pictures. Both of motorcycles.

"Nice place," I said.

"Thanks." His expression was unreadable. His shuttered eyes bored into mine, and he shoved his hands into his pockets.

His presence seemed to fill up the space as he stood there, saying nothing. Nerves choked me and the silent tension mounted. It was such a switch from outside, I wasn't sure what caused it. A muscle ticked in his jaw, and he looked away from me, making me feel that much more uncomfortable. The longer we stood there in silence, the angrier and more remote he seemed to get. It was as though he was pulling away from me until nothing but coldness masked his face. Confused by the change in him, my heart hammered in my chest. I took a step back, bumping into the wall.

A flicker passed over his eyes as he stepped back, his chin lifting and lips slashing into a frown.

At that moment, I saw it. Saw what he tried so hard to hide. Fear. He was terrified and the implication almost staggered me. This man, with all his strength and size, was scared. I was on his turf now, and I knew all the things he didn't tell anyone. Knew all the scars no one ever saw.

I managed a faint smile, and he almost jerked, his gaze searching my face. I slid a hand across his jaw.

He closed his eyes and took a deep breath. "Sorry for not being there to pick you up." He took my hand from his face and kissed my palm.

I tilted my head to look at him. "I understand."

He lifted his gaze and kept hold of my hand against his chest. "I said I would be there."

"It's all right, Jake—" My lips parted when he rumbled.

There was a spark in his blue-green eyes. His gaze intensified, and my breath caught. His eyes reminded me of the perfect storm. He pulled me flush against him. The hunger...the heat...made me breathless.

"My Angel." His rough hands slid down my neck.

His lips were so close to mine, I panted. I gripped his shirt and pulled him those few centimeters separating us and fused my lips to his. It was explosive. The heat of our bodies meshed together as we stumbled back against the wall. His hands cupped my ass and molded my hips to his as he slid me up the wall. His arousal pressed against my core, the muscles in his shoulders tight under my hands through his tee. He slid open-mouthed kisses along my throat.

I arched, crossing my ankles behind his back. Wanting closer. Needing closer. The fire he started in me consuming every thought.

"Hell, Bec. I swore I wouldn't do this," he muttered.

"What?" I asked.

Still holding me to the wall, he fixed me with a heated look. "Pounce on you like an animal."

I curled my hand into his hair and licked my lips. "I thought I pounced on you?"

His brow arched, and his mouth landed hard on mine, demanding I respond. But he didn't have to demand it. I gave. Without reservation. I couldn't get enough of his taste. I ached for him. Then he switched it up, slowed it down and ground his hips to mine in a circular motion. I felt everything. The muscles that bunched and flexed at a tortuous and leisurely pace. The hardness that ground against my core and retreated. I arched my back, trying to get air. My nails dug into his shoulders. He nipped my neck and soothed it away with his tongue.

"Jake," I groaned.

"That's a needy groan." His hot breath was on my ear. "What do you need?"

He kept up that slow grind as he held me pinned to the wall. My nails raked under his shirt. Sounds were emitting from me that I had never heard before.

"You," I begged.

"You got me, darlin'."

His darlin' panted in my ear made my pulse jump. I clawed at his shirt and somehow got it over his head. I suckled on his ear and was rewarded by his growl. He pushed up my shirt and bra and let it fall to the floor. Skin to skin. His body heat seared me. It was mind numbing the way he made me feel. With my heels, I slid off my shoes, and they clattered to the floor.

He threaded his fingers through my hair.

"You know what kept me up at night?" Jake rumbled. "Your pulse." He nipped my neck. "The way it flutters when I'm touching you."

"Like now?" I breathed, shoved my hands in his hair and pulled his head closer so his lips were on my skin.

His chuckle caused me to shiver from my toes to my scalp. "Just like that, darlin'."

I nipped his neck like he did mine and soothed it away with a lick.

"Are you using my own moves against me?" He ground his hips to mine.

I met his grind half-way. "Is it working?"

"Like a charm," he rumbled. He shoved me higher on the wall and captured a pert nipple. He suckled it and rolled his teeth across it.

237

"Oh, gawd," I moaned, latched onto his hair, and arched my back to shove more nipple in his mouth.

He whipped me off the wall and walked into the bedroom as he seized the other nipple. He laid me down on his bed and stretched my hands over our heads and held them there.

I opened my eyes as his stare lingered on my face, and his gaze slid down my neck and over each breast all the way down to the waist of my jeans. His look was so potent, he was caressing me with his phantom fingers, and it made me shiver.

With one hand he held my hands, with another he unbuttoned and unzipped my jeans. But his eyes zeroed in on my face. My hips arched when he dipped under the hem of my panties, and then he stopped.

His lips twitched, and his breath caressed over my lips, and down my neck, but staying just out of reach. His hand seared my skin, and I arched my hips again. I didn't care that it was the middle of the day. Or that I was half naked when it was light outside. He skimmed his hand back and forth, but not dipping lower. Teasing me.

"I need you," I panted, my eyes pleading.

His fingers slid in while he kissed me deep. I groaned in his mouth as his fingers slid in and out. My hips matched the time of his fingers. I broke the kiss to breathe. But it was impossible. He seized a nipple with his mouth while he rubbed circles on my clit and dove back in with his fingers.

"Oh gawd," I cried. My body tensed as he did it over and over. And would pause just before release, then start again. I felt feverish as chills swept me. "Please," I begged.

"Look at me." I did as he asked, and he stared into my eyes. "Come for me, Angel."

I bowed, shattered, and screamed, "Jake."

He growled and stripped off my jeans, taking my panties with them. Letting his shorts drop, he rolled on a condom and shoved me up in bed and paused. But I pulled his head down by his hair and kissed him. In a tangle of tongues, my hips curled up, searching, and he slid in.

"Yes," I hissed. Feeling complete. Whole. I clutched his shoulders and could feel his muscles flex and tighten. When he slowly rotated his hips, I saw stars. His calloused hand skated down one leg, then hooked it high on his hip and went deeper. Still keeping the pace slow, he kept up the circular grind.

"I want to make it last," he said against my lips.

I opened my eyes and got caught in his burning stare. I tilted my hips to match his thrusts. The pace quickened, and I met him halfway. Our breaths mingled and our gazes locked. It was so intimate. It felt so right.

I hit a peak and flung my head back with its intensity. "Oh, gawd."

"Fuck, Bec," he grated out. He grabbed my hips up off the bed and plunged in at a furious rate.

I gripped the covers over my head and whimpered. I forgot how to breathe. To think. I was just feeling. And oh gawd, was I feeling. Every move he made was potent…it was an out-of-body experience. When I reached my next high, I let out a low keen. I was vibrating from the force of it. A few strokes later, he met me and pulsed within.

SEVENTEEN
JAKE

Gawd damn…I couldn't catch my breath and couldn't keep my eyes off Becca. When I heard that low keen from her, that was, hands-down, the sexiest sound I'd ever heard. She still had fistfuls of covers in her hands above her head, and I felt her little after-shock tremors through my dick all the way to my spine. I slipped out and tossed the condom in the trash and braced my hands on either side of her head to stare at her.

When she leveled those brown eyes on mine and that smile toyed at her lips, I was lost. She was so far out of my fucking league. I never thought much about looks or even noticed looks, male or female, either way. But the way she was put together got all eight cylinders firing in me. I'd seen her two weeks ago, but I forgot the way she looked at me. The way her eyes warmed and the way her little tongue darted out to wet her lips.

Her hand reached up to scratch through my beard. "I missed you," she murmured.

I laid flush against her body but was propped on my elbows. My left hand threaded through her silky hair. "It's mutual," I said in a rough voice. She didn't know I never lingered like this. Never played with a girl's hair. Never missed a girl. But I was doing all of the above with Bec.

Her hand played with the hair at my nape, and she cocked her head. "What happened with your parents?"

I kissed below her ear. "Nothing."

"It wasn't nothing." She turned her head to give me better access.

I kissed the pulse in her neck, which was fluttering.

"I can keep you distracted like this all weekend." I growled against her skin, which brought a hiss and her leg hooked over mine.

"Don't say that," she whispered.

I lifted my head. "What?"

Her lashes flitted down and back up. "Don't remind me this is only for the weekend."

I should be freaking the fuck out at that comment. I barely did a few hours with a girl, not a long weekend. But I wasn't and— *that*, freaked me the fuck out. I rolled us so she was on top and ignored my thoughts. "Don't think any further than a few hours ahead. You can't stop time, but you can make each moment count."

Her brown eyes widened. "That's very insightful. You always surprise me."

I shrugged. "I assume, for most people, it's hard to be present and in the moment. They're thinking too far ahead. For the next thing. For the next move. I've had to take life moment by moment. If I didn't, I wouldn't have survived."

"I'm so glad you survived," she said. She peered into my eyes, pressed her tits against my chest, and our lips were almost touching. I slid my hand down her spine, and her breath kicked up a notch. She traced my lips with her finger. "You need to tell me what happened."

I didn't answer as my hand cupped the back of her head and I nipped her jaw.

She gripped my shoulders, and her lids lowered. "How can I need you again so soon?" And she melted into me, shoved her hands in my hair and crashed her lips onto mine.

She tangled with my tongue and wriggled down, so she was pressed against my dick. I groaned as she trailed kisses down my chest. Her nails drug along my skin as she went down. She encircled my cock and did that twisty thing. Over and over.

I looked down as she licked the tip, swirled her tongue around it and sucked it in. "Fuck," I grumbled. She met my gaze, and I gripped her hair to guide her strokes. Her lips around my dick was a beautiful sight.

"I need in you," I demanded. I fumbled to find a condom in the bedside table drawer. But she found it and rolled the wrap down. And in the full light of day, she bit her lip and lowered on me slowly—her lips parting, and her chin tilted up to expose that sexy neck.

I didn't know where she lost her shyness from two weeks ago, but I wasn't complaining. She might be on top, but I set the pace. I grabbed her hips and slammed up.

"Oh, hell." She pressed her palms flat on my chest for balance and widened her knees.

She turned me into an animal, and I had the sounds to go with it. I flipped her over, so she was on her back, and I stood up and dragged her to the edge of the bed, so her legs were dangling.

Her eyes popped wide. "What are you—"

I gripped her wrists and held them above her head and drove in.

"Oh, gawd," she said and arched her head back, and I bit right there at her pulse. Not hard but enough to leave a sting. She hooked her legs high on my hip, and she was doing that low keen again. It spurred me on to go deeper. Harder. Driving into her.

"You like that, baby?" I whispered in her ear.

"Jake," was her answer

The echo of my name spoken off her lips pushed me to the edge of sanity. I was almost mindless.

Sweat coated me.

My heart beat erratically.

My vision faded and in out.

But when I focused on her face, she grounded me. Her eyes were mere slits, and her mouth formed an O. She let out a high-pitched tone with every drive in. I released her wrists, and my hands framed her face. Her nails raked down my back, and I kissed her deep as I came. Pulsing within her, I continued that slow, strong kiss. As I ended the kiss, I noticed my hands trembled. Again. I pushed my hands down on the bed to steady my nerves.

She studied me with an expression of awe. We stayed like that, not moving, or saying anything. I stared at her, bewildered. I couldn't pinpoint my thoughts or feelings. It was a jumbled mess.

I lifted off her, tossed the wrap in the trash and slid her back up the bed, wrapped an arm around her. She snuggled right into me and tucked her head under my chin with a contented sigh. I laced my fingers in her hair. We stayed wrapped up like that in silence. Her arm was around me, and she traced random patterns on my back with her fingers.

How did she worm her way in? I didn't let anyone in. Most people were scared to even try. She even got in before I met her in person. How the fuck was that even possible? This tiny female scaled my walls, edged through razor wire, tunneled under my moat and reached me...unscathed. I tightened my arms around her. I hoped like hell she didn't regret it.

She cleared her throat. "I know you don't want to talk about it, but that's why you need to." She looked up into my face.

I sighed, knowing what she was alluding to. "Persistent, aren't you?" I grazed my knuckles across her cheek.

She arched a brow. "Yes. And you know that." She kissed my nose and wiggled out of my arms, and I watched her pull on her panties. I sat up, enjoying the scenery.

She turned her head my way and blushed. "Um, aren't you going to get dressed?"

"Does it bother you I'm naked?" I asked and smirked.

She pulled on her jeans, paused to glance at me and bit her lip.

"If you continue to look at me like that, I won't need to get dressed." I cocked my head and put a hand on my knee.

She jerked her head. "Mister, you are talking," she demanded and left the room.

I grumbled. I would rather have a vasectomy than talk about my parents. After throwing on my shorts, I walked into the living room as she was sliding on her pink flowy tank top. I scanned her from the holey, tight, blue jeans to the top that had little straps holding it up.

Her lips were kiss swollen, and her messy blonde hair framed her pink flushed face.

Her lips parted, and she was gawking at me. Her gaze seemed to be fixed on the undone button on my shorts. I walked to her and placed a hand on the wall by her head.

"Problem?"

She shifted her gaze back to my face and shook her head.

"You sure?" It's amusing to see her deer-in-headlights look, considering what we just did. Twice.

She opened her mouth and then snapped it shut and shook her head.

"Darlin', you can say whatever you want. This is a judgement free zone."

Her eyes glazed, pressed her hand flat on my chest and pinned me to the wall. "The way you look should come with a warning label," she murmured.

"The way you look at me gets my motor running." I snagged her by the waist and brought her body flush with mine.

She gasped and braced her hands on my shoulders. "But we need to talk."

I dipped my head, and she arched back, giving me more access. I wasn't touching her, but she was expecting it. "You certainly don't act like you want to talk."

Her eyes slanted at me. "It's your fault. You're very distracting."

I tipped her head back and grinned. "At least I have that going for me." I couldn't resist anymore and brushed my beard against her skin and kissed that pulse that was tempting me.

She pulled me down closer and bowed back, then suddenly she gripped my hair and yanked me back. "We need to talk," she said in a rush of words.

"You're not gonna let this go, are you?"

"No. Might as well get it out while it's fresh instead of letting it stew."

I shook my head and strode toward the kitchen. If we were going to talk about that shit, I needed, at the very least, a beer.

She gasped and touched my lower back. "Oh, my gawd. Did they do this?"

I didn't feel it until she said something. I shrugged and grabbed two beers out of the fridge. "Don't worry about it. It's nothing." I sat at my small kitchen table.

She planted her hands on her hips and scowled. "It's *not* nothing. It's the size of a dinner plate. Did they do that?"

She looked cute mad—*cute? What the fuck?* I rubbed the back of my neck, popped the beer bottle lid and downed half. "Yeah, it's nothing."

She crossed her arms. "Tell me."

I slouched in the chair. "As you know, Prick got out of prison and Jenny warned me he wanted to see me. But they chose this fucking day to show up."

As she sat in a chair across from me, I opened the beer for her, and she sipped it. She looked so pure sitting there. Her blonde hair in disarray, bare foot curled under her, and those soft brown eyes marked with concern.

"I have no clue why they wanted to see me. Jenny said something about money. Tomas was shocked when he saw me because he hadn't seen me since I was seventeen. He threw the first punch, then Jenny helped. Neighbors called the cops." I downed the rest of my beer. "Cops hauled their asses to jail. That's it."

She blinked. "You mean your mom hit you?"

"Yeah. She was pounding on my back. That's why I got hit. I stepped back and tripped over her. Tomas took a lucky shot."

I still heard Tomas' and Jenny's voice cussing me out. When the cops arrested her, she spit on them, and they used a spit hood on her. Throughout the ordeal, she fought and cursed at them nonstop. In fact, I could still hear her from the police car. Prick was more compliant, but the hateful glare said enough. I ran a hand over my face and looked down at the floor.

Then all I could smell was Becca. She stood and wrapped her arms around my shoulders. Her heart beat beneath my ear, and I tightened my hold on her waist. I lost myself in the feel of her. She didn't say anything, just ran her fingers through my hair and kissed the top of my head. Almost like she accepted me. Scars and all.

~

BECCA

My heart broke for him. I didn't understand how he could tell me what they did with no emotion. Like he was reading from a dictionary. Just flat. But I caught a glimmer of emotion when he looked down at the floor. The torment on his face was clear.

I struggled to hold back the tears, knowing he would hate it if I cried. But he clung to me, like he had earlier. And my heart swelled. I was falling hard and fast. I didn't know how to stop it, and I wasn't sure if I even wanted to.

When his phone vibrated in his pocket, he squeezed me one last time and retrieved his phone.

He shook his head, then stood up, and I was overwhelmed by how big he was. I shouldn't be, but the vulnerable side of him disappeared. Here stood a man with confidence. A bit of cockiness. And sexy as hell. I licked my lips.

He smirked. "Did you hear me?"

I blinked and flushed. Was he talking? I tried to hide how I was gawking at him, ran a hand through my hair and blew out a breath.

"What did you say?"

I squeaked when he picked me up and sat me on the table. He stepped in-between my legs and cupped my face.

"Tony said when we're done doing the horizontal conga we should head to Snookers."

His breath tickled my neck even though he wasn't touching my skin. I found out that he had a fascination with my neck. I wasn't sure if it was all of them or just mine—either way, it made my insides all gushy.

"Uh-huh." I wasn't sure what he said, something about Snookers, but as soon as his lips touched the corner of my mouth, I was spell-bound. I hooked my legs around his and pulled his head to my pulse. His chuckle-half-growl made it ten times worse. He pressed me flat and did that grind.

Where had he learned that move? I didn't know, but it didn't matter. I gripped his shoulders as he nipped my skin.

"Do you want to go to Snookers?" he asked, hooking my leg on his hip and cupping my breast.

"Uh-huh," I answered and shoved my hands in his hair and met his grind.

He shoved up my shirt and bra and latched onto a nipple. He suckled, and his teeth grazed it. The hunger I had for him was uncanny. He touched me, and I went up in flames. We had sex twice since I'd been here, and I wanted it again? *Obviously.* And he did too because he was rock hard.

He skimmed his lips between my breasts. "Do you want it?"

I flushed from embarrassment and bit my lip. "Uh…"

He smirked and unbuttoned my jeans and slid down the zipper. "Let's check."

The pads of his rough fingers scraped against my flesh, under my panties, and he slid a finger in.

"Jake," I pleaded and dug my nails into his shoulders. He aroused me so effortlessly, but I couldn't fight it. Everything about him mesmerized me.

"You're a greedy girl," he growled against my skin and stripped off my jeans and panties—again. He buried his head between my thighs like he was starving.

"Yes," I screamed. I grabbed fistfuls of his hair to keep him there. With both my legs over his shoulders, he teased and tortured me with his tongue. Teeth. Fingers.

I learned to be silent with Nick because he ridiculed me constantly. Jake made me feel things I'd never felt before. I couldn't be silent even if I tried. He gave me freedom to be however I was. And I was his for the moment. And this moment was all that mattered.

Once again, I hit my high…but it wasn't enough. I shoved at his shorts with my feet.

"I have to get a wrap," he said. When he kissed me, I could taste me on his lips. I was so turned on by it, I grabbed his head and kissed him deeper. I arched my hips to his and locked my legs around his waist. What I wanted was separated by one layer of clothing. But that was too much.

"Fuck, Bec." He pulled back a little. "I need to get a wrap," he repeated. "I'll only be a few seconds. I promise."

I panted and whimpered. I almost said fuck the wrap because I was on the pill. But I nodded and let him go. I peeled off my shirt and bra as he came back in.

He stopped and looked at me. "Gawd damn."

"What?" I didn't know what I looked like draped across his kitchen table naked. But I could imagine. My self-conscious-self smacked me in the face. I acted like a fool. *What was I doing?* I didn't behave like this. I sat up, ducked my head, and turned away. Tears pooled in my eyes at how ridiculous I was being.

He walked to me and put his hands on my shoulders. "You have nothing to be ashamed of."

I still wouldn't meet his gaze. I ruined the moment...again.

"Look at me," he insisted.

I glanced up into his eyes. Startling bright against his dark skin.

"I don't know what's wrong with me."

My own words shocked me. I was acting like a *whore*.

The word bounced around in my head—in Nick's voice.

As tears rolled down my cheeks, panic set in. I tried to scramble away from him, but before I could, he scooped me up, sat on the couch, grabbed a blanket off of it, and wrapped it around me. My nerves were somewhat calmed by being covered up.

"Hey," he said loud enough to break through the racket in my head and made me look at him. "Listen. Just breathe."

I stared at him and matched his breaths. He settled me. I realized how ridiculous I was being. But the fact was, Nick still had a hold on my life—it made me sick to my stomach.

"I'm messed up." I tried to look down, and he wouldn't let me.

"Hey, fuck that weasel dick," he said.

It never failed to bring humor to the situation, but right now, it just brought a brief smile.

"He accused me of being a whore when I wanted sex," I whispered.

I tucked my chin to my chest and wrapped my arms around myself. Fresh tears fell.

He put his arm tight around me and crushed my hair in his hand while I cried. Would I ever be normal? Would I ever get past this?

"I'm sorry for—"

"Stop." He lifted my chin with his knuckles and wiped my tears. "You did nothing wrong. That pathetic waste of human shit did. Let me ask you something. Do you blame me for what Tomas and Jenny did to me?"

"No," I said vehemently. "Nothing that you did..." I blinked and stared absently at the wall. That's when I realized I had no control over Nick, any more than Jake had control of his parents. I felt lighter, and I took a deep breath. The blame lay at Nick's feet. Nick's actions were his responsibility, not mine. I looked back at Jake. He had a crooked grin, and his head cocked sideways.

I planted my hands on his shoulders, straddled his lap, and the blanket fell away...we were skin to skin. I looped my arms around his neck and played with the hair along his nape. For all his rough and gruff demeanor, he was sensitive and caring. And very perceptive.

"You're amazing."

He scoffed. "I've been accused of a lot of things, but amazing isn't one of them."

"You are," I insisted. "You knew a blanket would help calm me. And you helped me realize I was sabotaging myself. Are you sure you're not the shrink?" A smile toyed with my lips, thinking how ironic the tables were turned.

That made him chuckle and really smile. He was beautiful when he smiled. I wrapped my arm around his shoulders, feeling the warmth of his chest against mine, and our lips so close, almost touching. My hand scraped through his beard. If I wasn't sure I was falling before...I knew it now. I didn't know of a single male who would be as patient and kind as he was.

Even Clay, my co-worker, was not as patient. We went out twice, and I spilled my drink, dropped my silverware, spilled his drink all over him, and knock my salad on the floor. He didn't say anything, but his expression said it all. I couldn't imagine he would understand a panic attack when we were trying to have sex.

But Jake did.

I didn't know how to say this, so I just blurted it out. "If you're clean, I'm on birth control. If you want to forgo the condom."

His brow arched. "I've never not used one. You trust me that much?"

"Yes," I breathed. "If you trust me." I widened my knees until we lined up perfectly. "Did I ruin the mood with my freak out?"

He smirked. "No, darlin'." He shoved my hips down farther. "We just hit pause."

Pause.

I gasped and fused my lips to his. And soon, I was panting, and he was growling, like we had never paused. Like I'd never had the freak-out. He leaned me back, so his teeth grazed my nipple from side to side.

"Jake," I breathed and fisted my hands in his hair.

"Are you ready?" he asked and switched to the other breast.

"Uh-huh." I bit my lip as he brought me to my knees.

He shucked his shorts, suckled a nipple and shoved me down on him.

He filled me. Completed me. He was doing that grind...again. My fingernails dug into his shoulders. I was on top, but he was doing all the work. He kept my hips still while he thrust and ground...thrust and ground. Over and over. Till I couldn't breathe.

I opened my eyes a fraction, and he was staring into my face. I wrapped my arms around his shoulders and returned the stare. His nostrils flared, breath harsh, and jaw clenched. I ran my nails over his scalp, and he rumbled. I felt it all the way to my toes, and I kept my eyes locked on him.

"Jake," I whispered against his lips.

He slammed me down and back up. My eyes popped wide, and when his foot shoved the coffee table forcibly away, we switched positions. I was on the couch, and he was on his knees on the floor. He hooked my legs over his arms and drove in. He would almost pull out and back in. He set a furious pace and all I could do was take it. But I loved how I could make him lose control.

EIGHTEEN
JAKE

My focus was where our two bodies joined, but soon my gaze traveled up across her stomach, to those teats that were hard as pebbles, to her flushed face—she was still looking at me. I had never experienced sex without a condom. The feelings shot all the way down my spine.

Raw possession built up in me. It demanded to be unleashed, and my mouth suckled the skin above her left tit. Hard. Her arms came around me, and she cradled my head to her breast. She released a high-pitched groan, flung her head back, and her walls closed in on me. I pulled her down off the couch, so she hovered, as I continued to drive in a few more times, until she milked me dry.

Laying my head between her breasts, I looked at the floor. I never felt that compulsion before. Marking a girl. It was an angry red with teeth indentions, and my hand clenched. I sighed and studied her face. She appeared dazed but met my gaze.

"I apologize. I was too rough." She should never be marked.

She didn't say anything for a few moments and framed my face with her hands. "It's okay."

I unhooked my arms from under her legs and touched it. "No, it's not. I've never left a mark on a woman."

She wrapped her arms around me and caressed my cheek. Her lips were an inch away, and her eyes fixated on me. She blushed, swallowed, and bit her lip. "I liked it."

My jaw slackened, and she turned her head. I shoved one hand into her hair and wrapped an arm around her waist with the other one.

"When I walked into the kitchen and saw you…you took my breath away. I don't know why, but you trust me enough to lie there like a fucking goddess. Naked. On my kitchen table, no less. When you should be terrified of me." I didn't understand her. "I even scare my friends' girlfriends…they said it last night. And probably everyone fear me."

She pressed closer to me. "You don't scare me at all. I know the real you." She closed her eyes for a moment. "Does it make me bad that…I like it?"

When I got a hold of Nick, I was boiling him alive. To take such perfection and treat her like gum on his shoes—I would take delight in boiling him inch by fucking inch, so he felt every ounce of pain.

"No. I was surprised. Like what you like. You don't need approval for that."

"Yeah?" Surprise lit her eyes. "You always say the right things."

"That's why I'm known as a ladies' man." I snorted. "Right. I'm not known for my tact."

She laughed. "I can see that, but I know the real you. I trust you with my life."

I jerked. Stunned. I growled and held her tighter. Never in my shit-show life had I ever thought someone would say that to me. "Even though I black out. Even then?"

She nodded and her eyes dilated. "I'm afraid for you, not of you."

"Fuck, Bec," I mumbled and pressed my lips to hers. I was not gentle. It wasn't slow. Her nails raked my scalp. And she pulled me closer, but we couldn't get any closer if we tried. I pried my lips away a fraction and stared into her eyes. She set me on fire in more ways than one. "Do you want to meet my shit-for-brains friends or stay home and continue to do the tango?"

She giggled. "That's not nice to talk about your friends like that. And conga."

"But they are. And what?" I had no clue what she was talking about. But I liked the way she giggled.

"Tony said horizontal conga. Not tango." She laughed.

"Whatever. What do you wanna do?" I nuzzled her neck. That's another thing I never did, but Bec was different. I didn't have a clue why—and I was beginning not to care why.

"Yes, I'd like to meet them, and I'm hungry," she murmured, while she pulled my head closer.

I kissed her skin and reluctantly leaned back. "Okay." I sighed. I could feast on her all night and that would be enough for me, but that would be selfish.

She giggled again. "You don't sound very pleased. Come on, it will be fun."

"Fun is what we're doing right now, being around people, isn't."

She rolled her eyes, stood up, and I grabbed her hips. I looked up at her, and her lips parted. Her pussy was level with my mouth, and I smirked at her. But I didn't do what she expected. I slowly stood up and dragged my beard along her skin. Up her stomach, between her tits, and along her neck.

"Oh, gawd." She swayed against me.

When I fully stood, I cupped the back of her neck, so she didn't have a choice but to look up at me. "Do you want to take the truck or bike?"

Her brown eyes glazed over. "Why is everything you do sexy? I didn't even hear your question." She blinked and shook her head.

"It's just what I do."

She arched a brow. "Cocky much?"

"No. I just like to rile you up." I kissed her shoulder and swatted her ass. "Get dressed. I'm gonna take a quick shower."

She squeaked, gathered her clothes, her bag and disappeared into the other bathroom.

Once in the shower, I realized I hadn't checked the time since she got here.

5:23 p.m.

She said she trusted me with her life.

I repeated her words over and over again in my head. What did I do with a statement like that? I looked at the shower floor as icy water poured over me. It was a compulsive need to mark her. And she liked it. I swore to myself I wouldn't do it again. She was way too beautiful to mar that way. She was a pure soul...my Angel. When my friends met her, I was sure they would warn her about me. She would see what they saw. I was sure of it.

I got out of the shower, got dressed and passed the bathroom door where Bec was. How long did it take her to get ready? If she was anything like Andrea, it could be hours. I went into the garage and opened the overhead door. She never answered my question, so I didn't know what she wanted to do. I was betting on her choosing the bike.

I stepped outside. It was cooling off and the weather tomorrow would be the perfect temperature for riding. A light breeze and the high would be 80. But the ride would be a long one. I hoped Bec could hold up.

BECCA

I stared at my reflection in the mirror. My lips were kiss swollen. My hair was a mess. He marked me above my left breast, and I touched it. My face flushed as I remembered my reaction to it. He did that sexy low rumble, and he bit me, then suckled. I'd never felt anything like it and was embarrassed to admit it turned me on. I squeezed my legs together just thinking about it. Then, my belly grumbled, reminding me I'd only eaten a banana at my house and the handful of nuts on the flight here.

I assumed we would take the bike, so I slid into tight, distressed jeans, a wide-necked black top that fell off one shoulder and was littered with pink flecks, and short black boots. After I freshened up my makeup, I pulled my hair back into a ponytail. I put both hands on my cheeks and tried to steady my nerves.

Jake didn't say, but I presumed, if asked, I would tell them we were friends. But it felt a whole lot more than friends. He didn't look at me like a friend did, and I didn't look at him that way either. He knocked me stupid and speechless.

I heard the garage door go up, so I assumed he was in there. I hoped my 'Emergency Care Kit' would fit somewhere on his bike. If not, I had a small backpack. My ECK consisted of a change of clothes, deodorant, toothbrush and paste, small brush, perfume and it all fit in a very small bag. It might be over the top for some people, but my mom had one and when my dad discovered I had the same clumsy trait, he passed the tip on to me. I grabbed my black leather jacket and draped my small crossbody purse over my head.

I blew out a breath. I could do this.

When I went into the garage, Jake was kneeling to inspect something on his bike that sat in the driveway. He turned his head and slowly scanned me from head to toe and back again. Good gawd...he visibly stripped me with his eyes.

Friends? Tony called it earlier. No one would buy it.

Then he stood up.

I visited a Harley shop near Richmond out of curiosity. It was the same outfit all the guys wore. Black biker boots, blue jeans, a Harley tee, a black distressed leather jacket, black Harley hat on backwards and a wallet with a chain—but those guys didn't make my mouth dry. The way he wore it made my pulse hammer. My palms sweaty. And when he shrugged off his jacket, he wore a couple of leather cuffs, a watch and two necklaces, also made of leather. He looked way too good. And sexy. And intimidating. He fit the bad boy biker persona. But I knew a side of him no one saw.

He walked to me...no, stalked me. Picked me up and placed me on his workbench. He pulled my hair free of the ponytail and stepped between my legs, and I could feel how hard he was. He angled my face up.

"If you continue to look at me like that, we'll never leave the house," he said against my lips.

I must have dropped my jacket and ECK, because my hands

knocked his hat off. "Just one kiss," I heard myself say. *Wait? What? I didn't mean* —

He kissed me like he needed my breath. Deep. His tongue swept into my mouth, exploring it. Slowly. He tasted of mint and his dark, musky scent enveloped me. I gripped his hair and locked my legs around his. He was enslaving me. I could fight it, but I didn't want to. I shouldn't want him this badly. We'd had sex three times since I got here. But I didn't want the kiss to end and whimpered when it did with the sound of a bike pulling into his drive.

"Fuckin', Tony," he grumbled and blew out a breath.

When the bike shut off, Tony was laughing. "Friends?" And he laughed again.

"This time I'm gonna kill him."

I giggled. I couldn't see Tony because Jake's body blocked him.

"You think this is funny?" He arched a dark brow.

I smiled. "You won't kill your best friend."

"Am I interrupting...again?" Tony asked behind Jake.

Jake picked me up and set me on my feet and faced Tony. "Is there a reason why you're here, asshole?"

Tony was wearing basically the same outfit as Jake. Even though, Tony was hot, bigger, taller—I didn't feel a thing. I glanced at Jake, who was looking at me, and I flushed and looked back at Tony. He was safer to look at.

"Matter of fact, I am," Tony replied. He leaned on the punching bag hanging from the ceiling. He eyed Jake. "I think it's a good idea Bec meets the gang before tomorrow. I was making sure you didn't back out."

I blinked and looked between Jake and Tony. They seemed to be having a silent conversation. I stepped closer to Jake. "Why?"

Jake's jaw worked. "Nothing you need to worry about."

I put my hands on my hips. "Which is precisely why I need to know. What am I not getting?"

Tony's chuckle was muffled by the bag. Jake leaned against his workbench and glared daggers at Tony. When Jake said nothing, I crossed my arms over my chest and glared at Tony.

"Obviously, you know. Spill it."

Tony's eyes widened. "Why are you glaring at me? I was trying to help you out, doll."

"Don't patronize me." I hated when people did that. Because I was small and appeared fragile, people continued to do that. "I'm not going anywhere until you guys spill it."

Jake smirked. "That works, because I didn't want to go anywhere, anyway."

I cut my eyes at him. "Fine. We won't continue where we left off before Tony interrupted us, either."

Tony howled with laughter. "Damn, doll. You got some spunk."

Jake punched the bag, and it swung to hit Tony. "Fuckin', Tony. She already knows most of it."

"Of what?" I asked.

"How you treat girls?" Tony questioned Jake.

"Yup."

"Does she really know?"

"Hello? You guys are not alone here." Did they do this all the time? Talk as if they were the only ones there. Because I felt ignored.

Jake looked at me. "Tony's worried that it might offend you how I treated girls in the past. But I've told you. I'm not hiding anything."

I nodded and looked at Tony. "Yes, he's told me."

He leaned on the bag again and eyed me. "He doesn't date. Ever. Never had a girl on the back of his bike. He doesn't take them to dinner. He sure as hell doesn't have a girl stay at his place. For four days."

"You've made your point," Jake said.

I got the feeling Tony was trying to protect me from Jake. I linked a couple of fingers with Jake's and looked at Tony squarely. "He's told me."

"All right. You two are gonna shock people. Be prepared." He headed towards his bike but turned back around. "You might want to claim her, Jake. She's a fighter. I'll see you guys in a bit." He winked at me and rode off.

I shook my head at the 'claim her' statement and turned to Jake. He was looking at the ceiling and tapping his foot. I wrapped my arms around his waist till I was flush up against him. He exhaled and looked at me.

"I know how hard this is for you. But I'm here. You're here. And someone reminded me we only have this moment. To just be present." His arms encircled me, and he breathed my name. Nothing sexual about it. This was more potent to my senses. Sex was off the charts with him...but this? This was wreaking havoc on my heart. I had a feeling he'd own it by the end of four days.

He sighed. "People will be shocked. I never thought about it till I told Tony you were coming." He brushed some of my hair behind my ear. "Just stay close to me or Tony."

"I'll be all right. I'm tougher than I look." And I was. I survived Nick and that unholy disaster. I could handle a few snide comments and rude glares.

He tilted my chin up with his knuckles and made me look at him. "I got enemies."

My lips parted and a bit of unease settled in my stomach.

"I never thought or cared about it until...you. Stay near us. Okay? For my sanity."

I sucked in my bottom lip and nodded. "I will." It reminded me of the barn, and then earlier today Tony telling me to lock myself in the truck to keep Jake safe. I shivered as I remembered his screams over the phone in the barn. He didn't sound human. I didn't even know how a human could sound like that. I hugged him tight. "I promise."

He kissed my forehead and let his lips linger.

Another piece of my heart was gone.

He looked behind him, retrieved my ponytail holder and held it out to me. He smirked. "You got your kiss, babe. Now, what are you hungry for?"

It was on the tip of my tongue to say you, but he already admitted he didn't want to leave. "A good burger and sweet tea."

That earned me a rare, full smile. "Now you're talking my language."

He picked up his hat and put it on backwards, handed my jacket to me, and put my ECK in the hard saddle bags of his bike. Never questioning it. Nick would've not only questioned it, but he would've also inspected the items, making sure they were to his standards. Jake punched a button on the keypad on the side of the garage, and the door rolled down. He slid on his jacket and braced an arm on the handlebars.

"Now, I'm nervous." I stood by his blacked out bike. No chrome anywhere.

"Naw, nothing to it. When I'm turning, lean with me. You'll see what I mean when we're rolling. Don't lean opposite of me."

"Won't I be holding onto you?"

"If you want. But that's why I got this padded sissy bar for you. So, you'll be more comfortable. It's a long ride tomorrow for a newbie."

I looked up at him. "You mean this is new? For me?"

"Yeah. I only had a solo seat. I added a back seat, foot pegs and a sissy bar."

I grabbed him by his leather jacket and hauled him down for a kiss. Nick never thought of my needs and wants. This tough biker with crude morals thought of everything, so I would have a great ride. I broke the kiss.

"Thank you," I whispered against his lips.

"It's nothing, but I like your response. Sure, you don't wanna stay home, darlin'?" he asked, and his breath was hot on my cheek.

There was something about the way he said 'darlin' that made me ache. "You don't play fair, but burgers sound delicious."

"I know what sounds delicious." He grabbed my ass. "You."

I put my hands on his chest and pushed him away a fraction and smirked at him. "Food is what sounds good."

He sighed. "All right. Let's go get you food, make an appearance at Snookers to appease Tony and go home so I can fuck you." He straddled his bike, kicked up the stand and fired it up.

I blushed at his coarse language, but he didn't even hesitate over the word. It reminded me of who he was. An admitted asshole who thought about my comfort.

His bike was loud. So loud I couldn't think.

I looked at the total package. Him on his bike…and I was so turned on I thought about pulling him inside for a quickie. I'd never done one of those, but I was positive Jake would be a willing participant.

263

He eyed me. "If I get off this bike, we're staying home," Jake said as a warning and pulled some shades out of his coat.

"Okay, okay." I could do this. I put sunglasses on and zipped my coat and balanced my hands on Jake's shoulders. One leg up and over and I was sitting behind him. A shot of adrenaline coursed through me. I couldn't stop the wide smile.

"You ready?" Jake turned his head.

I shifted and wrapped my arms around him. "More than ready."

He revved his engine a couple of times, and we took off like a shot. My breath caught. I wasn't sure where we were headed, but I didn't care. I had dreamed about riding on a bike my whole life. But dad shot down every fascination I'd had about motorcycles. Telling me how dangerous they were. I made the mistake of telling Nick one time and he laughed. Saying how I'd make the driver crash.

When we entered the highway, I held on tighter as we sped up— then I got why Jake rode.

I could only hear the wind rushing by as it stung my face. I felt the rumble of the bike under me. I looked up, and all I could see was endless blue. I looked down, and the road whizzed under us.

I felt alive. Free.

Exactly how Jake described it.

I got brave enough to lean against the sissy bar and spread my arms out wide and looked up. My skin prickled. My heart raced. I released tensions—concerns—worries. Just let it all go. I closed my eyes and felt weightless.

When Jake changed lanes, I opened my eyes and put arms around him.

"I love it," I said in his ear.

He squeezed my hands briefly. We pulled off the highway and there was a bike coming the other way. He leaned his hand low, and his fingers formed an upside-down V. I noticed the other biker did too. And every bike we came across, it was repeated. I was definitely putting that in the book.

Soon, we were pulling in a parking lot where the sign said Jester's Bar and Grill. Motorcycles filled the parking lot, and a band was playing on the patio. I'd never seen so many bikes and bikers in one spot.

"You need to get off first, babe," Jake said as he turned his head.

"Right." I got off with the help of his arm, steadying me. "Thanks."

"This place has the best burgers, and I thought you might like to experience a real biker bar."

NINETEEN
JAKE

I looked at her and stopped. Her eyes were bright, her face was pink by the wind, and she had the biggest smile. And I put it there. I didn't know how to react. On auto pilot, I locked the bags and put my grip-lock on.

"This is so awesome. What's that?" she asked and pointed.

"This is an anti-theft device." I unlocked it to show her. "You put it over the grip and brake lever and lock it. It won't roll. When you have a bike stolen, you learn your lesson."

"Someone stole your bike?"

"Not this one, but yeah. I found it later, but it was stripped. And I stripped the thief." That punk deserved everything that was done to him.

She shook her head. "I don't want to know what that means."

I smirked. "Smart girl." I slid a hand over her shoulder, and I couldn't resist another kiss on her forehead. "Just stay close to me."

She nodded. "I will."

I told her that for her own good, but a lot of women would have argued about it. But she listened and did so willingly.

I hooked a couple of fingers with hers and led her in. Jesters was the nicest biker bar in the state. And the biggest. A bar ran along one entire wall, and booths and tables were scattered about. There were several TVs on the walls and a waitress smiled at us.

"Do you want a booth, table, bar or patio?" she asked.

"Where do you wanna sit?" I looked at Becca, and she was staring wide-eyed. She shook her head and said nothing. "Patio," I told the waitress and followed her.

Becca tripped a few times, but I paused to let her get her footing and continued. Once we were seated, she wouldn't meet my eyes. I shrugged out of my jacket and peered into her face. Something was off.

"What is it?" I asked and tilted my head.

When she looked up, tears pooled in her eyes, but they didn't fall. "Nick never let me choose anything. He always told me where to sit, always ordered my food, my drink...everything. I've only gone on a handful of dates and those ended in disaster, partly because I wouldn't make a decision." She looked at the floor again. "But I've never told a guy about his abuse. Only you. I don't want to be like that anymore, but I struggle to be me."

It always came back to Nick. Rage boiled through me. I was an admitted asshole, but I didn't go around destroying people just because I could. Nick dismantled her identity. Took everything that made Becca who she was and destroyed her. I knew all about that. I grappled with something similar around the Paganos when I was a kid.

A waitress came over to our table. "What ya drinking?"

I glanced at her. "Give us a minute."

"Sure thing."

I waited till she walked off, took Becca's hand and leaned close because it was loud. "No pressure. Take all the time you need. I won't rush you. And fuck everyone else who tries to."

She gripped my hand and looked into my eyes. "Thank you for being patient." She wiped at her face with her other hand. "I want to get me back. I didn't really know how messed up I was until you."

"We all have battle scars. Some people allow you to grow through them, some assholes don't."

She managed a small smile. "Somehow, you always make something so serious seem so simple and lighthearted."

I huffed and sat up. "Me? Lighthearted? Nobody would agree with that."

She smiled wide, and she lit up. She damn near glowed—and I put the smile there. Again. *Damn.* I reached for my beer and realized we hadn't ordered yet. I yanked my hat off, raked a hand through my hair and slapped it back on.

She was sitting there, looking perfect, still smiling at me. "You seem anxious," she said and clasped my hand. "You've unknowingly given me the best gift." She leaned forward. "Permission to be myself. Thank you, Jake."

Her saying my name while looking me in the eye sucker punched me right in the chest. So hard, I physically flinched. I wanted to ride like hell away from her or pin her up against the bathroom wall and fuck her. But I did neither. Just stared at her.

She released my hand, grabbed a menu off the table and scanned it. "What do you recommend?"

I shook my head to clear it. "Everything's good here." I got the other menu, although I didn't know why. I knew what I wanted and glanced over at her. I wanted to put that smile back on her face.

The waitress came back and took our orders, then got our drinks and set them on the table. Becca took off her jacket and sipped her sweet tea. She looked hot as fuck in that shirt. That wide collar bared one shoulder and it brought attention to her neck. I took a drink of my beer, and she caught me staring. But I didn't look away. She blushed, pushed her hair over her ear and licked her lips.

"I'm surprised you wanted to sit out here. Because of the country music," she said and turned her attention to the band.

"You chose the patio in Virginia, so I assumed you would want to sit out here. But the music is shit."

She looked at me and parted her lips. "You were thinking of me?"

I cocked my head and fought the urge to kiss her. I didn't do PDA. I'd had a couple of girlfriends when I was a teen and decided they weren't worth the trouble. I'd flown solo ever since. They satisfied a physical need. Nothing more, nothing less.

I was saved by the arrival of our food.

"OMG," Becca said. "That's the biggest burger I've ever seen." She looked at me with wide eyes and watched me take a bite. "I'm going to have to eat it with a knife and fork."

I wiped my mouth with a napkin. "Eat it however you like, darlin'."

She narrowed her eyes and pointed at me with a fork. "Don't start that." She speared a piece of burger and ate it. She rolled her eyes back. "So good."

"Told ya."

We were about done when a female voice yelled, "Jake Korte, what's your sexy ass doing here?"

I downed my beer and turned my head. "Beer and food. That's why everyone is here."

Like usual, Hails wrapped me in a hug whether I wanted it or not. She kept an arm around my shoulders and patted my chest.

"I didn't see your bike—" She stopped when she saw Bec. Hails looked back and forth between the two of us. "You're not Andrea."

Bec smiled. "No, I'm Becca."

"Bec, this is Hails. She's Psycho's sister and also does tattoos." I weighed her reaction. I saw the tension leave her shoulders. "Bec is going on the poker run tomorrow."

Hails stared at us and tilted her head and put a hand on her hip. "So, she's riding with Tony? Where is he?"

"No. She's riding with me." I better get used to people's reactions. I couldn't give two shits about it, but Becca was going to catch a lot of heat. That wasn't fair to her. I could let her ride with Tony, but that option made me see red. Fuck that. The ONLY bike she was riding on was mine.

Hails put the other hand on her hip and continued to bounce her stare between us. "You're shitting me, right?"

I knew Hails was a lot to take in. With flame red dreads down to her ass, her curvy and tatted up body. She even had a hoop through her nose. Those creepy ice blue eyes that were fake. Who knew what her actual eye color was? She was short, but you wouldn't know that because she wore platform shoes all the time. She was a lot, and I had no idea what Becca thought, but it was probably all bad.

"Nope." I smirked at Hails and then Bec.

Hails blew out a loud breath and looked at the ceiling. "Damn you, Jake." She plopped her elbows on the table. "Spill it, girlfriend. How did you pin Jags down? I gotta know."

I raised my eyebrows.

Bec's eyes widened. "Jags?" She looked at Hails, then at me.

"My middle name is Jagger."

Hails sat in a chair and scooted closer to Bec. "Draw me a roadmap, so I'll know. I've been having sexy dreams about him for years. Never have I scored."

I choked. "Hails. Did you have to say that in front of me?"

"Why are you still here?" Hails asked.

Becca burst out laughing. She lit up again. I didn't know why she was laughing, but it didn't matter. "Are you laughing at me?"

"Yes. And the way Hails dissed you."

Hails leaned back in her chair, smiled, and was looking at me weird. And that was saying something because she always looked weird. "What?"

"If you don't know, boy. I'm not telling you," Hails answered.

"Huh," I said.

"Huh," she said back.

"I'm gonna take a piss." I stood up. "Hails, watch out for Bec."

"Sure thang, Jags," she said with a smirky smile.

BECCA

The fact that Jake left me alone with Hails said something. He trusted Hails. So much so, he didn't include her in his many one-night stands, and Hails blatantly wanted him. She made that fact clear. Hails was a lot visually, and I didn't know what to think at first.

"Where did you two meet?" Hails asked.

"In a biker forum. I'm writing a book and was looking for information about bikes."

"What kind of book?"

"A biker romance novel."

Her spooky blues widened, and she laughed. "Honey," she clapped me on the back. "He may know a lot about bikes, but he is short on the romance part."

I shrugged my shoulder. "I know nothing about bikes. Never been on one until now."

"For real?" Hails looked at my hair. "Sister, we need to do something about your hair."

"What? What's wrong with…"

Hails left the table and brought an enormous bag and a shot. "The shot is for you. Nothing wrong with your hair but riding with a ponytail will turn it into a rat's nest." She snagged the ponytail off and ran a brush through it.

"Owe," I exclaimed.

"See? Told ya. And if you're gonna be riding on the back of Jags' bike all day, you might want to invest in a headband like most of the girls here." Hails snapped the ponytail back on. "I braided it for ya, sister."

I smiled at Hails. "Thank you."

"Do ya line dance?"

I was taken aback by that question because Hails didn't look the country type. Platform shoes and a heavy metal shirt tied in a knot between her breasts that left her midriff bare didn't exactly scream country. "Yes, a little."

"Take the shot first," Hails directed.

I eyed the green liquid. "What is it?"

She laughed. "Don't worry, it's not poison."

I blew out a breath and downed it. It was surprisingly good until it hit. I swayed a bit for a moment. It felt like fire in my belly. "Is it Fireball?"

"Yes, ma'am." Hails dragged me to the small space in front of the band.

"Why was it green?"

"They put food coloring in mine cause I'm special. Hey, Rickie," she shouted to the singer. "Play a song that we can line dance to."

"You got it, Hails," he responded.

I laughed and looked back towards our table. Jake was seated, and he raised a beer. Evidently, he ordered a Bahama Mama for me because it was sitting on the table. He remembered my drink from Rockfish? The man stupefied me.

"Sister, get in the game," Hails said as a line dancing song came on. Several women joined us. "You can ogle Jags later."

The line dancing was different here, but not so different I couldn't adjust. After a few songs that left me winded and laughing till my sides hurt, we hooked arms and headed to our table.

"Your girl's all right, Jags." Hails kissed me on the cheek. "I'll see ya tomorrow, sister. Keep Jags in line."

I fell in the chair and sipped my drink.

"Having fun?" he asked and draped an arm over the back of his chair.

He was so distracting. Everything about him was potent. All those tattoos on his arms didn't hide his muscles, they only enhanced them. The black leather cuffs on his wrists added to his sex appeal....I really wanted to straddle his lap and kiss him. He leaned forward, laid an arm on the back of my chair and tipped his head closer to mine.

"Did you hear me, darlin'?" he asked in a low voice.

I parted my lips and tried to gather my wits. If he came any closer, I'd tackle the man. I shut my eyes for a moment to get myself composed.

"Yes. And yes." My words were just breaths, but he heard them. Fun would be an understatement...I was having the time of my life but couldn't form the words right now. His stare never wavered when I opened my eyes. But he didn't come any closer, thankfully. Or not. I wasn't entirely sure. But when he looked at me like that, everything and everyone faded. Till it was just us.

"Is Hails her real name?" I whispered and kept a lock on his eyes. He had beautiful eyes. Yellow rimmed the pupil, but blue was around the outer edges. The combo was striking.

"No. It's Hailey but don't call her that. She hates it." He leaned closer, and I was just about to pounce on him, but my phone chimed. And chimed again.

I blinked and shook my head to break the daze he had me in. I looked down, fumbled with my purse and dropped my phone under the table.

"I'll get it," Jake said. He scooted his chair back, fetched my phone and handed it to me.

"Thanks." I held back the urge to apologize and looked at messages from Tony. "Tony asked when we're going to be there. I don't have any idea how he got my number."

"Fuckin' Tony. He probably swiped it when he called you from my phone. Tell him—when we get there."

I rolled my eyes at that comment but relayed the message to him. "Hails said I need a headband like the girls wear. Where do I get something like that?"

"I don't know. Maybe the Harley shop? We can swing by there on the way to Snookers." He looked at his watch. "We have time before they close."

We swung by the Harley shop, where Jake bought two headbands and a shirt for me. I tried to pay for it, but he insisted on paying. The employees knew him by name and kept staring at us. I realized that tomorrow would be worse. Jake acted unaffected by it, but I kept tripping and dropping things because I was so nervous from the stares.

Soon, we pulled in and parked at Snookers. He put on his grip-lock and some girls called out, 'hi Jake' and he said, 'hey', in return. He didn't even look at them and missed the wide-eyed stares when the girls realized he wasn't alone. He hooked a couple of fingers with mine and opened the door for me, and we went in. It was loud and huge. Row after row of pool tables filled the place. The bar was in the center, and he led me to it. Along the way, several girls greeted Jake, and he said hey, never giving them more than a glance.

That's when I realized this was probably where he picked up his one-night stands. But I came with him and was going home with him. It didn't matter what happened in his past, I was here now. That should be enough—it was enough.

We snagged a couple of beers, and he pointed to a pool table in the far back corner. "That's where Tony is." Jake aimed his eyes at me. "You good?"

I nodded and put on a smile, but inside I was shaking. These were Jake's friends. Ones he hung out with, who had seen his random hookups. I wiped my palms on my jeans and took a deep breath. Tony had insisted we meet before the ride. I didn't know why, but it didn't matter as we approached the table.

"You made it," Tony said in a booming voice. He wrapped me in a hug. "You good, doll?"

I hugged him back, smiled and nodded.

Jake bumped fists with Tony. "We parked near a blue piece of shit Harley. Somebody should scrap it."

He laughed. "Fuck you."

I didn't think I could ever get used to their banter. I stood between Jake and Tony while they ribbed each other, and their friends stared wide-eyed at me.

Jake cupped the back of my neck and pointed at his friends. "That's Aaron and his girl Krista, Travis, his girl Sami and Mack. This is Becca."

I waved. "Nice to meet you guys."

Aaron had a full beard and appeared older than Krista. Travis had tattoos down each of his arms, and Sami had red hair. Mack had bleached blond hair and bright blue eyes.

They all said hi in return, but they still had dumbfounded expressions, which made it a lot of awkward. I sipped my beer because I didn't know what else to do.

"Where did you guys eat?" Tony asked.

"Jester's. And I met Hails," I replied.

Tony laughed. "You know she has a thing for Jake, right? And she's a lot. And, I mean, a lot, a lot."

"I know." I smiled, but Jake respected Hails enough to not go there. "She's a bit much, but she was nice, and we did line dances." I took off my jacket, hung it on the back of the chair and sat down at the bar high table.

"Nice to finally meet you in person," Krista said and sat at the table. "I talked to you on the phone. When Tony said you were flying in, I couldn't quite believe it."

Jake took off his jacket and hung it over mine. Our eyes briefly met as I leaned away from the back seat so he could. I watched him walk over to the pool sticks. His rolling gait and the way he moved with confidence made me want to lick my lips. I turned to see a smiling Krista and Sami, and I wanted to hide under the table. They were talking to me, and I didn't hear a thing they said.

"I'm sorry. What did you say?" Heat flooded my face.

They both laughed. "Honey," the red head Sami said in a low voice. "I'm devoted to Travis, but I even love the way he walks."

I sucked in my bottom lip and glanced at the brunette Krista.

"Guilty." Krista held up her hand. "But we've had years to grow immune to it."

And we all three laughed and looked at Jake.

He smirked at me.

"I don't believe it. I think Jake's finally toast," Krista said, mouth hanging open.

"I don't know whether to congratulate you or feel sorry for you," Sami added.

I looked at Krista and Sami. "Why?"

"He has a rep for being the most cold-blooded bastard around." Krista shook her head. "But you did make him say thank you when I gave him a ride."

He told me he was cold to girls, but I thought he was exaggerating because he wasn't cold to me. In the short time that I'd been here, he proved everything that he told me was fact. And that truth was sobering. His friends didn't know him at all. Was I the only one who saw the real him?

"I don't think he's cold at all," I said and glanced at the floor.

"He told us how you met the night I had to drive him home. I'd never seen him that drunk," Krista said.

Sami laughed. "It was the weirdest thing. He was having a conversation with the both of us. He never does that."

"Never." Krista shook her head. "You might get information about bikes from Jake, but Tony's the one you want to go to on the romance part. He's the womanizer, but he won't admit it."

"But you just said Jake's a womanizer," I said, confused.

Sami shook her head. "I don't know what Jake has told you, but he's only in it for the lay. That's it. Wham, bam, but I don't think he says thank you. Just shoves them out the door."

"Tony, on the other hand," Krista added. "Will wine and dine a woman until he finds something wrong with her. And drop her like a hot rock. Who knows what his reasons are? Maybe the girls are wearing the wrong toenail color."

"We've never figured it out." Sami sipped on her beer.

JAKE

I didn't know what the girls were laughing at, and I didn't care. Because Becca was smiling. I smirked at her, and her smile softened. When she did that, I wanted to hand her the world on a silver platter. With her, I was different. And I couldn't decide if that was good or bad.

"You claim her yet?" Tony asked and leaned against the pool table.

"What?" I asked.

Mack clapped my shoulder. "I never thought you'd end up with a girl like that."

"What?" I repeated and arched a brow.

Aaron leaned down to take a shot. "I know how it is. All it takes is the right girl."

My brows lowered. What the fuck were they talking about? "She's just a friend."

They busted out laughing.

"Nice try," Travis said. "She doesn't look at you like a friend."

"You oughta seen what I was interrupting at his house." Tony grinned. "And she threatened to cut him off."

As a group, the guys oohhed.

"Already? She hasn't been here twenty-four hours yet." Mack laughed.

"You done running your mouth, asshole?" I asked Tony.

"Hey," Tony held up his hands. "I'm just being honest, man. If you're gonna let a little thing like that boss you around, you might wanna re-evaluate things."

"Fuck you guys." I shook my head. I knew the guys were giving me shit because I hadn't had a girl around them. I studied Bec, and her head turned as though she felt my eyes on her. Our gazes clung. I couldn't deny the attraction, and I didn't want to even try.

Would it be fair to saddle her with me, though? And all my anger issues, blackouts, drinking issues and blind rages—she was an Angel. And she deserved better than to bring her into my hell. It wouldn't be fair to her. So, I was going to stick with the friend's title. Maybe add in some benefits while she was here, but I wouldn't claim her as mine.

As the night wore on, I noticed the stares. From the girls. From the guys. All directed at Becca. Every primal protective instinct flared… and I realized what I had done. I brought her to a place where I had a lot of random hook-ups. I didn't care what they thought of me. But I did care about what they thought of Becca. She wasn't dumb. She probably figured it out already.

"Hey, you all right, man?" Tony asked and stepped closer.

He noticed my agitation. Me and Tony might give each other shit, but when it came down to it, we had each other's backs. Then I noticed her yawn.

"Yeah, man." I walked to Bec. I slid a hand up her back, under her hair and cupped her neck. She looked up at me and gave me that soft smile. Again. "You tired, babe?"

"Yeah, a little."

"Let's go home." I glanced at Sami and Krista who were still at the table, and they both wore shocked expressions.

"I can't believe it," Sami mumbled.

I didn't care what their expressions looked like or the why of it. I wanted to get out of here. If I was alone, I'd ride all night. Nervous energy buzzed through me. But Becca was probably tired from travel, and we had a long ride tomorrow.

When she slid out of the bar-stool-high chair, she stumbled, but I caught her and waited till she got her balance before releasing her.

"Thanks," she said.

I slid my jacket on, and she did the same.

"We're out of here, guys." I clasped Becca's hand.

She said over her shoulder, "Nice to meet you."

I set a brisk pace, and soon we were outside and unlocking my bike.

"Jake?" Becca questioned.

Feeling like I couldn't breathe, I straddled the bike, fired it up and raised my gaze to hers. She had her hands on her hips and was giving me a puzzling stare.

"Get on."

She rolled her eyes, got on, and we peeled out of the parking lot. I focused on the ride. Getting home so I could sort through the rat's nest in my head.

On autopilot, I pulled in the driveway, and let Becca get off. Leaving the bike running, I walked over, punched in the code for the garage door, straddled the bike and pulled it in. Got off, without a word to her, pressed the button so the garage door would close and went in the house, Becca following behind.

I flung my jacket on the couch, my wallet, and keys on the table. It was a routine repeated over and over. But some random chick wasn't following me.

"You mind telling me what that was about?" Becca said.

I turned to her. "I should have never brought you to Snookers. My mistake."

I walked to the kitchen, poured a shot of whiskey, and promptly downed it.

"Why? Because you didn't want your friends to know me? Or I might ruin your other little flings? Don't worry, they'll never remember me once I'm gone."

I faced her and leaned my hips back against the counter. "No. It was a mistake because you shouldn't have been exposed to what type of person I really am. Hell, Bec, I don't give a rat's ass what they think about me, but I do care what they think about you. It was disrespectful to you."

"The type of person you really are? I know what type of person you are, Jake. Just because everyone else only sees what you let them, doesn't mean that's who you are." She crossed her arms over her chest.

"They know the truth. You are the one who sees something that's not there." I stepped toward her. And in some ways, maybe it was good that she saw what I was about. Maybe then she wouldn't have unrealistic expectations of me.

"Really? Because I think it's all an act. An act to keep people away." She glared at me. "I'm not stupid. I know why those girls were staring at you."

"Are you sure? Because I don't think you do. They were a mindless fuck," I said, making my words snap. "That's what they were."

She lifted her chin. "I knew that. Like I said, I'm not stupid. But there's one thing you haven't figured out yet—I'm not a mindless fuck, am I?"

That had my mouth gaping open like a fish, and I stepped back. *Gawddamn.* She was right. She wasn't a nameless, faceless fuck. She was in my house. Would be in my house for three more days. Staying with me. Nighty-six hours, give or take a few. I had only checked the time twice since she'd been here—she grounded me.

Goosebumps prickled along my skin.

I leaned against the counter again, and my hands scrubbed my face. What the fuck. I looked at the floor, and then she was there. Taking my hand, she stepped close. And all I could smell was mangos.

This girl—this girl brought me to my knees. I could snap a man in two, but she was cupping my hand against her chest…and that smile. That soft smile. It sucked me in.

"You shouldn't be anywhere alone with me."

"Why?" she asked and pressed her body to mine. She still had a hold of my hand between us. She tipped her head back to look into my face. "I'm safest when I'm with you."

Her trusting, big, brown eyes about buckled my legs. My heart hammered in my chest as my free hand slid up in her hair and tugged her braid loose.

"Angel."

"I don't know why you call me that, but when you say it like that…" She licked her lips.

"Like what?" I tilted my head down. My lips mere inches from hers.

She released my hand and grabbed a hold of my shirt. "I want to kiss you," she whispered.

"What's stopping you?"

"Nothing," she breathed. She raised up on her tiptoes to get closer.

I cupped her face between my hands, and she leaned her weight fully against me.

TWENTY
BECCA

I couldn't breathe. His stare locked me in place and our lips almost touched. My heart pounded. An ache settled low, and each passing moment was torturous. Our lips were just inches away, and a shiver ran through me. He brushed his lips with mine, but our stares still clung. This was more than physical attraction. We understood each other. His lips left mine and my hands slid under his shirt, around to his back. His muscles tensed and a jolt of pleasure rippled through me.

He tilted my head and fused his lips with mine. But he was slow. Agonizingly slow. He tasted of whiskey, and my senses were on high alert. I felt every move he made as I dug my nails in his back and melted into him. He took his time kissing me, like I wasn't already craving him. I wanted to feel his naked body against my bare skin. Gawd, the things he made me feel. I had nothing to compare it to. It was more than want, it was a need.

I pushed him back a little to break the kiss to try to get air in my lungs. I shoved at his shirt, and he helped me get it over his head, taking his hat with him. With his leather cuffs, a couple of leather neck-laces, and his tattoos…he was the stereotypical bad boy. But he wasn't a fictional character…he was flesh and blood.

My parents probably wouldn't approve. They would approve of Nick, the public version that he showed the world, but Jake had more integrity. He had no filter and said what was on his mind bluntly. But he didn't lie. Cheat, or steal. Or more importantly, he wouldn't hit me. He wouldn't threaten me. He let me be me.

"Are you gonna stare at me all night or what?" Jake asked.

Then, I noticed he was leaned back against the counter and looking at me with a playful smirk on his face. He had his arms braced behind him and had crossed his ankles. I closed my eyes a moment as embarrassment flooded me. I didn't know how long I had been ogling him, but long enough that he took notice of it. *Again.*

"I'm going to die of mortification," I mumbled.

Even his low chuckle was enticing. It slithered down my spine, and I reached for him. My hands landed on his waist and crawled up his body. Over his abs, up farther to his ribcage, over his chest that had minimal hair…just enough to know he was a man and not a boy. Where there was a red and black tattoo of a medallion, and I traced its outline.

By the time I got to his face, his expression shifted. The intense heat of his eyes startled me. He grabbed me around the waist and pulled me flush against his tense body. He slid one hand into my hair and tilted my head back.

I braced my hands on his biceps and gaped at him. My mouth suddenly dry, I swallowed. Thinking his lips would meet mine, I was surprised by the sensation of his breath against my neck. Not touching, but it was more potent with the promise of his lips on my skin.

"Did you purposely wear this shirt to tempt me?"

"No," I whispered. "Did you purposely wear those leather cuffs to be sexy?"

He leaned back his head to see my face. "What?"

"And do you walk that way to make women go crazy?" I curled a hand around his nape and tugged his head low.

He furrowed his brow. "What are you talking about?"

I studied his confused face and giggled. "You don't know do you?"

"I have no idea what you're talking about, but that shirt you're wearing was teasing me all night. I want to put my lips right there on that pulse."

I slanted my eyes at him. "What's stopping you?"

"Not a fucking thing."

He planted his lips right there, and my arms curled around his head. His lips on my skin started a buzzing through my body, all the way down to my toes. When his teeth scraped my neck, it intensified the buzz.

"Gawd, Jake," I hissed and shoved my hands in his hair.

His answer was a growl, and he whipped off my shirt and bra, picked me up and latched his mouth onto my nipple. Tingles prickled along my skin. I locked my legs around his waist and arched my back, pressing my breasts in his face. His coarse hands on my skin ignited the fire. I realized he was carrying me somewhere, but it didn't matter as long as he came with me. His teeth scraped back and forth on my nipple, and it popped out of his mouth when he tossed me on the bed.

I gasped, my eyes widening as I was thrown. He dragged me till my legs were dangling off the edge of the bed, then he braced his arms on each side of my body. It was dark in here, but I still felt his hot stare.

"You have no idea what you do to me," he said. His finger brushed against my lips and trailed down my chin and in-between my breasts.

"Same." I sounded like a teenager, but his finger tracked down my stomach and grazed along my jeans, making coherent thought impossible.

I felt him smirk. "Is that all your writer brain could come up with? Same?" He popped the button on my jeans, and I clutched his biceps.

"Mhum." My hips arched up when he dipped his finger under the hem of my panties. My breath was loud, erratic, and my body yearned for his touch.

"Do you want it?" His hot breath on my ear was about my undoing.

I gripped his shoulders. "Yes." I bit my lip to hold back the 'please'.

"How bad?" He nipped my ear.

"I don't want, I need." I needed him. Now.

He growled in my ear, stood up, and I whimpered in protest.

He took my boots off and grabbed my jeans and yanked them off, along with my panties, without a bit of protest from me. I sat up, looked up at him and undid his buckle on his belt. When he didn't stop me, I unbuttoned his jeans and slowly slid the zipper down. I slid closer to the edge of the bed, so his hips brushed my chest. His arousal was pressed in-between my breasts, with no underwear, and that made me pause.

"Um, do you always go commando?"

"Most times. Is that a problem?"

"No, I guess not. I've never known anyone that did." Once I got over the shock, it wasn't so surprising. He oozed sex appeal, from that smirk that he always gave me, to his scuffed motorcycle boots. My fingers traced around the waistband of his jeans and tugged them down a little, so that his cock was nestled in-between my breasts. My tongue traced along his waist.

"Fuck," he growled again. His dick jerked, and his body tensed. "If you ask me if I like it…"

I suppressed a giggle.

"Are you laughing at me?" He stared down at me.

I tried to bite my lip, but he sounded so incredulous, I couldn't contain it. I looked up at him and stroked down his length with a twist at the base, while giggling.

"Fuck," he repeated on a groan and thrust into my hand. Over and over.

There was one thing I knew I did right, and that was pleasuring a man. It just never was reciprocated. Bringing a moan to a man like Jake was empowering. Not to mention an instant turn on. My tongue swirled across the head, and I tasted precum.

"Ah hell no," he rumbled. He shoved me flat against the bed, kneeled on the floor and licked my center.

I cried out and gripped his hair. Sensation flooded me and my body bowed.

"Were you getting hot teasing the fuck out of me?" he asked, while his finger slid easily in and out.

"Yes," I hissed. My hips bucked with the rhythm of his fingers. I gave him my body. With no hesitation…he owned me.

One of his hands spread my legs, one finger slid and curled up and

I could make out the smirk on his face right before his mouth landed on my clit...and sucked. And again.

I saw stars. He swirled his tongue on that little bundle of nerves and used his teeth expertly. I clawed at his shoulders. "Please," I begged. His arms hooked under my legs, spreading me wider. He pressed a thumb on the bud and circled it, all the while his tongue fucked me. My entire body tingled, even my toes. Feverish. Hypersensitive to every brush of his hand. Every breath on my skin. "Oh, gawd. I need you," I panted. It was overwhelming how badly I needed him. My frame trembled, and I clenched his hair, keeping his head where it was. My hips bucked furiously into his face. I cried out as my body tensed and my thighs clenched on his head.

He rose and slammed his lips on mine. My legs worked his pants down lower, and he drove in.

"Yes," I yelled. His fullness completed me. It barely registered that his walk perfectly mimicked the way he moved his hips. "Your grind," I panted.

He bit under my ear. "Do you like the way I move, darlin'?" he asked as he slowed it down. His hands slid up my arms and held them above my head. He stopped and stared.

I opened my eyes. "Why did—"

He thrust in and rolled his hips. My mouth gaped, and I swore my eyes rolled back in my head. And again. While his hot stare bored into mine, I trembled. I didn't make a sound. It would have taken too much out of me. My breath exhaled with each thrust. Sweat beaded on us. The vibration started in my core and slowly made its way throughout my body. I whimpered from the force of it. It defied explanation.

"Jake," I pleaded. He released my arms, slid my legs high on my hips and buried it in. It was a race to completion. In and out. No fancy moves, but a low keen escaped my lips.

"I love it when you say my name like that," he grated out.

I exploded. There was no other term for it. I hung on to him, and he lasted a few more thrusts, then met me at our high. He pressed his forehead to mine as we took ragged breaths.

"Becca," he whispered.

One more piece, gone. *Poof.*

If he did this with all his random hook-ups, women would be beating down his door. I shuddered, sighed and grazed my hand across his beard.

~

JAKE

I was so far over my head with this girl. And she begged me—it should be me groveling. I wasn't worthy of her. But it was only one weekend. Right? *Right.*

"That is a satisfied sigh," I smirked at her. I was caressing her cheek like I never did.

She giggled. "Yes, it is. What gave it away?"

That smile. I couldn't see her eyes well, but I didn't need to. There was a light in her eyes that was only reserved for me. I'd studied her when she smiled at Tony and other people, and it wasn't there. Only me. I didn't do anything to earn it, she just gave it. I didn't understand her at all.

I kissed her on the forehead and went to the bathroom. I stared in the mirror. What the hell was she doing to me? That question rolled round and round in my head. She scrambled my brain.

I walked back into the bedroom, and she wasn't there. I went down the hall, into the living room and there she was in my kitchen. Wearing my tee shirt and sipping a glass of water. She turned and smiled at me, with a light in her eyes. She looked good in my shirt, in my kitchen and in my life. I shook those thoughts loose. She gave me the once over and bit her lip.

I strode forward and braced my arms on either side of her. She stepped flush up against me, slid her arms around my waist and hugged me. I never flinched at her touch, just hugged her back.

She tilted her head up. "Thank you for inviting me out this weekend."

I couldn't think of a response because this was all new to me. Everything with her was brand new. Instead, I hugged her a little tighter and kissed her forehead. Her response was that smile. And I wondered just what lengths I would go to keep her smiling like that at me.

Anything.

Damn.

"Let's get you to bed to sleep," I grumbled.

"You don't sound so happy about it." She laughed. "Well, I'm tired. And sleep sounds heavenly."

She released me, twined her hand in mine, and then she led me to bed. She climbed in and I shucked my boots and jeans and climbed in. She scooted her back to me, and I wrapped my arm around her. And if she noticed I was naked, she didn't comment on it. She fell asleep quick. I left the bathroom light on purposely so I could see her, then I leaned up on my elbow and watched her. I ran my fingers lightly through her gold hair and the scent of sex and mangos permeated the air.

Look at me? Getting poetic and shit. I grunted.

Only three days left.

My chest squeezed. *What the fuck was that?* And I forgot to check the time again.

11:17 P.M.

My eyes got heavy. I never went to sleep this easy. I wrapped an arm around her waist, and she scooted back closer to me. I'd never slept with a girl, I realized. Sex, sure. But sleep? Not a chance. I drifted off with my hand in her hair.

I WOKE WITH A JERK. FORTUNATELY, I DIDN'T WAKE BECCA. I SLID MY ARM from underneath her head, put on loose shorts and walked to my garage. I'd gotten just a couple hours of sleep when the nightmare-flashback occurred. I paced the garage, clenching my fists. When would I get peace? When would it end? I had not recalled that particular memory in a long time. I put my gloves on and dealt with it the only way I knew and swung at the heavy bag.

Fighting through all the bullshit in my head. I was on autopilot. Alternating between punches and kicks. My vision faded in and out, so I punched harder. Faster. I dodged the bag when it swung to me. Sweat ran into my eyes. I looked at the door and saw Bec. She was biting her lip and staring at my chest. I stopped. Not moving. My shirt on her hung to her knees. Her golden hair a mess. Her lips parted as she met my gaze.

~

BECCA

I came awake and smiled at the unfamiliar surroundings. I turned to Jake, but he wasn't there. A clock illuminated on the bedside table said 6:23 a.m. Rubbing my eyes and brushing my hair out of my face, I went in search of him. I padded down the hall to the living room, looked in the kitchen and passed the garage door that was ajar. I opened the door wider and peeked in.

Jake had on kickboxing gloves, loose gym shorts and was drenched in sweat. He had earbuds in his ears as he punched the bag that was hanging from the garage rafters. His hair was plastered to his head as he bobbed and weaved alternating kicks and punches. His moves were smooth. Flawless. The way his muscles tightened and flexed was mesmerizing to watch. He hadn't noticed me yet, but I was content to observe him. The way sweat rolled in rivulets down his chest, his abs and into the waistband of his shorts was nothing short of hypnotizing. That's when I realized he stopped moving.

My eyes met his. But he wasn't smirking. He was expressionless, and it startled me. It reminded me of when I first stepped in his house. Cold. Aloof. Blank. I swallowed.

"Um, sorry I interrupted your workout," I said as I turned to go.

"No," he stated. "Stay."

I froze and blinked. I didn't recognize his voice at all. So stern. His eyes were dark and stormy, but his facial expression hadn't changed. I twisted my hands in his shirt I was wearing. I wasn't sure what to say or do except stand there in silence. And then flashes. I couldn't breathe as images of Nick hit me all at once.

Standing over me. Berating me. Hitting me.

I choked and stumbled back against the wall. Tears slid down my face as I drifted down and curled in a ball on the floor. I covered my ears and rocked back and forth.

Dirty whore. Wanting sex. You're a perversion. I was dragged by my hair to the bed and stripped naked. He pointed out all my flaws. Too skinny there, too flabby there. He slapped me and squeezed my cheeks together. Till I was nothing but a shell. Then, he had sex with me, as I laid there. Not moving. Just staring at the wall.

When arms reached for me, I fought. Scratched. Clawed. And tried to get away.

"Becca, it's Jake. You're safe."

A voice penetrated my mind, and I stilled enough to open my eyes. I saw Jake's tormented expression. I launched at him, my arms curled around his neck and sobbed. I trembled uncontrollably. My throat constricted, and I breathed in gasps. I clung to him, and he put a blanket around me.

"Just breathe. In. Out." He rubbed my back. "You're safe," he said in a low voice.

I blinked and I realized we were on the couch. I buried my face in his chest and cried. I cried for the woman I lost. The time I lost. How Nick broke me to the point that I didn't fight back. No one knew the extent of the abuse. Only my therapist and Jake. But he didn't know all of it. I wiped my face on the blanket and looked at him.

"I'm sorry, baby." His brows were heavy with concern.

"You didn't do anything wrong," I said in a soft voice.

His jaw clenched. "I had a nightmare and was punching my way out of it. I shouldn't have snapped at you."

I agreed, but a normal person would have walked away to let him cool off. But I had a meltdown. I pushed some of my hair behind my ear, only to realize my hands still shook. I clenched them and looked down. "You didn't cause this. Nick did." I sniffed and continued in hushed tones. "I wish I was normal. I don't know how long it will take to be like I was before Dad died. Before Nick. I was going to be a famous author and was confident. Sure."

His brows lowered over his eyes. "You can't ever be like you were before. That's the sad truth." He took my hand. "But you can be stronger. Tougher than whatever life throws at you. Life is a shitshow you have to wade through to get a lil sliver of a spark. Sometimes the shit is so deep it swallows you up and you have no choice but to swim to the surface. And then it coats you until you shake it off. And start again. Each time you go under, you have a choice. Drown. Or come up for air guns blazing."

I studied his face while he talked. He was four years older than I was, but he seemed older. Wiser. He rendered me speechless. I wiggled the blanket down so I could feel his bare chest. I leaned my head against it and listened to the sound of his heartbeat. His arms came around me and he tightened his hold.

"Tell me." His fingers ran through my hair.

I shook my head and buried my head in his chest. I didn't even tell the therapist those details. The doc got the drift without having to go through all the gory stuff.

He sighed. "Bec, you gotta get it out."

I pressed my head right over his heart so I could feel the thump of it. "When I showed any interest in sex, it was always the same. Soon, I never wanted it, and I would try to avoid it at all costs. Sex with him was a means to an end," I whispered. "Are you sure you want to hear it?"

"Yeah, babe."

I blew out a breath and blinked once. "If he even perceived I wanted it, it was the same. He'd drag me by my hair, strip me, point out all my flaws." My throat closed, and I struggled to get the words out. "Pinch there, a slap here until I was nothing. He would have sex while I laid there." My last words were merely air.

JAKE

My body tensed with her last few words. My pulse pounded in my ears, and I wanted to see blood. Nick's blood. "That fucker raped you?"

She leaned back to look at me. "No. We were married."

I closed my eyes and looked at the ceiling to get a rein on my fury. Tomas raped my mother when I was present. So many times. Married or not, rape was rape. My hands gripped the sides of her face gently and I looked into her eyes. "Babe, it doesn't matter if you're married or not. If you were not a willing participant, it was rape."

Her eyes widened, and she shook her head vehemently. "No." Panic stricken...tears pooled in her eyes. "No. No." Her small fists struck me, as I watched the horror fill her face. "No, no. I won't accept it," she cried.

I wrapped her tight in my arms and cradled her head against my chest. Bile rose in my throat as she bawled, and her tears were absorbed by my skin. Every tear she shed scarred me. Her little fists beat my chest while she wailed. I knew she didn't want to hurt me, she just wanted to reject the reality of Nick's actions. After a few minutes, her tears subsided. Silence reigned except for a few sniffles from her. No number of words could take the pain away. None. I didn't even try. So, I held her tight. After a while, her head lay heavy on my chest.

Trying not to disturb her, I stretched us both out on the couch. She snuggled into the crook of my arm and her leg was thrown over mine. I draped the blanket over us and kissed her forehead.

Once again, I was shocked by the level of trust she gave me. To quote Bec, she trusted me with her life. If I'd been through what she'd been through...I wouldn't trust anybody. I looked down at her sleeping face. I caressed my knuckles across her cheek.

Did I trust her?

She knew my demons. She knew how I lived my life. Always chasing that adrenaline rush. Always on the edge. Anything I could do to feel. She made me feel alive without even trying. I inhaled her scent and closed my eyes. And focused on the here and now. And now she was in my arms. And that's all I needed.

. . .

I MUST HAVE DOZED OFF BECAUSE MY INTERNAL ALARM WAS GOING OFF. I looked at my watch.

8:03 a.m.

I didn't want to wake her, but the guys would be here soon for the poker run. I threaded my fingers through her hair.

"Becca." I nudged her.

She rubbed her face on my chest, opened her eyes and smiled. That smile that lit up her eyes for me. I was rendered speechless. My mouth went dry. My heart thundered so loud I was sure she heard it.

She raked her fingers through my beard. "Morning."

I cleared my throat. "Do you still want to go on the poker run?"

"Yes." She wet her lips. "Why do you ask?"

Gawd damn, she was fucking beautiful. The reality of her in my arms hit me all at once. So perfect. "I didn't know how you'd feel from earlier this morning." My hand traced along her cheek and laced into her hair.

Her lashes flitted down, then back up. "I'm not letting him rule my life anymore. He took enough of it."

"Brave girl."

"I don't feel brave." Her eyes closed. "I feel broken."

I shifted her, so she was on top of me, and she squeaked. I threaded my hands in her hair, so we were eye to eye. "Listen to me. You're not broken. You're healing. Doing the best you can with what you've been dealt. That's the definition of bravery."

Her eyes widened and then glazed over. Her lips were just a hair's breadth from mine. When she looked at me like that, it got my heart racing.

"They're gonna be here soon."

"Who?"

"Everyone from Snookers." She bit my bottom lip and trailed her lips down my neck. I groaned. "If you keep doing that, I'll lock the door."

"But I want to go." Her tongue and hands slid lower, and she bit my nipple.

"Fuck," I groaned again. I pulled her up to kiss her. Tongues tangled and she plastered her body to mine. She arched her hips, so she rode my erection through my shorts.

She broke the kiss and panted. "I need."

I grabbed her hips and ground into the vee of her legs. "What do you need, baby?"

"Oh, gawd." She sat up and pulled the t-shirt off. "I need you to fuck me."

I realized two things at once. One, she was completely naked under my tee, and two, it was hot as hell her saying the word fuck. I sat up when she tried to drag my shorts down.

Her hand dived under my shorts anyway and stroked down my length. "I need you now," she grumbled in frustration.

My hips answered as I thrust in her hand.

She panted in my ear as she stroked me. "See? You want me."

My eyes crossed. "Shit, Bec." I swiveled so my feet were on the floor, cupped her ass and stood up with her in my arms. Both arms came around me. She pressed her tits to my chest and moaned in my ear. "It's gonna have to be a quickie," I mumbled. Our friends would be here shortly, and she had me so hot I wasn't going to last long.

"I've always wanted to do a quickie." She giggled.

That comment cut our quickie in half. She had me out of my mind. I sat her down on the bed. She was sitting up with legs dangling off the bed and watched my every move while I shucked my shorts.

"Enjoying the view?" I smirked.

"Immensely." She eyed me up and down.

I growled and flipped her over, so she was on her hands and knees. I didn't even check that she was ready for me before I drove in.

She arched her back and flung her head. "Yes."

"Good girl. Nice and wet."

Being in her bare, I felt the ripples of her walls as she squeezed me tight. I remained standing, grabbed her hips, thrust in her. I didn't have time for fancy moves. By the way she was moaning, she didn't need it. I smoothed my hands down her back, and she shivered. I paused long enough to run both hands along her back.

"Oh, gawd." She tremble, pushed her ass back and rode me.

I let her do her thing. Her walls clenched me, and I grit my teeth trying to hold back till she got hers. When she emitted a low pitch, I took back control. I watched my dick slide in and out of her quick. But she was not nameless. And not a bitch. She was my Angel.

"Darlin, you better be close."

She gushed on me with those words and with a couple more pumps, I was spent. I pulsed in her and she shuddered with little aftershocks. I noticed she fisted the bedsheets in her hands. She went limp and fell flat on the bed, and her hair hid her face.

I laid on my back beside her. She blew at her hair.

"You're so good at that."

I quirked a brow at her. "What?"

She raised her head up, shoved her hair out of her face. "Really?" She shook her head. "You know what I'm talking about."

"Sex?"

She rolled her eyes at me. "How come everything you do or say turns me on?" She faceplanted a pillow and groaned.

"That's a needy groan."

"Smartass." She said in a huff and got up. "I'm going to get ready."

I sat up and whistled as she walked from the room with her little ass swaying. She partially turned around, so I saw her blush as she hurried in the other bathroom.

A cold shower later and dressed...I opened the garage overhead door. It was a perfect day. It was a tic cooler than yesterday, but there was clear blue sky as far as the eye could see. I rolled my wheels into the driveway and checked it out. I needed to make sure my ride was sound because it wasn't just me riding today. Bec said she trusted me with her life. And I took her trust in me seriously.

I checked tire pressure, any leaks, loose connections, and loose bolts. I heard Tony's bike before I saw him. He did a U-turn in my driveway, parked behind my bike and shut it off.

"Where's Bec?" he asked with a grin.

"Getting ready."

"She's still here? I figured you'd run her off by the way you acted last night."

"Yeah, asshole. She's still here." I wasn't explaining shit to anyone. It was between me and Bec.

"Nothing to say about it?"

"Nope."

"Why did you go off halfcocked like that?"

"No reason." I rested a hand on my handlebars. I didn't know what the fuck Tony was doing questioning me like this when he knew I didn't like that shit. I furrowed my brows as it dawned on me. "You like Bec."

"She's a good girl, Jake."

"You do." I clenched my hand.

"Easy. I like her, but not the way you're thinking." Tony raked a hand through his hair, stepped in close and lowered his voice. "I don't want her to get hurt. Come on, man. What are you doing with her if you don't claim her?"

Right about then, Aaron with Krista, and Travis, with Sami, pulled in. They all got off their bikes.

"Where's Becca?" Krista asked.

"Getting ready." My answer was curt, thanks to Tony and his prying.

She held up her hands. "Sorry I asked."

I glared at Tony and strode right past him to get a bottle of bug-off and sprayed some on my fender. It was going to be a long shit day if people didn't back off. I wiped both fenders.

"Did she cut you off?" Travis asked and laughed.

Tony grinned. "Naw, I was giving him shit."

"Already?" Aaron shook his head. "We haven't even left yet. Cut the man some slack. He's gonna get a boatload of it on the run today."

Then, Mack pulled up with a no-name girl wearing a helmet—then she took it off.

"Ah, come on man," Tony said. "Her? Are you fucking kidding me?"

I muttered curses under my breath and looked towards the sky. It was the girl talking shit about my back tattoo. The one where I about lost it and broke the pool stick in half.

"Hello to you too, Tony," she said.

Mack shrugged and grinned. "She wanted to come."

Tony shook his head. "Why do we always invite him?" He asked no one in particular.

"Cause we're gluttons for punishment," Travis said. "He always stirs shit up."

"Come on, guys. You know it would be boring without me around," Mack said. "So, where's Bec?"

"Getting ready," Sami said. She shook her head at Mack. "If your girl starts any trouble, she's out."

"You realize I'm right here and I can hear every word you're saying," the no-name girl said.

"Yeah. We know." Sami smiled none too sweetly. "Take it as a friendly warning."

Sami was a little firecracker. I had seen her tear a girl to shreds because a girl liked Travis. She said it wasn't jealousy, it was territorial. Protecting what was hers. And there's a difference.

I couldn't relate to her at all until Bec. Not like I was going to do anything about it. She was only here for the weekend, and I already went over reasons why I wouldn't. Was I still trying to convince myself? I looked at the garage door when she opened it and stepped out. When she glanced at the group and smiled at me, I had trouble remembering what those reasons were as she walked up to me.

She wore the t-shirt I bought for her. Pink, sparkly and a headband to match, black jeans and short boots. Her blonde hair was braided, and her leather jacket was over her arm. But the way she looked at me. That smile. The light in her eyes. *Damn.*

"Thank you for the shirt," she said and laid a hand on my arm.

"Yup," I mumbled and shoved my hands in my jean pockets. I didn't know how to react to her sometimes. Didn't know what to say most of the time. She made me feel different and it was hella confusing.

"Wait a minute…you're with Jake?" the no-name girl asked.

My hackles rose, and I cupped Bec's nape and glared at no-name. "You got a problem with that?"

Bec looked at her, then me and back at her. "Have we met?"

"No. But I think you should know he has a back tattoo with the words 'hell' written in big letters."

"I know. Is it a problem?" Bec put her hand on her hip.

"A nice girl like you shouldn't be with the likes of him." She flung her braid over her shoulder. "And I'm Ivy."

Tony inserted himself between Bec and Ivy. "Mack," he said as a warning.

TWENTY-ONE
BECCA

"Do you know her?" I asked Jake.

"No. I've only met her briefly." His jaw clenched.

I wasn't sure what was going on, but I wasn't about to stand down. I walked around Tony and faced Ivy. "You can't assume anything about someone you don't know. And you don't know either one of us, so back off."

Krista and Sami gaped and then smiled.

I glanced back at Jake, and he wore a stunned expression. I might be small, but I was done being stepped on. Jake told me I could never go back to the old me, and I realized he was right. And starting today, I was tougher, stronger, wiser. And it pissed me off that Ivy thought he was beneath her.

"I know your dad wouldn't approve of you being with the likes of him," Ivy said.

I was amazed at the audacity of her statement. "What gives you the right to even guess what my dad would think?" I looked at Mack. "How long have you been friends with Jake?"

Mack looked at Jake, then at me. "About fifteen years or so."

"Is Ivy your girlfriend?"

"Well, no." Mack shoved his hands in his pockets and looked down.

"And you're going to allow a girl to talk like that to Jake? A long-time friend." I crossed my arms and leveled a look at Mack. He was cute, in a way. I was sure he got a fair number of girls with those baby blues.

Mack looked nervous and swiveled his gaze from Jake to me to Ivy. He sighed. "Hell. Yeah, you're right." He straddled his bike and fired it up. "Get on, Ivy."

She buckled her helmet and got on. "Where are we going?"

"Your house to drop you off."

"What?" she screeched.

And they took off like a shot.

I turned to the group, and they were staring wide-eyed at me. Even Jake. "What?"

Tony burst out laughing, along with all the rest of Jake's friends.

"Damn, doll. You put Mack in his place," Tony said and continued to laugh. "You can hold your own."

Sami and Krista gave me high fives. It made me feel confident and I smiled. I recalled early this morning when I had a flashback of Nick. It made me feel so small and inadequate. Jake reminded me to fight those feelings…I wasn't powerless.

"I like her already, Jake." Aaron grinned.

I walked over to Jake and smiled at him. "I'm tougher than I look." He cupped the back of my neck, and it gave me a thrill. I felt protected and cherished when he did that. I laid a hand on his abs and looked up into his eyes.

"That you are," Jake murmured and pressed a kiss to my forehead.

My arm went around his waist, and I leaned my head against him and closed my eyes for a moment when his arm tightened. I opened my eyes to his friends who were staring at us slack-jawed. It was a shame he didn't let them see the caring, softer side of him. The him I knew. I better get used to that reaction today because we would be getting a lot of stares and comments.

I looked up at him. "I want to ride."

He smirked down at me. "Well, let's go."

Soon we were riding. We lined up two by two. Tony, Aaron and Krista, then Travis and Sami, and me and Jake. We rode in a planned formation it seemed. Goosebumps formed on my skin at just the thrill of riding. And when we came to a stoplight, Jake cupped the back of my leg, and when I glanced over at Sami, she had a huge grin. Travis was doing the same thing and Sami gave me two thumbs up. It was impossible to talk over the rumble of bikes, but I blushed. It made me feel like I belonged.

Jake turned his head to the side. "You okay?"

"I'm perfect," I said against his ear.

"Good." He squeezed my leg before taking off again.

Before long, we pulled into a parking lot of Psycho's Tattoos. My eyes widened. It was an overload of leather and testosterone. Most everyone was wearing vests, or cuts, that represented their club. Some women were wearing cuts that said, 'Ole Lady' and on the back 'Property of' and a biker's road name.

"What does RAMC stand for?" I asked Jake as we dismounted from his bike.

"Rolling Asylum Motorcycle Club." He put on his grip-lock. "Psycho is the club's Road Captain. He's been the one pushing me to get patched."

I glanced around at the stares, and I was more than a little nervous. They looked rough, and the women were not even hiding their glares. Jake grabbed my hand and spoke low in my ear.

"Just stay near me. I trust Tony, Aaron, Psycho, JJ and Hails. You'll meet JJ today. I don't want to frighten you but be aware. Okay?"

My grip tightened on his hand, and I nodded. I gave him a small smile and he winked.

"It's all good, yeah?"

As I gazed into his eyes, I relaxed. I might be doing research for my book, but it took a backseat to whatever was going on between us. "Yeah," I murmured.

We walked hand in hand and when I tripped, he paused and walked slower without me ever saying a word. For being the crude, asshole biker, his thoughtfulness of me left me in awe. We got in line, behind Tony, for registration and I tried to take it all in. The atmosphere, the lingo—the smell of cigarette and weed permeated the air. Krista and Sami were behind us with their boyfriends.

"Jags and Becca!" a female voice yelled, getting the attention of most everyone and heads swiveled in our direction. A smiling Hails advanced on us.

"So much for flying under the radar," Jake mumbled.

Tony laughed. "Fat chance of that."

Hails was wearing skintight black leather pants, a cropped bright green halter, which matched her eyes, and platform black boots with silver buckles. She was more flamboyant than yesterday, if that were possible.

Hails pulled me in for a hug. "You took my advice, I see." And pointed at my headband.

"Yes," I replied. "Jake took me to the Harley shop after we left Jesters."

"Did he, now?" She arched a brow, looked at Jake and grinned like the Cheshire cat. "That was mighty nice of him." And hugged Krista and Sami.

That's when I noticed Hails had fangs. I gaped a lil bit. She didn't have them last night. And her eyes were ice blue, not green. Hails hooked an arm around Jake's and Tony's waists and then her arms dropped lower to pat their asses.

"I don't mean to be feeling up your man, sugar, but you stole him from right under us. Give me this one."

"Uh," I stuttered. I wasn't sure who she meant by 'us', and Jake hadn't made it clear what our relationship was or wasn't.

"They say they're just friends," Tony piped up and laughed like it was the funniest thing ever.

"Yeah, right." Hails rolled her eyes.

The whole gang laughed, and I looked down and gripped Jake's hand again. My left with his right, which had the skull on it. Jake said nothing. Not surprising. We hadn't talked about *exactly* what we were doing. He didn't look at me or even glance down, but he squeezed my hand tighter, and it reassured me. I didn't know why. Maybe we shouldn't label it at all. It made sense to us, and who cared what anybody thought.

Hails tensed, stepped forward and placed her hands on her hips. Fury rolled off her. I followed her glare to Mack, who had a hand on a girl's ass. But at least not Ivy's.

"Now, Hails," Tony said.

She whirled on him and gave him a long, deep kiss. She created enough of a spectacle that whistles and whoops filled the air. And it seemed Tony was enjoying it because he cupped her ass.

Jake shook his head and leaned down to my ear. "Hails likes Mack, but he doesn't like her. Well...he doesn't like that she's sister to the MC's Road Captain. He won't touch her because of that."

"Why not?"

"MC's get protective of their girls. He doesn't want the whole MC after him."

When Hails broke the kiss, she smirked. "Not bad." She patted his cheek and walked off–her eyes trained on red faced Mack.

Tony grinned and wiped the black lipstick off his lip. "Damn, Hails can kiss," he said as he moved forward to register.

"Won't the MC be after Tony?"

"Nah. They all know it's just for show." We moved to the table. "How many hands do you want, Bec?" Jake asked.

"You can buy more than one hand?"

"Yeah," he answered as he filled his form out and pulled out a chip from the bag. Number sixty-seven.

I followed suit and replied, "One." I pulled out number twenty-two.

As we walked to Jake's bike, he tensed, and I studied his face. His expression didn't show it, but he held my hand and the muscles in his forearm stiffened.

I glanced up and a huge guy walked up to us. He was several inches taller than Jake and twice as wide. He smirked at Jake and focused on me and gave me a leering smile. The patches on his cut said 'Enforcer' and 'Kracken'. He certainly lived up to his name, and I recalled RAMC wanted Jake to take his place. I instinctively moved closer to him.

"Jags," Kracken said, but kept his eyes on me. It felt like tiny bugs were crawling all over me.

"Krack." Jake's expression followed his body and relaxed. I didn't know how he could do that because Krack was terrifying.

"Aren't you gonna introduce me to your little friend?" he asked Jake, but his eyes were undressing me. I swallowed.

Jake's stare never wavered from Kracken. "Becca, this is Myles."

Surprised when he gave a name other than Kracken, my gaze swung to Jake, but he never once glanced my way. Myles grabbed my attention when he emitted a sound so sadistic it reminded me of Nick. Myles stepped closer to Jake, puffed up his chest and stood breathing over him. Jake tugged me behind him.

"Stand down, Kracken," a deep voice said. Off to the left, two guys approached us. One was smaller than all three of them but couldn't miss the air of authority he gave off. He had dark caramel skin, and as he came closer, his eyes were burnt amber. The other one was as tall as Myles and had a long salt and pepper gray beard.

Kracken chuckled and cracked his neck. He lunged his head towards Jake's face, "Boo, motherfucker." And walked off laughing like he won the standoff.

Jake never flinched, but I did. I shivered, and my heart pounded. Myles' demeanor was like Nick on steroids. A lot of steroids. I pressed my forehead against Jake's back and tried not to panic. When he turned, I huddled into his chest and his arms came around me.

"What is it?" he asked me and tilted my head up.

"He reminds me of Nick," I said and wiped at my eyes. "Not in looks but attitude."

"You all right, little lady?" The one with the beard asked.

I nodded.

"Becca, this is Pope the VP and JJ the Sargent at Arms," Jake said.

JJ's position in the club explained his demeanor. He made sure all rules were followed.

"Nice to meet ya, Becca." JJ eyed us both and smirked.

"If you were patched, we wouldn't have this problem," Pope said.

Jake shook his head. "Not you, too?"

"Krack is creating issues. More than usual," JJ added.

"And why is this my problem?" Jake answered.

My gaze ping-ponged between the three of them. They sure wanted Jake to become a patched member. That was a side of him he hadn't shown me. His hand skated up my back to cup my neck and kept me close to him while they talked.

"I'm just saying," JJ continued. "He's an asshole and has an over-inflated ego. He likes to run that mouth of his when he should shut the fuck up."

"And again, why are you telling me this? I'm *not* part of your club," Jake said in a huff.

"Why do you want him to patch in?" I asked JJ and Pope.

JJ smiled. "He's quiet. An observer and reads people. And has a hell of a left hook." He paused. "I haven't seen you around. Where are you from?"

"I live in Virginia."

Bikes started up, and the noise was almost deafening.

JJ clapped a hand on Jake's back. "Just think about it. Nice to meet you, Becca, from Virginia." And they walked off towards their bikes.

"It never ends," Jake muttered, gripped my hand, and led me to his bike and stopped. "Are you sure you're okay?"

Nodding my head, I smiled at him, but he leaned down close to my ear. "I won't let anyone hurt you."

"I know." He brushed my lower lip with his thumb, and it sent shivers down my spine. When he looked at me that way, I felt cherished. Safe. Secure. Like it was us two against the world.

Soon, we were on the road. Dozens of motorcycles lined up two by two. It gave me goosebumps to see how far the line stretched ahead of us and behind us. We were still in town, and bikers blocked traffic at stoplights so we could ride together as a group. It was so well organized...it was like seamless chaos. Everyone knew their role. Once we hit the highway, it was on. At least fifty motorcycles going sixty-five mph was an impressive sight. I wished I could take pics, but knowing me, I would drop my phone. I noticed Krista and Sami taking pictures of the line of bikes and a few of me and Jake. I made a mental note to ask them to send me a few.

When Jake laid a hand on my calf, it gave me a thrill. Knowing that he'd made space for me in his life, when he let no one in, it meant something. I tightened my arms around his waist and rested my chin on his shoulder. He squeezed my calf.

"You okay?" Jake asked as he turned his head to look at me.

"I'm perfect."

JAKE

From the corner of my eye, I saw her smile. It knocked the air out of me every time. I had never let a girl ride with me since I was a teenager. But Bec looked right at home. After her initial nervousness last night, she rode like a pro.

Before long, we left the highway and were riding down some curvy backroads to Git Lost Bar.

"It's so beautiful," Becca said in amazement.

I looked back briefly to see what she was looking at. Rolling hills, cattle and very few houses dotted the landscape. I glimpsed a foal with its mother not far off the road. I didn't know what the country was like in Virginia, but nothing could beat an Oklahoma view.

"Wait till you see an Okie sunset."

"Are you saying you watch sunsets?"

I arched a brow. "Yeah."

She laughed. "You always surprise me, Jake. I didn't take you for the type."

There was that thump again right in the middle of my chest, but I tried to ignore it.

"When you had to catch an early flight home, I sat on the balcony of your hotel room and wished you were there to watch the sunrise with me." Her breath tickled my ear. She placed a kiss on my neck and laid her head on my shoulder.

As usual, I didn't know how to respond, and she didn't act like she needed a response. So, I let it lie. But thoughts had me tangled up. Word by word, she burrowed deeper into me, and I didn't know how to stop it. Her trust in me, I could never understand.

We pulled into the parking lot of the bar, parked and dismounted. She was all smiles when we took off our jackets because it was warming up. I put them in my bags.

"Do you want a beer?" I asked as I locked my bike.

She wrinkled her nose. "I don't care much for beer, but I like Smirnoff Ice."

I chuckled and grabbed a couple of her fingers and led her to the bar. Drinks in hand, we stood in line to get our second draw.

Psycho walked up to us, smirking. "When Hails told me you had a girl on your bike, I couldn't believe it."

I fist bumped him. "Becca, this is Psycho."

"Nice to meet you." She shook his hand.

He grinned at her, then at me. "How did you snag a girl like this?"

Mack stepped up to us. "They say they're 'just' friends." He made air quotes and walked off laughing.

Psycho raised his brows and looked down at our entwined hands. "Yeah. Right."

I knew what he was thinking but didn't comment either way. Between the stares and glares we were getting...I didn't want to feed to the rumor mill. At least, that's what I told myself.

"I was wondering if you had time to answer some question about being a patched member?" Becca asked.

"Hails told me about your book. I'd be happy too. But I can't tell you about club business."

Bec smiled. "I'm looking for basic information. Not specifics."

"Jake knows a lot already." He glanced at me. "If you were patched, you'd know more."

I sighed. "I'm gonna quit going on your rides if you keep hounding me about this shit."

Psycho laughed. "Did JJ and Pope already talk to you?"

"Yup." I tugged Bec's hand to draw a chip, and they wrote the numbers on our papers. I downed my beer, tossed it in the trash. "If you're gonna hang with Bec, I'm gonna take a piss."

He smirked. "Sure."

I walked off shaking my head. Between the MC nagging me and all the attention we were getting, I was ready to blow the entire ride off. And I would've if I were alone. Becca was the only reason I stayed. As I strode out of the bar, I overheard Bec's name from a male voice. I noted where Bec was, sitting and talking animatedly with Psycho and Hails at a picnic table outside. I turned the opposite way and walked over to the group of guys.

"I would like to bend Becca over and smack that fine ass," Kracken said, and a few guys laughed, but when they saw me, their lips zipped shut and they all looked down.

Krack turned around with a mocking smile. "Just the man I wanted to see."

I relaxed my stance and recalled the way Bec cowed down to Krack. The fear in her eyes was reason enough to beat his motherfucking ass.

"I heard you and her were just friends. I'm sure you wouldn't mind me tapping that," Kracken said with a sneer.

I watched his pulse. Expression. And the tiniest flex of a finger. I could read him like a book, and I knew he was right-handed. I'd watched him in several fights, but most were too scared to really fight him. He instilled fear with his size alone. But I wasn't one of them.

"Nothing to say?" Krack asked and stepped up to me, trying to intimidate.

My face remained in a bored, neutral state and I didn't say a word. Kracken knew the MC was looking to replace him with me. He had been trying to get me into a fight for a couple of years. When I still said nothing, Krack stepped closer. He was clenching his fists and breathing hard over me. I still didn't move.

"Fight," someone yelled over the crowd that was starting to gather around us.

If Krack backed down now, he would look like a coward. A vein throbbed in his bald head. This was it. I ducked his thrown fist. I landed a punch to Krack's kidneys and moved out of reach. He seemed surprised but came back and swung towards my ribs. I dodged it and landed a punch to his face, busting his lip.

I studied the way the muscles bunched and flexed and could see where the next blow would be. I'd had years of studying Prick's moves with heightened accuracy.

"I'm going to enjoy that hot piece you brought when I bring you down," Krack said, loud enough for everybody to hear.

Half of the crowd chuckled, but I remained silent. Words were a waste of energy. I dodged more punches, landed punches, and got hit a few times. But Krack was getting sloppy. He had muscle but no stamina, and he was a bleeder. Blood ran off his face and down his chest. His swings were missing me completely now. When I caught sight of a pink sparkly headband and Tony right behind her, it distracted me enough, I caught a fist to my jaw. Krack tried to double it, but I stepped back and returned the favor. An image flashed in my head…

Bec crying for me, but I couldn't find her. I saw Krack merge into Prick. *Becca…* the world came back into focus.

As I stood over Kracken, a stillness hung in the air, broken only by the sound of the ringing in my ears. Letting go of the fistful of his cut, I let his head loll on the ground. The crowd surrounding me was eerily quiet. For the second time today, I checked my watch. But it didn't do me any good because last I checked it was 8 a.m. and now it was 11:14 a.m. I assumed it wasn't a lot of time lost, but enough.

Fuck. I ran my fingers through my hair and realized my hat and sunglasses were missing. I spotted them in the dirt, snagged them off the ground, then slapped my hat on backwards and perched my glasses on my head. I spotted Becca with her mouth agape and eyes wide.

Double fuck.

I didn't care about the asshole coming to and groaning. I only cared about her. Trying to decide what I was going to say, I walked slowly toward her. I'd been in two fights since she gotten here…my record wasn't looking good. I got about halfway to her, and she jerked her arm away from Tony and ran to me. She wrapped her arms around my waist and my first instinct was to return her hug, but my arms stayed loose by my sides.

She looked in my face with such concern…it blindsided me. "Are you okay?"

I watched the crowd disperse with whispered murmurs. I sighed and focused on her. "Yeah."

"But your jaw?" She touched it.

"I'm fine. Bec, you should ride with Tony." I put my hands on her shoulders and stepped back out of her arms. Even though it killed me to do it.

"What?" she asked. "Why would I do that?"

I scrubbed a hand over my beard. "Because I'm dangerous. I don't—"

"No." She crossed her arms over her chest. "You don't get to do that."

"What?" I cocked my head at her. "I don't remember taking him to the ground. That should tell you enough."

She stood there shaking her head. "No."

I looked to the sky and then to Tony, who was watching with avid curiosity. "Tell her I'm unstable," I said to Tony.

She whipped her head around. "You keep your trap shut."

Tony held up his hands and walked off with a smile.

"And you," she said, bringing my attention to her. She stared me down, stepped closer to me and poked me in the chest. "You don't get to tell me you're unstable. You might appear that way to others, but not me. I know you. The real you. Don't shove me away because you're scared."

I blinked. *Scared?* I wasn't afraid of anything—I looked at all five feet of her. *Damn.* I blew out a breath. Yeah…she bewildered the fuck out of me. My arms came around her and she hugged me back.

"I was so scared," she mumbled into my shirt.

My fingers tilted up her chin so I could look at her. "Why?"

Her eyes widened, and she smacked my chest. "Because I thought he was going to hurt you, dummy."

I brushed my bruised and bloody knuckles against her chin. Even though she'd be better off staying here with my friends, I found myself asking, "Do you wanna take the long way, alone, to the third stop?"

She looked up, licked her lips, and mouthed, "yes."

I wanted to kiss her, but instead grabbed her hand and led her to my bike. Not saying anything to anyone, we got on my bike and took off. The cool wind off the lake was refreshing and cleared my mind a bit. Becca's arms were tight around my waist, but they shouldn't be. For the hundredth time, I wondered why I let her have her way. I should have demanded she stay. Hell, I should have never invited her out to Oklahoma to start with. But here she was, riding on my bike, and it felt right. Gawd damnit. It felt so fucking right.

"It's so beautiful here," she said next to my ear.

I nodded and pulled off on a side road, got closer to the lake and parked under a tree. It was quiet here. Isolated. Wooded. All you could hear were the bugs buzzing and the lake lapping along the shore. I found this spot when I needed away from the chaos and noise.

A downed tree was near the shore, and I propped up against it and looked out across the lake. She took the same position near me, and I felt her eyes on me, but I didn't look at her.

She took my hand. "You hurt your hands."

"Doesn't matter."

"It matters to me."

As I turned my head, concerned brown eyes met mine.

"What happened?" she asked.

I sighed. "He was talking shit and then swung at me."

"Tony was telling me this feud between you two has been brewing for a while."

"It was only a matter of time." Great fucking timing—again.

"When did you black out?"

I shook my head and started to move off the log, but Becca moved to face me and straddled one leg.

"Talk." She gripped the sides of my shirt.

"It doesn't matter."

She arched a brow at me and cocked her head.

"Geezus, you're like a dog with a bone." I gazed off in the distance at a heron perched on a rock on the opposite side of the shore, then looked back at her. "I heard you calling my name, but I couldn't find you. Krack merged into Prick and when I 'woke up', I was standing over that asshole."

She looked confused. "Was it a flashback?"

"Yes and no." I didn't bother trying to explain it. Hell, it wasn't even clear to me. "How did I bring him down?"

"Your eyes glazed over, and you ran at him, grabbed him by the waist, picked him up and slammed him on the ground. Hard enough, he was out when he hit the ground. Then you stood over him and punched him in the face multiple times." She looked down and was fidgeting with my shirt. "He's so much bigger than you. I don't know how you could pick him up like that. The crowd was silent when you did."

"And that didn't scare you?"

She looked back up. "No," she said with conviction. "You wouldn't hurt me."

"Becca, I don't trust myself, and you shouldn't either." She must be out of her mind.

She glared at me. "You listen to me. I trust you with my life."

"Why?" I braced my arms on the tree and tried to tame the turmoil in my gut. I would never forgive myself if I hurt her. Unintentional or not.

She pressed her body close to mine. "You've never hidden who you are. You're honest. Brutally sometimes. You don't cheat or steal. You're loyal. Thoughtful." She placed a hand on my jaw and lowered her voice. "But, most importantly, you're you. And you are a good man, Jake."

My heart thumped and flipped when she said my name, and she followed it up with that soft smile. It sucked all of the air out of my lungs. I gripped her head, and my lips were a hair's breadth from hers. My breathing ragged, and her hands tightened in my shirt. I wasn't sure what she was doing to me. In my head, I repeated the words she said... *You're a good man.*

Her breath rushed over my lips. "Please."

"Please what?"

"Kiss—"

I angled her head and kissed her. Deep. Thorough. It wasn't a gradual thing. I didn't bother to work her up slow. It was an assault. A direct attack. Then I stopped and pulled my head back, but she grabbed my shoulders and continued the kiss. I growled and grabbed her hips. Her scent. Her taste. I couldn't get enough.

I broke the kiss and trailed my lips down her neck. I bit her and soothed it away with my tongue. She grappled my shoulders and moaned. I did it again, this time a little bit harder. She hissed.

"You like that?" I asked as I scraped my beard against her skin.

"Yes." Her nails raked the skin under my tee. "I want you."

I picked her up and she straddled my lap, and her eyes widened when I shoved her hips down. So much so, she had to hang onto my shoulders to keep from falling. I ground up against her with a rotation of my hips. She gaped, and her nails dug into my shoulders. I leaned closer so my lips touched the shell of her ear.

"Can I make you come like this?"

She shook her head and hissed in air as I ground into the vee of her body.

"Oh, you think I can't?" My teeth grazed her chin, down to her shoulder and bit. "I bet I can."

She was meeting my grind, and her body fit perfectly to mine. Her softness melted into mine in the sexiest of ways.

"Yes," she panted.

"I bet you are dripping."

"Oh gawd, yes."

"I need to fuck you," I growled.

"Yes, please." She knocked my hat and sunglasses off in the grass and ran her fingers through my hair.

"Say please again." She had my blood boiling with her hushed words and demanding hands.

She leaned back to look me in the eye. "Please." She bit her bottom lip.

"Fuck." I growled a warning, picked her up, set her on her feet, turned her around and guided her towards my bike, in-between some trees.

"What are you doing?" she asked, looking over her shoulder.

"Doing what you asked me to." I unbuttoned, unzipped her jeans and my hand slid down her panties. I dipped a digit in her soaked slit.

"Oh gawd," she stuttered. She gripped my arms because her legs buckled.

I held her up and spoke low in her ear as I finger fucked her relentlessly. "Did you come already?" She shook her head. "No? I'll fix that."

I stopped, whipped off my shirt and laid it on the ground. I peeled her jeans and panties to her ankles and brought us to our knees. Her knees on my shirt, I leaned her back against my chest.

"Gawd damn, Bec. You're fucking beautiful."

TWENTY-TWO
BECCA

I looked back at him and saw the awe in his face as his hands traced over my thighs. His expression had me spellbound. I breathed in another piece of self-confidence I had lost. He gave it to me, whether he knew it or not. I closed my eyes when his hand drifted between my thighs, but he did the unexpected and gently worked my clit. Rolled over it and bit my neck. His other hand snaked up under my shirt, shoved up my bra and tweaked my nipple between his fingers. Between all three, it was an electric shock. My body bowed, and my hand curled around his nape and gripped it tight. "Jake," I mewled.

"Fuck," he muttered. His hands left my skin, and I whimpered.

He unbuckled his pants, and he filled me so hard I fell to my hands. It was primal. In the woods. Half-naked. But the craving I had for him far outweighed anything else. Our timing matched. Pants. Breaths. He gripped my hips tight, and I clawed the earth in my hands.

"More?"

I didn't know how there was more, but I wanted it all. "Yes."

He grabbed my shoulders and set the pace, rhythm, and all I could do was take it. It was brutal, and he gave me more. It was pleasure that bordered on pain…and I reveled in it. I lost the ability to moan. To breathe. I shook with the force of my orgasm.

He was on the heels of my completion. My eyes widened, my heartbeat erratically. I trembled and almost fell to the ground, but he caught me and bundled me up against his chest. His arms safely tucked around me. His heart was thundering like mine, and we stayed quiet. I heard the birds and the sounds of the lake all around us. His arm around my waist, his shirt was under my knees, and I craned my head to look back at him. He brushed his hand across my jaw, kissed my forehead and let it linger. I swallowed.

Another piece. *Poof.*

He tugged me and we stood up. We got our clothes straightened, and he picked his shirt off the ground, brushed the dirt and grass from it and put it on. We stood there in silence, staring at each other for a hot minute. Something shifted. I couldn't tell what it was, but it made me nervous, and I sucked in my lower lip. He pulled me into his arms.

"You okay? Was I too rough?"

"No." I smiled, embarrassed. I wished I was good at hiding my thoughts like he was.

"What is it?" Jake peered into my face. "You liked it, didn't you?"

I looked down. It was hard to block Nick's voice out of my head. I knew Jake wouldn't say those nasty words, but it's hard to retrain your brain to not think them.

His knuckles tilted my head up. "Never be ashamed of what you like. Yeah?"

I nodded because I didn't trust my voice yet.

He gave me another kiss on the forehead. "Let's roll."

We didn't say anything on the ride. Another ride through seemingly never-ending winding roads along the lake when we arrived in a town shortly thereafter and pulled up to a bar. I stared at the sign.

"Hidden Pickle Bar?"

"Joe Bob owns it, and he makes his own pickles."

I looked around the mostly empty lot. "Are we early?"

"No, we're late." Jake grabbed my hand, and we went inside.

"It's about time, fucker," Tony said with his hand on his hips. "I was about to send a search party."

"We're adults, if you hadn't got the memo," Jake replied and stepped up to draw a hand.

I had to hold back a laugh at Jake's reply. He wasn't wrong, but heat hit my face. I was sure they knew why it took so long for us to get here.

"I was about to bail on you guys," the guy with the chip bag said.

"Bec, this is Sprocket. He's the tail gunner," he said as he drew a chip.

Sprocket had an infectious grin, hazel eyes and dark brown hair. He was young and wiry. "Nice to meet you." I shook his hand and drew a chip.

He wrote the numbers down. "I knew you could take him down," Sprocket said with a grin. "That body slam was epic."

I looked at Jake, and he said nothing, just shook his head. He took down a man roughly twice his size and a lot of men would gloat. He was confident. Cocky. But he didn't boast or brag about anything.

"I didn't have any doubt either," Tony added.

I saw him glance down at his watch. "We're late."

He grabbed my hand and led me out of the bar. By his tense jaw, I knew he didn't want to talk about the fight. But I had a feeling he was going to have to talk to the MC about it.

We were on the road in no time. Tony, Sprocket and me and Jake. I laid my head on his shoulder. Something he said was bothering me. He said yes and no about the flashback. I wasn't sure what it meant. Maybe he merged the present and the past together. When his eyes glazed over, I knew there was something wrong. It was like he was there but wasn't, and I was terrified for him. He had that similar expression in the garage this morning. Just blank.

We rode through a city, through countryside and into a small town where we pulled up to another bar called Rusty's Buzz. This time it was crowded with bikes, but we didn't have to stand in line for the chip bag. We got our numbers, and everyone started mounting their bikes. Seemed we'd arrived, just to leave again.

But this time, we rode as a pack. Two by two. We rode near the back, and it gave me goosebumps all over again. The roar from the motorcycles was all I heard. I took a deep breath, smiled and absolutely loved it. I tightened my arms around Jake, and he cupped my calf as we rode.

Forty-five minutes later, we slowed and crept along, waiting in line for the riders to get parked.

"Is this the last stop?" I asked.

"Yep. It's the MC's clubhouse."

"Is there food here? Cause I'm starving." I dismounted.

He got off, locked his bike and smirked. "Yeah. There's food here."

"What?"

He cupped the back of my neck, and his rough thumb caressed my skin. He dipped his head low and turned his head to focus on me. "For such a little thing, you sure like your food."

Gawd. When he looked like that...it was sinful. I licked my lips and sucked in my bottom lip. The energy he gave off was addicting.

"Did you hear what I said?" he asked.

I shook my head and closed my eyes. "No. But it doesn't matter."

He smirked, gripped my hand, and led me through the throng of people.

Music blared from a live band that was set up on a flatbed semi-trailer, and they had a dozen picnic tables in front of the clubhouse. They had a line of kegs, an outside bar for liquor, and had a bonfire in the center. The scent of charcoaled burgers along with an overpowering whiff of weed drifted in the air.

Some scantily dressed women hanging off bikers, and a few of them looked like they were having sex for everyone to see and obviously didn't care. I tried not to stare, but it was so much to take in. Jake seemed immune to it.

We got the last number, grabbed some burgers, some beers and sat at a picnic table with the Snookers crew.

JAKE

I studied Bec as she watched people with wide eyes. Nothing new to me, but it was probably shocking for her. I glanced at the crowd and rested my gaze on her. She held my complete focus. The urge to make her mine clashed with my common sense. She had me tied up in knots.

"You okay?" I asked.

She blinked at me and nodded. "Um-hum."

"Man, I can't believe you took Krack down so easily," Mack said with a grin, as he walked up to us and sat down.

I took a deep breath and said nothing.

"Are you gonna get patched and become the enforcer?" Mack asked.

I glanced at him and didn't bother to answer. Krista and Sami would hardly look at me. Figured.

Becca smiled at me. "Are you not going to answer his question?"

"No," I said flatly to Mack and looked away.

Aaron sat down beside me. "You know, the MC are gonna hound you."

I snorted and chugged my beer. "They already are."

"If I was given six months to prospect, I would give it a go," Travis said.

"Over my dead body," Sami said with outrage. "Like hell you are going to."

"Calm down. I'm not." He slung his arm around Sami.

She glanced at me and quickly looked back at Travis. "I'm going to the restroom." She got up, and Krista followed her.

I got the feeling the girls were more scared of me. Not one girl greeted me at the clubhouse, not that I cared. But it was a noticeable difference from the norm. Most of the members turned away when I looked at them. They were afraid of me. More so than they already were. I met Becca's stare, and she smiled. Why was she the only one not afraid of me?

There was a pause in the music to call out the winners for the high and low hand. Nobody in our group won and the music continued.

I noticed Pope, JJ, Psycho, Hails and Beezy, the prez, headed toward me. *Welcome to the shit show.*

Hails met me with a wide smile and smacked our table and looked at Becca. "Come on, sister, let's dance." She tugged Becca up, and she had no choice but to follow her as she led her in front of the band.

"We need to talk," Beezy, the prez, said.

I sighed, stood up and looked to Aaron and Tony. "Keep an eye on Bec."

Tony and Aaron lifted their chins in agreement.

I followed the MC board members into the clubhouse. It was a grey and black house that had been added on over the years. There was a covered porch over the front door and the first room was a large bar. Complete with pinups, dart boards, a jukebox and an L-shaped bar along the back and right wall. Behind the wall were a few offices and 'church'. I had never been in there because only members were allowed. Off to the right was the kitchen and several bedrooms upstairs. It smelled surprisingly clean. Round tables were spaced around the room and two pool tables. A few members were there, and all the talking stopped when I walked in. Just the music echoed in the room.

We went into Beezy's office. I would guess he was in his early fifties by the gray in his hair and beard. He sat in the chair behind his wooden desk and propped his feet up on it. The wall behind him had a painting of the RAMC logo. It filled it completely. It was a joker skull with the tongue sticking out. Psycho, Pope and JJ filed in and sat in the chairs that were along the wall. I leaned back on a window that you could see out of, but not in, and crossed my arms.

"Krack is history. It's not official yet, but he disappeared after the fight. Pussy," Beezy said, disgusted. "Figures he wouldn't be a man."

I said nothing, but I knew where it was going.

"We need a good man for the position. A man who demands respect," Beezy added.

"We've shortened your prospect time by half," Pope said.

Psycho chuckled. "No member in his right mind would give you shit orders. I sure the hell won't."

JJ slouched in his chair and looked at me. "The way you took him down was impressive. But it's more than that. You got the demeanor we're looking for. You're calm and not a fuckin' idiot like Krack. He caused way more trouble than he's worth."

Beezy ran a hand over his beard. "We respected you before this. You would be a good fit."

I eyed all four of them. They didn't know about my blackouts and rages. Only a handful of people did. I worked my jaw. I didn't want to tell them anything, but they wouldn't get off my back.

"You don't want me. I'm unpredictable," I said.

Pope raised his brows. "How do you mean?"

"You're more predictable than Krack," JJ added.

I clenched my jaw and met Beezy's gaze.

He pondered me for a minute and said, "I want to talk to Jake alone." The guys promptly left, so it was just me and him in the room. "How so?"

"I don't talk about it."

"I make it my business to know everyone in the club and those who hang around the club. And I know about you too. Not the full story, but enough," he said.

I crossed my legs. "If you knew, you wouldn't be telling me I'm a good fit."

"I know and because of that, you would be perfect for the role."

I scoffed. "Right."

He swung his feet off the desk and stood. "PTSD. Blackouts. I know."

I swore under my breath. "Has Tony been running his fucking mouth?"

"No," he said. "I know because I have them, too. I was a Marine."

I wasn't surprised often, but I was now. Beezy was always watching and listening and never talked much. Exactly like me.

Motherfucker. How did I miss it?

"I got twenty years on you," he said, somehow reading my mind. "Even if you don't prospect, my door is always open."

I forced a nod. I had nothing to add.

"Just think about it." He knocked twice on the desk and left.

After a few minutes to get my head wrapped around that piece of information, I wandered out of Beezy's office and stopped at the bar for a couple of shots. People got quiet when I entered and didn't resume their chatter until I was almost out the door.

It was near dark, and the party was in full swing now. I knew it wouldn't burn out anytime soon. In my search for Bec, I found JJ and Tony first.

"Are you gonna prospect?" JJ asked with a red cup held loosely in his hand.

"I don't know," I said honestly.

"That's better than a fuck no." JJ took a drink. "No one would fuck with the MC if you became one of us." Then he nodded and walked off.

"Where's Bec?" I asked Tony.

"Still dancing." He pointed near the stage. "You serious about maybe joining the club?"

I spotted Bec laughing. "Maybe." I looked back at Tony.

"Damn. You were dead set against it an hour ago. What changed?"

"I'm not sure." I knew, but I didn't want to voice it. "Did you know Beezy was a Marine?"

Tony jerked his head back. "No. I had no idea. That explains a lot though."

"Yup. A lot."

I looked back at Becca, and she was looking in my direction. Even from a distance, she smiled, and it softened like it always did when she looked at me. It made my heart thump.

"Fuck it," I muttered under my breath and marched right up to her.

BECCA

I watched Jake make a beeline straight for me. His swagger and the way he walked should be a carnal sin. Determination was set in his jaw as he stopped in front of me. His eyes blazed. He grabbed my hand in the middle of a line dance and tugged me after him. After I tripped for the third time, he hauled me up over his shoulder and picked up the pace.

"Jake," I hollered. "I don't think this is necessary."

Hails whistled loudly, but most of the bikers parted like the red sea and didn't utter a word.

"Where are we going?" I asked him.

Still no response, which was typical, but at least I had a good view of his ass. He set me on my feet and stared at me with hands on his hips. His brow furrowed, but other than that, his expression was unreadable. We were away from everyone, the faint light from the bonfire the only illumination.

"Are you okay?" Maybe something happened in the meeting with the MC members.

His jaw worked and he paced back and forth in front of me, muttering under his breath, but I couldn't make out what he was saying.

"Fuck it," he said, stopped his pacing and looked me dead in the eye. "Do you want to be mine?"

I inhaled, and my heart beat so hard I was sure he could hear it. I swallowed and clasped my shaking hands in front of me.

"I have anger issues, social issues, drinking issues…the list goes on and on. If you don't—"

"Yes," I blurted out.

"Shit, I never should have asked." He looked up and raked a hand over his beard. "I've no right—"

I stepped up closer, grabbed his belt and stared into his eyes. "I've been yours," I murmured. "Since I first met you."

He looked at me. "At the beach?"

"No." I was crazy for telling him this, but here goes nothing. "Since I met you in chat."

His head jerked back. "But you didn't know me then."

"You've been on my mind ever since then. But the only question is, will you be mine?" I searched his face for some sign.

He stepped back, forcing me to let go, and gave me a fiery stare up and down my body. I sucked in my bottom lip. The intensity in his gaze had me trembling. The hunger in his eyes. The way his nostrils flared like he was scenting prey, heightened my senses. Not to run away. Never. I wanted to be consumed by him. In every way. And the honesty of my thoughts shocked me.

His arm wrapped around my waist, and his other hand tipped up my chin with force. I braced my hands on his shoulders, and my eyes widened. The heat from his body seared me and my breath froze in my chest.

"Yeah, baby," he said gruffly.

His voice left chills in its wake. So deep. I whimpered and tried to pull his head closer.

"Do you need something?" he asked a hair's breadth away from my lips.

"I need you to kiss me."

His lips crashed on mine. He was ravenous, like he was starved for me. He grabbed my braided hair and forced my head back, arching my body. He breathed along my exposed skin.

"Oh gawd." I gripped his shoulders tighter. I couldn't think straight. If he was intense before, it didn't compare to now.

His teeth grazed back up my neck and bit right under my ear. Hard. And he growled, "Mine."

My legs turned to jelly, and if he were not holding me up, I would have fallen to the ground. I hissed at the bite and shivered at the word. My head spun, and I felt out of control. It was too much to absorb. A man like him—wanted me.

He took my chin and made me look into his eyes. "Mine," he repeated. And resumed his brutal kiss. He delved deep and explored my mouth with equal parts of dominance and hunger.

I gripped his hair and hung on tight. I couldn't get enough of this man, who played by his own rules. "I want you," I murmured against his lips when I came up for air.

A whistle rent the air, and I abruptly turned my head.

"Damn," Hails said. "You guys need a room?"

Jake turned to Hails and smirked, but he never loosened his hold around my waist. "Naw. I'm gonna take my girl home."

She smiled wide. "You're finally claiming her, huh? About time."

What was it about these people? You couldn't claim people like property. But I'd seen a few women sporting a cut wearing 'Property of' and a biker's road name. I looked at Jake, bit my lip and turned to Hails.

"My guy is taking me home," I said on impulse.

Hails burst out laughing. "Fair enough."

Jake arched a brow and leaned toward my ear. "I'm gonna fuck you so hard you'll be begging me to stop."

My eyes crossed, and I forgot Hails was even there. I laid a hand on his beard. "Promise?"

He smiled, but it was feral-like. "It's a promise and a threat."

A short time later, we were on the bike. His words echoed in my head. My hand slid under his jacket and tee, and my fingers traced along his waistband. His answer? Roll the throttle, so we got home quicker.

When we reached home and parked the bike in the garage, he said, "Get in the house."

I looked at him askance at the tone in his voice. He walked to me and smacked my ass, and that got me moving.

"Keep on moving to the bedroom," Jake said from behind me. He turned the light on in his bathroom and tossed his cap and wallet on the side table with a clank. But he didn't touch me.

His behavior made me fidget, and I couldn't get a read on him. He stepped up to me and slowly took my headband off and worked loose my braid till my hair framed my face in waves. He slid my jacket off and tossed it on a chair.

"I've reached my control limit," he said in low tones. "I could work it out on the bag to take the edge off, or make you scream my name till the neighbors hear. Your choice. Either way, I'm fucking you tonight. It all depends how nice you want me."

I gulped and stared at him. "What do you mean? Your control limit."

"I can only handle being around people for so long. I get very agitated. I'm usually alone when I'm like this." He laced his fingers through my hair and cupped my head. "I won't hurt you, but I'm raw. I'll be rougher than I've been."

Rougher than at the lake? I hadn't seen this side of him. And the way he devoured me with his eyes, it was a promise and a threat, like he said. It reminded me of his intensity when he lifted Krack and slammed him to the ground. I should be terrified...but I wasn't. A strange thrill shot through me. My panties were soppy wet before, but now? I wouldn't be surprised if I had a visible wet spot on my jeans.

I licked my lips. "Take me."

"You sure of that?"

I raked my nails up his chest under his tee, and I got a growl from him as a reward. Then I smiled and said, "Yes."

He stepped back. "Strip."

My lips parted, and my insecurities reared their ugly head, but the way Jake was looking at me gave me courage. I peeled off my shirt, revealing the pink shelf bra underneath. He made no moves to take his clothes off, but a muscle in his jaw twitched. He even kept his jacket on as he studied my every move. I sat down on the bed, took off my boots and stood up to peel my jeans off.

"Leave the bra and panties on." He stepped closer and dragged a finger across my lips, down my neck, in-between my breasts. "Gawd damn, you're beautiful."

I felt beautiful in his eyes, and it made me feel powerful. I swayed towards him and trembled under his scrutiny. He tweaked one of my nipples with his finger, and I gasped. He picked me up, so my legs wrapped around his waist, and he latched onto a nipple through the lace bra.

"Jake." Sensations of the wet lace combined with his mouth created a new friction. I held his head there, loving the feel.

He laid me on the bed with my legs dangling off. But he never let go of my nipple and shoved his hand under my panties and two fingers slid in. He used his body to spread my legs wider and finger fucked me hard. It felt like electric currents running through my body. He wasn't gentle. He demanded, and I reveled in his rawness. I was already on the edge, and when he bit my nipple, I exploded on a cry, as my hands tangled in his hair. I thought he would let up, but he kept on. Never slowing down using two fingers and his thumb.

"You were ready for me." He slid up and bit my shoulder sharply.

All I could smell was leather, musk and our spicy scent...it was a heady combo. The familiar tension in my body built up, and I tried to buck my hips to his frantic pace, but his leg pinned mine so I couldn't move.

"No, baby. Don't move and don't come." He stopped moving. "Put your hands above your head."

I hesitated a moment, then did what he asked. He placed one of my wrists over the other and restrained my hands with his. Now I was truly at his mercy.

"Just say no, and I will let you go. You have the power, baby." I nodded.

He resumed his torture of my body. Two fingers in and out. Thumb on my clit. The tension coiled up again and sweat beaded on my body. "Please, Jake," I moaned.

"Not yet," he whispered in my ear.

I trembled and shook my head back and forth. His hand on my wrists pressed deep into the mattress tightly. I whimpered and panted. He sent my body aflame, every muscle tensed.

"You're so wet," he growled against my skin before he bit down.

"Ah. Gawd. I can't hold back anymore."

He immediately released me, tore my panties off, slid his arms under my legs, lifted my hips off the bed, and replaced his fingers with his mouth. Instantly I came apart. He feasted on me till I was spent, but his tongue slid along my sensitive flesh. Lapped it up, and he sucked hard on my clit.

"Oh gawd," I cried when it started building up again. He brought me to climax faster every time, and he stopped right before I came and dropped my hips to the bed. "Please." I sawed my legs back and forth. I was a big whopping pile of need.

He stared at me and started dropping his clothes. I scooted to help him unbuckled his pants. "On your hands and knees."

I didn't even hesitate this time. He shoved my head down into the mattress.

"Put your hands behind your back." I did, as I took big gulps of air.

He held onto my wrists at the small of my back and buried himself in me. I almost came right that second. I couldn't meet his thrusts because he held me so secure. My moans turned into whimpers with every drive, and I lost count how many times I came. I was in a lust filled haze that seemed never-ending. He alternated between pinching my clit and rolling it. He was relentless.

No pause.

No break.

He was like a machine.

Hard. Edgy.

And I loved it.

"Becca," he grit out. He swelled in me and pulsed. He let out a low growl, shortening his thrust. Then he let me go, and I fell flat on the mattress—spent. My body trembled from sheer exhaustion. My arms tingled from being held so tight. It felt amazing.

He slid into bed naked and gathered me in his arms. I snuggled into his chest and the last thought I had was, *he's mine*, before falling asleep.

TWENTY-THREE
JAKE

I stared at her sleeping face and wondered what the hell I did right to win her. I moved some stray hairs behind her ear like she always did. I shouldn't have given her a choice. Should have taken out my aggression on the bag first. Yet again, another mistake on my part. I was fucking up left and right. She didn't deserve to be treated like that. She was my Angel.

I was hyped up from the day—the fight—the MC—the attention.

I'd snapped.

Did I regret making her mine? Fuck no. Could she do better than me? Hell yeah. Was I gonna let her go? Fuck no. But I vowed I wouldn't let my demons take over like I did tonight. No. It wasn't happening again.

I pressed a kiss to her forehead. She scrambled my brain.

After a few hours' sleep, I woke to her calling my name. Tears ran down her cheeks, and I nudged her awake.

Her eyes popped open. "You left me," she murmured as she clutched me.

"Shh. I'm right here. It was just a nightmare." I wiped the tears away.

"You left me," she repeated.

"You might leave me, but I won't leave you." That's the realest statement I had ever said.

Her eyes were still unfocused. "Make love to me, Jake," she whispered.

I froze. Suspended in time, her words hit me like a throat punch. It had to be because she wasn't fully awake. "Shh. Go back to sleep."

"Please," she said in a small voice. She touched my lips and raked a hand through my hair.

"Babe." I groaned in defeat. That's the pull she had over me.

I rolled on top of her, kissed her slow. Gentle. Took my time and built her tension gradual. I made love to her in place of words. I had never said I loved another person. Ever. Actions spoke louder than words. And gawd damn, if anyone deserved to be worshiped, it was her. I kissed every part of her and when she clenched around me and moaned my name, my soul cracked. Her warmth and colors seeped in. She was like a tiny invasion and threatened my very being.

"Becca," I breathed in a ragged voice.

She nestled in the crook of my arm and fell back to sleep, unaware of my turmoil. I was thirty years old, yet this was brand-new territory. My heart flipped. Then stuttered.

I love her.

I tried to breathe through the shock of it. I wasn't capable of loving someone…was I? I didn't do relationships. Or I hadn't till last night. I stared at her peaceful face as she slept. And I wondered, for the millionth time, how this tiny female had broken into my self-imposed cell.

~

BECCA

The next morning, I woke up smiling. He had claimed me. He was my boyfriend. I stretched and rolled over. He wasn't there, which was not surprising. I tugged on his shirt from the day before and went in search of him.

He was in the kitchen drinking coffee, staring out the window, his back to me. He had on loose gym shorts. I couldn't help but admire the muscles in his back, the two indents right above his waistband and the large tattoo that covered the left side of his back. I bit my lip as he turned around. He had an honest-to-gawd vee that disappeared in his shorts. It just screamed—look there. My gaze traveled up over his chest and to his face. His smirking face.

"Did you hear me?"

Oh gawd. Was he talking? I fiddled with my shirt. "Sure. Yeah, whatever."

He placed his mug down, reached for my hand, and tugged me closer. "You didn't hear me, did you?"

I blew out a breath. "No. But it's your fault."

"Did you sleep well?" He stared into my eyes as though searching for something.

"Yes. Did you?" I pressed flush against his body. There was an odd look in his eyes. A question, though he asked nothing.

He nodded and wrapped an arm around my waist. "I apologize for last night. I should've taken out my aggression on the bag. Not you."

I tucked my chin to my chest. "No," I whispered. Just thinking about last night made my thighs press together with need.

He shook his head. "It was uncalled for—"

I put my fingers on his lips to silence them. Despite my embarrassment, I admitted the truth. "I liked it. No. I loved it."

He arched a brow. "It didn't scare you?"

I shook my head, and my hand curled around his nape. "Is that bad?" I swallowed. Being held down by Jake didn't even remotely compare to when Nick held me down. Jake made sure I knew that *I* was in control. And I trusted Jake. That right there was the difference.

"Babe," he said, and his fingers threaded through my hair. "You tell me?" His breath tickled my cheek and ear.

When he said babe in that low voice, it made my knees weak and mouth dry. "I don't know," I mumbled.

He dragged his lips down my neck while he crowded me to a wall. He braced his arms on the wall on either side of me, leaned back so we were eye level, and cocked his head. "My demons were in control last night."

I twisted my hands in the shirt again and embarrassment flooded me. "I want the real you. All the different facets of you. Even your demons."

He stilled with wide eyes. "Gawd damn," he growled and fused his mouth to mine.

I curled my arms around his shoulders and opened my soul to him. I wanted to live and breathe him. That fact frightened me, but I couldn't resist. Didn't want to try.

He bit the side of my neck. "You like when I'm rough?"

My head fell back, and I hooked a leg on his hip. "Yes," I hissed.

He grabbed my bare ass and picked me up. I locked my legs around his waist, and his erection rode perfectly between my thighs. He dug his fingers into my ass cheeks and did his slow roll. I saw stars.

"Oh gawd."

He paused to stare into my eyes. "Take off your shirt."

He didn't have to tell me twice as I quickly pulled it over my head and dropped it. I pressed my bare chest to his and scratched through his beard and into his shaggy hair.

"Perfect. I can't get enough of you," he said.

In one move, he kissed me, pulled down his shorts and rammed in. He rolled his hips, hitting every nerve ending. Tremors raced through me, and I broke the punishing kiss so I could get air. He bit me on the neck hard, and I cried out. I could feel his teeth pinching tighter, and I held his head there to savor the feeling. His chest rumbled, and he tilted my hips. And he hit deeper, if that was even possible.

"Eyes on me," he ordered.

In the full light of day, I did as he asked. I saw his intense eyes blend and darken like a perfect storm, and he picked up the pace. His jaw tightened, and I felt the muscles in his back flex. Tension coiled tighter, and I whimpered against his lips. I was on a Jake high, and I didn't want to come down. Every thrust forced air out between my lips.

"Mine," he said harshly.

"Jake." I clawed his back as I came.

He continued his relentless drive, not giving me time to catch my breath. There was no room for thought. My head flung back into the wall as I cried out. He slowed his thrusts as he came. He whipped me off the wall, kicked out a dining room chair and sat down with me straddling his lap. I settled my arms over his shoulders and played with his hair.

"I marked you again." He sighed.

"I like you marking me."

His hands squeezed my hips. "You surprise me. I'd never thought you would because of your ex."

"I'm bewildered too, to be honest." I raked my nails through the scruff of his beard. "All this is new. I never liked sex, before...you."

He trailed one hand up my spine and cupped the back of my neck, leaving tingles in his wake. "Yeah?" He smirked, but it was only fleeting.

The odd look was back, and I couldn't decipher it. He was very hard to read, but I knew something had changed. I could see the gears turning in his head.

"Mom's having a cookout and we're ordered to be there. Tony ran his fucking mouth again, and told her you were coming down," he said on a frown.

"Do you not want to go?"

A muscle ticked in his jaw. "Yeah. It's fine."

I arched a brow. "You're lying."

He nudged me off his lap, put on his shorts and handed me his shirt. "I didn't know about it, and if she says to be there, you better be there. Whether you want to be or not. She's stubborn, and well, it's easier to do what she says. If we didn't show up, she would come get us."

"Evidently, that's nothing new to you. So why are you pissy?" Crossing my arms over my chest, I watched his mouth open and close like a fish. It was almost funny the way he struggled for an answer. "Don't worry. I know the answer to this one. It's because I'm here and you don't know how to handle it. Me being around your family and friends."

His nod was slow in coming and barely discernable, but he remained silent and even took a step back. It reminded me of when I first got here. He was scared. Shitless.

I reached up and took his hand. He gripped my hand tight and then pulled me into an embrace. His arm went around my waist and the other tangled in my hair. His shuddering breath seeped into my bones. There was nothing sexual about it, and once again, I felt needed. I hugged him back and he brushed his lips over the top of my head.

Poof.

I buried my face in his chest, inhaling his musky scent.

"We have to be there in about an hour. I thought I would take my dirt bike. There's a track out there, so I need to get it loaded up." He released me and moved toward his garage, but not before he turned his head to give me a faint smile.

A FEW HOURS LATER, I WAS WATCHING OUT A WINDOW AS JAKE AND TONY tried to outdo each other on the track. When they first took off, hit the first jump and flew into the air, my heart leapt in my throat. I didn't know how many feet off the ground they were, but it scared the hell out of me. They both wore helmets, so after the twentieth lap around and they were still upright, I relaxed a bit.

Maria handed me a glass of sweet, iced tea and smiled. "Don't worry. They always act like juveniles."

I took the glass. "Thanks. I've figured that out about them."

I moved away from the window and sat on the plush sofa. Maria had made me feel welcome instantly and I couldn't help but like her. She had salt-and-pepper hair with Tony's bright blue eyes. Carl, Tony's dad, had wrapped me in a bear hug like I was someone he knew and hadn't seen in a while.

Their home was cozy. Pictures lined the walls and on every table. It was so obvious they loved their family. Such a stark contrast to the house Jake lived in. This one was filled with personal touches.

"I thought you might like to see some pictures of Jake when he was little," Maria said and pulled out a large photo album. "Yes, this is the one." She sat on the sofa next to me and laid it in my lap. When I opened it, I couldn't help but smile.

There they were. Three dark-headed kids standing knee-deep in snow. "I'm guessing this is Andrea?" I asked and pointed to the girl in the center.

"Yes, it is. Hard to believe she's married now. How I miss her."

I looked up into the sad smile on Maria's face. "Jake said she lives in Virginia now. Where at exactly?"

"She moved to Highland Springs. Not far from Richmond."

"Yes, I know where that is. I've lived in the Richmond area all my life."

"You two would be good friends. And don't be jealous, but she used to have a horrible crush on Jake. She was ten when Tony and Jake became friends, and she was just discovering boys." Maria smiled. "But he always treated her like a sister. Just as overbearing as Tony and her dad."

I listened while I flipped through the album. I began to notice that he was in all the holiday pictures. "From the looks of these pictures, it seems you pretty much adopted him. Although, it doesn't surprise me all that much since he calls you Mom."

Maria's smile disappeared. "If I could have done it legally, I would have. That boy," she paused and looked up at the window where the sound of dirt bikes whizzed by, then leveled her eyes on me. "He is my second son. And he knows that. He may not express much to people, but I know what's going on in his heart. That's why I was so happy when I heard about you. He's never brought a girl home, Becca. Never. Even though he had a couple girlfriends when he was in his teens, we never met them."

I didn't know how to respond to that. Tears glistened in Maria's eyes, the kind of concern a mother should have.

"I don't know what he's told you about his life, but...he was abused. Horribly so," she said and took my hand. "And I know they still emotionally abuse him, so I try to counteract all the harm they cause. The first time he ever spent the night, he woke up with nightmares. Not just normal nightmares. The kind that makes a twelve-year-old-boy lash out at anyone who comes near him. It wasn't long before I realized what was going on, and I let him know he was welcome here as much and as long as he wanted."

I swallowed hard and looked down at a picture of him on a bicycle.

A barely there smile on his face as though hesitant. I traced it with my finger and nodded. "He's told me. I know what they did to him." I glanced at Carl, who was sitting in the recliner. Our eyes met briefly, but he didn't mention anything.

"He was just a kid." Jake's screams still echoed in my head from the barn incident. It left a sick feeling in my stomach. "You probably saved his life."

Maria's smile was faint. "Yes. But he was worth saving. And I hope I'm not being presumptuous, but you can give him a reason to live."

Realizing what she was asking of me, it seemed the weight of the world landed square on my shoulders. I might desperately want to give him that reason, but it was too early to see how far we would go as a couple.

Maria wrapped me in a hug. "I know you are that reason. I can tell by the way he looks at you." Maria pulled back and cocked her head. "Those boys are done playing, I better get some drinks and food ready."

"But they just ate," I pointed out.

Maria laughed. "Darling, boys are never full. Especially boys that play." Then she got up and went into the kitchen.

I stepped outside onto the back porch, and the humidity made it hard to breathe. I was sure glad it wasn't like this yesterday. Sweat trickled down my spine as I glanced around for Jake but found Tony.

"He's on the other side of the barn," he said, a goofy grin on his face, water dripping from his hair. "And if you're wondering, he lost."

"He lost?" His only answer was a laugh as he walked by me and into the house. I followed his direction and passed the opening of the barn. I stopped and stared in for a few minutes. A tremor ran through me, and I closed my eyes a moment and continued on.

I stepped around the corner and found the other side of the building to be shaded. A slab of concrete, big enough for a car, was set against the edge of the barn. Jake was standing there holding a running water hose over his head, his eyes closed. Water streamed down his bare chest and into the waistband of his riding pants, which sat snug on his hips. My gaze followed the rivulets, and I couldn't hold back a sigh of appreciation.

"Hot?" I asked, barely making it a question.

He opened his eyes and smirked. "Yeah. You couldn't stay out here with us?"

"No. Maria was showing me pictures." I tugged at my short sundress, the fabric already sticking to my skin. "And what did Tony mean, you lost?"

"Did that asshole tell you that? He's a liar, don't believe him. I beat him," he scoffed.

"Beat him at what?"

"Racing. We always race on the track. And I always win because he's old."

I laughed. "But he's only one year older than you."

I could tell that he considered this his home. He appeared relaxed, his playful banter flowing effortlessly.

When he glanced back and forth between the hose in his hand and me, a mischievous twinkle shone in his eyes.

I took a step back. "No. Stop. Don't you even—"

I gasped as the cold water rained down on me. Laughing, I fought with him for control of the hose. Water sprayed everywhere and his low laughter joined mine. I couldn't even begin to get a hold of the slippery hose, not to mention he was bigger than me and had no problem keeping it out of my grasp. He stopped the same time I did, our breathing heavy, and that's when I realized he had a wide smile on his face. The first I'd ever seen.

The shadows that always lurked in his eyes were gone for the moment.

I slid my arms around his waist, looked up into his face, then reached up on tiptoe to kiss his chin.

He dropped the still running water hose and framed my face with his hands.

My breath caught at the intensity in his eyes. So much emotion right there at the surface, yet so far out of reach. His thumbs slid over my cheeks. So gentle. His mouth brushed the corner of my lips with the lightest of touches.

My heart hammered in my chest—and I was gone. *Poof.*

I was in love with him.

My heart. My mind. My body...belonged to him. I swallowed. There were so many reasons why it wasn't a good idea. But I couldn't help it. The more things I learned about him, the deeper I got.

He picked up strands of my wet hair and put it behind my ear. "You're wet," he said with a smile.

I pulled myself together enough to say, "Seems this punk drowned me with a water hose."

"I don't know why someone would do that," he replied, his voice mocking.

"Hmm. I don't either."

He kissed me full on the lips, hugged me, then stepped back to turn off the water. I pulled at the soaked fabric of my dress. "And what am I supposed to do about clothes?"

He looked up, his fierce gaze leaving me hot. "Oh, I don't know. You look good to me."

"Sure. But I can't go into Maria and Carl's house dripping. I didn't bring extra clothes like you did." My ECK was at his house. I couldn't believe I'd forgotten it.

He looked thoughtful and said, "No problem." He grabbed my hand and led me around to a side door into the house. Stepping inside, I realized it was the laundry room, complete with a sink.

"Hey, Mom." Jake said, then after a pause hollered again. "Mom."

"I'm coming. What is all the ruckus about?" When she stepped into the small room, she said, "Good grief. You're dripping all over my floor." She tsked, snatched a towel out of a cabinet and dropped it on the puddles.

"We got wet," he said.

"I can see that, Jake," Maria huffed.

Then he stepped to the side to reveal me and said, "She started it."

I punched him playfully on the arm. "I did not. You drowned me with a hose."

"Now kids. It doesn't matter. Jake, run along. I know you have spare clothes. Becca, sweetie, we'll get your clothes dried in no time."

Jake winked at me as he took off out of the laundry room.

"Try not to drip all over my house, mister." Maria hollered through the doorway, then looked at me and sighed. "I swear that boy forgets all the manners I drilled into his head."

"Yes, ma'am." A voice carried down the hall.

A laugh bubbled up until I couldn't contain it.

JAKE

That evening, I was sitting on the sofa, Becca curled up in the crook of my arm, while we watched a NASCAR race and munched on pizza. Ever since my revelation early this morning, I'd been memorizing her. The way she laughed, the way she moved, the way she looked at me when I was looking at her.

All of my friends, the MC, Carl and Maria loved her—which wasn't surprising. They probably liked her more than me. Correction, I knew they liked her more than me.

She looked up at me. "I've really enjoyed this weekend."

I ran my knuckles against her cheek. "Me too."

She turned, straddled my lap and snuggled against my chest. My arms went around her. I'd never touched someone so much in my life, and I didn't flinch from her touch like I did with other people.

"I can't believe I have to go home tomorrow. I don't want to." She sighed.

"Maybe I'll fly out to see you." I'd been thinking about it all day.

She abruptly sat up, mouth gaping. "Really?"

I smirked at her. "Really."

She squealed, her eyes lighting up, and she bit her lip. "When?"

I chuckled at her enthusiasm. "Maybe mid-June."

Her arms wrapped around my neck, and she planted little kisses all over my face. I turned my head to capture her lips and deepened the kiss. My hand was on the back of her head, and my tongue delved into her mouth as I squeezed her hip. Her taste, her scent—she was like a drug. And I was more than addicted. I broke the kiss and leaned my forehead against hers.

"I don't want to go." Her fingers laced in my hair.

I didn't say it, but I didn't want her to go either. I gripped the back of her head, crushed her against me and held her tight. The thought of her leaving strangled my throat. Maybe I could fly to her sooner.

She sat back and held one of my hands. "It's been only two months, but I feel like I've known you forever."

I watched her trace the palm of my hand. Her light caresses zapped my brain. I never had someone touch my hands like that. She touched the rounds scars on my palm and furrowed her brows.

"What are these from?" she asked and looked up.

I clenched my jaw. "It's nothing, just some old scars."

She grabbed my other hand and looked it over. I wanted to jerk my hand back but didn't.

"No, it's not nothing. Tell me. I noticed the same scars on your neck."

"Fuck," I mumbled and ran a hand through my hair. I looked away, then back at her and sighed. "Cigarette burns."

Her hand covered her mouth, and her eyes widened. "Your parents," she whispered. "That's why you have so many tattoos. To cover them up."

I nodded. "Part of the reason. I have to work with my hands. That's why I haven't tatted my palms. I haven't gotten around to my neck yet."

She brushed her fingers along the front of my neck, touching a few of the scars. Her eyes were glassy, like she was going to cry.

"Don't cry. It was a long time ago."

"How young were you when they started doing that?"

I shrugged. They'd always done it.

She raised up to her knees, put her hands on each side of my face and leaned forward. "You are so strong. You could have given up easily. I'm so glad you didn't."

"Don't pity me, Bec."

Her finger trailed along my lips. "I don't. I admire you."

"Don't admire me either."

Her lips pursed. "Too bad. I already do."

That antsy feeling was back, and my chest squeezed painfully. I slid her to the side and bolted to the garage without a word.

"Jake?"

I pulled off my shirt and turned on the blue-tooth speaker, so it blared. I swung at the bag as she followed me.

"Jake?" She put her hands on her hips.

I didn't answer her, just hit the bag with my bare knuckles. Feeling so much was overwhelming, especially when I was used to being numb. I didn't know how to deal. I usually chased the high, but to feel for three days solid…it was stifling. The pressure kept building until I felt ready to explode. I wanted to be alone, but I didn't want her to go. There was a tug of war going on—in my mind—in my body.

In my heart.

I breathed through the force of it. My heart thumped in my chest. My throat tightened. My vision faded in and out.

She moved in between me and the bag. Arms crossed, glaring at me.

"Bec," I warned.

"Talk. Don't get all evasive."

"Fuck." I turned off the music. "What?"

"Talk."

I stared at the ceiling. "What do you want me to say?" I knew what I wanted to say—I wanted to admit I loved her. But I closed my eyes and kept my mouth shut.

"Tell me what you're feeling."

I shook my head and ran my hand through my hair. I couldn't catch my breath. My hands shook, and I fisted them. I rubbed the center of my chest and paced.

"Out with it."

"What do you want me to say?" I had to force the words out.

"Talk to me," she huffed. "I only said I admire you. You don't get to decide how I feel about you."

I backed up. "You shouldn't feel anything regarding me." My thoughts were racing, and they tumbled on each other. This girl had me in knots. I wanted to pull her closer as badly as I wanted to push her away.

She got up in my personal space. "I feel everything about you."

I stared at her, shocked. Did she really say that? I advanced on her.

TWENTY-FOUR
BECCA

I blinked and took a few steps back as I realized what I'd said. I sucked in my lower lip as he crowded me against the workbench.

"What did you say?"

His arms caged me like they did at the beach. His eyes were as tumultuous as an angry sea, and he vibrated with unleashed energy.

"Uhh." I couldn't form the words. My heart in my throat, I barely shook my head. No, it was too soon. I couldn't say that I loved him. Even though he probably read my face like a book.

"You demand I talk, and then you clam up." He grabbed a random tool, then flung it into the wall with a crash.

I flinched, although he didn't see it. He was too busy staring at the ceiling with his hands laced on his head.

"Jake," I breathed.

He visibly flinched when I said his name. He whirled on me with a rumble from his chest. "What?"

I swallowed. "I'll give you some space." I went back into the house and clasped my hands together.

Maybe space was what he needed right now. I couldn't believe I said that. What was I thinking? I took a deep breath, went into his bedroom, and got my laptop. Setting it on his kitchen table, I decided to go over the notes for my story. But my mind drifted to him and his sudden shift in moods. What set him off? Maybe my intense feelings for him spooked him. I couldn't hide my feelings for him even if I tried. Didn't matter if I said it or not, he was a master at reading people. I sighed and refocused on my story.

When a few hours passed, and he didn't come in the house, I finally went to him. He had the seat off his dirt bike and was working on it. His hands were greasy, and he was still shirtless. He shouldn't look this good even when he looked at me with a blank expression.

We stared at each other for a few moments in silence. "I'm going to bed."

His gaze roved my form, and it made my breath catch. "Okay," he said and turned back to the part he was working on.

I blinked, turned on my heel and went to bed. Silent tears seeped into my pillow. Not only sad that I was going home tomorrow, but his dismissive attitude hurt. I'm sure he didn't mean it. The noises in his head were probably too loud. He needed his alone time, or that's what I told myself.

I woke to an arm tightening around my waist. And it kept getting tighter. Jake flinched hard in his sleep, jerking me. He was slick with sweat, and I realized he was dreaming. Correction, having a nightmare.

"Jake." I tried to tap his arm. "Wake up." But he wouldn't and his arm was like a vise squeezing me. "Jake," I said louder.

He yelled and punched the mattress by my head, and I cried out. He blinked awake.

"Fuck," he mumbled. "I'm sorry. Did I hit you?"

I couldn't stop the tears. "No. It's okay."

He sat up in bed and scrubbed a hand over his face. "No. It's not okay."

I blew out a breath. "You can't control what you dream."

He glanced at me and frantically got out of bed. "I could've hit you." He went into the bathroom and slammed the door shut.

I flinched and sat up, put my hands on my head and rested my elbows on my knees. I was going home today, and I didn't want to leave with us like this. To be honest, I didn't want to leave period. To say this weekend was an emotional rollercoaster would be putting it mildly. I went to the other bathroom and got ready for the day. Determined to talk to him and get to a stable place before I left.

When I went into the kitchen, he was sitting at the table. I had left my laptop open, and he was reading.

I smiled. "Do you like it?"

His gaze jerked to me. His nostrils flared, and he abruptly stood up. "What the fuck is this?"

Confused, I cocked my head and stepped closer. "What do you mean?"

"Was this your plan all along?"

I blinked. The rage coming off him was like a storm. Beautiful as it was terrifying. "It's just my story."

"Don't play games with me. This is a story about my life." He wasn't yelling. His voice was deceptively even, a direct contradiction to the vibe he was giving off. "Who gave you the right to write about my life?"

"No. It's not about you." I tried to explain. "I would never—"

"Don't fucking lie to me." He swiveled the laptop around, so it was facing me. Like I didn't know what I had written. "It's your typed words. It's all right there."

"No. It's minor bits and pieces." I admit, some of him leaked through in my writing. I couldn't help it, but it wasn't his life. I would never do that to him.

"You wrote about the fight with Kracken. Word for word, in detail." He didn't have a shirt on, and I saw his muscles tense and veins pop. He slammed his fist down on the table, and his lips slashed in an angry line. "I fucking let you in."

"Jake, I—"

He flinched, then backed up a step. "Enough of the bullshit. You got what you came for," he sneered. With a look of disgust, he whirled around and left the kitchen.

I gaped and followed him into his bedroom. "Please, let me explain. It was a fight scene. If you want me to, I can change it." My heart in my throat, I watched him change clothes into jeans, shirt and riding boots. Never once glancing at me. "It's not about your life," I insisted.

When he slapped a Harley cap on his head and totally ignored me, my heart skipped a beat. "Are you leaving?"

He strode into the living room, with me right behind him, without a word and put his wallet in his pocket and clipped the chain on his belt loop.

I grabbed his arm. "Jake, please. Let's talk about this."

He shook off my grasp. "Lock up when you leave."

"What?" My heart beat painfully in my chest. "Where are you going?" I followed him to the garage, trying to think of something to say to stop him. To make him listen to reason. "Why will you not talk to me?"

He looked me dead in the eye when he got on his bike, his gaze deep and dark. It sent chills down my spine. "You got what you wanted. We're done here." With those parting words, he fired up his bike, and I felt the blood drain from my face.

I was rooted to the ground as he walked his bike backwards out of the garage. When he started to turn in the driveway and point his bike at the road, I sprang into action and ran to him.

"Please, Jake."

He put his shades over his eyes and without pause…rode away.

I was left there stunned and shattered in the driveway. Tears tracked down my face as I watched his taillight disappear. Surely, he would come back once he had a chance to think about it.

He didn't.

He never answered my text messages. His phone went straight to voicemail. I had no other choice than to call a cab. My flight left at one thirty. I couldn't stop crying, and I also couldn't believe he didn't give us a chance to talk about it. But he shut me out. All the things we talked about and all the traumas we shared were swept away with a little misunderstanding. I wrote him a note before I left. At the airport, I searched for him. Hoping he would show up.

He didn't.

I boarded my flight and steeled myself not to cry. The guy sitting next to me frowned and put his earbuds in, like I was going to talk to him. *No, I'll keep my sob story to myself, thank you very much.* The flight attendant offered me water and nuts, as I replayed the weekend like a broken wheel. A few rogue tears escaped. I looked out my window and there was blue as far as I could see, but I didn't really see it. All I kept seeing was Jake's eyes when he left. So cold and angry. He really believed I betrayed him. More tears rolled down my face. I hoped he read the letter I left on his kitchen table. I hoped I hadn't lost him just when I had gotten him.

In hindsight, I probably put too much of him in my book inadvertently. My thought process was to get it all out and then edit and pull most traces about him out. But if he didn't listen to me, I'd never get the chance. In my heart, I could understand his knee-jerk reaction. But at the same time, he didn't even tell me bye. He left, leaving me to get to the airport myself. I rubbed my forehead. A sharp shooting pain was forming behind my eyes. But it was nothing compared to the vise around my heart.

Roughly three hours later, I met Summer at baggage claim. I tried in vain to hide how upset I was.

She narrowed her eyes. "What happened?"

I shook my head. "I don't want to talk about it here. I'll talk when I get home."

She pursed her lips. I could tell she wanted to say something else but refrained.

On the car ride, I checked my phone for missed texts. Nothing. Not a peep. I stared at it, willing it to vibrate. My heart pounded like a drum and by the time I stood in my apartment, I was panicking.

As soon as Summer closed the door, I turned on the alarm. Alan assured me Nick was in custody, but I didn't want to take any chances.

"What happened?" Summer demanded.

Immediately, the dam broke. I covered my mouth as tears went unchecked. The pain was so intense, I bent over, wrapping my arm around my waist. Summer led me to the couch and held my head to her chest. I sobbed. Ugly tears. What if he didn't reach out? What if he really meant what he said—*we're done here.*

Eventually, my sobs turned into silent tears, and I relayed my whole story to Summer. Even my freak-outs during sex. My head hung low, my elbows on my knees and my hands fisted in my hair. I was at a loss about what to do. Maybe I could call Tony.

"He's a dumbass if he doesn't answer you." She got up and popped open a bottle of red wine, poured her a glass, and sat back on the couch and handed me the bottle.

I bit back a small laugh, took the bottle and swallowed a drink. "I love him," I whispered.

Her shoulders dropped. "Oh, chica. Did you tell him?"

"No. But it was probably written on my face." I sighed. "He's really good at reading people."

She nodded. "And your face is an open book. Except when you were with *el cabrón*. That asshole Nick."

Nick's abuse had been gradual and, before long, I was a master at hiding it. But I knew what Jake saw on my face last night. I closed my eyes and fresh tears fell.

"What am I going to do if he never talks to me again?" I looked at Summer.

She gripped my hand. "He will. Eventually. Depends how long you want to wait."

I took a deep breath and tightened my grip on her hand. Somehow, I knew it would be awhile. If ever. *No.* I couldn't think like that. My heart couldn't take it. Even with all his flaws, he was perfect for me. No one understood me so well. He had to talk to me. There was no other choice.

∾

JAKE

I looked at her. All I could see was deceit. "You got what you wanted. We're done here." With those parting words, I fired up my bike.

I was more than done. I mistakenly gave my heart to a conniving woman who played my emotions perfectly. Well—game over.

I rode but this time it didn't clear my head. I didn't pay attention to where I was going and didn't care. I ended up at Rolling Asylum MC headquarters. Only a few bikes were parked here, and I dismounted, locked my bike and headed straight for the bar. Midway, I stopped. There was a gym onsite, and I switched directions to go there. Drinking wasn't going to help. Nothing would, I was guessing.

It squeaked when I opened the door, and the sound echoed throughout the metal building. A few guys looked up, and I ignored them. I had never exercised here, but it had everything a professional gym would have. Machines, free weights and a boxing ring. There were a few free-standing boxing bags over on the far side, and I strode straight for them. I took off my shirt, tossed it on the floor near a bag and swung, putting my entire weight behind it.

The impact was loud in the building, and I almost toppled it over, but I countered a hit on the opposite side. Who the fuck cares if I was wearing jeans and motorcycle boots?

Every time I closed my eyes, I saw her and my blood crashed through my veins.

I screamed at her in my head as I pummeled the bag. I didn't care about the pain in my knuckles...I reveled in it. I could deal with physical pain, but this? This sharp stabbing in my chest kept getting deeper and deeper. I couldn't get away from it, no matter how much sweat poured off me. No matter how much blood dripped off my knuckles. She twisted the knife as I pictured in my head how she would smile at me.

I screamed out loud and hit the bag harder. Faster. No matter how hard I tried, I couldn't block her out. My body finally gave out, and I slumped on the floor. My vision came back into focus, and I spotted Beezy in a chair. He stood up, walked over to me, and handed me a Gatorade.

I propped myself up against the bag and took it. I drank half and realized it was just us in the building.

1:02 p.m.

My knuckles were raw and caked with blood, but I didn't feel it.

"My guys let me know you were in here. Said you were out for blood. You want to talk about it?" Beezy asked. He brought the chair closer to me and sat down.

I drank the rest of the Gatorade and said nothing. My head was full to the fucking brim, and I wanted to talk about it. That thought shocked me, and I dragged a hand through my wet hair.

"I almost hit her because of a nightmare." I stared at a random spot on the floor and clenched my jaw. I'm not ready to tell anyone more than that. The buzz under my skin was still there, but less intense.

I glanced at Beezy, and he nodded. "I've been there."

I didn't know much about him, but I knew he was single. I didn't make it a habit of asking for advice because I had raised myself with little input from anyone else. Didn't even want it. But Beezy had blackouts and nightmares like me. "What helped?"

He leaned his elbows on his knees and laced his hands together. "Time. Talking through emotions. Meds."

"Fuck." I leaned my head back against the bag and looked up. Everything I didn't want to hear. "I've avoided and distracted myself. It worked until it didn't."

He nodded. "Me too." He straightened and looked at me. "My advice. Talk to someone. A psyche doc or a friend."

I snorted. "A doc would throw me into a mental asylum."

He smirked. "I thought the same thing. Or you can talk to me. Whatever you're comfortable with."

"I'm comfortable not talking at all."

"How's that been working for you?" He stood. "Offer still stands about being a prospect. And I know a doc I used to see."

I stood and threw my tee over my shoulder. I never answered his question because the state I was in was obvious. "I'll think about it."

We walked out of the building and into the clubhouse. It was busier than a few hours ago, but a hush fell over the place. The jukebox played low, much like Saturday. I walked to the bar, not looking at anyone.

"Sprocket, get him anything he wants. It's on the house," Beezy said. "Jags, if you want to crash here, there's extra rooms upstairs," he told me as he walked into his office.

Sprocket grinned at me as I slid on a barstool. One of the few people who hadn't treated me different since the fight with Kracken. "Are you gonna prospect?"

"I don't know." I wasn't focused on that. I pictured Bec's face. How could she look so innocent and yet betray me in the worst way? I clenched my hands so hard they hurt. Fresh blood seeped out of my torn and ragged knuckles.

"Jake?" Sprocket got my attention. This time, he had a serious expression. Not the usual jokester. "What are you drinking, man?"

"Oilfire." He set a up a shot glass, and I waved him off. "Just the bottle."

"Damn. Are you sure?" His brows raised to his hairline.

I nodded. He shook his head and let me take it. I spotted an empty table in the back corner next to Beezy's office. No one could come up behind me this way. I sat down, propped my feet in a chair and crossed my ankles. I flung my shirt on the table and took several swallows. MC members eyed me warily, and I thought about baring my teeth just to fuck with them. I settled on getting comfortable in an uncomfortable chair and getting shitfaced.

Bec had texted me, but I deleted them without reading them. I did the same with her voicemails. I wanted nothing to do with her. She was just using me for her own gains.

A couple hours later, I had a good buzz going and pulled a joint from my pocket and inhaled a long drag. But she was still there. In my head. And if I went home, she'd be there. Not physically. She was probably in Virginia by now. But my house would smell like her. I would see her everywhere. In my bed. On my couch. Laid out on my table naked. I slammed my fist onto the table.

I blinked and looked up. Straight into the face of Hails, and she glared at me.

"What?"

"What are you doing?" she asked.

I closed one eye. "It's a bar. You drink in a bar." I offered her the bottle. "You want a drink?"

She rolled her eyes and slid into the chair beside me. "It's empty."

I eyed the bottle. So it was. "I can get a new bottle. Sprocket, get me another one."

"Was it a fresh bottle before you started?" Hails asked.

"Yes," Sprocket responded as he walked to my table. "It was. And no, I'm cutting you off."

"How are you even upright and talking coherently?" Hails asked me.

I huffed. "You don't want to know." I lifted the bottle to my lips and then remembered it was empty. Sprocket took the bottle, and I took a drag.

Hails threw up her hands. "And high. Oh, I know. Becca's gone home."

I whipped my head around to stare at Hails. "We're done."

"What did you do?"

Sprocket slid into the other chair.

I eyed him. "Don't you have something else to do?"

"Nah, prospect got it covered," he said with a grin.

Hails tugged my arm with an expectant expression. I gritted my teeth and breathed through my nose. "She was writing about me. My life." As drunk as I was, I still felt the knife twisting in my chest.

"Oh no. Surely not. She's a good girl, Jags. It was probably only a misunderstanding."

I looked down at the table. "No. I read part of it. It was word for word my fight with Krack. And my..." I stopped. The fewer people who knew about my blackouts, the better. "I trusted her," I muttered under my breath and stubbed out my joint.

I stood up and the world spun. I swayed on my feet, and Sprocket and Hails tried to catch me, but I was almost dead weight. They corralled me back in the chair. I think. I wasn't sure because I couldn't feel my face, or anything, for that matter. But I still felt her betrayal. The one thing I wanted to numb.

They were talking to me, but I couldn't understand them. And I didn't care what happened to me.

TWENTY-FIVE
JAKE

I woke up from my phone alarm blaring in my pocket and sunlight piercing my eyes. Mother fucker. I rolled over, sat up and turned my phone off. I scrubbed a hand over my face and glanced around. Where was I? I still had my jeans on, but someone had removed my boots. I spotted Tony sprawled in an armchair, sound asleep. I must be in the clubhouse, but I don't remember how I got here.

Then it hit me all at once. Bec. The twisting in my chest was excruciating.

I had to work today. I had a mild headache, and my throat was parched, but that was all. I laced my boots, tugged on my shirt, stood and toed Tony. He woke with a start.

"Why are you here?" I asked.

He rubbed the heel of his hand against an eye. "You don't remember?"

I blew out a breath. "Who did I fight?"

"A table." He stood. "It didn't fare too well. What the hell happened with Bec?"

I looked away and a sick, twisted feeling coiled in the pit of my stomach, and it wasn't from the alcohol. "Doesn't matter. We're done. And I need to go to work." I strode out of the room and downstairs.

"Hey, asshole." Tony hollered and followed me. "You're not gonna tell me anything?"

I turned to face him. "She was writing about my life in detail. I read part of it by accident." The knot in my stomach made me nauseous.

He stopped and raised his brows. "Seriously?" I nodded. "Hails told me why, but I couldn't believe it. Are you sure?"

"I. Read. It." I snapped off each word.

"Did you talk it over with her?"

"No. There was no point." I turned away and strode out of the clubhouse with Tony right behind me.

"Of course, you didn't talk it through. That would've made sense. And your stubborn ass doesn't like to talk about anything. Becca doesn't have a mean bone in her body." He crossed his arms and glared at me. "When you finally pull your head out of your ass, it might be too late."

I clenched my teeth, got on my bike without a word to Tony and sped off. It figures that everyone would take her side. I pushed those thoughts away and got through my workday. Later, I pulled in my driveway and opened the garage door.

Memories flipped through my head like a broken gear. The way she ran to me in the yard. The way she sat on my workbench. I entered the house, and I could see her everywhere. Like I predicted, her scent lingered. On my couch. On my table. In my bed.

I saw a note addressed to me on the table and picked it up. My name was written in a flowy script. Crumpling it up in my fist, I could hear my breath and slammed my hand on the table. I grabbed a lighter, lit the letter on fire, dropped it in the sink and I waited till it turned to ash. But I didn't feel better. A searing in my chest spread outward toward my limbs, and I wanted to destroy everything.

I picked up a kitchen chair and smashed it against the edge of a wall, until just wooden pieces remained. I clenched my fists and crashed them down on the table.

Over…and over…again.

Until it was broken into pieces.

Breathing hard and slick with sweat, I staggered back.

I couldn't stay here. That much was clear.

I grabbed a couple of duffle bags, loaded it full of my clothes and grabbed my laptop.

An hour later, I knocked on Beezy's office door.

"Come on in," he answered.

I strode in and shut the door behind me. "I want to prospect and want to room here. Also, I'll pay for damages for the table and whatever else."

He nodded his head and steepled his fingers. "Okay." He pierced me with his blue eyes. They saw way more than I wanted him to see. "Why don't you tell me about it?"

"About what?" Instead of demanding answers, he looked at me. I clenched my fists. "Nothing to tell. We're over."

"I need to keep my MC family safe. You do realize we're family. We have each other's backs."

This is the part I had the most trouble with, but I would deal with it. "Yup."

"I don't care if you keep it to yourself, but as prez, I need to know your headspace." He leaned back in his chair and waited.

Fuck. "She was writing a biker book. Turns out, she was writing about me." I felt my face heat from rage all over again and looked at the floor.

He stood. "I think there's more behind what you see." My head jerked to face him, but he was reaching in a closet and pulled out a cut. He tossed it to me. I noticed it already had a patch on it that said 'Jags', along with 'prospect' on the back. "I'll let you have a few days to settle before you start your prospect duties. And you can room where you spent the night." He handed me a key and clapped me on the back.

I got my shit settled in my new digs, and I was surprised that it had its own bathroom. The rooms were outfitted like small studio apartments. Love seat, TV, microwave, fridge, small table and two chairs. However, nothing met my cleanliness standards. After locating the laundry area and cleaning supplies, I soon had it how I wanted. I didn't say a word to anyone, and no one talked to me. Matter of fact, everyone avoided me, which suited me just fine. I deleted more messages from Bec and ignored messages from Tony and thought about everything.

Bec.

My job.

Bec.

What I wanted.

Bec.

I sat my laptop on a small table in my room and searched for a new house.

~

BECCA

It had been weeks since I heard from Jake. Tony called me asking what happened, and I explained through my tears. Tony said Jake wasn't talking to anyone about anything. But he assured me he was fine, just being more of an asshole than normal. Tony's words, not mine.

I understood how Jake would interpret what he read. I just did not expect to be shut out without a conversation. His words echoed in my head, *I let you in.* He'd never let anybody in, and he thought I betrayed him. If I was in his shoes, I would've probably acted the same. He'd been dealt a shitty hand, and I couldn't blame him for being wary.

I put my elbows on my knees and threaded my fingers through my hair. Tears dripped off my face. How many more tears could I shed? I never cried this much over Nick, but I realized I never loved him. Jake showed me the difference. When you love someone, you do the small things to make life easier. Like Jake feeding me crab. Remembering my favorite drink. Making sure I was comfortable on his bike. Him matching my stride without pause when I tripped.

My eyes widened, and I sat up straighter.

Jake *loved me.*

How did I not see it sooner?

Because I was too busy falling for the crude biker. *Duh.* I put my hand on my forehead. The last night I was there, he was feeling overwhelmed. The last morning with him, he almost punched me because of a nightmare. He was looking for a way out. I saw it all clearly.

Because he loved me and said, many times over, he wasn't good for me.

My hand covered my mouth. I was ecstatic and sad. I grabbed a couch pillow and sobbed into it. How could I reach him when he wouldn't even listen to me?

3 MONTHS LATER...BECCA

This was a mistake. I had agreed to have lunch with Clay, as a friend, but he wanted more. Matter of fact, he insisted on walking me to my door, after me repeatedly assuring him, I would be fine. I was determined to tell him at the door and remind him, we would never be more than friends. Period.

But a tall man relaxed beside my door, and I stopped walking. Stopped breathing. Black boots, worn jeans, black leather cut, hat on backwards and sunglasses perched on his head. His legs were crossed at the ankle, and those incredible blue-green eyes glowed—it had my heart racing.

"Are you okay?" Clay asked, getting my attention.

"Yeah," I mumbled absently as I resumed walking to Jake. He straightened off the wall and seemed bigger than I remembered. I swallowed a nervous breath and stood before him.

"Do you know this guy?" Clay asked, but I couldn't take my eyes off Jake.

"I do." I licked my lips. My body hummed at his nearness. "What are you doing here?" I asked in a breathy voice, as though I took the stairs to the fourth level and not the elevator.

His gaze flicked to Clay and then back to me. "I was in the neighborhood." He shrugged.

I blinked. "A thousand miles is in the neighborhood?"

"Who is this guy, Bec?"

I shook my head and looked at Clay. "You can go."

"Not until I'm sure you're safe." He stepped in front of me. "Where do you know him from?"

Jake stepped in Clay's direction, and I stepped between them. "Clay, just leave. I know him, and I'm perfectly safe." I felt safer than I had been in three months. I could feel the heat emitting off Jake's body behind me, and I had a difficult time not swaying into him. And when his hand cupped the back of my neck, a thrill shot through me, and I quit fighting and leaned against him. I looked at Clay. "Thank you."

"You heard the lady," Jake said, but his voice dropped to that low octave I knew too well.

Clay looked like he was going to say more but then said, "Fine." He turned on his heel and left. I felt bad, I really did. But I all I could think was, *Jake was here.*

Jake stepped away from me a pace, and I stumbled.

"Can we talk?" Jake asked.

I blew out a breath, trying to get my libido in check. "Yeah." I unlocked the door, went in, he picked up his bag and followed me in. I shut the door behind me, and he dropped the bag beside my couch.

"Nice place." He flicked his intense gaze over me.

I didn't know if he was talking about my apartment or me. With the way he was looking at me, I wasn't sure. I don't know if he walked to me, or I walked to him, but suddenly we were standing mere inches from each other. His jaw was tight as he stared down at me. I had so much I wanted to say—yell—scream—kick—punch. But the words lay strangled in my throat.

"Jake," I managed to whisper, as I grabbed a hold of his cut and dragged him down. At the same time, he wrapped an arm around my waist and brought me flush up against him.

We both groaned as our lips crashed together. It was a violent tangle of tongues. My arms encircled his neck, he picked me up and my legs wrapped around his waist. We collided against the kitchen table, and he set me down on it. I pushed off his hat and glasses and tangled my hands in his hair. Then he did that grind into the vee of my legs, and I broke the kiss to hiss in air.

"Oh hell," I panted and pushed off his cut, and he helped me shed his shirt. All the while keeping up the grind. Somewhere in the back of my mind, I knew we should talk before this, but I was starved for him. His kisses and nips along my skin said everything. I dug my claws deep into his back.

"I'm so pissed at you," I mumbled, as his hands tugged off my shirt and bra.

"I know, darlin.'" He shoved me flat on the table and captured a nipple. I arched and pushed it farther into his greedy mouth.

"I need you," I panted. "Now." I toed off my shoes and he stripped off my jeans, taking my panties with them.

He paused to look at me. "Fuck, you're beautiful."

I sat up and undid his belt and jeans and slid my hand over his length. He growled, pushed me flat and slammed in. I about came on the spot. He paused again to stare into my eyes and hooked one arm under my leg. He hit that precise spot as he slowly thrust in and out. I gasped every time he drove in.

"Becca, look at me," he said in a low voice. I did and drowned in those sea-colored eyes. His breath hitched, and he stopped moving. He brushed his rough hands along my cheek, and I clung to his hair. He seemed to want to say something.

"I…fuck this is so hard."

I pressed my hips up to his, and I couldn't wait any longer. I needed to say it like I needed air to breathe. "I love you, Jake."

His nostrils flared and both hands cupped my face. "Say it again," he whispered.

I licked my lips and tilted my hips up. "I love you."

He growled low and drove in. My table banged loud against the wall at the furious pace he set. My legs locked around his waist, and his hot breath caressed my skin, leaving tingles.

"Are you still mine?" He bit me between my shoulder and neck, and I couldn't help but moan.

"Yes." I dug my nails in his back. "Are you still mine?" I was mindless with pleasure but needed to know.

"Fuck, yes." He bit me hard, and I hissed at the pain. But I relished his answer and the pleasure as he took me higher and higher.

"Oh gawd," I keened.

"That's it, darlin'," he coaxed.

I spiraled on a wave of rapture, and he came quickly after me.

His breath was harsh, and he lifted his head to look at me. Our frantic breaths mingled for a few minutes. We just stared at each other.

Gawd, I missed him. His scent. His everything.

He closed his eyes a moment. "I don't have a clue how to love, or if I'm even capable of it," he said in a raspy voice. "But I don't want to exist without you. And if that's love, I'm drunk on it."

I tilted my head and smiled at him. Only Jake would phrase it like that. I scraped a hand through his beard. "Yes. It is. I love you too."

He let out a breath. "Can you teach me?"

"Teach you what?"

"To love."

"Jake, you already know how to love."

His brows lowered, stood up and ran a hand through his hair. "I don't know the first thing about it." He looked so serious and worried, my heart stumbled.

I sat up and captured his hand. "Love isn't something you only say, it's what you do. You showed me you cared by all the little things you did. You cared for my well-being. Was patient with me. You showed me love in the million little things you did."

~

JAKE

When I saw her walking down the hall with a guy, I wanted to pummel him. But once she came closer, she was breathless. And I knew I hadn't lost her by my dumbass actions. It was my intention to talk, not pounce on her like she was my last meal.

And here she sat, holding my hand, and giving me that smile when she had every right to cuss me. I didn't deserve her. She tugged my hand over her heart.

"You own this."

But if the last three months were any indication, I knew I'd be lost without her. "You own all the broken edges of me."

"You're not broken. You just have rough edges," she said.

I tipped her head up. "We need to talk."

She snorted out a laugh. "That's funny. You demanding we talk?"

She slid off the table, picked up my shirt and pulled it on over her head, while I zipped my pants. She went to the restroom, got us a couple of bottles of water, and we sat down on the couch. She turned sideways and put her legs over my lap and waited.

I blew out a breath. "Sorry about taking off when I should have talked to you."

"I accept your apology. Go on."

I raised my brows. "That easy?"

"Yes. I understood the why of it."

Even I didn't understand it, but she did, but it shouldn't surprise me. I scratched my beard and laid my hands on her silky legs. "I agreed to prospect the day after you left. After about three months, I was made a member and took position of Enforcer."

"What happened to six months?"

"Members didn't give me jobs as a prospect, so Beezy took it to a vote."

"They were probably too afraid."

I shrugged. "I also bought a house with a large metal building, quit my job at Ford and opened a motorcycle repair and custom shop. I named it Octane Junkie. Sprocket and a Tug, a prospect, help out."

Her eyes widened. "You've been busy. Did you sell that other house?"

I couldn't help but trace up and down her legs. "I was renting it. But there's more," I said as my hand traveled up higher on her hip, pushing the tee up.

Her lids lowered. "More?"

I nodded and stopped. This was harder to admit. I swallowed. "I've been seeing a psych." Her mouth gaped and eyes widened, but I continued. "Beezy has PTSD, blackouts, and he hooked me up with the doc he used." I looked down and then back up at her. "I don't want to hurt you when I have a nightmare or blackout. And the doc and Beezy are helping me deal with it."

Tears pooled in her eyes, and she straddled my lap. "Jake. I don't know what to say."

I took a deep breath. "You don't have to say anything." I pushed her hair over her ear and wiped away a runaway tear. "I didn't mean to make you sad. Don't cry."

She laughed as tears streaked her face. "I'm not sad. I'm ecstatic." She draped her arms around my shoulders. "Your actions prove you know how to love. I'm so proud of you. I know it wasn't easy." She cocked her head and rewarded me with a soft smile.

I still didn't know how to take compliments, but the doc said I shouldn't reject them. "It wasn't, but I'd do anything for you, Bec." It was a risk, but it was a risk I was willing to take. To have a real chance with her.

She settled on my lap and her lips were inches away from mine. "I wasn't writing a story about your life," she whispered.

"It doesn't even matter. My dumbass was overwhelmed. At least, that's what Doc said." I kissed her beneath her ear, and she automatically leaned her head back and pressed closer. My hands slid up under her tee, gripped her bare ass, and pressed her hips down to mine. "Fuck, I missed you."

I scraped my teeth along her neck, and then she pulled my head back.

"No disappearing or running," she said as her breath heaved. "If you need air, that's fine. I get that. But after, we talk. Communicate."

"Okay." I pressed my forehead to hers. "I don't deserve you, but I'll be damned if I'm going to let you go."

Her fingers trailed down my nape. "I never want to hear you say that again. I need you. I love the man you are. No one understands me like you do. No one else is you."

My eyes squeezed shut for a moment, and my chest expanded. She shook me to my core, and I couldn't convey how much she owned me. Nothing terrified me more than this little woman. She could crush me but breathed so much life into me. I stared into her eyes, hoping she could see all I couldn't say.

She tipped her head sideways with tears in her eyes. She nodded. "I know, Jake."

I crushed a hand in her hair, gripped her ass and slanted my lips over hers. She moaned in my mouth when I shoved my hips up. She ground down on me as I whispered near her ear. "You're mine."

"Yes," she said as her hands slid through my hair. "I'm yours."

"To lick." I licked her ear. "To taste." I suckled her skin right beneath her ear. "To bite." I clamped my teeth on that same spot.

She hissed in a breath and gripped the hem of the shirt and flung it across the room. She flattened her breasts against my chest and narrowed her eyes at me. "Fuck me, Jake."

With a low growl, I effortlessly lifted her in my arms and made my way to her bedroom. I didn't let one inch of her flesh go untouched. I teased and suckled till she screamed my name. Over and over. Never would I get tired of the sounds she made. I would be perfectly happy with my mouth on her skin forever.

9:39 A.M. SUNDAY.

I woke first, my arm around her waist. I leaned up on my elbow and looked down at her peaceful face. So much had changed in me because of her. All for the better. After she left, it didn't take me long to realize I fucked up. If I hadn't figured it out myself, all my friends were telling me to pull my head out of my ass and talk to her. I didn't even tell her bye the last time I saw her, and she welcomed me with open arms. She was my Angel. The sun filtered in the window, and I pushed some of her hair out of her face.

She opened her eyes and smiled. "Hey you."

I kissed her shoulder. "Hey, babe."

She turned on her back and put her hand on my face. "When do you have to go back?"

"Monday morning. It's a long ride home."

"I have you for just one day?" A tear sneaked out and tracked down her face. And she had the sexiest pout. "That's not enough time. You disappear for three months, and I only get one day?" She smacked my shoulder and shoved me onto my back. "That's not fair. All the ways I tried to get you to answer, to make you hear me." She straddled my lap, fisted some of her hair and looked up at the ceiling and cried.

It started out as a few tears, and then she sobbed and covered her mouth.

I sat up and gathered her in my arms, and she bawled against my chest. I had no excuse for the way I had treated her. No matter how many times I said I'm sorry, it would never erase the pain I caused.

"I wanted to make sure I was safe around you." I kissed her head. "But it wasn't fair to you."

She pushed back to look at me. "No. It wasn't fair. You could have let me know you were working on it."

"I didn't know if I'd be safe around you. Ever. I didn't want to give you false hope."

She glared at me. "You would've just let me think it was my fault?" She crossed her arms over her chest. "And went on about your life?"

"No." I sighed and scrambled for what to say. "I don't know. I know that I'm a fucking mess without you. That I just tried to get through the day, and gawd damnit, I was doing everything I could to get to here. With you. I didn't think any further than that." I ran my hand through my hair and looked away.

"I thought I'd lost you. I thought you were never coming back to me."

"I'm so very sorry. I should have let you know something." There was so much desolation on her face, I was ashamed of how I acted.

"Never do that again. I couldn't take it. Promise?"

"I promise."

She pushed me flat and planted her lips on mine. I wasn't good with words, so I answered with hunger. I grabbed her head and kissed her like I had all the time in the world. Savored everything about her. I nipped her bottom lip, kissed each corner, and scraped my beard to her ear.

"Oh gawd," she panted.

My fingertips traced her spine. "I wanted to be here. With you." I grabbed her ass with both hands and slid her against my erection. Her nails dug in my shoulders.

She arched her back, and her eyes closed. I slowly slid in her, and she clenched tight around me. I loved all of her. Every emotion was written on her face. She was on top, but I controlled her hips. Pushing and pulling her at an easy pace. Until she opened her eyes to mere slits and bit her bottom lip.

She pushed up till she was sitting and balancing her hands on my chest. She spread her legs wider and sat fully down. Her groan was about my undoing as she rode me faster. She took my hands and placed them on her tits. I loved the way she let me know what she needed. I pinched her nipples, and she almost shot off me.

I sat up and tweaked a bud with my teeth. She twisted her hands in my hair and hissed.

"You," she moaned.

"What?" I asked as I switched to the other breast.

"You make me need you." She parted her lips and locked her legs around my waist.

In one solid move, she was on her back, and I laced my hands with hers above her head. It was like coming home every time I sank into her. "I swear. I'll never leave you again. Even if you tried to leave me, I wouldn't let you."

I slammed in and she cried out from the force of it. No longer slow and easy. I needed her to know that she belonged to me. I wanted to brand her. Sear her body with mine. Make her feel cold and hollow when I wasn't in her. The intensity bordered on madness as I drove into her. My vision faded in and out, on the edge of control. Then she tightened and released a high keen, and my vision returned. I freed her hands and moved them to her hips. I was frantic. Fucking her like an animal, but I couldn't stop. She cried out my name and trembled all over as her nails dug in my skin. I lost it. Coming. Pulsing. I buried my head between her shoulder and neck. I released the bruising grip I had on her hips.

She shuddered and laid a hand on my nape, and I lifted my head to look at her.

"Wow," she said and trembled again. "That was…" She placed a hand on my face and traced my bottom lip with her fingertip. "Intense," she whispered.

Her skin was flushed pink and damn near glowed. I wanted to keep it there, so thinking about leaving Monday made me physically sick. Being apart wasn't going to work. That was clear. Seeing how we just got back together, I didn't have a clue when we should talk about living a thousand miles apart.

Then the doorbell rang, jerking me out of my thoughts.

She stilled. "Shit. I forgot about meeting Summer for brunch." She scrambled out of bed, tripped on my jeans and caught herself by the wall.

"Brunch?" *What the...?*

"Where's my phone?" Becca dug through our piles of clothes on the floor.

"Open up, chica," Summer hollered through the door.

Becca ran out of the bedroom as I pulled on my jeans. I used the bathroom and heard Summer shriek.

"What? That asshole is here? And you let him in?"

I rounded the living room corner, and Summer's eyes narrowed on me.

"You have a lot of nerve traipsing back in here as if you owned her." Her face red with rage, she stepped in front of me and poked a finger at my chest.

"Summer," Becca said in a high voice. "We worked it out, and I forgot about brunch. I'm sorry." She threw up her hands. "I don't even know where my phone is."

Summer glared at me. "A few hours don't make up for months of absence or the countless nights spent consoling her." She pointed at Becca.

"Summer, stop," she yelled.

I put my hands in my jeans pocket and looked at Becca. "I know." I flicked my eyes back to Summer. "I have no excuse."

That seemed to deflate her a bit. But it didn't last long, and she crossed her arms over her chest. "Where have you been?"

"Bec knows." I left it at that. It wasn't anyone's business but mine and Becca's.

Summer's anger flared again. "Not good enough. She was devastated. Do you hear me?" She poked my chest again, but I said nothing.

Becca grabbed Summer's arm. "Please. Let it go. I'll tell you the complete story later."

"Seriously?" Summer huffed. "Why can't he tell me himself?"

I bit my tongue, but I wanted to say *it's none of your fucking business.*

Becca got in-between us. "I know you're mad. But let me handle it. I'll give you all the details later."

She glanced at Bec and scowled at me. "You hurt her again, and I'll have your balls on a silver platter." She hugged Bec and marched out the door.

Bec sighed. "Sorry about that."

"I deserved it." I folded her in my arms. She turned and hugged me back. We were silent for a few beats.

"I'm gonna go get cleaned up." She smiled at me before she padded to the bathroom.

I thought about joining her, but I needed to get my mind straight. I washed my face in the kitchen sink. Retrieving my toothbrush from my bag, I brushed my teeth. Now that I knew she wouldn't reject me, I needed a plan. I was sitting at the kitchen table with a cup of coffee when she came in the room. Dressed in black leggings and an over-sized tee that slipped off one shoulder, she smiled.

"I hope you don't mind. I dug around in your cabinets to make coffee."

"It's fine. I needed coffee too." She poured herself a cup and sat down across from me.

I struggled to voice my thoughts, so decided on my usual bluntness. "This may be premature on my part, but do you have any thoughts about us living a thousand miles from each other?"

She sipped her coffee and shoved some hair behind her ear. "I hate it, honestly." She looked down and back up with a serious expression. "But I want to be sure you won't run again. I think, as much as I hate the thought of being away from you, it's best to not rush for a drastic change right now."

Every cell in my being rejected that idea. Made me antsy. My knee bounced with nervous energy. "That's fair."

"Hey." She grabbed my hand. "Just for now, okay?"

I fixed my gaze on her face. "I'd be willing to move here. Wherever you are is where I want to be."

Her lips parted and her eyes widened. "But the business you just started? Your house? The MC? What would you do about that?"

I shrugged and looked down. "Doesn't matter. I'm not trying to rush you, but I need you to know where my head's at." I stared at her as my desire to be transparent battled with my inner voice. The hateful voice in my head that said I was nothing. Would always be nothing. Deserved nothing. I swallowed.

"Nothing matters except you," I said in a rough voice.

She came around the table, straddled my lap, and ran her fingers up and down my neck. I pulled her hips in closer, and her eyes sparkled. Love shone brightly in her eyes, and if I was standing, she would have brought me to my knees. My chest tightened—it was hard to breathe. I felt exposed. The power she had over me scared the fuck out of me. I blinked a few times, trying to name this feeling.

She lifted my hand and placed it on her chest. "Breathe with me."

Gazing into her eyes, I matched my breath with hers. Bit by bit my tension eased. She kept caressing my neck until my shoulders loosened.

A tear escaped from her eye. "That is the most beautiful thing anyone has ever said to me." I didn't have a reply to that, but she wasn't done. "I know what it took for you to say that. I know you don't let anyone in. I'm so glad you let me. I know your instinct not to trust is ingrained deep in you, but I will never, intentionally, break that trust because I know what it cost you."

It felt like she was holding a gun, and I just gave her the bullets. Resting my head in the hollow of her throat, she laced her fingers in my hair. I slipped my arm under her shirt to feel her bare skin and crushed her tighter against me. Placing a chaste kiss on her shoulder, I breathed in Bec. Mangos.

I would fucking level the world for this girl. I slid my hand up her back to cup her neck and lifted my head. My lips mere inches away.

"Mine," I grated out.

She melted into me. "Yours," she sighed.

TWENTY-SIX
BECCA

J ake stayed till Wednesday, much to my delight, but the distance was too great to drive or fly out to see each other every weekend. When I wasn't with him, it was as if a piece of my being was missing. We went over our options many times. Him move here or me down there.

Jake said he'd do whatever it took to make me happy—even give up his way of life. Sell his business he just started, sell his house, and even cut ties with the MC. It was too much. I'd fell in love with the beauty of Oklahoma and the people in the MC, anyway. Summer threw a fit, but in the end, she helped me pack. I missed her already, but looking at Jake, I knew I had made the right decision. I would still work for the paper, remotely, and I had sent my book to agents and already started writing a follow-up book. A month after that decision, we drove the moving truck to Oklahoma and parked in the drive of Jakes house—now our home.

Tony, JJ, Sprocket and Tug helped unload all my stuff. Jake's new house had four bedrooms, two baths, and had more square feet than his rental. There was a bedroom that faced the shop entrance, and I chose that room as my office. I wanted to see him as he worked. When the guys left, Jake came into my office as I was putting books on the bookshelves.

He wrapped an arm around my waist and nuzzled my neck. "Finally, I don't have to spend another night without you."

I turned, smiled, and gripped his shoulders. "You mean sexy video calls weren't good enough?"

"Fuck no." I laughed, and he picked me up and sat me on the desk. "Are you laughing at me, darlin'?"

I gasped. You would think I would get used to him saying that. But I had the same reaction every time. "Yes. I am." My lids lowered and my hand grazed his beard. "I'm trying to unpack."

But it was hard to think, much less work, when he bit my delicate skin.

"So?" He pulled me to the edge of the desk. "We never fucked on your desk." His hand slid up under my shirt and traced my spine, making my back arch.

"That's about the only place we haven't." He started that grind again, and I was helpless. All thoughts got swept away. He was good at that. He was annoyingly good at everything he did. An hour later, we were both sweaty and sated.

I still had moments when I seized up because of Nick, but they were few. Jake still had flashbacks but not blackouts. We worked through them together with the help of therapy. When he asked me to attend with him, I was stunned. The more I learned about his parents' abuse, the more horrified I became. Especially at the hands of Tomas. If it wasn't for the kind neighbor, Cellie and the Pagano family, Jake wouldn't be here.

I had been to a few bike gatherings, and Jake still didn't converse with many. But I finally felt safe. No more looking over my shoulder, wondering if Nick was going to show up. Hails gave me a vest, or cut, that had patches on it that said, 'Angel' on the front and 'Property of Jags' on the back. I would have been offended six months ago, but every time I wore it, Jake's eyes darkened and reminded me of the sea. He said nothing about it, but he didn't have to.

. . .

A MONTH LATER, I WAS IN MY OFFICE WHEN I HEARD A KNOCK ON THE front door. I was expecting Hails, so I grabbed a light jacket, my purse and then opened the door.

My breath seized. Standing on the threshold was a man I never, ever wanted to meet. He gave me a leering smile that made my insides shrivel, and I stepped back.

"Well, well. Jake got him a pretty thang."

As he scanned me with cold, dead eyes, I stood frozen to the spot. All I could think was, Jake's in the shop. So close, yet so far away. I swallowed. "How can I help you?"

I hadn't met Jake's father, but he was an identical copy. The eyes were different, and it made me physically sick thinking of all the things he'd done to Jake. This man was capable of evil. He chuckled, and it slithered down my spine.

"That's the way you're gonna play the game?"

I didn't know exactly what game this was, but I wanted out of it. "I don't know what you mean. I've never met you before."

He sneered. "I'm Jake's old man. Like you hadn't figured that out." He clucked his tongue and so quick I didn't see him move, he had a hand around my throat and squeezed. I dropped my purse and jacket and clawed at his arm. He turned me, my back against his chest, pulled a gun and held it to my temple, and his hand covered my mouth.

I recoiled from the cold bite of metal as my heartbeat roared in my ears. His skin reeked of alcohol, as if he'd been dunked in it, and my chaotic thoughts scrambled for some means of escape. Instinctively, I bit his hand, and he slammed my head into the doorframe. A sharp pain exploded in my brain, making me feel woozy, and I saw black spots before my eyes. He pinned me there, the wood biting into my skin.

"Bitch." He chuckled while cocking his gun against my head. "Fight. I dare you."

My whole body shook with the overwhelming sense of dread. He could kill me. I knew he was capable of it. He dragged me by my throat across the gravel driveway and every crunch of stone echoed loudly in my head. I pushed back with my legs when I realized we were headed for a car.

"No," I cried out in a panic.

His hand tightened around my neck so I could barely breathe. "Do you want this gun to go off accidentally?" Before I could react, he opened the door, shoved me in the backseat and followed me in. Jake's mom, Jenny, was in the driver's seat, cackling.

Tears streaked down my face. This couldn't be happening. Jake was *right there*. But he couldn't see the car even if he stepped outside. "Where are you taking me?" I choked out as I tried to loosen his hold on my neck. My answer was a high-pitched laugh from Jenny. She started the car, and we drove off. I whimpered when I felt Tomas' tongue lick my face.

"The little mouse is crying," he said with glee. He ran the tip of the gun through my tears, and it made me cry harder. He pushed me flat on my back by my throat. His hand was so tight around my neck, my mouth opened trying to get air. My hands tore at his, but he pushed the barrel down my throat till I gagged.

I froze. Terror gripped me. The cold steel forced me to open my mouth wide. I could see he had the gun still cocked. One wrong move and it could go off. He let go of my throat but shoved the gun in my mouth deeper, making me gag again till my eyes watered.

"If you puke, bitch, I'll let you drown in it." He shoved my shirt up, baring my chest, then twisted my breast, and I let out a garbled cry. The man was smiling—he was getting pleasure from my pain.

I focused on the torn headliner, disengaging from reality. The worn tan fabric frayed, and I memorized each individual thread as silent tears seeped from my eyes. I could only feel the pressure from the gun in my mouth. Barely felt the pinches and slaps. Barely heard their voices. My body shut down until the car stopped.

He pulled me out of the car, jabbed the gun in my side and forced me into a run-down trailer. I tripped, and I screamed as he dragged me by my hair down a hallway. It felt as if I were reliving Nick's actions all over again.

"Scream all you want. No one is gonna hear you." He shoved me into a room and shut me in. I tried the handle, and it twisted, but it was locked from the outside. I flipped on the light switch, but it didn't work.

Standing against a wall, I hugged myself, desperate to keep it together. If I gave into despair, I'd be useless. My gaze darted around, looking for an escape. The lone window was busted and boarded up from the outside. A dingy mattress lay on the floor. There were holes in the walls, a busted-up dresser and a pile of trash in the corner. Mildew and mold grew on the ceiling, and the stench burned my nose. I heard Jenny and Tomas arguing from somewhere in the house. Why they were fighting, I hadn't a clue, but it didn't matter. I needed to find a way out.

I spotted a closet and opened the door, but it was held on by one hinge. It banged against the wall, and I cringed at the noise, but they were yelling and slamming things. After a minute, I gathered my courage to grope around the dim interior. I felt something metal and snatched it back to see. It was a toy car. The red paint was chipped and worn. I turned it over and could just make out the words written on the bottom...*Jake.*

I blinked and looked around the room again. This was his room. Had this been the room he grew up in? I choked back a sob at the horror. This was no place for a child, or even a pet. It was uninhabitable.

Refocusing, I found a lone wire hanger on the rod. Tucking the car in my pocket, I grabbed the hanger. It took some effort, but I untwisted it, doubled it up and gripped it in my hand like a knife. It wasn't much, but it was better than nothing. I crouched in a corner and hoped Jake found me soon.

But he didn't know his parents had taken me.

He didn't know where I was—*I didn't even* know where I was.

I swallowed bile and panic that clogged my throat.

He had to find me. There was no other choice.

I don't know how long I crouched there. It seemed like ages. Sweat covered my body and my teeth chattered. Hearing heavy footsteps down the hall, I stood up, braced myself, and my hand tightened around the wire hanger as the door swung open. I held it high and stabbed down, and it caught his cheek. He howled and blood seeped from the wound.

"Fucking cunt." He grabbed my arm and slammed my hand against the wall, forcing me to let go. He slapped my face, whipping my head to the side, and I cried out. "Didn't Jake teach you manners?"

Shoving me back onto the mattress, I tried to scramble away, but he caught me and sat on my legs. He ripped my shirt in half, tore my bra and caught my flaying arms and pinned them down. Then he smiled at me. Tears rolled down my face as I struggled, but I couldn't move.

"Jenny," he hollered. "Bring the stuff in here."

My eyes widened. "What are you going to do?"

He gave me a menacing smile. "I wouldn't want to ruin the surprise."

I choked back a sob as Jenny came into the room. He flipped me over, and I tried to push off the mattress, but he was straddling my legs again. Wrenching my arm back, I howled in anguish, and he clamped a metal cuff on my wrist, so tight it bit into my skin.

"No," I yelled. I fought harder despite the pain.

With the help of Jenny, they caught my other wrist and secured it with the cuff. Twisting his hand in my hair, he jerked back my head to the point of agony, and I screamed.

"The little mouse is caught. Time to play," Tomas said.

I whimpered—*This can't be happening.*

~

JAKE

Wrench in my hand, I was working on a fellow MC member's bike. Ever since I was patched, members were more relaxed around me. They still said little to me and kept a respectful distance, but I didn't silence a room anymore. Bec still didn't know what I did as an enforcer. She knew the PG version, but not the reality.

The shop door banged open, and Hails rushed in. "Something happened to Becca," she said breathlessly. She had Becca's jacket and purse.

"What?" I dropped the wrench with a clang, and I hurried over to her, with Sprocket hot on my heels. My brows furrowed and tingles shot down my spine. "Where is she?"

"She's not at the house. I looked everywhere," she said frantically. "Her phone is in her purse. And the door was left wide open."

My eyes widened, and I shot for the house with Sprocket and Hails. We searched everywhere. Her Jeep was still here, and she didn't go anywhere without her phone. "Fuck." I ran my hand through my hair.

"A pale blue piece of shit car was pulling out as I was pulling in, but I only saw one person," Hails said.

My breath stalled. "Was it a woman driver?"

"Yeah, but—"

"Those motherfuckers." I paced back and forth. Where would they take her?

"What do you think happened?" Sprocket asked.

I stopped and took out my phone. "My parents. I'm calling Tony." I punched in his number as I ran toward my truck. He answered. "We got a problem. My parents took Becca."

Hails climbed into my truck, and Sprocket followed on his motorcycle, as I peeled out. Chills swept my body. They just issued their death warrant. But if they harmed her, they would die a slow and painful death. I knew every hellhole place they frequented, but I'd try home first.

The king of hell on earth.

Fortunately, Hails didn't ask any questions as I sped north with dread creeping over me. I never came here. For good reason, it was steeped in ugly memories that triggered my sanity. The closer to 'home' I got, the more suffocated I felt. I knew every corner, avenue and place in this shithole. Where to get the best hookers and drugs. Where to hide if you didn't want to be seen.

Adrenalin surged through my body, making me grip the wheel tighter. I knew Tomas was capable of anything and everything. There was no limit to the depravities he would go.

What if he hurt her?

What if he killed her?

What if I was too late?

My vision went in and out. I sped through town to their place in the middle of no-wheres-ville. I slid to a stop, blocking their car.

"That's the same car I saw," Hails said.

"Stay here."

I broke down the front door and ran inside. The stench was overpowering. The room was a mess, with broken furniture scattered haphazardly and piles of trash accumulating in every corner. Memories tried to suck me back in, but I refused to let them. I was stronger than any memory or flashback.

Then I heard screams—Becca's screams.

Jenny stepped out of my old bedroom. I barreled toward her and flung her into the wall, like she did me so many times before. My gaze swung into the room, and Prick was kneeling on the mattress, and blocking my view of Becca. But I heard her shriek, and I spotted a syringe on the floor beside him—*He was going to drug her*.

Stomping the needle, I drug him back by the scruff of his collar and hit him so hard he spun to the floor. Becca scooted to a far corner, and I got between them. I didn't have time to check her injuries. She was alive, and that was enough for now.

Prick shook his head and glared at me. "Well, if it isn't our snot nose little brat." He wiped the blood on his face, crouched and dove towards my legs. We crashed into the closet, tearing down the dangling door in the process. Fists flew as we fought in that tiny closet, until I got my feet on his chest, and I sent him flying into the wall.

Getting to my feet, I looked at Becca whimpering and huddled in the corner. Blood ran from an injury on her head. Her face and throat were varying shades of red and her arms oddly behind her back. Her brown eyes were wide against the pallor of her skin.

I seethed and heard blood rushing in my ears as I clenched my fists tighter.

"Jake, watch out," she shouted.

I ducked in time to see his thrown fists, landed a punch to his kidney and then an uppercut that knocked him flat on the floor. I relished in the surprise expression on his face, but I didn't stop there. I kicked him in the face and stomped his ribs. He'd done me the same way when I was a kid.

Stepping back, I said in a deceptively level voice, "Get up, Prick."

Blood dripped from his face as he stood and swayed on his feet. "You've gotten cocky."

He swung but missed me, and I pinned him to the wall by his shirt and punched him multiple times. He tried to slide down the wall and cover his head, but I shook him and made him stand back up.

"Don't be a coward." I tossed the words back as he hurled at me. "Be a man."

I shook him and beat his face again till he was cowering on the floor before me, trying to cover the blows that rained down on his head. "Please," he said.

"Please didn't work for me, motherfucker." I bared my teeth, held him by his shirt and hit his face over and over.

For Becca. For me. For every mother-fucking-thing he touched and destroyed.

Something liquid sprayed my face, but I didn't care. Over and over, I pummeled his head like it was my punching bag. All of these years, I imagined him dead. The buzzing in my ears was deafening. There was no concept of time, but an arm dragged me back and I swung as Tony backed up.

"Jake," he shouted. "He's dead."

It took a few moments for his words to penetrate, for my breathing to slow. I blinked and swayed into the wall. Dizziness washed over me. I focused on Becca and the shock on her face as her gaze swung back and forth from me to Prick. I looked down. His skull was caved in. His brains splattered the floor like bugs on a windshield. Blood was everywhere. I swallowed and glanced at Bec.

"Jake," she cried and attempted to stand up, but she fell over.

That's when I saw her handcuffed wrists, ripped shirt and bra that left her bare-chested. I rushed over to her, gathered her in my arms and picked her up. Trembling uncontrollably, she pressed her face in the crook of my neck and let out a soft, strangled cry. I took one last look at the man who commanded my nightmares. He was just a bloodstain now. Unrecognizable.

I carried Bec into the living room where Sprocket had trussed up

Jenny like a hog, with duct tape over her mouth. And he'd propped his legs on her like she was a coffee table.

He gaped at us as he stood. "Holy fuck. It looks like you bathed in blood."

I didn't care what I looked like. All I cared about was Becca. "Do you have anything to remove handcuffs?"

"Yeah. Lock picks are in my bike," he said as he strode out of the trailer.

Sitting on the couch with Becca in my lap, I pressed her tight to my chest. "You're safe now," I whispered. Her answer was a small sob. Sprocket returned and sat on the couch with us, and in no time Bec was free from the handcuffs. Immediately, she clung to me.

Tony walked down the hallway into the living room with a cold, blank expression. "Get her out of here. And burn those clothes."

"What do you want to do with this?" Sprocket pressed a foot on the back of Jenny's head and smashed her face on the floor. She squealed like a pig.

I met Tony's eyes. "Do whatever you want with her. I don't fucking care."

I stood with Bec in my arms—I couldn't get out of here fast enough. Striding out the door with Bec, Hails got out of the truck when we walked out. "Can you drive us home?"

She never blinked. "Sure thing."

I sat Bec in the truck's backseat and followed her in. She had a death grip on my cut and buried her head against my chest.

"Is she okay?" Hails asked.

I nodded and pressed my lips to the top of Bec's head. If I'd been five minutes later, she would've been raped. Or dead. I caressed her hair and tightened my hold on her. I had not seen my parents since that day Bec visited. And I'd moved and mistakenly thought I'd seen the last of them.

"I'll have Screwy detail your truck," Hails said, and our eyes met in the rearview mirror. "He's good at that shit."

I nodded. When we got home, I carried Bec into the house and to the bathroom. I turned the shower on, stripped us both, and we got in. Bec's eyes were still glazed and her body shook. I held her under the warm spray of water to rinse the blood away. Then I gently lathered her hair and washed her body. The scent of mangos filled the shower. I studied the mars on her skin. The handcuffs left red marks on her wrists. Her lip was busted, and her eye was going to swell. Several teeth imprints were on her breasts. Bile leapt towards the back of my throat.

He got off too easy. *Too fucking easy.*

She blinked, clutched my arms and her gaze aligned with mine. Her lip trembled, my knees buckled, and we collapsed on the shower floor. Sobbing, she clung to me, and I crushed her against me.

"I'm so sorry." My vision swam. I never cried. I couldn't even remember the last time I cried...but I was crying now. Prick was moments away from raping her. Drugging her.

Just like the blond girl from my past. A shiver shook my frame in revulsion.

Once her sobs subsided, she fixed her eyes on me. "You killed him."

"Yeah, I did." I swept her wet hair away from her face.

"They're going to take you away from me," she said in a choked voice.

I put my hands on either side of her face. "No. It's taken care of. I'm not going anywhere."

"What? How?" Confusion and panic etched her features.

I took a deep breath. "Bec. I promise you...it's taken care of." Between Tony and JJ, they would have it covered. They would make their dead bodies disappear...and no one would ever miss that brand of trash.

Her jaw slackened, and she stared wide-eyed at me. "What?" she repeated.

"I'm the enforcer. The muscle. I make shit happen and JJ and Sprocket order the clean-up." I waited for the judgement—the rejection.

I didn't come out and say I hurt people, but Bec was a smart girl. No way in hell I was letting her go. She chose this life by moving here. Maybe I wasn't being fair, but I never thought that I'd have to tell her in this way.

"How many?" she said in a shaky voice.

I sighed. "Does it matter?"

"Did they deserve it?" She gripped my biceps, and I saw a determined gleam in her eye.

I raised a brow. She got some of her spunk back. "Yeah. They did." I gently brushed each bruise. "I'm so sorry."

She was staring, and I waited. I had infinite patience with her. Always had. But she was Bec. And there wasn't anything I wouldn't do for her. She grounded me. Kept me sane. She was my Angel. My savior.

I would burn down the world to keep her by my side.

"Do you still believe you're safe with me?" It would kill me if she didn't.

She took my hand and laid it over her heart. Taking a deep breath, she looked up at me as steam from the shower billowed around us. Face to face. Eye to eye.

"It changes nothing." She laid a hand on my jaw. "I embrace all of you. No matter who you are to the world, you will always own every beat of my heart."

"Gawd damn." Chills swept me.

I wanted to kiss her so damn bad, but she had a busted lip. I laid my forehead against hers, and her hand tangled in my hair. She brushed her lips with mine, and I pulled back.

"Your lip is hurt."

"I don't care." With tears in her eyes, she said, "Make me forget."

My breath froze in my chest. Just like the first night we talked—it all came full circle.

We stood up, and my lips crashed on hers. We stumbled back onto the shower wall. I gripped her hips, and she clawed my back as I slid her up. Her breath became mine, and I drove home. She broke the kiss to cry out, and I nipped the skin beneath her ear.

"Mine," I growled.

"Yours," she moaned.

ABOUT THE AUTHOR

Keep up with Ashlynn other books & socials all on her linktree & website:

https://linktr.ee/AshlynnPearceAuthor

http://www.ashlynnpearceauthor.com/

ALSO BY ASHLYNN PEARCE

Next up : Toxic Edge #2 Rolling Asylum Motorcycle Club series

Made in the USA
Monee, IL
17 March 2025

14075579R00223